"I have *not* been plotting your *seduction*," Natalya cried in tones of outrage.

She felt a change in the cadence of her heart, and her palms grew moist as Grey looked at her, waiting patiently and trying not to smile.

"You're spoiling it all, you know, making me explain!" she burst out in a furious whisper. "This was not the way it was supposed to happen. I came here because I want to become a . . . woman, in the true sense. I mean—"

"I think I know what you mean," he said dryly.

"And since I don't intend to marry, I began to doubt whether I would ever have another opportunity after I reach Philadelphia. I'm not one of those women who could have love affairs, and they sound like such a bother, don't you think?"

"Well, there wouldn't be any question of *this* being a love affair, would there?"

NATALYA

Cynthia Wright

BALLANTINE BOOKS · NEW YORK

Copyright © 1991 by Cynthia Wright Hunt

All rights reserved under International and Pan-American Copyright Conventions. Published in the United States of America by Ballantine Books, a division of Random House, Inc., New York, and simultaneously in Canada by Random House of Canada Limited, Toronto.

Library of Congress Catalog Card Number: 91-91977

ISBN 0-345-36781-2

Manufactured in the United States of America

First Edition: October 1991

FOR TOM E. HUFF
A true professional among writers and
a cherished friend, who was always there
with wisdom, encouragement, or a quip
that could make me howl with laughter.
I miss you, Tom, and hug you in my heart.

PROLOGUE

Unbidden guests
Are often welcomest when they are gone.
SHAKESPEARE
(1564–1616)

"SOON IT WILL BE DARK, M'SIEUR," THE MAN IN
the black cloak said gruffly. "I've drunk your ale and paid for
it. Now, kindly direct me to the château."

Brogard, the diminutive, white-haired proprietor of Le Chat
Bleu, peered at the stranger. Other patrons, thirsty after a day's
labor in the vineyards, were arriving, and his time was limited.
"I don't like to send a man I don't know up to the château,
although I owe M'sieur Beauvisage no allegiance. His father
is the marquis, strictly speaking, but the elder Beauvisage has
been in America since my youth, and besides, we have no
aristocrats in France anymore." He winked almost impercep-
tibly. "At least not at the moment."

"Vive le roi!" slurred a man seated at the next table.

The stranger glanced over sharply. "Is it true that Louis the
Eighteenth is returning from England to assume his brother's
crown, and that Napoléon is expected to relinquish his power
in a matter of days?"

"Where have *you* been, my good fellow? Locked in
prison?" Brogard demanded, with a hearty laugh. "Those
rumors have been circulating for weeks!" He paused again,
stalling, trying to ascertain the character of the man before
him. Late thirties probably, educated, and most likely English,
though he spoke French with ease. Yet something was not
right. The stranger had an air of . . . danger, Brogard decided.
He was tall and powerfully built, an imposing physical pres-

3

ence in the rustic taproom with its low, beamed ceiling. Brogard knew enough of the wellborn to recognize the man's
sculpted bone structure for what it was: odds were that his
blood was blue. But something had brought the fellow low—
he was unkempt and looked as if he hadn't eaten in days. And
the light in his gray eyes sent a chill down Brogard's spine. It
was the look of a hunted animal, although the innkeeper sensed
that this was a quarry that would fight back savagely if cornered.

"I cannot tarry another minute," the stranger said, with
growing impatience.

"Will you not at least confide the nature of your business
with Nicholai Beauvisage? You're a stranger to me, m'sieur,
while I've known the Beauvisage family for thirty years.
They've been good to me—and I won't have you or anyone
else disturb them unnecessarily, if I can help it. How can I
direct you when I don't know whether you are friend or foe?
I don't mean to offend you, m'sieur—"

"Spare me this long-winded speech, my good fellow," the
man broke in, a trace of amusement softening his curt tone.
"I assure you that I bear no ill will toward your revered Beauvisage. Now, I must insist that you tell me how to reach the
château. Nightfall approaches, and a storm is brewing over the
Loire. If you will not tell me the way, I'll ask elsewhere. Pretty
girls are often more forthcoming." He smiled thinly.

"D'accord," Brogard agreed, with a sigh. "I have not the
time to argue this further. I will walk with you to your horse
and direct you."

They emerged onto the crooked rue de Juin, in the middle
of the little village that staggered down to the golden banks of
the Loire. Shadows were lengthening along the narrow, ancient streets as clouds gathered ominously overhead. Brogard
turned and pointed out the roads that would take the stranger
to Château du Soleil, which perched on a hillside a fair
distance west of the village. There was a gatehouse at the
end of the drive, Brogard said, but admittance was usually
easy to obtain, unless the Beauvisages were entertaining or
away.

"Tell the gatekeeper that you are a friend of the family," he advised. "He probably won't question you, though he ought to. You certainly look suspicious enough. Ambrochette is a kindly sort, and very fond of his afternoon wine. If I know him, he's dozing even as we speak, and probably won't rouse enough to think much about you. His wife is as fat as a cow, and a harridan as well, so no one blames him for drinking the way he does. If *my* wife—"

"I appreciate your help," the stranger interrupted. "Thank you." He studied his route, shading his eyes against the setting sun. "Beautiful." His voice was barely audible as he gazed at the white stone château's airy towers, turrets, and pinnacles, bristling against the green background of the forest of Chinon. It looked like a fantasy.

The sound of distant hoofbeats roused him, and he stared down at the stone bridge that spanned the Loire far below them. Two men were rapidly approaching on horseback. One fellow had vivid auburn curls that glinted in the patchy, fading sunlight, while his companion was remarkable only for his steed, a black-maned gray.

Brogard saw the light intensify in the stranger's eyes. "Do you know them?"

"I realize that you have no reason to trust or believe me, m'sieur, but I give you my word that those two men are thieves, intent on robbing me of my life. I hope to find a means of escape from my predicament through the generosity of Nicholai Beauvisage. If you care at all for justice, you will tell those men that you have not seen me." The man swung onto his stallion, black cloak swirling out behind him, and added, "I must warn you, though. They will say that I am an escaped prisoner, a murderer, and an enemy of Napoléon."

The stranger flashed Brogard an enigmatic grin, then rode off up the steep cobbled lane, bound for Château du Soleil.

PART ONE

Thus I live in the world rather as a
spectator of mankind than as one of the species.

JOSEPH ADDISON
(1672–1719)

Chapter One

Château du Soleil
March 27, 1814

HIGH IN ONE OF THE FANCIFUL WHITE TOWERS OF Château du Soleil, Natalya Beauvisage was writing a novel. Her scarred desk was positioned to afford her an ideal view through the three narrow windows that pierced the wall, and she spent much of her days dreamily appreciating the luminous beauty spread below the château.

It was a long way from Philadelphia, where she had lived until traveling to Europe nearly six years ago, at the age of twenty. Natalya might have grown used to her surroundings, but she refused to take them for granted. The Loire Valley was, she'd decided, unquestionably the most beautiful place on earth. The river itself swirled over blond sand, past light willows, shimmering poplars, and vineyards that spread over voluptuously curved hillsides. The valley's magical element was its golden, pearlescent light, which washed the soft landscape as if it were an endless watercolor.

As a writer, Natalya reveled in the history that saturated the Loire Valley and its châteaus. She had grown up in a newly formed country that had the personality of a headstrong youth with good instincts. America was still raw in many ways. France, on the other hand, was redolent with history and style. Each day Natalya found herself looking out over a meandering river where centuries exchanged memories across the banks. Sometimes she felt as if she had stepped into one of the fairy tales her mother had read to her during her childhood. Rumor

9

had it that this very château had been the inspiration for Charles Perrault's ''Sleeping Beauty,'' but fortunately she had stopped believing in fairy tales a long time ago. Times had changed, and Natalya was certainly a far cry from the damsels of the past who may have languished in this very tower, waiting for brave knights to ride up and carry them off. She had dreams, certainly, but they did not center around the appearance in her life of a handsome prince. With her usual sense of dramatic originality, Natalya had chosen dreams that she could pursue and realize all by herself.

Shaking her head, Natalya smiled and looked back down at the last page she meant to write that afternoon. The approaching twilight seemed to be in league with a spring storm. Purplish clouds burgeoned against a glowing gray sky, and the light was waning by the moment. When fat raindrops began to pelt the leaded-glass windows of the tower, she put down her pen, stored her day's work in the top drawer of her desk along with the other one hundred seventeen pages of her manuscript, and left the tower study.

Lisette Beauvisage heard the soft tapping of Natalya's footsteps on the circular stone staircase that led from the tower to the family quarters. Peeking into the corridor, she called to her, and when Natalya came into sight, Lisette gave her niece a radiant smile of greeting.

''I'm just about to soak in my bath and sip tea. Won't you share a cup with me and chat for a few minutes?''

''Gladly,'' Natalya replied, her face alight. ''You know how ready I am for conversation after a day in the tower. If I hadn't seen you, I would have been forced to converse with the tapestry in the gallery!''

Laughing, Natalya followed her aunt into the spacious bedchamber that had been refurbished at the turn of the century. The white paneled walls were now lightly embellished with gilded wood relief, and the windows and bed were hung with draperies in a vibrant shade of powder blue. Lisette had chosen furnishings from the Louis XVI period, which featured rich, inlaid woods and classical lines. Two paintings of sylvan woodland reminiscent of Fragonard adorned the walls, and vases of daffodils splashed the room with yellow. Lisette's delicately painted porcelain bathtub had been moved from her dressing room to a spot before the hearth, within which a fire blazed cheerily.

"Doesn't that look heavenly?" Lisette asked, gesturing toward the bath. A maid was just pouring in the last pitcher of steaming water. "It's going to rain like the devil tonight, you know, and I love to bathe in front of the fire when the weather is gloomy." She turned to the maid, a petite young black-haired girl named Marie-Helene, and spoke in French, requesting tea for two and some tiny cakes. Then she shed her silk dressing gown and stepped into the bathtub.

Natalya reclined on her aunt's chaise and smiled. "I hope that I am half as beautiful as you are twenty years from now."

"I'm sixteen years older than you, not twenty, but if that was a compliment, I accept."

At forty-two, Lisette Hahn Beauvisage had long been secure in her beauty. Her elegant, willowy figure and lovely face, offset by curls of sunbeam hue and eyes that sparkled a deep, rich blue, had changed little over the years. At twenty-one, when Lisette had been the proprietress of Hahn's Coffeehouse in Philadelphia, she had cared little for her appearance and was in fact eager to dissuade men from admiring her. Since Nicholai's entrance in her life, however, Lisette had come to appreciate *all* her gifts and take pride in her feminine attributes. She had mellowed, although she continued to cherish her rights as an individual. True, she respected her husband and secretly thrilled to his masculinity, but that did not prevent her from insisting she stand with him as an equal in their marriage. Her children had grown up watching her not only work alongside their father, but also pursue her own love of painting. Moreover, she had never backed down from Nicholai just to keep the peace. Her feelings and moods were known to be as valuable as his, and she believed that this was a great lesson for their children.

"I dreamed last night that Adrienne came home from London," Natalya remarked, accepting a cup of tea from Marie-Helene.

Lisette gestured for the maid to set her tea on a side table, then returned to the task of lathering her arms. "I wish that Adrienne *could* come home. She's so far away, or she might as well be, and this hideous war makes travel so dangerous that we're afraid to let her join us even for holidays."

"Don't forget that the war is the reason you sent Adrienne to school in London. Uncle Nicky seems safe enough here, probably because he's been in this part of the country since before the Revolution and has won the loyalty of the locals. But it's hard to know how Adrienne would be treated if she tried to carry on a normal life here." Natalya sipped her hot tea and smiled. "She's much more outgoing than James. After all, at seventeen . . . well, she's a young lady and needs the company of others her own age, while James is perfectly content to stay here at the château where it's safe. As long as he can play the man alongside his father, and have his horses and books, he's happy."

"For the moment." Lisette's tone was wry. "Have you noticed his voice getting deeper, or the fact that he's grown two inches since Christmas?" She sighed. "Already fifteen . . . He'll be ready to go off in search of female companionship, if you take my meaning."

Natalya reclined on the chaise and closed her eyes. "James seems remarkably sensible to me. Perhaps he'll listen to his dear cousin Talya and be wary of romance. Life can be so enjoyable without the complications of *affairs de coeur*."

Stifling an impatient response, Lisette turned her head to regard Natalya. How innocent she looked with those astonishing blue eyes and that pretty mouth, with its full lower lip. Except for her eyes, which darkened from aqua to turquoise when she was angry, she was the image of her mother. Caroline had the same luxuriant, honey-colored tresses, the same profusion of soft curls frothing about the edges of her winsome face. And, like Caro, Natalya was petite, slim of waist, with gracefully curved hips and legs and utterly lovely breasts. She had every gift necessary to attract men, but she seemed totally oblivious to her charms. Lisette couldn't help sighing as she noted the concealing white cashmere shawl that Natalya wore over her pale peach chemise frock with its fashionably low neckline. If her niece had her way, her physical charms would remain a family secret.

Lisette sympathized with her to an extent, remembering how resistant she had once been to attracting men or yearning for romance. Marriage had been the last thing on her mind when she was young, until fate had stepped in and brought Nicholai into her life. By the time Lisette was Natalya's age, she was not only a wife, but a mother as well. At twenty-six her niece showed no inclination to marry at any time in the near—or distant—future. She insisted that she was now able to make her own way in the world, as an author, and therefore had no need of marriage.

"What was that sigh all about?" Natalya queried, looking up at her aunt.

Lisette laughed. "Oh, I was just meddling in my own mind again. Worrying about you, wishing you'd fall in love and marry and—"

"Live happily ever after?" Natalya finished. "Unfortunately I have seen enough of life to know that marriages like yours, and my parents', are extremely rare. Why don't you be honest, Auntie, and admit that if you hadn't met Uncle Nicky, you probably wouldn't have been married at twenty-six, either! You'd have gone on supporting yourself at the coffeehouse, determined not to settle for some bland barrister simply because society preferred that you have a husband." She was leaning forward now, eyes dancing mischievously. "Can you deny it? I'm absolutely right, aren't I?"

Lisette wrinkled her nose, frowning. "You needn't behave as if I have been matchmaking at every opportunity. Why, it's been more than a year since I even invited a man to dine with us." She put on an innocent expression, and Natalya giggled in response. "And you're right. I never thought I would be fretting over the word *spinster*, but I suppose I'm getting old and turning into a mother. You're still young, beautiful, and completely enchanting, and part of me wishes that you had someone to share life with. . . ."

Realizing that they would never reach complete agreement

on this subject, Natalya sought to divert her aunt's attention. "Well, perhaps I will meet the man who will change my mind about love and marriage if I can ever arrange to go home." She sighed. "That's really uppermost in my mind, you know. It's just astonishing how much I've come to miss Philadelphia of late. Today, as I worked on the character of the mother in the new book I'm writing, wondering what she should be like, I was struck by the most overpowering longing to be with Maman. The thought of seeing her and Papa and Kristin, of coming in the front door of Belle Maison, sleeping in my old bedroom, visiting Grandmama . . ." She paused, her voice catching. "I yearn for it so, it brings tears to my eyes."

Lisette sipped the last of her tea and gazed at her niece. "I miss Philadelphia, too, and I don't blame you for wanting to go home. It's been nearly six years. And you know that Nicholai is exploring every possible way to get you back to America, but—"

"There is a war on, I know." Natalya's eyes blazed a brilliant turquoise. "It makes me crazy that I cannot travel where I please!"

"Sometimes I cannot help wondering if part of the reason you're so determined to sail for home is the fact that everyone tells you you cannot," Lisette said mildly. Stepping out of the bathtub, she wrapped herself in a thick towel.

"I'll find a way," Natalya insisted. "And I'm not motivated by stubbornness, or a whim. Something inside"—she pressed a hand over her heart—"tells me it's time to go home. It's the same inner voice that bade me leave Philadelphia and travel to Europe after my twentieth birthday. Whether it is God or my own best instincts, I trust it enough to do my utmost to obey."

Everything Natalya did and felt seemed to be *bigger* than normal, Lisette thought as she formulated a tactful reply. However, before she could speak, Marie-Helene appeared in the doorway.

"Madame, there is a stranger outside, insisting that he speak to M'sieur Nicholai." The little maid's eyes were wide with trepidation.

"M'sieur Nicholai and James have not yet returned from their ride to Saumur?"

"No, madame."

"Well, I'm sure that they'll be back momentarily. It's started to rain, hasn't it? You must ask our visitor in, give him a drink, and assure him that M'sieur Beauvisage should arrive home within minutes."

Marie-Helene looked pained. "Madame, this man is . . . a *stranger*."

"Whatever do you mean by that?" Lisette was losing patience. "If he is a friend of my husband's—"

"He does not look like any friend of M'sieur Beauvisage's that I have seen before. He looks almost—dangerous. . . ." The maid began to wring her hands nervously.

"Oh, for heaven's sake," Natalya exclaimed, "I'll go down and deal with the man!"

Standing, she drew her shawl close around her slim shoulders and hurried out of the room. Marie-Helene scuttled along behind, head down. They descended the curving, white marble stairway, Natalya's fingers skimming the rail of the intricately carved, black wrought-iron balustrade. At the bottom stretched the château's long gallery, magnificent with its floor of black-and-white marble squares and its renaissance tapestries. Through the gallery's long windows, which overlooked terraced gardens, Natalya could see the stranger who struck such fear into Marie-Helene. Clad all in black, he stood inside the arched doorway to the château's east wing. A slight breeze billowed his cape and caused him to lift his head, giving Natalya a glimpse of a rakish, dark, bearded face.

Baby hairs prickled along the back of her neck, a novel sensation that startled her.

"*Voilà!*" hissed Marie-Helene. "You see? He is a devil!"

Natalya blinked. "I see nothing of the kind. Your imagination is driven wild by this ferocious weather."

"*Je t'implore*, do not open the door to him!" the maid cried.

As she crossed the stone entry hall, Natalya realized that Marie-Helene was scurrying in her wake like a child trying to hide behind her mother. She put her hand on the latch and warned, "You needn't cling to me if you're so terrified of this person. I can deal with him on my own."

"*Mais, non!* I cannot leave you, mam'selle. I am here to serve you with my very life, if need be!"

Natalya stole a brief glance heavenward and tried not to smile. "I'm sure I don't deserve such blind devotion. You'd better brace yourself, then. I'm going to open the door . . . *now*!" She was nearly laughing as she pushed back the bolt, lifted the latch, and dragged open the heavy door. Her eyes were sparkling with merriment, and a silken honey-gold curl came loose to brush the side of her cheek.

Then, Natalya focused on the stranger. Her body stilled and her smile faded, while the pounding of her heart grew deafening. Never before had she seen so striking a man. The effect was intensified by the angry twilight, which hurled raindrops, faster and faster, at the black-clad giant.

Perhaps he wasn't really a giant, Natalya amended, ever aware of her tendency to embellish reality; but he was bigger than her father or Uncle Nicky, both of whom were tall and broad-shouldered. The stranger's size was made more menacing by his black cape, which swirled out over worn trousers stuffed into muddy black boots. Most arresting of all, though, was his proud head, with a profile that bespoke arrogance and danger, and a keen intelligence. Natalya was struck by his wild, wet black hair, which was laced with silver, and by his pale face with its sculpted bone structure and steely eyes. He wore a trim beard, and his mouth looked sensual and hard all at once.

"*Bonsoir, madame,*" the stranger said in a voice that sounded hoarse and tired. "I beg your pardon for this intrusion, but I have come a very long way to speak to your husband."

Startled, Natalya exclaimed, "You're English!"

"I'm afraid so," he admitted. "And you are . . . American?"

"Yes. Monsieur Beauvisage is my uncle. My aunt is upstairs at the moment, but my uncle will be back directly. Would you care to come in and—'' She heard Marie-Helene gasp and felt her tug urgently at the back of her shawl. Natalya gave her a quelling glance. ''You must excuse our maid. She has taken it into her head that you are a dangerous character and—''

The man turned his head sharply, as if he had heard an expected but unwelcome noise. ''If you don't mind, I'll accept your invitation and come in now,'' he said hurriedly. ''This weather is devilish.''

Before Natalya could step out of the way, he pushed past her, causing Marie-Helene to cry out. Natalya herself was beset by a sudden wave of apprehension as she realized that he knew her uncle was not present. In the interest of fairness and good manners, she had written off his appearance to the rain, wind, and duration of his ride, but now she could see that beneath the cape his clothing was frayed, his hair and beard were overdue for grooming, and there was an evil-looking scar across the hand that reached out to push the door closed. When he turned again to look at her, she immediately recognized the threat in his gleaming gray eyes. She wasn't surprised when he put his hand under his cape and drew out a long, sharpened dirk. At the same time, she became aware of the clatter of hoofbeats entering the courtyard of the château.

''Do as I say,'' the man said curtly, ''and neither of you will be hurt.'' He stared hard at the trembling Marie-Helene. ''Compose yourself! When the two men who have just ridden up come to the door, they'll describe me, and you must tell them that you have not seen me, do you understand? You must be calm and convincing, little girl, else your beautiful mistress will feel my blade.'' He waited for the maid's crazed, wild-eyed nod, then lifted Natalya off the floor and carried her into a tower alcove just a few feet from the door. ''Don't fight me,'' he ground out. ''Be silent!''

The hand covering Natalya's mouth was wet and smelled of horse and sweat and damp wool. His other arm clasped her waist, and now she felt the tip of the dirk press upward between her breasts, the steel cold through the thin muslin of her gown. His body seemed to surround her: powerful, musky, terrifying. As more unknown and potentially dangerous men pounded at the door, Natalya waited for her heart to explode.

"Shh. Don't move," the stranger whispered, his breath madly ticklish against her ear. "If you're very good, perhaps I'll give you a kiss after they've gone."

This sudden burst of teasing humor, so peculiarly and arrogantly male, made Natalya long to sink her teeth into his palm. Never had she met a man whom she despised more!

Chapter Two

 March 27, 1814

  Two men, as stormy in appearance as the sky, were looming over Marie-Helene, shouting questions and demanding answers. Somehow she rose to the occasion, shouting right back at them.

"Tell us! You *have* seen him, haven't you?" cried one of the intruders, a tall, thin, balding man. "There is no mistaking St. James. He's huge, with black brows and flashing gray eyes, and his hair is black as a raven's wing, with strands of silver. He is terrifying to behold!"

"No, no! No one has been here all day except you," Marie-Helene insisted.

"Let us speak to your master, then."

"He isn't here. He's gone to Saumur. No one in the château has been near the courtyard for hours, except for me, and I have seen nothing."

"You lie at the peril of your own life, *ma petite*," warned the other man, the one with the bright auburn hair. "The one we seek is an escaped prisoner, an enemy of France, a thief and a murderer! He would think nothing of invading this beautiful château, raping you and your mistress, and then"—he drew his finger across his neck, eyes wide—"*slitting* your *throat*!"

Natalya flinched involuntarily, and the stranger tightened his grip. The fist that held the blade pushed against the softness of her left breast. Suddenly she was aware of the heat of his flesh, aware of the fact that she had not been this near a man, for this long, in years. Wedged between his powerful body and the stone wall, Natalya was forced to turn her face upward, brushing the rough, hard curve of his cheekbone with her temple. She felt the warmth of his breath. It smelled, not unpleasantly, of ale and tobacco. The realization that this was very much a flesh-and-blood male seemed to intensify her fear. Had he been serious about kissing her? His tone had been rather light and mocking, but what if the men at the door were telling the truth? Was this horrible Englishman capable of rape . . . and murder? Never had she felt more vulnerable, confused, and terrified; and because all three were emotions she abhorred, she was angry as well. How dare he hold her captive, cause her such fear, threaten her, and then make jokes in the next breath?

"I tell you, this monster you describe has not been here!" Marie-Helene insisted, stamping her foot.

The redhead glared at his companion. "The gatekeeper was snoring when I approached to question him, so there's no way of knowing for certain if this one is lying."

"No sign of St. James's horse," the other man pointed out.

"M'sieur Beauvisage will be returning home at any moment," Marie-Helene cried out. "If he finds you here, making such trouble, he will be furious!"

Sighing, the auburn-haired man glanced at his companion and admitted defeat. "We can hardly search the château, can we, Poujouly?" He shrugged. "*D'accord, ma petite*, we'll go, but do not forget our warnings. If Grey St. James appears at this door, do not admit him. He is dangerous—and an enemy of our emperor. He must be returned to prison with all possible haste. Tell your master what I have said . . . and if you should happen to see St. James, do give him this message from Jules Auteuil. Inform the criminal that he shall not escape permanently." His voice shook for an instant. "We will not stop until he is back—"

"In our *care*," Poujouly finished. His mouth curved slowly upward, then twitched.

"Au revoir, messieurs," Marie-Helene rejoined impatiently. "I have work to do."

Natalya's body had begun to ache after being forced for so long into an awkward position, and she was feeling short of breath. When she heard the door close, she squirmed, but her captor only tightened his grip. They remained immobile until they heard the other men mount their horses and ride off down the drive. Finally, after the sound of hoofbeats had died away, Marie-Helene appeared in the alcove.

"I did as you said, m'sieur. Now, release mademoiselle!"

Natalya made a muffled sound behind the Englishman's hand, and, abruptly, she was freed. She sagged against the stone wall and looked over to find his dark head bent as he casually replaced the dirk in its sheath.

"I must say, I'm glad that's over." His tone was conversational, and he laughed wearily. "I appreciated your cooperation—uh . . . Excuse me, mademoiselle, but I'm afraid we've not been properly introduced. I do not know—"

"This is unbelievable!" Natalya yelled, outraged. "You can't *really* mean to behave as if you didn't just threaten our lives a few moments ago?"

"I wasn't serious, though." He gave her a surprisingly boyish, appealing smile. "Don't you see, there wasn't time to explain properly, so the only way I could be certain you'd do as I said was to frighten you both sufficiently. I really had no choice."

Natalya was aghast, particularly when she saw Marie-Helene softening. "You—you— I can't think of a name bad enough to call you! Whatever the crime was that you committed, you deserved to be caught by those men! You deserved to be shot—guillotined—drawn and quartered—"

"Please!" He held up a hand, laughing. "Don't go on."

She refused to be disarmed. "Your behavior was despicable, sir. I must ask you to leave." Lifting her chin, she walked regally into the entry hall. Marie-Helene stood between them, looking back and forth with trepidation.

"I came to see Nicholai Beauvisage," the man said, his voice deep. "I cannot leave until I have spoken to him."

"I'm afraid that's impossible," she declared, without turning back to look at him.

Another voice answered Natalya. "Impossible? Hardly."

She gasped and spun around to find her uncle Nicholai and his son, James, standing in the doorway to the courtyard.

Not a moment too soon, Grey St. James thought wryly as he walked toward Nicholai Beauvisage and introduced himself. The pace of the past two days had been unforgivingly brutal, and his reserves of charm were low. Another second and he'd have been hard-pressed to scrape together a credible response for the intense mademoiselle.

"St. James," Nicholai repeated thoughtfully, drawing off his gloves. "Have we met before? Is your father the Earl of Hartford?"

Grey nodded. "Yes, and yes. I was visiting at Father's London house the last time you and your wife stopped for tea, a few years back."

"Of course! You're the elder son, aren't you. I can't tell you how pleased I am that you managed to find us. You know, your father spared my brother Alec's life during our revolution in America, and we've all been indebted to him since." Nicholai, who was still vigorous and handsome at fifty-three, looked the Englishman over with clear green eyes. "If there is anything I can do for you, you need only ask. I hope I won't sound rude if I observe that you look a little less . . . yourself than when we last met in London."

St. James gave a laugh sharpened with irony. "You're very tactful, sir, and kind. My circumstances have changed drastically in the last year. To be perfectly frank, my life is in danger, and I do need your help."

"I hope there is time for you to have a long hot bath, and then join us for dinner before my assistance is required," Nicholai said, with a calm, reassuring smile. "My manservant will attend to your needs, and then we'll discuss your situation over some good wine and hot food, all right?"

Grey closed his eyes for a moment and sighed. "My prayers have been answered."

Nicholai patted him on the back, then glanced back at his son. "Ah—I've been remiss. Grey, I would like you to meet my son, James. James, this is Grey St. James, Viscount—"

"I don't use my title," Grey said. "Life is much simpler without it. Hello, James. I'm glad to meet you."

James Beauvisage put out his hand and tried to match the Englishman's grip. At fifteen, James was blessed with shining chestnut curls, clear gray-blue eyes, and a ready smile. He had much of his height, but he had yet to fill out and was at that precarious age when he was no longer a boy but not yet a man. "How do you do, sir?" he said politely.

Nicholai started to walk toward the gallery, and Grey kept pace. "God, I need a bath," Beauvisage muttered, brushing dirt from his buckskin breeches. "It's not a day to be on the roads, hmm?"

Natalya remained in the entry hall, fuming. When her uncle didn't miss her, she cleared her throat before the men were out of earshot.

Nicholai glanced back. "What is it, little Talya?" When she tensed, blushed, and glared in response, he took a guess. "Don't say that you have not been formally introduced to our guest! My dear, I do apologize," he said, eyes twinkling, and beckoned her over. "Grey St. James, may I present my niece, Natalya Beauvisage?"

She wanted to make a scene, but somehow she suffered through her uncle's introductions, giving St. James what she hoped was a poisonous smile as they ascended the long, winding stairway to the second floor. Upstairs, Nicholai presented the Englishman to Lisette, who was now clad in a chemise frock of pale yellow muslin. Her blond hair was caught up with tortoiseshell combs so that loose curls framed her lovely face, and around her neck she wore an exquisite gold locket that contained a miniature of her husband and a lock of his hair. Nonplussed by the sudden appearance in her home of such a bedraggled, dangerous-looking stranger, she nevertheless managed to greet him warmly. Then, enlisting the aid of Nicholai's manservant, Honoré, she hurried off to show St.

James to a bedroom and arrange for his bath and fresh clothing.

Natalya waited impatiently for her cousin to retire to his own bedchamber. By the time she was finally alone with Nicholai, he was already peeling off his damp coat, now-limp cravat, and shirt. Marie-Helene had been dispatched to heat water for two baths, and she and another serving girl would be returning any moment with the first steaming pitchers.

"Uncle Nicky," Natalya burst out, "I *must* speak to you about that . . . person!"

"This isn't the most opportune time," he replied mildly, sitting down to pull off his top boots.

"You don't understand, you must send him away immediately! He's a *criminal*, escaped from prison, or some such thing. There were men here, looking for him, and they said that he's an enemy of the emperor, and—"

"My darling niece, don't you realize that St. James is an Englishman and France is at war with England?" Beauvisage laughed gently. "Of *course* he's the enemy, and regarded as a criminal, especially if he was able to harm France in any way. But, you know that I have always tried to remain neutral. My loyalties are really American, after all, and I've no right to judge Grey St. James." He watched two maids pour steaming water into the porcelain tub and waited until they had left the room to continue. "Talya, you don't give a damn for Napoléon. I should think that you'd be congratulating St. James if he's managed to be a thorn in that tyrant's side. And, apart from that, the Beauvisage family owes a debt to his father. I wouldn't dream of turning Grey out."

"But he threatened me to keep me quiet while those men were here. I was afraid for my life! I cannot believe that you could take his side over mine."

He came over to her and patted her cheek. "It's nothing to do with that, and I think you know it. Must I make a choice? I have come to trust my instincts about people, and I sense that Grey St. James is a good man at heart. Let's allow him to bathe and have a hot meal, hear him out, and then decide, all right?"

Furious, Natalya bit her lip and started toward the door.

"Talya, this is between the two of you, isn't it? There's no reason for you to be angry with me," her uncle reminded her.

"I cannot bear to be *near* that man. He is insufferable." She paused in the doorway and added, "You may give him my place at dinner, Uncle Nicky, because *I* won't be there." With that, she swept from the room and narrowly missed slamming her hem in the door.

"I must say, you do look transformed, Mr. St. James," Lisette proclaimed. "Will you have more *feuilleté solognote*?"

Grey glanced at his dwindling portion of puff pastry filled with pheasant and partridge. "Perhaps I should wait for a moment. It's been a long time since I have eaten so much delicious food."

Sitting across from the Englishman, Natalya longed to mimic his polite tone or engage in some other shockingly rude behavior designed to drive him from the château. She had changed her mind about staying in her room during dinner when it occurred to her that St. James would be free to lie and connive as much as he pleased if she weren't present to monitor the conversation. Her first sight of him in the vaulted dining hall had made her glad she'd reconsidered.

It was hard to believe that this could be the same man who had appeared so menacing and uncivilized just two hours earlier. Honoré had done a splendid job as barber, and now Grey's clean, gleaming hair was cut into the current windswept style. His ragged beard had been shaved, uncovering a chiseled jaw and arresting mouth. In truth, although pale and in need of some added weight, Grey was magnificent to behold, from his keen eyes to the expert knot of his borrowed cravat. His strong good looks only intensified Natalya's antipathy.

For his part, Grey was more than a little intrigued, and even amused, by Natalya Beauvisage. Holding her lush body in his arms earlier had reminded him painfully of appetites too long suppressed through no choice of his own. She was exquisitely lovely, self-assured, intelligent, and obviously well past the age when similarly blessed maidens took husbands. Was hers off in the war? Dead? Yet she was American . . . and still had the name Beauvisage. What the devil was she doing in France? Knowing that it would make her furious, Grey decided to inquire openly.

"I hope you won't think me too bold, but I've been wondering, Miss Beauvisage . . . are you a spinster?"

Her mouth dropped open and she gasped. "What . . . an extraordinary thing to say!"

"You're married, then?"

"No, but—"

He nodded shortly, as if attempting to gloss over some terrible secret he had accidentally learned about her. "I see. Believe me, it was not my intent to call attention to your rather . . . sensitive circumstances." He had to bite the inside of his lip to keep from grinning at her outraged expression. "You appear to have adapted very well, and are doubtless grateful to have such understanding relatives offer you shelter."

Lisette, torn between horror and a mad urge to giggle, interceded. "Natalya's situation is not what you think, Mr. St. James. She is unmarried by choice, and supports herself independently. Her first novel will be published in England next month."

Natalya glared at him, nostrils flaring. "Not that it is any of your business, *sir*."

"I'm certain I can speak for my sex," he replied, with a straight face, "in mourning the fact that you have chosen to deprive some lucky man of the bliss of sharing a lifetime with someone as warm and charming as you, my dear Miss Beauvisage."

Desperate for something, anything, to say before his niece lunged across the table and assaulted their guest, Nicholai heard himself remark, "Talya is longing to return to Philadelphia, but I don't know how we'll ever get her there as long as this war, and the war between England and America, continues."

"I wish I were in Philadelphia right now," Natalya declared.

"To tell you the truth, so do I," Grey said, with heavy irony.

"Well, I wouldn't want to be there if you were there!"

"For heaven's sake, stop it," scolded Lisette. "Natalya, I don't know what went on between you two before Nicholai came home, but whatever it was, you must put it aside while we are all at the dinner table. Mr. St. James is our guest. If you cannot be friendly, at least be civil."

As their plates were cleared, a dish of cheese and fruit and a bottle of calvados appeared on the table. Natalya pressed her lovely lips together and folded her hands in her lap.

"Grey, perhaps now might be a good time to tell us what has brought you to Château du Soleil, and how I may help you," Nicholai said.

St. James sat back in his chair and sipped the fiery brandy made from Norman apples. "My story is a long one, but I will try to confine myself to the pertinent facts. I was the commander of one of Britain's finest warships until it was captured, and I was taken prisoner. I was considered a prize, because I am a cousin to Wellington . . ."

"And quite a favorite of the regent's, as I recall," Nicholai said.

Grey nodded. "Yes, he and my cousin have both tried to have me freed, which has only whetted Napoléon's interest in me. He sees me as a bargaining chip—and came to see me in my prison at Mont St. Michel this past autumn. He took an immediate dislike to me, no doubt in part because I am at least a foot taller than he is. At any rate, he gave orders that I was to be guarded more carefully than any other prisoner, and that if the Allies should win the war, I must be shot."

Natalya took a sip of her calvados, trying not to listen, determined that nothing would soften her heart toward this man.

"I won't go into the details of how I managed to escape. Suffice it to say that, as rumors continued to reach the prison regarding the imminent end of the war, many of the regular routines were forgotten. Meanwhile, the warden, a brutish man named Jules Auteuil, taunted me with promises of my death. When I escaped he followed me, he and his henchman.

No doubt he thinks I'll lead him to Wellington! They were the men who came to your door today. I couldn't risk even the slightest chance that they'd discover me, so I . . . well, I threatened Miss Beauvisage and your maid with death if they betrayed me.'' He smiled tentatively at Natalya, who refused to meet his eyes. ''I fear that she'll never forgive me for frightening her so cruelly.''

''You're quite right,'' she murmured.

''That's an amazing story,'' Nicholai said slowly. ''Now that you have found a safe haven, what do you want to do next?''

St. James met his gaze with keen gray eyes. ''Like your niece, I am determined to get out of France. Perhaps I might be able to deliver *both* of us safely to England. From there I could arrange passage to America for Miss Beauvisage, but it would mean spending several days in my company. She would doubtless consider that a fate worse than death.'' He looked across the table at Natalya, whose heart had begun to pound, and arched an eyebrow. ''It's insane for me even to hope that you might agree, isn't it?''

She took a deep breath. ''Tell me your plan.''

Chapter Three

March 27, 1814

NICHOLAI AND LISETTE STARED IN ASTONISHMENT. Natalya pretended not to notice. Only the two spots of color on her cheeks betrayed her awareness of the humbling leap she'd just taken. Meanwhile, James alone seemed oblivious of the dinner table conversation. He was more interested in the wedge of caramelized apple tart that had just been put before him.

"What are you looking at?" Natalya finally demanded of her aunt and uncle. "There's no need for shock. I've only agreed to hear the man out, not become his mistress."

St. James lifted his brows mildly. "What a relief." After a well-timed pause, he began to explain. "The difficulty of my situation is that Auteuil and Poujouly—the prison warden and his assistant—know my horse, and they'll be looking for me alone. The perfect solution, as I see it, would be not only a disguise and a different horse, but also a *wife* to travel with me. Knowing my past—the year in prison, and before that, the war—they'd never think to find me with a woman cooperative enough to pretend to be my wife."

"Well, they would be right, wouldn't they. It's ludicrous!" Natalya's turquoise eyes registered stunned surprise. "I guessed that you were mad, sir, but I was hoping that perhaps I'd judged you in haste. Now there is no doubt that I was right all along."

"Right about the fact that you judge too hastily?" he replied

29

innocently. "I fear I must agree; but it's heartening that you are examining your character defects—"

"If you play with me, Mr. St. James, I shall leave the table without listening to one more word of your so-called plan," she ground out between clenched teeth.

"Then spare me your sharp-tongued interruptions," Grey said coolly. "I can assure you, Miss Beauvisage, that my reference to needing a wife was in no way a declaration of love and proposal of marriage for *you*. I only need someone to *pose* as my wife, for a mere week, perhaps, and although it would be pleasant if that person were also someone whose company I enjoyed, it would seem that I am not in a position to make such demands." He paused, fine nostrils flaring slightly, and took a sip of calvados. "That was a very long-winded way of saying what is perfectly obvious to me: you and I can help each other in ways that are critical. We both need to get out of France, and the odds are against either of us doing so alone. Together, we can be successful. I'm not asking you to do me a favor. We would each benefit equally." He shrugged. "I suppose it depends on how much you want to leave this country at the moment."

Natalya took a deep breath. "I do. I do want to go, so badly that my heart aches with the yearning to see America. I apologize for my rudeness. Please, tell me more."

Nicholai, hearing the throb in his niece's voice, leaned forward to give St. James his complete attention. "I should warn you—you'll have to convince us all," he murmured.

Grey smiled. "My plan is fairly simple at this point. Since both of us speak French well, we can travel as a married peasant couple, which would draw little or no suspicion. I'm certain Auteuil and Poujouly expect me to travel to Paris and thence to England by way of Calais. Or else they hope I will go to join Wellington." His long fingers caressed the stem of his glass. "It wouldn't occur to them that I might go right back over the ground we've just covered, which is why I've chosen St. Malo as our destination. As you know, it's very near Mont St. Michel."

Natalya, caught off guard by the sudden flash of his grin, smiled back. "Could we sail from St. Malo, then?"

"Absolutely. I couldn't do so when I first escaped from prison because Auteuil was right behind me. Also, it may take a bit of scheming to get to a British ship, but I'll have no problem once that damned warden and his henchman are off my mind. It may even turn out that my own ship will be lurking somewhere off the coast. If so, we'll bribe a fisherman or a smuggler to transport us. Once on board a British vessel, we will be guaranteed safe passage to England. The war may very likely be finished by then."

"What's Natalya going to do once she arrives in England?" Nicholai asked soberly. "Did you forget while in prison that your country is at war with America as well? I hardly think that she can book a pleasure voyage from London to Philadelphia."

"You're right, of course," he agreed, nodding. "I can assure you that I shall not desert your niece once her usefulness to me is past." He stretched his legs and rubbed a sore muscle in his right thigh. "I will personally arrange her crossing to America. I am an officer in the British Navy, and I also own a trading ship of my own, so I'm critically connected for Miss Beauvisage's purposes—"

"You may as well call me Natalya," she said lightly.

"All right. And I'm Grey," he replied, the barest smile touching his mouth when she nodded in response. "Uhm . . . as I was saying, I shan't leave Natalya at the dock once we arrive in London. She will stay at my father's house until I have settled on safe passage for the rest of her journey. At least she will be out of France—"

"I don't know," Nicholai said, his tone dark with doubt. "I love Talya with all my heart, and I am responsible for her. She may not want to be here anymore, but sometimes we cannot have what we want exactly when we want it. An important lesson, my darling niece." He pointed at her, his rebuke warmed by an undercurrent of affection. "Here, at least, I know that you are safe."

"Uncle Nicky! For heaven's sake, I am not a child. I'm twenty-six years old."

Grey managed to hide his surprise at this revelation when she glanced at him, reddening at having given herself away. He covered the awkward moment by returning his attention to Nicholai. "If it will put your mind at ease, sir, I'll promise to deliver your niece personally to America if I am unable to find suitable means for her journey."

"Excuse me, but this decision is up to *me*." Natalya threw her uncle a stubborn look that reminded him of her childhood. He half expected her to stick out her lower lip.

"She *is* twenty-six, darling," Lisette reminded him gently. "And don't forget that your own daughter lives in London, and Adrienne is barely seventeen."

Beauvisage drained his glass of calvados. "Fine. I can see that I have no influence whatsoever."

"You might as well become accustomed to feeling ignored, Papa," James remarked between bites of apple tart. "Your own children will undoubtedly stop listening to your advice long before we turn twenty-six."

"You stay out of this," Nicholai barked. "And, incidentally, Lisette, it's no use bringing Adrienne into this. She's safely deposited in London's finest private school for girls, where she is chaperoned twenty-four hours a day. You cannot compare the two situations."

Natalya held up her hands in protest. "Everyone is getting all worked up before I've even decided what I'll do." When her dinner companions all stared at her expectantly, she laughed. "Let me think about it overnight, lest I be accused of behaving rashly or childishly."

"How very mature you are, my dear," Lisette proclaimed. "Did you hear, Nicky? She's going to think this matter over carefully, weighing all the factors, positive and negative, before coming to a decision. Now you'll be able to relax and enjoy your apple tart." She nudged his arm. "Take a bite, darling. I made the crust myself, with my favorite old recipe from the coffeehouse."

Nicholai sighed and ran a hand through his crisp chestnut

hair, now liberally salted with white. "All right!" Staring
defiantly at his wife, he speared a large bite of tart and stuck
it into his mouth. In muffled tones, he added, "Now I know
how Napoléon feels. Powerless!"

"You have a very illustrious history in this château, monsieur," Grey remarked as he and Nicholai wandered through
the great hall with its gilded, coffered ceiling and mammoth
fireplace. Two silken-eared spaniels slept before the cheery
blaze. "These paintings are Beauvisage ancestors?"

Nicholai was torn. He wanted to play the kind host to his
guest, but now he was afraid that any displays of friendship
might further encourage St. James's mad scheme. If only Natalya hadn't become involved . . . Then, reminding himself of
the debt owed by the Beauvisages to the St. Jameses, Nicholai
decided to adopt a manner that was polite but not . . . familiar.
Smiling, he led Grey to the painting nearest the doorway.

"These are all my ancestors, but not all of them are named
Beauvisage. A hundred and twenty years ago, the only son of
Paul Mardouet, seigneur of St. Briac, died in a hunting accident. Paul's eldest daughter, Marie, then married a nobleman
named Beauvisage, and Château du Soleil passed to them. Our
family tree gained a new branch."

Grey gestured toward the painting. "By the look of this
fellow's jeweled doublet, I gather that he must be a Mardouet."

"Correct. This was Thomas Mardouet, one of St. Briac's
earliest seigneurs. He was a great friend of King François's,
and it was he who razed the château's north wing when the
enlightened age of the renaissance did away with the need to
fortify one's home against attack."

"He looks . . . fulfilled," Grey observed. The painting revealed a handsome man with curling chestnut hair, a trim
beard, and turquoise eyes that seemed to dance with pleasure.
"And I can see a family resemblance."

Nicholai smiled. "Thomas's eyes and hair have turned up
on descendants all through the years. And I think you're right
about the look of him. Although he lost his first son in child-

hood, that was his only real tragedy. Thomas had two daughters and another son, and according to all reports he was passionately in love with his wife. They shared a long life together, and they made some fine wine here."

Grey's eyes wandered to the next portrait, of an enchanting, raven-haired woman with clear spring green eyes. Garbed in a gown of rich emerald velvet embroidered in gold, with long sleeves and a low, square neckline, she appeared alluringly alive. "Don't tell me that this was his wife . . . ?"

"Hmm? Oh, yes, I'm afraid so. That's Aimée. Exquisite, wasn't she?"

"She certainly accounts for his contented look."

Nicholai laughed suddenly, the furrow disappearing from his brow. "We Beauvisages have ever been a romantic lot. My father, who grew up here and was the rightful heir to this château, had no taste for playing lord of the manor. He chose to be a pirate, during the days when such practices were tolerated. He did a great deal of illegal trading with the colonies—America—when trade with England was so expensive and troublesome. By all accounts, Papa was the consummate rake. My mother, who is Russian, met him when he captured the passenger ship on which she was sailing to America. Theirs was just one in a long line of passionate romances in our family."

Grey inclined his head. "Your own included, it is clear to see. My own family, on the other hand, is littered with acrimonious arranged marriages and cold-blooded infidelities. I myself—" He broke off with a bitter smile that was not lost on his host. "Growing up, I never saw anyone genuinely in love—most especially not my own parents," he went on after a slight pause. "As a consequence, I've never put much stock in notions of romantic love. If there is such a thing, I'm convinced that it's magical—and transitory."

"Well, Natalya has had good examples to observe since birth, and she's more cynical about love than most men I know . . . at least when it comes to her own life. She hasn't let me read the manuscript for her novel, but my wife has confided that the heroine of *My Lady's Heart* is incorrigibly romantic."

"Miss Beauvisage wouldn't be the first person to discover that affairs of the heart are safer conducted at a distance," Grey remarked ironically.

Chuckling, Nicholai stifled a yawn. "It's been a long day—longer than I realized. You must be exhausted as well. Shall we go up?"

"Would you mind if I remained behind for a bit? I think that I need a little solitude after the chaotic events of the past few days. It will all begin again tomorrow morning. . . ."

"You needn't leave so soon."

"My friend, I couldn't bear the suspense, waiting to discover how this adventure will turn out." Grey's tone was ruefully amused. "I think you must know what I mean."

"I do." Beauvisage nodded. "It's just that danger is likely in the offing, and it would behoove you to be rested and well fed before you confront it."

"Which is your way of implying that you don't want your niece to accompany me," Grey murmured. He gave his host a sidelong glance under arching brows. "I have already assured you that I will lay down my own life, if need be, to insure her safety."

"There's really no point in discussing this with me, St. James." Nicholai held up his hands in surrender. "Didn't you hear Natalya tonight, telling me to mind my own business and reminding me that she is far past the brink of independent adulthood? If she decides to embark upon this wild escapade with you, there's not a damned thing I can do about it short of locking her in one of the towers." He ran a hand through his gray-flecked hair. "On the other hand, if she doesn't want any part of you or your scheme, no amount of urging from me could persuade her to go. In short, my friend, my beautiful niece would seem to hold all the cards!"

"I'm not going."
"Indeed?"

Natalya, wearing a plain nightgown and wrapper of gossamer-thin white batiste, sat on the edge of her aunt and uncle's grand testered bed while Lisette braided her hair.

"Who would pamper me and love me and brush my hair at bedtime if I left here?" Her delicate nostrils flared as she considered one possible answer. "Heaven knows I wouldn't let that *oaf* touch me, not under any circumstances. Aside from the fact that it would be an utter nightmare to be forced to share that *person's* company for days on end, I've just begun to recollect that it's a harsh world outside our lovingly civilized château." Her tone was light, but she was only half jesting. "I've grown appallingly spoiled, I know it, but it's a fact, and ought to be accepted. Don't you agree?"

Lisette wrinkled her nose as she wove her niece's rich, honey-hued hair into a thick plait that nearly reached her waist. "I can speak for myself, thank you. Aren't you being rather melodramatic? First of all, I don't find Grey St. James hideous in the least. I personally think that he is immensely attractive."

"Auntie!" Natalya gasped, looking back over her shoulder with an expression of mock horror. "If you torture me with one more nauseating word of praise for that savage, I'll repeat it all to Uncle Nicky."

"Oh, no, please, not that!" Laughing, she pulled on her niece's braid. "Silly twit, do you imagine that Nicholai would fly into a rage if he heard that I admired another man's beauty? On the contrary—it doesn't bother him that I appreciate other men because he's completely secure in the knowledge that I am his alone."

Natalya sniffed dismissively. "In my opinion, the two of you spend far too much time dwelling on the pleasures of the flesh."

"Just wait." Impulsively Lisette hugged her niece from behind. "One day you'll discover those pleasures for yourself, and—"

"I'd really rather not," she broke in, stiffening.

They were silent for a long minute as Lisette finished the braid and fastened it with a wide bow of sea blue silk. Natalya's eyes were downcast, seemingly fixed on the edge of her wrapper, which she was twisting this way and that. Lisette never ceased to be struck by her niece's ripe and radiant beauty. She almost seemed lit from within.

"Do you know what I think?" Lisette murmured.

"Dare I ask?"

The older woman bit her lip, hesitating, knowing that Natalya would be incensed if she spoke her mind. "I think that you are attracted to Grey St. James, in spite of your protestations. You are frightened to death of flesh-and-blood men, who you cannot control the way you do the heroes you create on paper, and so you have decided to do the *safe* thing and stay behind with us rather than travel to England with Grey." She shrugged slightly. "To tell you the truth, I'm a bit disappointed. You've always put on such a show of bravado that it comes as a bit of a surprise to discover it was false all along. The only risks you're willing to take are in your imagination, with the characters in your books."

Natalya turned slowly to stare at her aunt, her eyes huge with outrage. "That's simply ludicrous! Are you implying that I am a *coward*?"

A trifle too emphatically, Lisette shook her head. "Of course not. Quite frankly, I don't even think that you are aware of what you're doing. . . ."

"Perhaps I'm more aware than you know. Auntie, that St. James person threatened me to keep me quiet when those men from the prison came today. He pressed some sort of terrifying dagger between my ribs, and I was frightened for my life. And, I was furious! To make matters worse, when the men had gone and I confronted him, he merely brushed the matter off with a jest. What do you think about *that*?"

"I think it sounds rather thrilling, to be honest, but I can see that your pride was bruised—"

"*What?*" Natalya jumped up and paced across the chamber, turning to face her aunt with arms outstretched. "Perhaps you didn't fully comprehend what I just told you. I might have been *killed* by that barbarian. Do you really think that it would be safe for me to travel alone with him?"

Lisette shrugged. "Well, you seemed to think it might be

safe when you were responding to his plan at the dinner table tonight. . . ."

"It must have been the calvados. I wasn't thinking clearly. Since then it has also occurred to me that St. James has been locked up in prison for the past year. Who can predict what might happen now that he is at liberty?" She widened her eyes meaningfully.

"Aren't you being just the tiniest bit theatrical?" Lisette fought an urge to laugh. "Grey St. James is not a savage who was put behind bars because of some heinous crime; he is an English nobleman who was captured as a prisoner of war. He's a hero, for heaven's sake!"

"He still hasn't had a woman for a very, very long time," Natalya muttered stubbornly. "And he certainly didn't act very noble when he was threatening to kill me. Honestly, Auntie, I should think that you would be more concerned for my welfare. Do you really think that it would be prudent to entrust me to the care of this stranger?"

"I suppose I'm viewing this as a woman, not an aunt. I think that you've been locked up yourself for too long, darling. This scheme of Grey's promises to be a rare adventure." She shrugged again. "Of course, the choice is yours."

Nicholai appeared in the doorway then, loosening his cravat. "I'm exhausted. I must have had too much fresh spring air today."

"Talya has decided not to go with Grey St. James," Lisette told him.

"No?" He glanced toward his niece for confirmation. "Well, I can't say I'm sorry to hear that. You're a woman after all, Talya, and he's definitely a man. Why tempt fate?"

"Spoken like a true uncle," Lisette murmured dryly.

Natalya smiled. "Yes, well . . . I'm awfully tired myself. I think I'll go to bed." She hugged and kissed her aunt and uncle good night, then hurried into the corridor and closed their door. A cool breeze swept through the wide stone hallway, causing her to shiver and hug herself, but she did not turn toward her own bedchamber. Feeling restless and strangely unsettled, she started down the curving stairway, her robe and gown whispering behind her.

A light burned faintly from the far end of the gallery, as if someone had forgotten to put out a candle in the great hall. It was a welcome diversion, and Natalya decided to investigate.

Chapter Four

A NARROW ROOM ADJOINING THE GREAT HALL HAD been transformed into a library by Lisette Beauvisage, and Grey had discovered its pleasures. After shedding his cravat, opening his collar, and plucking several volumes from the carved bookshelves, he reclined on a flame-stitched wing chair and gazed at the pages by candlelight.

How inexpressibly sweet it was to be at liberty after more than a year! In prison, he had been deprived not only of good food and warm clothing, but of nourishment for his soul. He had missed his books desperately, the glorious feeling of sunlight on his face, freedom to come and go as he pleased, stimulating conversation with friends, the sensation of holding a woman's body in his arms . . .

"Oh!" Natalya passed through the low, arched doorway and started at the sight of Grey. "Excuse me! I saw the light and assumed that Uncle Nicky had forgotten to put out a candle. I thought that you had already retired for the night . . ."

"You aren't interrupting. My mind's too busy to slow down enough to really read, but it's a tremendous pleasure just to touch fine books again." He half rose and gestured toward the chair next to his. "Would you care to join me?"

"Well . . . perhaps for a moment." As she crossed the cozy library, it seemed to Natalya that the air fairly crackled with male energy. She found that she couldn't look at Grey, and her cheeks were growing warmer by the minute.

Grey, meanwhile, was grateful for her averted gaze, because he seemed to be unable to stop his own eyes from feasting on the vision before him. Natalya's beauty was a delicious treat for his starved senses. The light batiste of her loose nightgown and wrapper covered her more completely than the décolleté, form-fitting gown she had worn earlier, yet this ensemble was much more alluring. He found himself imagining the feel of soft batiste against his hands and the warm, naked curves of her body beneath the nightgown. When Natalya curled up on the other wing chair, artlessly tucking her bare feet under her bottom, Grey caught a whiff of her scent and was beset by a sudden stab of arousal.

Natalya tried to look straight at the Englishman and found that it was like meeting the gaze of a silver-eyed panther. Panicked and confused, yet curious nonetheless, she swallowed hard, then looked away. They were completely alone; no one even knew that they were downstairs together. Despite the fact that St. James had held her at knifepoint and threatened her life, she realized that she wasn't really afraid of him. She wasn't even certain that fear was one of the cluster of emotions that raced through her body. Moistening her dry lips, she managed to inquire, "What were you reading?"

"Chateaubriand's *René*."

"That's my copy. Why don't you take it with you? I know how it feels to be hungry for books. I'd like you to have it."

"Thank you." His finely wrought mouth curved upward. "It's been years since I read it."

Natalya smiled at him. Grey was intrigued to discover that he couldn't stop looking at her. She possessed a beauty unlike any in his experience. Most of the women he had known in London had been fashionably pale and slim in their high-waisted chemise frocks, but Natalya's skin was dusky and her body was lush, womanly. Her hair was luxuriant, like silken honey twisted into a liquid braid, and her face was mesmerizing with its sensual mouth, tip-tilted nose, glowing complexion, and great turquoise eyes. Part of the secret must be her age, he decided. She was more mature than girls in their

first Season . . . and yet he would swear that Natalya was still
innocent.

Natalya watched as a bemused-looking St. James rubbed an
elegant forefinger across his lower lip. She was experiencing
an assortment of very unsettling feelings and was certain that
Grey St. James was the cause. Was it possible that Lisette had
been right? Was she attracted to him—and was that the reason
she was afraid to travel with him? The possibility that she
might really be a coward was distinctly unnerving.

"Have you made up your mind?" Grey asked suddenly, his
voice low and firm.

She had been twisting the corner of her dressing gown, staring at it as if it were a project that required all her concentra-
tion. Now she bit her lip and looked up at Grey, her brow
furrowed. "Yes, I think that I have."

"Wait!" He held up a hand, laughing. "I sense a refusal
coming, so to be fair, you must first give me the opportunity
to convince you. I realize that I did not create the best first
impression earlier today, and I apologize for that. Will you
come with me if I promise not to threaten your life again?"

Natalya listened with half an ear as he went on, all easy
charm and artful persuasion. She tried to talk herself out of
her attraction to him. Certainly the man was handsome, but
he was also pale and far too gaunt. She told herself that she
really had nothing to worry about. Never before had she lost
her head or her good sense when dealing with men. That sort
of romantic weakness was merely a plot device in her books,
designed to throw her heroine together with the hero.

The thought pleased her, and she smiled. Yes, that was it!
She'd simply been spending too much time in her own novels,
and was confusing her heroine's emotions with her own. She
must plunge ahead fearlessly, treating her association with Grey
St. James as a business arrangement. There was no reason to
be anxious. He was only a man, after all, and therefore infe-
rior. However, in this instance he could prove highly useful,
for he knew how to get her back to Philadelphia, and that was
more important than any other consideration.

"Yes," Natalya said suddenly, interrupting him.

His black brows flew up. "Do you mean to say I've actually convinced you?"

"Certainly not! I wasn't even listening. I simply changed my mind." She stood up. "This is very, *very* exciting. I'm going home tomorrow!"

More than a little amused, Grey replied, "It may not be as simple as saying it."

"If I concentrate on the goal, all the rest will be tolerable. I'll even be able to endure your company, sir, if I think of Philadelphia." She laughed, eyes dancing. "Do you want to leave at dawn? Shall I stay up all night packing?"

"Packing what?" He stood up facing her, looking down, and wondered what he was getting himself into. "We're going to have to travel in disguise, which also means that we'll take no more than we can carry. Roll up your plainest gown with clean stockings, a comb, and a chemise inside. Don't bother to dress or arrange your hair in the morning. I'll bring you something to wear at about seven o'clock. There's no need to leave at dawn."

Natalya nodded dutifully in response to everything he said. "I understand."

"I must say, this cooperative, obedient pose is very impressive, but I'm not dim. It's obvious that you are a strong-willed woman. I respect that, but if this arrangement is going to work, you will have to agree to take directions from me. There can be no arguments in moments of crisis."

Her eyes flashed for an instant, then she managed to smile sweetly. "I promise to do your bidding, sir, as long as your directions preclude physical contact between us."

"I promise you, nothing could be farther from my mind," Grey reassured her, with a slight incline of his head.

Feeling oddly insulted, Natalya nodded. "Good. Good! Well, then, I ought to go to bed, hmm? I'll see you at seven o'clock."

"Sleep well, Miss Beauvisage."

She glanced back from the doorway, trying not to respond

to the splendid sight of him standing in the candlelight, white shirt open to expose part of his broad, muscled chest. "I shall," she said. "I'll dream of Philadelphia."

"Each to his own," Grey replied, and gave her an enigmatic grin.

"I think that I should get up," Lisette mumbled, without conviction. A thin ray of early sunlight parted the bedhangings, informing her of the time.

"Why?" Smiling, Nicholai slipped his arm around her waist and pulled her more snugly into the curve of his body. "Mmm." He kissed the back of her neck.

This was their morning ritual, wherein they pretended to debate whether to get out of bed at all. Nicholai, naked between the soft linen sheets, would fit himself to the elegant curve of Lisette's back and derriere, and they would slowly come awake together, murmuring reminders of the love they'd shared the night before. Sometimes, if they were feeling especially decadent, they would mate again in this sentient, dreamy state.

Today, however, Lisette turned on her back and stretched in her husband's embrace. He ran his hands lightly over her breasts, smiling.

"You look as though you have a secret," she remarked.

"I was just thinking about the night we made love in the bathtub at Lion and Meagan Hampshire's house."

"You took advantage of me!" Hair splayed across the pillows, Lisette beamed at Nicholai and caressed his roughened cheek. "I was only in the same room with you and that bathtub because I was nursing you after that cursed duel. I had no idea you were capable of bathing yourself . . . let alone—"

"It was a long time ago," he whispered.

"More than twenty years. You know, I fell in love with you during those weeks at Hampshire House, when you were helpless and I was taking care of you."

Nicholai laughed at her choice of words, then retorted, "My dear, you insult me. You fell in love with me the instant you saw me." He gathered her into his arms and held her fast so that her breasts pushed against his chest in a way that was both familiar and keenly exciting. "You are even more beautiful now, if that's possible. Truly."

Lisette knew he meant it, and that was more important than reality. She kissed the hard, flat surface of his chest and inhaled the scent of his skin, smiling. "Thank God we found each other." She wanted to stay in the warm cocoon of their bed, to let their kisses deepen with passion, to feel Nicholai's strong fingers caressing her . . . but her instincts told her that she had already tarried for too long. "Darling, I must get up. Look at the sun!"

Nicholai released his wife and propped himself on one elbow, watching as she moved around the bedchamber, pouring water to wash her face, then brushing her hair and slipping on a dressing gown of sea green silk.

"I suppose that St. James may have already gone," he remarked, then seemed to reconsider. "He didn't say his goodbyes last night, however, so he must not be in any hurry. Thank God Natalya had the sense not to take part in that insane scheme of his. If she'd agreed, I don't know what I'd have done. . . ."

In the midst of fastening her dressing gown, Lisette glanced at him under her lashes. "I think I'll just go and check on both of them. You ought to prepare yourself for the possibility that your niece may have changed her mind. It's a woman's prerogative, you know."

He was scrambling to the edge of the bed in an instant, yanking open the bedhangings. "*What?* Is that your notion of humor, or are you just testing my reflexes?"

Halfway to the door, Lisette looked back over her shoulder and shrugged. "I just think that Natalya's feelings regarding this matter were a bit more complicated than she admitted to us—or to herself. So, I'm merely suggesting that you brace yourself in case she's had a change of heart."

With that, she strolled out of the bedchamber, leaving her husband to stare after her in consternation.

* * *

"How did you ever find so many horrid articles of clothing?" Natalya asked Marie-Helene as she stood before the pier glass and surveyed her reflection in disbelief.

The little maid giggled. "M'sieur St. James and I have been searching together since dawn. He's a very charming man, mam'selle! *Bien sûr*, I should be quite pleased to enter into a masquerade with him. We inquired of all the servants, and it was Colette, the milkmaid's grandmère, who provided most of this. She even had a trunk of her late husband's trousers and coats, and M'sieur St. James paid her a shocking sum of money for all of it. He came away as happy as a little boy who has discovered buried treasure!"

"Well, who can blame him?" Natalya remarked dryly, wrinkling her nose as she stared at herself. She was wearing the ugliest assortment of clothing she'd ever seen. A whalebone corset and rusty old side hoops reshaped her body, while Marie-Helene had added insult to injury by stuffing in padding to fill out strategic areas. "I certainly feel *disguised*."

"No one will know you, mam'selle."

"I should certainly *hope* not!" She was almost afraid to touch the musty-smelling gray gown that covered her padded, boned undergarments. Like the corset and panniers, the rest of her costume was distinctly out of date. "Why in the world would the milkmaid's grandmother have kept these old things?"

Marie-Helene giggled. "She was still wearing them, I think. She prefers the fashions from her youth, when Louis the Fifteenth was king." The maid leaned forward and pulled two tattered cords hidden near the gown's waistline. Magically the skirt parted in the middle to reveal a discolored red silk petticoat.

"Dear God. How hideous!" Natalya grimaced. "I wonder when these last saw soap and water?"

Crossing the ends of a water-stained fichu over her mistress's bosom, Marie-Helene stepped behind her to tie them in back. "I really couldn't say, mam'selle. *Vraiment*, I think that is also part of m'sieur's plan. If you should encounter the men who are searching for him, he intends that both of you will appear so authentically decrepit that they will not suspect for a moment—first that he could be the criminal they seek, and second, that you could be the sort of person M'sieur St. James might choose as his accomplice.''

"Exactly, my dear Marie-Helene. I couldn't have explained these bizarre costume choices more convincingly myself.''

Hearing St. James speaking from the doorway, Natalya turned, then squinted in surprise. The man standing before her bore no resemblance at all to the imposing, black-haired, bearded madman who had pressed a knife between her ribs upon their meeting less than a day ago. Gone were the stark black clothes, the appealingly virile good looks.

"How reassuring to see that someone in this château is uglier than I this morning," Natalya said brightly.

Grey cocked an eyebrow at her. "But you haven't done your hair or painted your face yet, my dear Miss Beauvisage. The best is yet to come." With a flourish, he brought his hand out from behind his back to display a long, large white cone that Natalya vaguely remembered had been used many years ago to protect the face while a person's hair was being powdered. She took a step backward, and Grey laughed. "You may as well submit without a struggle. Otherwise I'll have to restrain you while Marie-Helene applies the powder, and that wouldn't be pleasant for any of us, would it?''

She felt like crying with frustration. It was obvious, looking at him, just how horrid he intended her to be. His own appearance bordered on the grotesque. He wore a powdered bag-wig under a huge tricorn hat, and his face was virtually unrecognizable. He had applied powder to heighten his pallor, then added dark smudges under his eyes and cheekbones to make himself appear even more gaunt. His eyebrows were thicker and the lines bracketing his mouth more pronounced. Moreover, he had chosen a costume that was just as antiquated and unflattering as hers: a flowing lace jabot that was torn and stained, a long pink brocade waistcoat, baggy green knee breeches, and a matching, ill-fitting green coat with wide soiled velvet cuffs and gold buttons, several of which were missing. His square-toed black shoes had large buckles, and his calves were covered by sagging grayish stockings. The entire effect was that of a loathsome old man who had not changed his clothes since the storming of the Bastille.

"How can you bear to appear in public looking like that?" she asked.

"My dear Natalya, you must hold fast to your sense of whimsy if we are to succeed with this little plan. Words cannot describe the fun I had unearthing these costumes for us, and I needn't remind you that my objective is to look as far from *me* as possible. Traveling with you will help, but I'd like to make this as simple as possible. Hence, our amusing new identities." Grey leaned on his long, amber-knobbed walking stick with one hand and reached into the deep pocket of his coat with the other, producing a tarnished silver snuffbox. He flicked it open, inhaled a pinch of imaginary snuff, and struck an attitude. "Madame, meet your husband, Maurice Galabru. What name would you like?"

"Do you mean to suggest that I have a *choice* in the matter?" she retorted.

He favored her with an imperturbable smile. *"Mais, oui, ma chère marié!"*

"You're too kind." Natalya stared at herself in the mirror, watching as Marie-Helene arranged her long hair in an elaborate style that would have pleased Marie Antoinette. "I believe I'll be Antoinette, in honor of our late queen."

"Very good," Grey said approvingly. "I'm pleased to see that you're beginning to enjoy yourself."

Before she could stick out her tongue at him, Marie-Helene placed the cone over her face, covered her dress with a sheet, and began to squirt powder at her head from a cloth bag fitted with a special nozzle. Her victim made outraged choking noises all the while. When she was finished, the sheet and cone were set aside, and the little maid produced a voluminous mobcap, which she drew over Natalya's coiffure until it was nearly covered.

"Voilà!" Marie-Helene cried proudly.

Grey nodded. "Well done."

"I look like an old witch," wailed Natalya.

"But I am not yet finished," Marie-Helene protested, reaching for a tray of cosmetics. Quickly she covered her mistress's beautiful face with white powder, then painted her cheeks dark pink and her mouth red, adding a black patch near her lower lip. At last she stepped back to admire her handiwork.

Natalya was so repelled by her own garish reflection that she didn't know whether to laugh or to cry. Slowly her crimson lips turned upward. "At least no one will guess who I really am."

"That's the spirit!" Brandishing the walking stick, Grey crossed the dressing room in his buckled shoes and extended his hand. "Come to your husband, my beautiful Antoinette."

When Natalya placed her hand in his, he bent to kiss it, smiling into her eyes.

"I was afraid of this." Lisette stood in the doorway, her expression one of bemusement. Shaking her head, she remarked, "Either there are two very bizarre strangers in my niece's dressing groom, or Natalya has decided to travel to America after all. . . ."

Chapter Five

March 28, 1814

THE RAINS HAD PASSED, LEAVING THE LOIRE VALley washed clean and glowing with the innocent luster of early spring. Out in the courtyard of Château du Soleil, Nicholai, Lisette, Grey, and Natalya stood together near a large wagon that looked as if it had been in use since the construction of the château.

"Why do we have to travel in *that* broken-down old thing? Haven't you a decent closed carriage that you could loan us, Uncle Nicky?" As she spoke, Natalya tugged at her padded corset, struggling to arrange it more comfortably.

Nicholai tried not to look at his niece, for each time he did he was nearly overcome with laughter. She reminded him of one of the old crones who had knitted at the guillotines during the Reign of Terror. His amusement was almost enough to distract him from his misgivings about the adventure she was about to embark upon. "I offered Grey a perfectly nice phaeton, but he insisted upon this ancient vehicle."

"But, what if it *rains*?" She turned on Grey. "Not to mention the likelihood that we'll lose a wheel or the entire thing will simply collapse. And look at that *horse*! It's half-dead."

"Shh." He pressed a finger to his lips, eyes alight with mischief. "She'll hear you. That bay is a very faithful steed, and, like the wagon, will do perfectly for the first day of our journey. Tomorrow morning I'll hire a carriage, but I have

50

other plans for our departure from St. Briac. I intend that we shall be noticed.''

While two stable boys loaded a large cask of wine into the back of the wagon and filled the rest of the empty bed with straw, Grey turned to his host. ''I must thank you, sir, for your many kindnesses to me. I shall guard your niece with my own life.''

Nicholai sighed. ''I don't like this at all, but I suppose there's nothing to be done. Can I count on you to find a maid for Natalya when you reach London? I don't have to tell you that it's unheard of for a gentlewoman to be traveling alone . . . particularly alone with a man.''

''I was planning on it, I assure you.''

''It's hard for me to realize that she's of independent years. Still, at any age, certain rules of propriety ought to be observed.''

Lisette leaned toward her husband. ''Darling, why were you so little concerned with those rules in *my* case?'' she teased. ''Besides, there's the war to consider. Only fathers—and uncles—bother with propriety at times like these.''

''Why don't you go and give Natalya some sound, motherly advice regarding the maintenance of her virtue?'' Nicholai's stern words were belied by the twinkle in his green eyes.

''Speaking of the war,'' Grey said, ''I meant to ask you about that last night. I understand that it is all but finished, and so is Napoléon. What news can you give me? Is there any possibility that we might encounter fighting on our way to St. Malo?''

''No. The battles, if they continue even now, are being fought in the east. If that jackass Napoléon weren't so proud and stubborn, the bloodshed would have ended long ago. As it is, the Allies offered him an armistice last month, but Napoléon refused unless they left France its newly enlarged boundaries. Naturally that ended the negotiations.''

''And now?''

''Yesterday, in Saumur, I heard that all the armies left alive in France are en route to Paris, where one hopes that Corsican will see that his cause is doomed and surrender before any more blood is shed. Of course, he couldn't be bothered with fortifying Paris, believing himself invincible.'' Nicholai shrugged. ''It is a tragedy that a land as beautiful as France must struggle continually with turmoil, is it not? When I first came here thirty years ago, I fell in love with my new home, but soon it was torn apart by that barbaric revolution. Now, Napoléon has seen to it that the beautiful villages are ravaged and most of the fine young men are dead. And still his pride will not allow him to admit defeat. To that madman, no one's blood has any value but his own.''

''I agree; it is a tragedy.''

''Well, with God's grace, peace will come soon. They say Paris is a lost cause. Perhaps Napoléon will take pity on the mothers of France and spare us all another battle.''

''I know that anyone will be an improvement over Napoléon, and that the restoration of a king would mean peace for France,'' Grey remarked, ''but I have to tell you that Louis the Eighteenth hardly meets the requirements of the savior so desperately needed here. I knew him in London.''

''I have met him myself and found him to be slow and genial,'' Nicholai agreed. ''However, to be perfectly honest, I think that France has had enough of dynamic leaders for the time being. And I feel certain that a great deal will change within the government. Louis the Eighteenth will never have the power his brother did.''

Across the courtyard, Lisette embraced Natalya as tears sprang to her eyes. ''You know that I shall miss you desperately, my dear, but in truth I am glad that you are going. You won't be young forever, and I think that it is important to have great adventures. This certainly qualifies!'' She drew back to give her niece a smile that radiated love.

''Lisette,'' whispered Natalya, glancing around to make certain she would not be overheard, ''I'm *scared*.''

''I know you are, sweetheart, but that is only fear of the unknown. You've been insulated here at our château, living through your writing, yet you will not be able to write after a time if you don't enrich your own life with new experiences. This journey can be wonderful fun if you let go of your fear and trust God to guide you. And soon you'll be back in Philadelphia, beginning an entirely new chapter in your life.''

The men were walking over to join them, and James had just burst from the château, running toward Natalya to bid her good-bye.

''I overslept,'' he apologized.

She began to weep as she hugged him, reaching up to brush back his tousled chestnut curls. ''I'm going to miss you terribly. When sea travel is safe again, you must come to America, James.''

''I wish I could go with you now.''

''The next time I see you, you'll be a terribly handsome grown man, and all the girls in Philadelphia will be fighting for your attention.''

He stood up a little straighter. ''Do you suppose?''

She giggled. ''Absolutely!''

His eyes wandered over her costume, taking it in for the first time. ''You certainly look different, Talya. I would never know it was you.''

''That's just what I like to hear,'' said Grey.

''Can that be *you*, Mr. St. James?'' the boy queried in amazement.

Amid the laughter that followed, Lisette tucked a basket of food and wine under the wagon seat, and Nicholai turned to his niece, opening his arms. She stepped into them and pressed her face against his shirt.

''I love you, Uncle Nicky,'' she murmured, her voice thick with tears.

''Watch that you don't spoil that splendid coiffure or your artfully painted face,'' he teased. ''I love you, too, Talya, with all my heart.''

''I can still remember when you came to visit us in Philadelphia, during the revolution here. I was very little, and you were so handsome and dashing. You held me on your lap and told me stories, and you used to give me part of your dessert.''

Nicholai's eyes were warm as he hugged her closer. ''You were a beautiful, enchanting child, and you remain so as a

woman. I'm grateful that you came to Château du Soleil and
lived with us. You've been a bright light in our household.''

"I wouldn't trade these past years for anything.'' She drew
back to look up at him. "But I suppose it is time to move on.
And I do miss Maman and Papa terribly.''

"As do I. Will you be certain to visit Adrienne while you
are in London?''

"Of course! And I will tell her everything that is happening
here.''

Nicholai gave her one more hug and then released her. ''I
must let you go now. Remember, if you change your mind,
you need only send word and I will come immediately to bring
you back.''

"I'll remember, Uncle Nicky.''

Grey helped her into the wagon, where she perched uneasily
on the narrow, splintered seat. Then, after bidding a final farewell to his hosts and their son, the Englishman climbed up
beside her, picked up the reins, and they began to roll forward
down the château's long drive. Natalya turned back once to
wave, seeing her relatives through a blur of tears.

As the wagon with its two eccentric-looking occupants
turned onto the road and disappeared into the chestnut trees,
Lisette took out her lace-edged handkerchief and dabbed at
her eyes. "I truly think that this was the right thing for Talya
to do. It's time she emerged into the world and discovered love
for herself. I've tried not to meddle, trusting God to bring her
to a crossroads.''

Nicholai gave his wife a sidelong glance. "Hmm. I hope
you don't have Grey St. James in mind when you say that. As
a woman, you are probably blinded by his looks and breeding,
and I admit that he seems to be a nice enough man, but he's
hiding something. I can't quite remember what it is, but I'm
certain there's something in his past that disqualifies him as
the husband you've dreamed of for Talya. . . .''

Clinging to its hillsides, the village of St. Briac-sur-Loire
overlooked a dawdling bend in the river. This morning, merchants arranged their wares or swept the rain-washed stone

steps in front of their shops and chatted amiably about the weather. Dogs chased one another up and down the crooked tangle of streets, and wives carried baskets over their arms as they chose bread, meat, cheese, fruit, and vegetables for the day's meals. Then, when they were done, they gossiped and sometimes indulged in tiny tarts or cream-filled pastries that tempted them from the window of the *pâtisserie*.

Le Chat Bleu, perched on the edge of the village, was quiet so early in the day. Brogard, the tavernkeeper, was standing outside replacing a broken shutter hinge when two men on horseback rode up.

"Bonjour, m'sieur," said the first. A few locks of his red hair blew free from under his cap. "We have returned to find out if the fellow you described to us last night has come back."

Brogard shook his white head. "No, I have seen no one. Did you not find him at the château?"

"Oddly enough, no."

"Perhaps he was refused entrance, or he might have changed his mind," the old man said, with a shrug, turning back to the broken shutter. "Or more probably, I was mistaken. I told you that I was unsure. . . ."

"Somehow, I doubt that you were unsure, or that St. James changed his mind." The redhead looked toward his thin-faced companion with indecision. "What do you think?"

The man shrugged. "I don't know, Auteuil. If he was here in this village, I doubt that he's stayed. The question is, which way should we go? Where did you say Wellington was last sighted?"

They were distracted by the sound of a rickety wagon making its way precariously down the cobbled lane next to the tavern. All three men looked over in curiosity, their eyes widening at the sight of the wagon's bizarre occupants.

"Ah, bonjour, messieurs," the man driving cackled, grinning to display stained teeth. His powdered hair, caught back in a sloppy queue, was covered by a huge tricorn hat that came down to his eyebrows. In flawless French he continued, "I was just saying to my beautiful wife that I have rarely seen a finer morning."

"Do I know you, m'sieur?" Brogard inquired, squinting in the sunlight.

"I do not believe you have had the pleasure of an introduction, my good fellow. I am Maurice Galabru, and this is my wife, Antoinette. We are simply passing through en route to visit our daughter in Malestroit."

While Grey extracted his snuffbox and took a pinch, Natalya peeked at the trio of men from under her mobcap. "This village is one of the most charming I have ever seen. Is this your tavern, m'sieur?"

"I am Brogard, madame, the proprietor of Le Chat Bleu. Perhaps you and M'sieur Galabru would care for—"

"*Attendez!*" Auteuil interrupted, dismounting and walking over to the wagon for a closer look. "What are you doing with this wine barrel?"

"It is filled with wine from the château." Grey pointed over his shoulder toward the white castle on the hill above them. "We paused there to greet our cousin, who is a milkmaid for the Beauvisage cows, and the seigneur gave us this wine. A fine and generous man."

"Have you not heard?" Auteuil sneered. "There are no more seigneurs. France has done away with the aristocracy. He jabbed a finger at Grey's chest but avoided touching the dingy green jacket and pink waistcoat. "I demand that you open that barrel for us, old man. There is an enemy of the emperor at large, and you and your wife strike me as the sort of scum who would be ripe for a *bribe*. How much did he pay you to carry him out of town, secreted in that barrel?"

Natalya gasped loudly, while Grey grumbled, "You insult us, m'sieur. We will take our leave now."

"I think *not*." Auteuil produced a large pistol and aimed it at them. "Poujouly, open the barrel!"

The sharp-faced man dismounted, then heaved himself into the back of the wagon. "How very shrewd you are, *mon ami*," he said to the warden approvingly. "Nothing escapes your notice." Then, pulling a knife from his boot, he set about prying the top from the barrel.

"This is outrageous," Grey cried. "You have no right!

M'sieur Brogard, you must stop them. We are poor, simple people, undeserving of such treatment.''

An evil smile spread over Auteuil's face. "Frightened, hmm? I can't say as I blame you. The emperor does not deal lightly with traitors.''

A heavy silence fell over the group as Poujouly forced the nails out of the barrel one by one. Even Brogard came over to watch, favoring the eccentric-looking old couple with a sympathetic smile. Although he disapproved of the tactics of this prison warden, he had allowed himself to be intimidated by the man's threats the previous evening, enough to hint that the prisoner they sought might have gone to the château. Now he regretted his action and decided to at least try to make amends. "See here, my good fellows, must you harass these poor people?''

Auteuil's eyes flashed as he looked back to snarl, "Stay out of matters that do not concern you! The emperor does not favor those who obstruct justice.''

His face burning, Brogard nearly exclaimed that their exalted emperor was nothing more than a pathetic cornered rat whose conceit was greater than the power that remained to him. However, at that moment Poujouly pried out the last nail and gave a grunt of triumph.

Auteuil craned his neck. "Well?''

His companion's face fell. "There's nothing in here but wine. Just as the old man said.''

"Then he's in the straw! Search through the straw, damn you!'' Auteuil's face was as red as his hair.

Poujouly obeyed. Then, reaching the other end of the wagon, he turned and shrugged elaborately. "Nothing.''

"Are you satisfied?'' Brogard said. "Put down your pistol, m'sieur, and let these innocent people be on their way.''

"*Oui*, m'sieur,'' Natalya implored, "do not threaten us further. We are simple folk, and quite unaccustomed to violence.''

Scowling, Auteuil acquiesced. "Something about this doesn't smell right.'' He bent down and looked under the wagon in search of a hiding place. Then, straightening, he fixed Grey with an enraged stare. St. James glanced away instantly and adopted a submissive posture. *"Eh bien*, you may go. But do not forget that I have taken notice of you. If you have any connections to one Grey St. James, I suggest that you sever them if you value your lives!"

Grey hunched over even farther and picked up the reins, while Natalya clung to his arm and whimpered. *"Merci*, m'sieur. We shall not forget. Good day." The bay mare lifted her hooves and started forward. The wagon lurched in response.

Watching them go, Jules Auteuil narrowed his eyes and clenched his fists. "I don't know what it is about that fellow, but I am positive that I have been deceived in some manner."

"Forget about that old popinjay and his painted hag," Poujouly advised. "You're looking for someone to blame, but I've never seen two more unlikely suspects!"

Leaning back against the splintered barrel, Natalya basked in the spring sunlight as the wagon jogged along. Suddenly she giggled. "I simply cannot recall the last time I had so much fun!"

"There's no need to repeat yourself, my dear," Grey said mildly. "I believed you the first time you said so two hours ago."

It was nearly noon. They had made slow progress on their journey to Angers, where Grey had determined that they would spend the first night. It wasn't far, though any destination seemed distant given their mode of travel, but there was much to be done once they arrived. Grey had friends there who would shelter them, help them to dispose of the wagon and the bay, and hire a proper carriage to speed them on to St. Malo.

"That awful man was so furious—it was all I could do not to laugh at him," Natalya continued, unfazed by Grey's teasing. "I may have forgotten to congratulate you on the good sense of your plan. If so, please accept my compliments."

"Good sense?" he echoed, silver lights dancing in his eyes. "Don't you mean *brilliance*?" He didn't mention the doubts he had about whether Auteuil had been completely fooled, preferring to reassure himself with the conviction that his old enemy would have torn off his disguise on the spot if he'd even suspected the truth.

"Please," Natalya rejoined, "you know that I would not praise you with undue enthusiasm. It would be very bad for you."

The road they traveled afforded a breathtaking view of the cerulean Loire, meandering dreamily between its golden banks. Curtains of poplars and groves of birch shimmered, as if dancing to celebrate their budding spring leaves, and new sights appeared with every bend in the road. It was, thought Natalya, like the unfolding of an exquisite tapestry, of ancient villages, mills, fisheries, vineyards, and hunting lodges, all crowned intermittently by magical châteaus high on the surrounding hills.

"I'm simply ravenous," Natalya exclaimed suddenly, bending over to pull the basket from under the wagon seat. "I was so nervous this morning that I couldn't eat a thing—" She broke off, realizing that he might interpret this as a sign of weakness on her part. "Actually I wasn't *nervous* so much as busy. And it was wrenching to bid farewell to my uncle and aunt and James and everyone else at Château du Soleil."

"It's perfectly acceptable to be nervous, my dear Miss Beauvisage. I'll admit to suffering a qualm or two myself from time to time." Grey turned to give her a kind smile. "Right now, though, I'm suffering only from a desire to get out of these clothes and have a bath in the river. I don't know if I can bear this until evening."

"Well," Natalya said briskly, "you must. But take heart. I look just as hideous as you do, and I'm a woman, so my suffering is greater." She pulled the cork from one of the bottles of excellent Vouvray wine Lisette had packed, lifted the bottle to her lips, and drank deeply. Seeing that Grey regarded her with uplifted brows, Natalya laughed. "I thought I ought to stay in character. It seemed just the sort of thing Antoinette would do, don't you agree? Would you care to partake, Maurice?"

"You're quite a little minx," he remarked, accepting the bottle and following her lead. The white wine was dry and fresh and tasted utterly delicious.

To her surprise, Natalya felt the blood rushing to her cheeks in response to his words. "Goodness . . ." She pressed her hands to her face. "It must be the wine."

A wry smile touched Grey's mouth. "Probably." He looked around as she broke a baguette in two and handed half to him. Inhaling deeply, he sighed. "I know that this sense of peace won't last, and that there are problems ahead of us beyond imagining, but at this moment I am a happy man. Liberty is sweet indeed. . . ."

Natalya took a bite of her baguette, and fragments of the thin, crisp crust showered her lap. She smiled at him and nodded vigorously, her outrageously painted face more eloquent than words. From a nearby tree, a tiny gold-and-green willow warbler sang out, as if in acclamation.

"That's right," Grey said, chuckling. "We're going home."

Chapter Six

March 31, 1814

MOONLIGHT STREAMED OVER NATALYA'S EXCEED-
ingly uncomfortable bed on the third story of one of St. Malo's
less prestigious inns. The legendary fortified town was nearly
silent, save for the rhythmic crash of waves against the battle-
ments, yet Natalya had scarcely slept all night. She couldn't
stop thinking about the day to come, about their escape from
France; most of all, however, she couldn't stop thinking about
Grey St. James.

Her heart raced with a jumble of mixed emotions. How
different the past three days had been in comparison to what
she had expected. There had been little cause for laughter
since they had shared wine and bread on the road to Angers.
She had slept on mean, narrow beds in the homes of Grey's
friends, Paul in Angers and Louis in Bain-de-Bretagne. At
least she had *tried* to sleep while the men sat up talking and
drinking wine. Neither house had offered much in the way of
amenities or hot, nourishing food, for neither man was married. To make matters worse, after discussing their situation
with Paul, Grey had decided that time was of the essence and
that he and Natalya would ride to St. Malo rather than hire a
carriage. If Auteuil and Poujouly were in pursuit, they must
not be allowed to catch up. And so their journey had been
arduous, with little time or opportunity for meals and rest, let
alone conversation. Natalya's body ached and her heart was
beginning to ache as well.

In spite of everything, she felt safe with Grey, and she realized that other traitorous feelings had also taken seed. Galloping along beside him, she would find herself studying the shape of his shoulders or the play of his lean hands on the reins, and his face had become an object of fascination. Gaunt he might be, but she had realized that he had the same rouguish, piratical look her father had possessed in his younger days. She was startled by her attraction toward this daring Englishman. He could be maddeningly arrogant, yet he possessed a lighthearted side that appealed to her sense of whimsy. And he was keenly, undeniably intelligent.

Now, turning on her straw tick, Natalya stared out the diamond-paned window set high in the wall. Her eyes were large and luminous with confusion and excitement, anxiety and wonderment. Perhaps, she told herself, she was only drawn to Grey because he seemed to have pulled so far away from her. She had expected him to flirt, but instead he held her at arm's length, treating her with a careful sense of propriety that had begun to annoy her. They never touched except by accident or necessity, when he was opening a door for her or helping her dismount from her horse. By the third night, when he had brushed against her while they climbed the stairs to their rooms, she'd found herself aching for more.

What was happening to her, and why was it happening now? Certainly she had enjoyed herself with men before, and more than a few had fallen in love with her, but none of it had ever been more than a diversion for her. The main reason she had left Philadelphia was boredom—boredom with the rounds of parties, boredom with the pressure to marry that grew with each passing year. By the time she'd turned twenty-five and begun to write *My Lady's Heart*, Natalya had decided that her only talent for romance lay in writing about it.

Tonight, however, in this colorful town, which she had yet to view in the daylight, she lay awake, bemused by the stirrings of her own heart. Closing her eyes, she conjured up the image of Grey's face when he laughed. She ran her hand lightly over the curve of her hip, imagining that his fingers were touching her. . . .

"Natalya! Open the door!"

She sat straight up in bed, blushing in the moonlight. "Grey?"

"Hurry!" His voice was low and hoarse with urgency.

Without another thought, she scrambled up and ran barefoot across the tiny chambers, ghostlike in her white nightgown. She lifted the wooden bolt, fingers trembling, and threw open the door. Grey stood before her clad only in his trousers. His face was pale, his eyes silvery above the strong tapering expanse of his chest.

"Get back!" he hissed, pulling the door closed and bolting it.

"What in heaven's name is happening?"

He clamped a hand over her mouth. "Shh! They're here, searching the inn. I saw them come in from my window. Don't ask me how, but I *knew* that cursed bloodhound would sniff me out. Now you'll have to hide me and then persuade them of your innocence when they get to this room."

Her palms began to sweat and her heart thudded. "But, Grey—"

He was looking desperately around the room, which was hardly big enough for the bed and a little table that held a basin and pitcher. "Dear Christ," he muttered.

"If only we weren't so high, you could go out the window."

His black brows flew up. "You're brilliant!" Swiftly he climbed onto the bed, threw open the casement, and looked outside. Turning to glance at Natalya, he whispered, "The rest is up to you. Call me when they've gone." And with that, he pulled himself up and out the window and disappeared from sight.

Natalya stood rooted to the spot, dumbstruck. In the next moment she heard pounding on other doors around her chamber. She was grateful that Grey had insisted they arrive separately, as if they didn't know each other. At the time, she had thought him overcautious, particularly as he wore the large tricorn hat that proved an effective disguise all by itself. Now she realized that, thanks to him, the innkeeper would be fooled on two counts: he would not connect Auteuil's description of

St. James with the man in the tricorn hat, and he would not connect either of them with Natalya, who had explained that she was meeting her father there at dawn. Who would suspect a sweet and proper young maiden of entertaining a man in her tiny bed in the middle of the night?

Natalya told herself that she had nothing to fear as she listened to the approaching tumult. Still, her heartbeat nearly drowned out the noise. She tried not to think of Grey or worry that he'd fallen to his death.

Bang! bang! bang! "Open this door immediately!"

Recognizing Auteuil's shrill voice, Natalya broke out in a cold sweat. "Who is it?"

"You'll not be harmed. Just open the door, or we shall enter by force!"

She pulled the threadbare quilt from the bed and wrapped it around herself, then gingerly lifted the bolt and opened the door a few inches. Jules Auteuil's face filled the space—and in the next instant he had pushed his way in, followed by Poujouly. Clutching the edges of the quilt against her breasts, Natalya backed up against the edge of the bed.

The lovely picture she made in the virginal nightgown, hair spilling over her shoulders, was not lost on the two men. Auteuil's belligerent demeanor altered as his eyes raked her body. He stepped into the room.

"*Pardonez-nous*, mam'selle." He advanced upon her with an evil leer. "We are officials from the Emperor Napoléon's prison at Mont-St.-Michel. It was rude of us to disturb you in this manner, I know, but perhaps you can help us."

"I don't see how that is possible," she said meekly.

Looking back at Poujouly, he muttered, "Why don't you continue our search. I hardly think that both of us are needed to question this young lady."

The other man frowned but did the warden's bidding. When he was gone, and Natalya found herself alone with Auteuil, she fought a rising tide of panic. "What are you searching for, m'sieur?" she inquired politely. "Whatever it is, I hardly think you'll find it here."

"You have nothing to fear, my dear girl. Are you trem-

bling?'' He put a hand on her arm, and she flinched. ''There
is a criminal at large here in St. Malo, and I have come to
recapture him. I have reason to believe that he is here in this
very inn. Ah, I see that I have scared you, and that was not
my intention. Perhaps you have seen a tall man with black hair
and gray eyes? He is English.''

''I have seen no one. I only just arrived tonight, and am
waiting for my father. He is due at any time.'' She was swept
by a wave of revulsion. When Auteuil smiled, she saw that
many of his teeth came to points as if they had been filed. He
emitted a rank odor, and his reddish hair stuck together in
clumps. ''Please, sir, leave me in peace.''

Awkwardly Auteuil tried to put his arms around her. ''Why
so skittish? I am here to protect you, until my assistant has
finished searching for the criminal.''

''There's really no need!'' Natalya's voice rose; instinctively she put her hands up to push at his chest. When she did
so, the quilt fell away, revealing the gossamer-thin nightgown
she wore underneath.

Auteuil's eyes gleamed. Licking his lips like a starving man
presented with a feast, he ran one hand down her slim back.

''My father could arrive at any moment!''

''I'll take that chance.'' His breathing grew ragged as he
bent closer.

''Loose me, or I'll scream,'' Natalya threatened.

''Oh, I don't think so.'' Auteuil lunged toward her mouth with
his own, but she squirmed wildly and turned her head. ''Hold
still, wench!'' he hissed, fumbling for Natalya's breast.

The casement on the window opened above the bed, but the
warden was too preoccupied to notice. Then a man's body
swung toward him feet first, seemingly out of the night sky,
and Auteuil stepped backward, lifting his hands to his face as
he was knocked to the floor. Flooded with relief, Natalya
scrambled out of the way as Grey grabbed the other man by
his shirt and struck him hard across the chin with his closed
fist. Auteuil's head sagged, but still he reached up blindly,
clawing at his adversary's eyes.

"I see that you leave me no choice, m'sieur," Grey ground out in tones of icy fury. He put both hands around the warden's neck and struck the back of his head against the floor. Auteuil went completely limp.

"Is he dead?" Natalya whispered after a moment.

Grey stood up and brushed off his hands. "Unfortunately, no. I know I ought to kill him, but I've never had a taste for murder, no matter how excusable it might be."

Natalya had begun to shake. "What an odious creature he is!"

"I know." He gathered her into his arms stroking her hair. "Are you all right? Did he hurt you? I needed only to hear you raise your voice to guess what the devil was trying to do."

"I'm fine. Truly." She felt so safe in Grey's embrace, her face pressed against his bare chest. "Thank you for . . . interceding. It was a most impressive display."

"I was a fool to leave you alone."

"Oh, my—I nearly forgot! The other one is still in the inn. Auteuil sent him to finish searching the chambers."

"Then we have work to do."

Grey dragged the warden's body away from the doorway and instructed Natalya to sit on the bed, against the wall. Then he picked up the pitcher from the little table and stood behind the open door, waiting. His patience was soon rewarded. Poujouly came into the room as innocently as a lamb to slaughter. Squinting at Natalya in the shadows, he said, "*Eh bien*, mam'selle, I see you're still—"

The pitcher came down over his head with a crash, and the tall man crumpled to the floor. Natalya scrambled up, and she and Grey set about tearing her quilt into strips, which they used to gag and tie Auteuil and Poujouly. When they were finished, Grey stood over the two men and murmured with heartfelt irony, "If only this were permanent. Unfortunately they'll awaken all too soon, so we must away."

"Do you think he saw your face?"

Grey gave a harsh laugh. "It doesn't matter. He'll know who it was." He glanced down at Natalya, who looked like a frightened fawn, and his eyes softened. "I'm going to give you the late Maurice Galabru's knee breeches to wear, and we'll put a hat on you. A woman would attract too much attention on the quays. Gather up your things now and come with me.''

Natalya obeyed without question and hurried after Grey down the darkened corridor of the inn, her white lawn nightgown billowing out behind her.

Built on a granite rock in the English Channel and joined to France's mainland by a causeway, St. Malo had served as a lair for privateers since the Middle Ages. An aura of romantic adventure clung to the town like the ocean that pounded the wide ramparts surrounding it. Behind the walls rose steep, slate-roofed buildings, a graceful cathedral spire, and the grand homes of shipowners, many of whom had made their fortunes in the slave trade.

As she followed Grey through the maze of cobbled streets and alleyways, Natalya found herself wishing she had time to explore St. Malo properly. Many of France's most legendary men had been born here, including Jacques Cartier, who had discovered Canada; Francois-Auguste-René de Chateaubriand, the illustrious writer; and Surcouf, the fabled corsair who had become the terror of the English in the Indian Ocean and a great favorite of Napoléon's. Natalya was particularly fascinated by Chateaubriand and Surcouf, who were still very much alive and at the peak of their creative powers.

Unfortunately she was destined merely to sweep through St. Malo before leaving France, and at the moment she could hardly complain. As Grey pulled her along, she stole an occasional glance over her shoulder, expecting each time to see the redheaded Auteuil rounding the last corner, bearing down on them with all manner of murderous weapons.

Heather-tinted streaks had begun to lighten the eastern sky, and the dawn lured people out of their beds and onto the streets. They stared at the tall man and young boy who hurried by, the boy holding his old-fashioned hat in place with one small hand. Natalya's legs had begun to ache, and her throat burned; she was about to protest that she could not go on when they arrived at the Porte de Dinan. Grey took them through the arched stone gate, and as they emerged under the ramparts onto the Quai de Dinan, Natalya stared in wonderment at the sights she beheld.

The harbor was a hive of activity, reminding her of Philadelphia's bustling waterfront at dawn. The shore was teeming with sailors, peasants, merchants, donkeys, and monks who wound their way through the crowd with their crosses. On this side of the ramparts, Natalya was suddenly aware of the noise: human voices were nearly drowned out by the salvos of guns and the pealing of bells. Longboats were pulling into the harbor from the sloops and brigantines anchored farther out.

"The slave ships and privateers are blocked in port by the British warships in the Channel," Grey explained, pausing to catch his breath. "Only the fishing boats go unchallenged if they attempt to leave the harbor . . . although many of the corsairs are sly enough to slip by at night."

With that, he grabbed Natalya's hand again and drew her into the crowd. His keen eyes scanned faces as they passed, until, finally, he settled on a sorry-looking old cod fisherman. Grey drew him aside, speaking rapidly in French. The old man peered at him in disbelief, paused, and then nodded. Minutes later Natalya found herself on board M. Oiseau's rotting boat, pushing off into St. Malo Harbor.

Grey pulled her down onto the malodorous deck, shoving aside a pile of nets, and they leaned back against the stern. "Just stay down. I'm in no mood to take chances." To Oiseau, who was adjusting the sails, he called in French, "I'll take the rudder and direct our course."

Drawing a ragged breath, Natalya found that she could scarcely speak. "How. . . ?"

"I bribed him, naturally," Grey told her, with a thin smile. Borrowing her hat, he rose to a crouch and turned the rudder, his eyes fixed on a distant schooner that flew the Union Jack. "I told him that I'd come ashore to fetch my French wife, and now I had to get you safely back to my ship. It was a plausible enough lie, and considering that I was asking him to break the law, it at least allowed him to accept my proposition in exchange for a generous sum of money. Obviously,

M. Oiseau's boat is about to sink, taking with it his livelihood, so he has decided that God sent me to save the situation.''

In a state of crazed exhaustion, Natalya almost began to laugh. "I cannot believe this is happening! Dear Lord, if Uncle Nicky could see me now—"

"I'd rather not think about him at the moment, if you don't mind," Grey replied, with exaggerated irony. "He'd have my head if he had any idea what transpired at the inn."

"You mustn't blame yourself," she protested. "Just the opposite, in fact. You saved my life."

Grey stared at her with intense, silver-gray eyes. "My dear, it was my fault that your life and your honor were in jeopardy at all. That cursed monster should never have gotten close enough to touch your sleeve, let alone—"

"I suggest that we forget about it," Natalya broke in firmly. "In fact, I insist. I'm far too ravenous to argue about something that is already a memory."

M. Oiseau appeared before them and held out a pottery jug.

"Water!" she exclaimed. "How thirsty I am!"

"Let me be your taster," Grey said. Lifting the jug, he swallowed, drank more, then handed it to Natalya with a grimace. "It's calvados. Or, the cheap equivalent. It's bad, but it *is* wet."

Laughing, she drank deeply and felt the strong cider spirit spread its warmth through her tired body. Almost instantly she was swept by a wave of giddiness. Before Grey could stop her, she had turned and risen on her knees to look over the stern, back at the shore. On the verge of waving, she froze at the sight of Auteuil, his auburn hair a banner at the forefront of the crowd. Grey turned to pull her back down, but not before he, too, beheld the narrowed eyes of his nemesis. Could Auteuil really have spotted him? he wondered.

Natalya was startled by the fleeting look that crossed Grey's face. Was it fear? "We're safe now, I'm certain of it," she said impulsively, covering his big hand with her own. "He can't pursue you any longer."

St. James nodded slowly. "Is that possible?"

* * *

"Good God, it's Captain St. James!" The first lieutenant of the *Essex* leaned over the quarterdeck rail and stared in disbelief at the dilapidated fishing boat. "Is that you, sir?"

"Yes, Harrington, it is I," Grey shouted.

The young man turned around, calling, "Captain, come immediately! It's Captain St. James!"

Moments later the plump face of Grey's old friend George Bumblethorpe appeared high above the water. Resplendent in his red, blue, and white uniform, Bumblethorpe gaped at the sight of his fellow captain in the Royal Navy. He could smell the old fishing boat from the quarterdeck, and a pale, shabby-looking St. James stood in the middle of that dubious vessel flanked by a grimy old man and a girl in baggy breeches. After a moment Bumblethorpe regained his voice and exclaimed, "God's eyes, man, let's bring you aboard!"

Grey laughed. "Old boy, I thought you'd never ask!"

Before he and Natalya were transferred into a longboat that could be hoisted up, Grey turned and gave the old fisherman a handful of coins. "You have my sincere gratitude, m'sieur."

Oiseau grinned, revealing a gap in front where several of his teeth were missing. "I was glad to help." He held out a folded pamphlet and said enigmatically, "Chateaubriand speaks for me as well."

Natalya was feeling exceedingly dazed, thanks to Oiseau's calvados and the turmoil of the past several days. By the time they reached the *Essex*'s quarterdeck and George Bumblethorpe bent over her hand during their introduction, she found that she had difficulty focusing. British seamen seemed to swarm around them and to leer at her from the masts.

"Grey?" She reached for his arm. "I believe I may be going to faint. . . ." With that, her knees gave way and she slumped to the deck.

Chapter Seven

March 31, 1814

"SHE ISN'T ILL, IS SHE? OR INJURED?" CAPTAIN Bumblethorpe peered anxiously at the young woman who lay across his cabin bunk, unconscious.

"I doubt it," Grey replied. "I think that a mixture of exhaustion and the excitement of our narrow escape from St. Malo are to blame." He added wryly, "I doubt there's cause for alarm, however. She's a feisty little sprite, and I'll wager that she'll be fully restored to good health after a few hours' sleep."

"I daresay you could use a bit of that yourself, my dear St. James. Sorry I can't offer you better accommodations, but as you know, my cabin is the only oasis of privacy on board." He patted the younger man's back with a beefy hand. "I hope Miss Beauvisage isn't the sort of chit who carries on about propriety? . . ." Bumblethorpe asked, wondering briefly if she were more than just a traveling companion.

"I would hazard a guess that, under the circumstances, a sensible girl like Natalya will not concern herself with propriety just now," Grey replied wearily, sitting down at the captain's desk to remove his boots. "We'll worry about appearances in London. In the meantime, I'm exhausted."

"Never fear. I'm the soul of discretion," Bumblethorpe assured him. "Do carry on, old boy, and sleep if you can. We'll be more than happy to ferry you across the Channel. This blockading nonsense can be frightfully boring, particularly as

71

we all know that the war is virtually ended. In any case, the regent will probably thank me personally for delivering you safely back to British soil. Might even get a medal! I heard a rumor or two that you were dead.''

"That's cheering." Grey yawned, hoping Bumblethorpe would take the hint. "D'you suppose they'll be glad I'm not?''

The captain laughed heartily. "Never knew you very well, St. James, but I can't recall an occasion in your company when I didn't laugh. Lovely wit you have.''

"It will doubtless improve with sleep. . . .''

"Right, then . . . I'll leave you alone. You're certain you don't want food first?''

"I'm too tired to eat just yet.'' Grey looked longingly at the bunk, then smiled at Bumblethorpe, who was backing out into the gangway. "My thanks, George. You're a splendid host.''

"Sleep well, old boy.''

When the paneled mahogany door closed at last, Grey leaned back in the captain's chair and sighed deeply. His body felt leaden and his eyes burned with fatigue, but he needed a few moments to reflect before he could surrender to sleep. The past few days had been so filled with tension and urgent activity that he'd had neither the time nor the energy to think beyond the moment.

He stared at Natalya. Now that they were safely out of France, he no longer needed her help, but he owed her a great deal. And he had made promises to Nicholai Beauvisage that he meant to honor. Very soon, he would see England for the first time in four years. He ached for his homeland. The prospect of being reunited with friends and family, of revisiting familiar haunts, was almost more than he could fathom. Earlier in the war, he had learned to block out the bittersweet memories of the life he'd left behind. How difficult it was to realize that freedom was his again, freedom of thought and of action!

Yet he could not forget Natalya during his homecoming. She was his responsibility, and a prickly one at that. Perhaps she'd spend her time writing while he investigated possibilities for her passage to America—and caught up on his own life.

Yes, his own life. . . . What of Francesca? he mused dispassionately. Would she still be at Hartford House, waiting dutifully for him, or were the rumors he'd heard true?

He almost hoped for the worst: hoped that Francesca had left him and that he'd be able to make a new beginning unencumbered by marriage to a woman he didn't love. . . .

"Please, don't," Natalya whimpered, turning her face toward Grey as she slept on. She looked kittenish to him with her long-lashed eyes that tilted upward at the corners and that tangle of honey-colored curls. Seeing the way her little hands suddenly balled into fists as she slept, Grey felt his heart soften, and he went to her.

She was curled on her side, her attractive bottom pushed against the paneled bulkhead. The boy's costume she wore made her look both comical and endearing, Grey thought as he lowered himself tentatively onto the bunk next to her. Sensing his nearness, she reached toward him. Then, the instant her cheek found his chest, her features softened and she sighed.

"You're safe now," he murmured, his voice barely audible. "We're both safe."

Grey found those words strangely comforting. Cradling Natalya in his arms, he allowed his eyes to close. Almost immediately sleep overtook him and drew him under.

"Devil take it, Auteuil, you're mad!"

Natalya's heart jumped, her eyes flew open, and she would have cried out if her mouth hadn't been pressed to Grey St. James's shoulder. Totally disoriented, she struggled to get her bearings. Gradually she realized that she and Grey were alone and that he was talking in his sleep. But where were they? The rocking of their bed and the *swoosh*ing sound of water against creaking walls suggested a ship. Vaguely she remembered coming on board the British schooner in St. Malo Harbor. It was difficult to sort out dreams from reality.

Her head throbbed, her mouth tasted like cotton, and her stomach rumbled; she was on the verge of nausea. Through the narrow transom above the bunk, a soft, rosy-amber shaft of sunlight slanted in. Was it still early morning, or was twilight already stealing around them?

Natalya was rather disconcerted to realize how comforted she was by Grey's presence, perhaps even more now than she had been that morning in St. Malo. She was unused to leaning on a man, and it went against her principles, but this adventure seemed far removed somehow from her *real* life. Everything had been turned topsy-turvy, and she found it necessary to make up new rules on the spot.

"No!" St. James shouted suddenly, and his long, lean body jerked against hers.

Natalya wrapped her arm around his back and patted gently, feeling the sharpness of his shoulder blades. "It's all right, Grey," she whispered. "You're only dreaming."

His eyes opened, so piercingly silver gray as they stared into hers that a shiver ran through her body. "Dreaming," he repeated, his voice thick with sleep. "Of course."

Natalya's eyes fell on his hand, examined the angry scar across it, and she nearly asked if it was a souvenir from Auteuil, the villain who haunted Grey's dreams. But at that moment they both seemed to become aware of their intimately entwined limbs and disengaged hastily. Grey pushed himself up against the pillows and rubbed his eyes with long fingers. Then he studied Natalya with a slight, mysterious smile that made her blush.

"What amuses you?" she demanded, Auteuil and the scar flying from her thoughts. "You may as well know that I can't remember a blessed thing since we boarded this ship, so if I did something horrendously embarrassing, I'd appreciate it if you would make me aware of my . . . lapse."

"I find it interesting that you assume this sudden onset of amnesia must be a result of wicked misbehavior on your part," Grey remarked, laughing. "I know I shouldn't tease you, and I apologize. But I couldn't help myself. You've had a devil of a time since we left St. Briac, and deserve only my gratitude and highest praise. You're an extraordinary woman, Natalya."

She digested his kind words, then narrowed her eyes. *"And . . . ?"*

"What do you mean?" Grey ran a negligent hand through his hair and lounged against the pillows.

"There's nothing else? Nothing I should know about?"

"If you are concerned that you may have climbed the mainmast, wantonly displayed your admittedly display-worthy charms, and then sung or perhaps recited poetry for the entertainment of the crew . . ." He paused, eyes twinkling, as Natalya waited with an expression of mingled suspicion and alarm. "You may rest easy, my dear. You were not nearly that diverting. Moments after you had been deposited on the *Essex*'s quarterdeck, you fainted. It wasn't your finest moment, but I hardly think that you need feel ashamed."

"I thought you'd decided not to tease me," Natalya said, with a trace of petulance, then declared, "I vow, I'll never touch calvados again!"

"I imagine that some food might lift your spirits—and mine," Grey said. The sight of her brightening face gave him an odd sort of pang in the middle of his chest. He'd never tell her so, but he was beginning to think that he'd never known a more enchanting-looking female than Natalya. And she was looking more enchanting than ever at this moment, sitting on Bumblethorpe's bunk in her voluminous white shirt and old man's breeches. Her face had a warm, winsome appeal accentuated by her lively aqua eyes and unexpected, incandescent smiles. Her honey-gold hair was a mass of disheveled wisps and curls that framed her delicate face and tumbled riotously down her back. Obviously Natalya was one of those rare women whose beauty was even more apparent in the absence of artifice. Grey decided that it was fortunate for him she was so advanced in years. An unmarried woman of twenty-six could only be a spinster or a worldly mistress; she could not be viewed as a proper candidate for romance and/or marriage. He might find her attractive, but nothing could come of it.

Still . . . it was difficult not to think about the other, more intimate discoveries he had made about Natalya when he had cuddled her in his arms in sleep. In spite of all she'd been through, she smelled as if she'd just had a bath scented with meadowsweet. He tried now to forget her fragrance, to forget the warm, firm pressure of her breasts against his chest. Upon awakening, he had had to suppress an unconscious urge to pull open her shirt and nestle between the pale, warm curves—

"I'm utterly ravenous!" Natalya announced suddenly, interrupting his reverie. She scrambled off the bunk to pace across the cabin. "What time is it? How long will it be until we arrive in England? And where will we land?"

Rather disgusted with himself for his mental lapse into lechery, Grey sat up and reached for his boots. "Bumblethorpe, the captain, is a friend of mine, and he was eager to bring us food when we first arrived. I needed sleep more, and you had already made your choice. I'll go above and see what can be arranged now." Pulling on the second boot, he stood up. "And I would guess that it's about sunset, which means that we ought to be nearing the English coast. I'll have to ask George where he intends to put us off the *Essex*. He may take us straight up the Thames to London."

Natalya watched Grey open the door to the gangway, then declared to his back, "How self-important you are. We are at war and you expect this Captain Bumblethorp to deliver you to your front door as if he and his ship have nothing better to do. Pardon me for laughing, sir!"

But it was Grey who laughed as he glanced back over his shoulder and took in the sight of her standing there, arms akimbo and chin lifted insolently. She could still hear him chuckling through the closed door after he'd left the cabin. For some reason, the memory of his flashing teeth and dancing, dangerous eyes made her shiver all over. . . .

"What are you reading?" Natalya asked as she took another bite of tangy cheddar cheese and tore off a fifth generous chunk of baguette.

"Didn't your mother teach you not to speak with your mouth full?" Grey had finished his plate of bread, cheese, apples, and smoked salmon. Now he sipped a glass of fine Grenache wine and perused the booklet M. Oiseau had pressed into his hands when they'd said farewell on the fishing boat.

"Didn't *your* mother teach you that it's criminally rude to *read* when sharing a meal with someone else?'' Natalya countered.

"Touché.'' Grey gave her a nod of dry respect, then held up the pamphlet for her to see. "It's quite extraordinary. Chateaubriand has just published this review of Napoléon's offenses, called *Des Buonaparte et des Bourbons*.''

"I'm not surprised,'' she replied, with studied nonchalance. "Today is the fifth anniversary of the execution of René Chateaubriand's brother, Armand. Do you know the story?''

"Vaguely. Refresh my memory.'' Each time he was reminded of her keen intelligence, Grey felt a slightly unnerving twinge of surprise.

"In 1809, Armand was arrested for transmitting dispatches from the emigré Bourbon princes to their agents in France. René wrote to Napoléon and asked for mercy for his brother, but he was denied, supposedly because the letter was too proud.''

Grey began to nod. "Yes, I remember. Armand Chateaubriand was tried, found guilty, and then shot, wasn't he?''

Natalya's eyes were huge with pain as she finished the story. "René recounted the episode to us when he visited at Château du Soleil last year, and the memory of his face, his voice, will never leave me. He said that Armand was killed on Good Friday, and that he himself arrived just a few moments after the shots were fired. He found his brother lying dead, his skull shattered by bullets, and . . . as he put it, 'a butcher's dog licking up his blood and his brains.' ''

"I heard from prison that Chateaubriand had been in seclusion these past five years, writing quietly, but by no means forgetting what Bonaparte did—not only to his brother, but to France,'' said Grey.

"All along, René has been incensed by Napoléon's limits on freedom of the press. He's been aching to speak out, but I imagine he has been saving his eloquence for when it is needed most.'' Brushing crumbs from her fingers, Natalya reached for her wineglass and continued, "René told Uncle Nicky that when the Allied armies made their final approach and the end of Napoléon's empire was at hand, he feared the French, out

of pride, would make a last show of heroic resistance in spite
of every Frenchman's secret wish to be rid of Bonaparte.
Which, of course, is exactly what is happening. I'll wager that
this pamphlet is René's way of urging France to be reasonable
and welcome the Allies with open arms." She leaned forward,
her eyes agleam with interest. "Do tell me what he's written."

"Well, you are quite right. Chateaubriand contends that
'God Himself marches openly at the head of the Allied
armies,' and then he goes on to list Napoléon's crimes—
executions, tortures, and the rest—and reassures his read-
ers that only a man with a 'nature foreign to France' could
have done such things." Grey smiled at Natalya. "Furthermore, he says that Napoléon's offenses must not be
charged to the French people. . . ."

"How sly of René," she exclaimed, reaching for the pamphlet and scanning its pages. "By assuring the French that
Napoléon is not *really* one of them, he gives them permission
to withdraw their loyalty from him now that the Allied armies
are closing in." She looked up and met Grey's eyes. "I hope
that René's approach helps to end this madness before more
lives are lost."

"You sound as if you love France," he observed.

"How could I not? The land charmed me instantly—its
beauty and style, its history—and over the past five years I
have felt more and more at home. Perhaps it's because my
father is French. My grandpapa spoke with a French accent,
and I learned French from infancy. There has always been a
bond. It's in my blood—"

A loud crashing noise on deck interrupted Natalya. Grey
jumped to his feet and strode out into the passageway to investigate. Moments later he returned, pale but calmer, to report that part of a yardarm damaged in battle had broken loose
and fallen to the deck.

"There's no cause for alarm," he assured her.

"You've turned positively white! Did you think we were
under attack?" Natalya asked, without thinking. "Were you
afraid that those men had somehow followed us?"

"Nonsense. You have the overactive imagination of a melo-

dramatic novelist.'' Grey gave her a quelling look. ''To return
to the situation at hand, George tells me that he is taking us as
far east as Dover, and that's fine. He simply cannot spare the
time to sail all the way up the Thames and then back again.
We're nearly to Dover now. We'll go ashore after the tide
comes in early evening, spend the night at an inn, hire a coach
in the morning, and then be in London by midafternoon.''
Smiling to himself, Grey dropped onto his chair and stretched
out his long, muscular legs. ''I own I couldn't be happier to
be going home. For the past few years, I've learned to block
out thoughts of my old life, and now that I no longer have to,
I find I am most anxious to return.''

Natalya studied him pensively. ''I know exactly what you
mean. I feel the same way—about holding back on thoughts
of home, forcing my mind not to dwell on memories of my
old life. Now I worry that everything I long to rediscover may
have changed, that nothing will seem quite the same as it did
when I last was home.'' She sighed. ''People say that that's
the way it is. . . .''

St. James arched a black brow and turned his face away. ''It
hasn't been that long . . . and I wasn't dead after all. I trust
that my loved ones and friends have kept a spot in their hearts
for me. They've more sense than to credit a lot of nonsensical,
hysterical rumors. I have no doubt that they're expecting my
return.''

''I'm sure you're right.'' Natalya reached out to pat his hand,
but Grey lifted his wineglass at the same instant. She watched
as he drained it, then stood. Restlessly he strode across the
low-ceilinged cabin.

''I'm going up on deck to wait this out. Would you like to
come?''

Natalya beamed. ''Indeed! I'll be with you as soon as I put
on my shoes.''

''You'd better wear my cloak, too. The ocean breeze is
chilly.''

Minutes later, enveloped in the worn black wool of Grey's
cape, Natalya emerged from the dark gangway with its fumes
of pitch and bilge water onto the H.M.S. *Essex*'s main deck.

She barely remembered her arrival on board that morning, but now she was fully alert and quite determined to take in every detail in case she ever needed to write a scene set on board a warship.

The barrage of sights, sounds, and smells was exciting and impressive. Her eyes swept over scrubbed decks and spotless brasswork, triple lines of guns, and masts and yards high overhead that were nearly obscured by a forest of ropes. Smart-looking, straight-backed officers oversaw the movements of gaunt sailors who wore reefer jackets with mother-of-pearl buttons, straw hats, and loose white canvas trousers. They surged over the decks and ratlines, unfazed by the rocking of the ship. Natalya closed her eyes for a moment and listened to the piping of whistles, the rushing of waves, the clanking and creaking of pulleys, the trampling of feet. Her nostrils were filled with the smells of tar, brine, and cold, moist air.

"What an adventure this is!" she cried suddenly, trying to grasp Grey's arm through the folds of her cloak. "I am so very grateful to you for making this extraordinary experience possible."

"What a minx you are," he replied. His bemused eyes held a glint of silver as they stared at her searchingly. "Do you not realize that I would still be trapped in France right now if not for you? I should be expressing *my* gratitude to *you* on bended knee."

"Then why aren't you?" Natalya demanded, her laughter laced with mischief.

Grey smiled and drew her forward. "Perhaps another time, my dear," he replied. "At the moment, it seems more appropriate that we join Captain Bumblethorpe on the quarterdeck. The English coastline is at hand, and the view should be excellent from there."

As they were climbing to the higher deck, a voice bellowed from a platform on the main mast, "Land ho!"

Bumblethorpe trundled forward to meet them. "Ah, my dear lady, what a pleasure it is to see you up and about, and looking so pink-cheeked and lovely!" He caught her elbow through the cape and led her to the polished rail, pointing with one stubby, weathered finger. "Behold, the white cliffs of Dover!"

Natalya gasped, and behind her she heard Grey's sudden intake of breath. "How lovely," she murmured, struck by the sight of the vast promontory, rising up before the churning whitecaps. The cliffs were burnished by a chalky sunset in hazy layers of lilac, gold, and rose. "It's exquisite. I've never been to Dover before. The last time I sailed to England, we docked at Falmouth."

"I happen to think this is an especially pretty place to arrive," Bumblethorpe told her. "The beaches here are quite the rage lately, and the Dover Road to London is profoundly historical, not to mention beautiful."

Natalya nodded politely as the rotund captain chattered on happily, but her eyes were drawn to Grey. He stood a short distance behind them, staring over her head toward the Dover cliffs. The golden orange light of the sinking sun softened the pale, rugged contours of his face and the hard set of his mouth . . . but his eyes! Natalya had never seen the like. His eyes caught the fading rays of the sun and positively gleamed with intensity as he beheld the majestic coastline. At last, becoming aware of Natalya's scrutiny, Grey glanced down at her and appeared to give himself a mental shake.

"It's been a long time," he muttered.

Natalya didn't answer. The aura surrounding him surpassed that of a man who simply missed his homeland. She sensed that there was more at stake for Grey St. James than a mere desire to see old, beloved friends and places from his past.

It was becoming clear that Grey had secrets of some weight. Whatever he kept from her about the bad blood between him and Auteuil was probably the least of it, she realized. A little thrill ran down her spine.

The adventure was just beginning.

PART TWO

Man plans, but God arranges.
THOMAS À KEMPIS
(1380–1471)

Chapter Eight

April 1, 1814

IN THE MORNING, GREY OVERSLEPT, AND NATALYA had to tap on his door at the Ship Inn to rouse him. It was nearly ten o'clock when he finally emerged into the inn's tap-room, looking appealingly sleepy, and rakish in a white shirt and cravat, black breeches, and top boots. Accepting a wedge of cold pigeon pie from the innkeeper's wife, he paid their bill, gestured to the waiting Natalya, and led the way into the yard.

Natalya had certain qualms about the mode of conveyance Grey would arrange for them on this leg of their journey, but when she saw the elegant green-and-black Daumont-style lan-dau he had hired for their passage from Dover to London, all her fears vanished. A pair of prancing chestnuts and a wiry little driver completed the stylish picture. Spring was on her best behavior; the sky was an azure canopy above budding trees, purple crocuses and blue scillia, singing birds, and sunny breezes. As London was only a few hours away, the low-slung, open vehicle seemed not only appropriate, but inspired.

Joy and anticipation lit Natalya's face from within. "What an unsurpassably excellent morning this is. And in all fairness, sir, I must give *you* the credit!"

Grey smiled in spite of himself. "I'm relieved beyond words that you approve of my choice, Miss Beauvisage. May I assist you?"

Natalya smiled prettily and clasped his outstretched fingers, lifting her skirt with her free hand. Today she had packed away the breeches, choosing instead to wear one of the chemise dresses she'd managed to squeeze into the small bag she'd been allowed to bring from France. Although a trifle crumpled, the charming frock of blue-sprigged white muslin, with its tiny puffed sleeves and silk sash, lent her the air of a young girl in her first Season as she arranged herself beside Grey on the landau's leather seat. Her honey curls, freshly washed at the Ship Inn, were caught back in a ribbon to stave off the wind's ill effects, emphasizing the exquisite beauty of her skin, mouth, and sparkling eyes. And her enthusiasm was contagious.

"I'm surprised you're not driving yourself," she said as a boy Grey had hired sprang up to his perch. "I thought it was a point of pride with men of your ilk."

Grey crossed his booted legs on the seat opposite and chuckled. "Dear God, deliver me from falling into anyone's ilk!" When Natalya continued to look at him expectantly, he sighed and went on in a tone of capitulation, "You'll find, if our acquaintance continues, that I am not one of those tiresomely vigorous men who stride through the day constantly reaffirming their masculinity. I enjoy tooling a curricle or phaeton as much as the next fellow, but today I have other matters on my mind."

"Oh, I see." Natalya didn't know what else to say, since it was evident that Grey's thoughts were far from their conversation. So, she left him to them and turned her own attention to the scenery as the landau rolled away from the Ship Inn and began to speed up the Dover Road.

England's appearance of dazzling rural prosperity was all the more impressive in light of the ruin Natalya had witnessed during her recent journey through France. As their landau bowled along the fine metaled highway, she stared at the fat meadows and downs with their well-fed flocks of sheep and herds of cattle. The villages looked idyllic. Laughing children and fat geese frolicked on the greens, and whitewashed cottages clustered around the church and manor house in a cozy fashion. Even the people looked more prosperous than their French counterparts. On the coast, fishermen wore striped jerseys, grey aprons, leather leggings, and fur-lined caps. In villages, Natalya noticed that the country squires sported snowy shirt frills under their wide overcoats. Some farmers wore long-tailed coats, and even the gamekeepers strutted out of shops in green coats and gold-laced hats.

"Has the war had no effect at all on these people?" she asked at last, turning to Grey. "Are there no poor here? Most of the farm animals I've seen this morning appear to be fatter than the majority of people we encountered on our way from St. Briac to St. Malo!"

Her traveling companion appeared to be deep in thought, his countenance more drawn and rugged than usual. However, when he looked at Natalya, he managed a grudging smile. "You do have a singular way of expressing your opinions." He looked around then, as if truly focusing on the countryside for the first time. "I'm sure I don't know how to answer you, Natalya. I've been inhabiting a worse world than you these past years. I hope that England has somehow benefited from the war, and no doubt it's been easier here at home because all the fighting's been going on elsewhere. Not that that is much consolation for all the men risking their lives in Europe and America." Grey paused, sighing as he inhaled the fragrant air of early spring. "I pray that all of England has been prosperous—that nothing changed while I was away, except for the better."

With that, he forgot her again, returning to his own private world of memories and expectations. Natalya swallowed her disappointment at his indifference and self-preoccupation. She had no idea what she felt about Grey anymore, or what she hoped for. She only knew that the sight of his hand resting on his hard thigh, long-fingered and taut, made her heart ache, and she had the same wild stab of pain when she stole a glimpse at his chiseled profile. She had never felt so exhilarated and terrified all at the same time.

This was much more than a silly female reaction to the company of a passably attractive man, she decided. In fact, it probably had very little to do with Grey St. James at all. Life itself was undoubtedly the cause of her euphoria. Every single second that had yet to occur was unpredictable and part of an entirely new experience. She was overjoyed to be alive!

Relieved to have the matter settled in her own mind, Natalya relaxed and stole another glance at Grey. His arms were folded across his wide chest, his eyes were closed, and he was napping in the sunshine, apparently peacefully.

When at last the green-and-black landau gained the top of Shooter's Hill, Grey sat up, fully alert. It was a delightful afternoon. New daffodils were opening ruffled, lemon-bright petals as the travelers sped across Blackheath and spied, through the woods and windmills and hedgerows, the stately hospital of Greenwich and the masts lining the Thames. Then, under the hills of Highgate and Hampstead, appeared London herself. Natalya's first impression was of a maze of brick, steeples, and chimneys spewing smoke high above twisting streets.

"It's been a very long time since I've been here, or to any city, for that matter," she said, with a measure of awe. "It's beginning to dawn on me how isolating the war has been."

"Even the smell of the smoke is familiar," Grey remarked, as if to himself.

Natalya gathered her courage and turned to look him full in the face. "I hope you'll pardon me if I'm being overfamiliar, sir, but I feel that we have become friends of a sort, and I can't help forming the opinion that something or *someone* is haunting you. You have an almost . . . tormented look." Her voice rose dramatically in spite of the way his brows suddenly flew up. "Would it help you to talk about it? Is it Auteuil? I cannot help wondering what passed between the two of you to cause him to hold such a need for vengeance in his heart." Natalya's huge aqua eyes fell for an instant on Grey's scarred hand before she looked away.

"Are you puzzling out a plot device for another novel?" he responded in a tone of amused patience. "A brooding man with a mysterious *secret*? If so, I fear you've come to the wrong person for inspiration." He ran lean fingers through his hair and laughed. "I have no score to settle with Auteuil, and I must assume that my association with him ended in France."

"You dream about him," she countered.

Grey gave a harsh sigh. "Leave it alone, Miss Beauvisage. If I'm preoccupied, it's due to my return to London and no other reason." He looked away from her, out over the city. "God knows there's enough waiting in London to keep me perpetually preoccupied. . . ."

She sniffed. It was certainly his right to keep the truth to himself. If he wanted to pretend that a lot of nonsense from his life among the London beau monde was responsible for his distant, worried demeanor, fine! She, however, preferred to think that Auteuil and his unspeakable crimes of torture were behind it all.

"What shall we do now that we're here?" Natalya asked as they drove along Piccadilly. Her face shone with excitement and her beribboned hair gleamed in the sunlight as she looked right and left, taking in the sights. Through the crush of phaetons, tilburies, landaus, curricles, and tim-whiskies all drawn by stunning thoroughbred horses, she could make out the elegant shops and hotels of Piccadilly. She'd nearly forgotten the extent of London's singular, lively style. Seeing the dandies who strolled about, impeccably turned out in their close-fitting buff trousers, outrageously high starched collars, and windswept hairstyles, she wondered briefly if Grey could have ever been one of them. Realizing that he had not answered her question, she turned and spoke again. "Where shall we go first?"

Grey seemed to remember her presence with an effort. "I . . . uh . . . I think that it would be best if we take you to a hotel so that you can settle in . . . freshen up—" He cleared his throat and finished lamely, "That sort of thing."

"Surely you cannot mean just to deposit me all alone in a hotel with strangers!" Natalya protested in tones of outrage. "I distinctly recall that you assured Uncle Nicky you would take me to your father's house!"

Grey's own face grew stormy. "And I distinctly recall that

you accused us both of treating you like a child. I would have thought that, at your age, you would prefer the more sophisticated situation of a hotel, located near the finest shops. I would have expected you to insist on being able to come and go freely, without having to account for your whereabouts!'' He took a breath and added, ''I'm not trying to push you off in some dingy inn, my dear lady. On the contrary, I thought I'd book rooms for you at the Clarendon, which is probably a good deal more comfortable than my family's town house. And, of course, it goes without saying that I shall send over a ladies' maid at once.''

Natalya cut quickly through his arguments. ''You are trying to get rid of me!'' she cried, then gasped at her own reaction. If she hadn't grown so attached to Grey St. James, for whatever mysterious reasons, his plan would have met with her enthusiastic approval. And, knowing her as he did, he was obviously aware of this. Feeling his silver-eyed scrutiny, she strove for an attitude of nonchalance. ''Never mind. You are one person whose rejection cannot hurt my feelings.'' She feigned a mischievous laugh. ''I shall be overjoyed to escape from our enforced proximity. Considering the difficulty I had even being civil to you when we first met, I think I've done remarkably well during this trying journey, but it would be wise not to test my nerves too severely. How far are we from the Clarendon Hotel? Perhaps it is situated near the offices of my publisher, John Murray, in Albermarle Street. As soon as he learns of my presence in London, I probably shan't have a moment's peace. He's written me the *most* flattering letters.'' Natalya tilted her chin up and to one side, hoping her manner would convince Grey that she had already forgotten his very existence.

Grey gave her a long, bemused look. To be honest, he really did have doubts about leaving Natalya at a hotel, but he simply couldn't have her around, underfoot and asking questions and demanding his attention, during his first days back in London. Before he could inform her of the location of the Clarendon, she startled him by rising abruptly out of her seat and pointing as if crazed toward Hatchard's Bookshop.

"Good heavens!" she cried. "We must stop! It's Adrienne!"

Fearing that she might tumble out of the landau and be trampled in the traffic, Grey grasped Natalya by her shapely hips and pulled her back down beside him. "What the devil are you ranting about now? Quite frankly, I am beginning to wonder if you—"

Fortunately Natalya's excitement prevented her from hearing the rest of her companion's observation. "Grey, do please ask the driver to stop as near to Hatchard's as he's able. Can you see those three females who've just come out? One of them is Adrienne Beauvisage, my cousin!"

Grey did as he was asked—no easy feat considering they were hemmed in by the crush of vehicles filled with London's *ton*, most of whom were more concerned with seeing and being seen than attending to any specific errand.

Natalya was oblivious to it all, however. No sooner had their landau drawn up beside the pavement, which was elevated for the use of pedestrians, than she was out, never thinking to wait for male assistance with the carriage door. Grey considered interfering, then surrendered and sat back against the leather upholstery to watch the marvel of Natalya. In the sunlight, her hair was like a long, luxurious stream of molten honey, accented by the vivid blue ribbon at her neck. Charmingly she was the only woman in sight who was not wearing some sort of headdress. Her delicate features were lively, particularly her turquoise eyes, and excitement and pleasure infused the movements of her body with a new dimension of beauty. Grey smiled slightly to himself as he observed her, pleased with his own air of detachment.

"Adrienne!" Natalya exclaimed, running up behind three fashionably dressed females. Two of them appeared to be quite young, seventeen years old at most. The third woman was at least twice that age, with a commanding presence and heavy russet-colored hair, which she wore piled atop her head and crowned with a green crepe toque.

Natalya was exchanging a series of enthusiastic embraces with the more beautiful of the two young ladies, whom Grey assumed must be her cousin. Although willowy like Lisette, and blessed with her mother's engaging smile and dimples, Adrienne Beauvisage had inherited her father's coloring. Chestnut curls, shot through with red-and-gold highlights, framed her lovely face with its merry emerald green eyes. Grey didn't know if Adrienne was old enough for her first Season yet, but it was obvious that she would be a heartbreaker. He guessed that if Nicholai had any inkling that his daughter was in possession of such a bounty of feminine charm—and was displaying it freely before all of London—he'd have her back at home, locked up safely at Château du Soleil.

"How simply wonderful it is to see you, Talya!" Adrienne was exclaiming. "And how exciting that you're going home to Philadelphia! However, once you get a taste of London society, you won't want to leave. Here, I'm forgetting my manners. You must meet my dearest friend, Venetia Hedgecoe. We're at school together." She paused as Natalya and Venetia exchanged greetings, then drew the older lady forward into their circle. "And this is dear Mrs. Sykes. Mrs. Sykes is an old friend of Venetia's parents, and she's been kind enough to let us come and live with her this year. Staying at school had become unspeakably dreary, Talya, and there is so much to see and do here in London! Thanks to Mrs. Sykes, I am now able to truly *live*, rather than simply exist, locked up at school with a lot of dusty old books and priggish girls."

Natalya was taken aback. "I understand your point, dear cousin, but do Uncle Nicky and Aunt Lisette know of the change in your circumstances?"

" 'Tis difficult to post letters to France," Mrs. Sykes put in. "But, we'll try. I've been penning a missive to Adrienne's parents myself." When she smiled at Natalya, her strong chin seemed to grow even longer. Although tall as a man, with broad shoulders and big hands, she was possessed of a certain regality. "I don't mind having the girls with me in the least. They came for tea a few times, and I found that my heart went out to them, shut up in that school during what ought to be one of the most exciting times of their lives. Books are all well and good, mind you, but I believe that there is more to life, particularly when you're young and pretty.''

Events progressed rapidly from that point. Upon discovering that Natalya was going to stay at a hotel, Adrienne declared that she must come and stay with them at Mrs. Sykes's lodgings in Bennett Street. Natalya agreed, if only to see for herself in exactly what sort of environment her cousin was living. Then, suddenly remembering Grey, she whirled around to discover him leaning against the landau and watching them.

Despite his pallor and gaunt appearance, he made an astonishingly attractive sight with his keen gray eyes and chiseled features. His black hair, with its strands of silver, was windswept and gleaming in the sunlight. People stared at him as they passed, particularly the women, and some offered hesitant greetings. Grey acknowledged only those who dared address him, giving them a sudden flashing smile in exchange for their uncertain words. An animal magnetism underlay his smooth, mannered exterior, reminding Natalya of a stallion waiting for the hunt to begin. She realized with a qualm that this was not the way Grey had planned to spend his first hour back in London.

Natalya's cheeks were pink as she drew him forward and made introductions. Feeling Adrienne's astonished, curious gaze, she hastened to explain, ''Uncle Nicky is well aware of this arrangement, so you needn't look at me that way, cousin! You would also do well to bear in mind that I am a decade older than you, which alters my situation considerably.''

''Do you mean that you needn't concern yourself with propriety any longer, Tayla?'' the girl inquired, with studied innocence.

''I haven't a particularly strong desire to continue this discussion,'' Natalya replied primly. ''I will add, however, that because of the war, we were forced to bend the usual rules a bit. I wanted, above all, to return to America, and this was the only way I could accomplish that goal. Now then . . .'' Briskly, she turned her attention to Grey, whose eyes revealed far more to her than words. ''I know that you may be dubious about my new plans, Mr. St. James, but there's no need to concern yourself. I am quite capable of seeing to my own needs during my time in London, and it will be much more pleasant for me to stay with Adrienne than be all alone in a dreary hotel.'' She gave him a bright smile intended to put an end to the subject.

Grey opened his mouth to protest, then thought better of it. Although it was clear to him that her proposal was far from sound, or even sensible, he kept his opinions to himself. He would take her at her word and let her control her own affairs.

''If you say so, my dear Miss Beauvisage,'' Grey replied in his mildest tones, adding a polite, if insincere, smile. ''I shall leave you, then, in the company of Mrs. . . ?''

''Sykes,'' the older woman supplied firmly. ''Perhaps your lordship's forgotten, but you and I have met before. I'm an old friend of your father's.''

Grey's eyes opened wide as awareness dawned. This was one of the women whose company the Earl of Hartford had come to depend on soon after the death of his wife, Grey's mother. At her own husband's death, Grey recalled, Mrs. Sykes had been left with a fine house in Bennett Street, a staff, and creditors. Past her prime, she had used her compelling personality to attract men of substance and thereby maintain her life-style. Nothing out of the ordinary in London, certainly, but why was she taking in innocent young girls to live in her house?

''Ah, yes, Mrs. Sykes,'' he said, with a cool smile. ''Of course, I remember you. You're looking very well. Have you news of my father? I'm just back from France, as Miss Beauvisage has doubtless informed you. Haven't been home yet.''

''The earl is in good health, I believe,'' she said. ''I haven't spoken with him for some weeks, but I will tell you that there's a rumor about that you were lost in the war. It may be quite a shock for him to see you.''

A shadow of cynicism crossed Grey's countenance as he replied, ''Somehow I doubt that, Mrs. Sykes.'' He might have added that he had never known his father to display any emotion as strong as shock.

Natalya was watching him curiously, while Mrs. Sykes studied him with a critical eye. ''I hope you'll pardon me for

speaking my mind, your lordship, but you look terrible. You
need someone to look after you. How horrid that your—'' She
broke off suddenly, as if realizing that she was about to say
too much. ''But I'm taking up your time, when you doubtless
have more pressing business.''

Francesca's name hung unspoken between them; Grey's jaw
was clenched as he glanced away. ''Very true, madam. I really
must be going.'' He turned to Natalya. ''I'll be in touch with
you as soon as I have settled the plans for your passage to
America. If you need me, I'm certain Mrs. Sykes will assist
you in reaching me.''

Natalya's heart began to ache as she realized that they were
parting, and that she was more nervous about her new situation
than she would ever admit. She longed to touch his hand, but
Grey had never seemed more distant. ''Thank you for bringing
me this far,'' she murmured, mustering a brave smile.

''It is I who am indebted to you,'' he replied gracefully. ''I
shall see you soon. Have you sufficient funds?''

''Oh, yes, certainly.'' Natalya flushed. ''I brought with
me the very handsome advance that Mr. Murray paid for *My
Lady's Heart*.'' She didn't mention the fact that Nicholai had
given her a far larger sum of money than the rather meager
payment her publisher had made.

''Ah, yes, a woman of independent means,'' Grey murmured. ''I beg your pardon for forgetting with such annoying
frequency.'' He smiled into her eyes, adding, ''I hope that you
enjoy London, Natalya.''

With that, he sketched a bow to the other females, made his
farewells, and returned to the landau. The driver brought Natalya her small bag, then hopped back to his perch and guided
the beautiful landau into the sea of vehicles. Natalya stared
after him, trying to keep Grey's dark head in sight.

''Cousin!'' Adrienne exclaimed next to her. ''What tales
you must have to tell of your flight from France with that
exceedingly thrilling man! Are you *desperately* in love?''

''He's a viscount, you know,'' Mrs. Sykes put in bluntly.
''Not so long ago, every well-born female's mama had her
sights set on Lord Altburne. He was a rake, but so irresistibly

charming that no one could hold his faults against him. The war's aged and hardened him, but I'll wager he's still the sort of man women can't help falling in love with.''

Natalya felt herself redden. ''Grey doesn't use his title anymore,'' she mumbled. ''And you mustn't be so silly, Adrienne. There's nothing to tell. The arrangement between Mr. St. James and myself was purely one of convenience. Once he arranges my passage to Philadelphia, our business will be ended.''

''How dull and depressing,'' pronounced the younger girl. ''I don't know that I believe you, Talya.''

Mrs. Sykes turned to lead them toward her carriage. ''I wouldn't depend on hearing from Viscount Altburne any time in the near future,'' she said in the tone of one who knew much more than she would divulge. ''He will soon discover that he has a rather messy plate of his own business to attend to.'' Reaching back, she took Natalya's arm in a firm grip. ''Come along, my dear. I'll see to it that you are not bored while you await his lordship's attention. To begin, we must acquire a proper bonnet for you!''

Chapter Nine

April 1, 1814

"Ah! I see you're back," the Earl of Hartford said mildly as he stood to greet his son. "Do come in, dear boy."

Torn between a familiar twinge of disappointment and the stirrings of amusement, Grey was surprised to feel himself smile easily. His lordship, having been informed by the butler that his long-lost elder son was in the vestibule, had done no more than lay aside the *Gazette* and inform the rather stunned-looking Dimbleby that he might bring the viscount up to the library. Now, as Grey crossed the softly hued Aubusson carpet, his father regarded him with polite interest.

"You're looking extremely fit, sir," Grey said by way of greeting. As he shook his father's hand, he thought how well the elder man wore his seventy years. Hartford was always impeccably turned out in the finest and most subtle of taste. His tall, lean figure never seemed to change, though his hair had gone completely white and his ice blue eyes appeared to be even more piercing under the snowy tufts of his brows. Grey decided now that perhaps this was one of his parent's positive attributes: he was reassuringly predictable. And most predictable of all was his impassivity.

Hartford believed that it was bad form to show emotion. He had once remarked to his son that while there must be occasions to warrant such displays, he had yet to encounter one. He had weathered the birth of three children, the death of his

97

wife delivering their daughter when Grey was ten, and more recently the loss of his second son, David, in the battle of Salamanca. If none of these had caused him openly to shed a tear, why should the return of his heir from rumored death be an exception?

"I look well?" Hartford repeated, as if trying to make sense of his son's remark. "Why should I be otherwise?" He glanced up as two maids came in with tea and cakes. "Ah, just the thing. Can you stay for tea, my boy?"

"Father, I've come home," Grey said, with labored patience. Why had he allowed himself to hope that the earl might show some sign of affection or relief or even simple pleasure when he presented himself after a two-year absence? The old man behaved as if his son had merely dropped by as a matter of course to indulge in speculation about the weather.

"So I surmised, but I thought you might have other matters to attend to." Hartford sipped his tea, then inquired, "The war is over, I gather?"

"Nearly so, sir. I've been in prison at Mont St. Michel this past year. I escaped and found a way back to England, thinking that, perhaps, I might be allowed to take leave. Matters seem so nearly resolved on the continent that I felt the Allied forces could doubtless manage without me." His tone was dry and laced with irony, a match to his father's spare conversational style.

"Prison, hmm? So that's where you've been. No doubt that was unpleasant, but certainly preferable to David's fate." Hartford glanced longingly toward his *Gazette*, but forced himself to chat a few minutes longer. "I'll own that you don't look well, dear boy. But then, you're getting older. I tend to forget that you're . . ."

"Thirty-six," Grey supplied.

"Hmm. Yes, of course. Well, you look as if you could do with a good meal and a good bed."

"Father, where is Francesca?" Grey asked abruptly, tired at last of not knowing for certain what he sensed was bad news.

The earl drew his mouth into a tight line and appeared perilously near visible annoyance. "How very tiresome. I'd hoped that you had already been told. You know, Grey, I never did care for that girl—"

"I need not remind you that I only married her at your behest, Father," Grey put in firmly. "I was tired of being badgered to marry and sire an heir, and tired of being chased by the mothers of every girl in England. Francesca was beautiful, and eminently suitable, *you said*. For my part, I was simply glad to have it settled so that I might devote myself to the war with Bonaparte."

"I'll not deny that there were many practical advantages to that marriage, nor that I encouraged it," Hartford replied in Franchill tones. "The competence Carsbury settled upon his daughter discharged debts that were a threat to our fortune, and that affected *you*, my boy. No one coerced you to agree, however." He gave his son a shrewd glance, thinking of the passion he had seen in Grey's eyes before his wedding to the hotblooded Francesca Carsbury Burke. The young woman's first marriage to a corporal in the King's Own Third Dragoons had been short-lived, thanks to the war, and she had emerged from mourning one year later wearing a restless, knowing expression that had roused the interest of every healthy male she'd encountered. "You had an odd kick in your gallop that spring, my boy," Hartford continued. "I never did know whether it was boredom with your mistress or an urge to cause a stir among the *ton* that sent you to the altar; I certainly didn't ascribe your compliance to any desire to please me."

Grey nearly laughed aloud, longing to declare his belief that the earl had spared little energy worrying about his son's motives or state of mind. Instead he remarked cynically, "It was an interesting wedding night."

"And then you returned almost immediately to your ship, leaving *me* to share this house with the new Lady Altburne." The earl's gaze wandered as he reached out with a thin hand to touch the *Gazette*. Sniffing, he added, "I couldn't like her."

"Father, our apartment is quite separate from yours. I highly doubt that you had occasion to encounter Francesca with any regularity.'' Grey's eyes were steely as he leaned forward and said, ''Now, kindly tell me the whereabouts of my wife.''

''Have you heard nothing at all?''

''A rumor,'' he allowed. ''I would appreciate facts in its stead.''

''Well, your bride has flown,'' Hartford said placidly, with a wave of his hand. ''Run away, you know.''

''Father, I would be obliged to you if you would simply lay the thing bare for me! I'm in no humor for struggling to elicit each scrap of information.''

''Unfortunately, dear boy, I am in possession of relatively few facts. One day, a few months after you returned to sea, your wife disappeared. Left a letter that claimed she had no marriage and couldn't bear such a life any longer. Something about a premonition that you'd be killed in any event, so what was the point? Such a lot of nonsense.'' The earl opened a golden snuffbox and gracefully took a pinch before continuing. ''Since you're keen on hearing everything, I'll add that rumors were flying at the time that Francesca had run away with a lover, but I've no idea whether there was any truth in that.''

''Do you not?'' Grey queried coolly. ''And have you no news of her whereabouts?''

His father stared thoughtfully into space for a moment as if searching his memory. ''I do believe that I heard she'd somehow gotten herself to America. Michael Angelo Taylor mentioned to me when we last met at Brook's that she had written a letter to her father that took six months to arrive. I wouldn't rely on Taylor's word, however.'' Hartford brought the folded journal back into his lap and let his eyes roam over the printed columns. ''No doubt you're fatigued, dear boy. The servants will be delighted to fuss over you.''

Taking his cue, Grey stood. He had a thousand questions more to ask, but it was evident that the earl had already exceeded the time limit he placed on filial conversations.

''I'll be dining out, Father.''

Hartford nodded absently, not looking up. ''Fine, fine.''

* * *

Grey was aware of an almost overpowering sense of unreality as he stood in the bedchamber inhabited by his bride for so short a time. He found new holland covers on the furniture, but the soft gold walls and gold, green, and cream carpet were poignantly familiar. Drawing the cover from the testered Hepplewhite bed, he stared at the rich mustard brocade counterpane and pictured Francesca lying across it, her auburn hair spread out to frame a pale face with slanting, thick-lashed green eyes and a luscious red mouth. Her legs had been long, pale and smooth as alabaster, and her breasts—

Grey gave himself a mental shake. It was true that his bride had been a tigress in bed, and in those days he had been satisfied with the match if only for the most carnal reasons. Now, however, as dusk cast a pall over the bedchamber, the entire affair seemed a rather unsavory dream. It was difficult to remember exactly how it had all come about. In part, he blamed his fondness for spirits during the weeks of his leave in England that spring of 1812. Drink had dulled his judgment. Then there was his boredom with Alycia, just as the earl had suspected. His longtime mistress had been overpreoccupied with her desire to have him buy her a house, gowns, jewels, and assorted other treasures during his brief stay in London. Francesca had sparked the sort of lust he hadn't known for a long time, and he remembered having some notion of getting her with child to leave an heir behind in the event of his death.

Thank God there had been no child, Grey thought now as he wandered into the dressing rooms and bathrooms that connected his wife's bedchamber to his own. Four-year-old suits of clothing hung neatly in his dressing room, and it was as if they belonged to a dead man. It was obvious that he'd need to pay a visit to his tailor on the morrow. Where, Grey wondered, was Clive Speed? His devoted valet of nearly two dozen years was an authority on all matters of male style, taste, and breeding. He had taught his master to shave and to tie a cravat that would rival any of Brummell's; Grey would have gladly taken Speed with him into war had it not been for the man's advancing years.

Somehow, even though he'd sent no word of his impending

arrival to Hartford House, he had rather expected the valet to be waiting beside his shaving stand with a fresh neckcloth. Perhaps, Grey thought, he was taking a turn in the park. There doubtless had not been a great deal to occupy the proud man-servant during his employer's two-year absence.

A few gowns and personal possessions remained in Francesca's dressing room. Grey had an odd feeling when he touched the gossamer-thin muslins and rich silks, remembering how the fabrics had clung to her body. They had lived together as man and wife for less than two months, yet Francesca was burned indelibly into his memory. Out of bed she had been difficult to deal with, although never boring, and their lusty encounters between the sheets had had a combative edge. Once or twice, when they had coupled in daylight, Grey had glimpsed a light in her eyes that had seemed calculating. At the time he had dismissed his vague sense of unease, but now the memory gave him a chill. Today, with the war nearly over and his life spared, he was glad to be rid of Francesca and their marriage. It had been an impetuous, foolish busi-ness, the sort of thing that occurred all too frequently in time of war. He knew that his pride should be bruised, but he thanked God that his wife had been shallow enough to run away in search of excitement rather than wait for him out of stubbornness or greed.

She'd given up quite a lot, he had to admit. Francesca's father and her first husband had been wealthy, so his own modest fortune was not of great importance. However, he knew that she had been impressed by her new title, the history of their ancestral estates, their position in society, and the heirlooms that passed to her as his wife. It must have pained her to leave behind his mother's jewels, which she had worn constantly in the weeks after their wedding. Grey knew that Francesca had dreamed of the day when the earl would die, passing on his title to Grey, and she would be the Countess of Hartford.

Just to set his mind at ease, Grey found his own key to the secret drawer in Francesca's satinwood dressing table. Insert-ing it in the tiny golden lock, he slid open the drawer and withdrew the carved mahogany box that had always held the jewelry belonging to his mother and, more lately, his wife. They were exquisite pieces, many of which had been in the family for more than two hundred years, and it had always made Grey feel a bit odd to see Francesca wearing them. Somehow, he sensed that his mother would not have approved.

Assuming that the jewels would be inside the box, he opened the lid. His heart froze. All that lay against the velvet interior was Francesca's wedding ring, along with the pearl-and-emerald choker he had given her as a marriage gift.

Speed had doubtless put the other pieces away for safekeeping, he decided immediately. He pulled the bell cord and waited restlessly for Dimbleby, who had been pacing in the passageway in anticipation of his lordship's request for a bath or a hot meal. The old man appeared in moments.

"How may I serve you, my lord?"

"Where is Speed? Has he gone out for the afternoon?"

"No, my lord. Were you not aware that he had taken another position?"

"What?" Grey stared in disbelief. "Are you roasting me, Dimbleby?"

The butler was mortified. "Of course not, my lord! I would never do such a thing! Mr. Speed was never himself after you went away, sir. Quite at a loss, he was. Then he was offered an excellent position as valet to Lord Faircastle, and although the decision was difficult, he had to go for his own peace of mind. There was no telling how long the war would go on, or what the outcome would be."

Grey was visibly shaken. What a fool he had been to expect his world here to stand still until his return! But to lose Clive Speed was almost more than he could bear. Had he not made it plain to his manservant how deeply he valued him? Then, remembering the fog he had operated in during his wedding leave, he felt a wave of self-loathing. Speed had been more than a perfect valet; he'd also been father, companion, and confidant. From the time of the countess's death, he had been Grey's anchor, discreetly guiding him through adolescence and into manhood. How would he manage without him?

"Faircastle, you said?" he murmured, looking pained.

"Yes, my lord."

"Well, I cannot fault him. Faircastle is head of his own household, so it was a step up for Speed, hmm?"

"Might I venture the opinion that Mr. Speed was motivated more by the fact that Lord Faircastle is *present*, my lord? He needed to be occupied."

It occurred then to Grey that Clive Speed might be lured back to his former employer if a heartfelt plea was made. "Dimbleby, I would like a hot bath. I'm going out." His thoughts bounced back and forth between the challenge to recover his manservant and his desire for the company of Alycia Hamlyn, the mistress he had cast aside so heartlessly on the occasion of his marriage. After settling matters with Speed, he would go to the tenderhearted, loyal Alycia, and beg her pardon. Fortunately the evening was young.

"Yes, my lord. I'll have a bath for you straightaway. And I shall send someone to see to your clothing."

"Thank you." Grey started to turn away, then remembered to ask, "Dimbleby, you don't happen to know if Speed or my father put Lady Altburne's jewelry away for safekeeping after she . . . uh, departed?"

"No, my Lord. I haven't a clue."

A shadow passed over Grey's face. "I feared as much."

Edward Meadows, the sixth Marquis of Faircastle, lived in Faircastle House, which had been built by his grandfather on the west side of St. James Square in 1755. The fifth marquis had perished in a duel while his son was still at Oxford, and Edward remained uneasy in his title. He was eight years younger than Grey, so they had never been friends, but Grey remembered him hanging about at White's and Brook's soon after inheriting his earldom, and he'd seemed a genuine sort of fellow.

Standing outside as he waited for a response to his knock, Grey decided that he almost preferred Faircastle House to his own family residence. Its facade was plain, but there was a top-lit staircase in the center of the building around which, on the first floor, ran a circuit of magnificent reception rooms. He'd attended a memorable rout here soon after his wedding and had found the house to be richly colorful and warm. Hartford House, on the other hand, was a cool place. Its huge, high-ceilinged rooms were filled with priceless works of art that made Grey feel as if he lived in a museum. Briar Hill, the family estate in Hampshire, was a pleasantly different matter, but he'd spent little time there as an adult.

When Faircastle's rather courtly butler admitted him into a splendid entry hall lit by a glittering chandelier, Grey began to sympathize with Clive Speed's decision to defect.

"Lord Altburne, it's a pleasure to see you safely returned from the continent," the butler dared to remark. "I'm sorry to inform you that his lordship is not at home this evening."

Relieved, Grey felt a fresh surge of confidence. Perhaps all had not been quite as he left it two years ago, but he would soon have matters restored to their proper order. "Actually, Forbes, I have not come to see Lord Faircastle. This may sound rather odd, but I'd hoped to have a word with Mr. Speed, his lordship's manservant."

"Ah, I see, my lord. Well . . ." Forbes paused, as if wondering how to proceed.

"I'll be happy to go belowstairs to meet with him."

"Certainly not, my lord! Follow me, please."

The butler took Grey to a small study near the back of the house, furnished him with a glass of champagne, and then excused himself. Grey stood near a cheery fire burning in a small, tiled fireplace and drank the champagne. Idly he surveyed his own appearance, knowing he'd earn a scold from Speed. His clothing might look impeccable to an unschooled eye, but the manservant would notice immediately that his buff pantaloons were not as snug as they ought to be, his cravat was not as fresh and crisp as new snow, and his blue coat was a trifle outdated. Grey might have turned ladies' heads on St. James Square, but Speed was a genius for the fine points of dressing a gentleman.

The paneled door to the study opened, and Clive Speed entered, unannounced. He looked considerably older than

Grey remembered him. Always small and wiry, he was now
slightly bent, and the light dusting of gray hair atop his narrow
head had disappeared completely. The gleam in his snapping
brown eyes was unchanged, however, as was his habit of clearing his throat whenever he tried not to show emotion.

"When they told me it was you, my lord, I thought they
were having me on," he said softly.

Grey strode forward and shook the older man's hand with
feeling. He would have hugged him, but he knew that Speed
would be horrified by such a breach of propriety. "Speed, how
good it is to see you! I'll confess that it was a terrible shock
to find that you'd left Hartford House."

"You shouldn't have come here, my lord. You had only to
send word and I would have been before you in a trice." His
sharp eyes wandered quickly over the form of his erstwhile
master. "What did they do to you, my lord? How thin and
pale you've grown, and—"

"I've probably tied my cravat improperly, hmm?" Grey
interjected, with a grin. "I've been in one of Boney's prisons, Speed, but that's over now and I'm home. A few days
of sun, good food, and sleep and I'll be fine. Tell me about
yourself. Am I really doomed to rattle through life without
benefit of your guidance?"

Speed went to stand before the fireplace, staring at the dancing flames. "I've dreaded this day for a year, my lord. The
only thing that frightened me more was the possibility that you
might not come home to give me a dressing-down. You must
know how fond I am of you. I've no right to say it, but there
were moments when it felt as if we were father and son . . ."

"I felt it as well!" Grey answered, with feeling.

"How can I explain what led me to leave my position?
Perhaps, if you hadn't gone off for so many years, I might be
there still, yet there is more involved than the boredom I felt
with nothing to occupy me until your return. I had years to
think, and I began to realize that I was no longer as useful to
you as I had been. I began to regard you as a—a beloved son
who had grown up and no longer relied on me, or needed me,

as you once had.'' Speed paused to draw a pained breath. ''I began to feel blue-deviled. Old. Useless.''

''Speed!'' Grey exclaimed. ''You are neither old nor useless. I have always depended upon you more than words can express and finding you gone was a worse shock than discovering I no longer have a wife!'' He gave a short, bitter laugh.

''Let me say again that my regard for you, my lord, is beyond expression. But, quite simply, it began to dawn upon me that I had already taught you all that I knew, and you have had years to practice. You're better at shaving yourself and tying your own neckcloths than I am, and that's a fact.'' Smiling philosophically, Speed rubbed a wizened hand over his bald head. ''Then Lord Faircastle came to me, said he was marrying and in need of the best manservant available. He'd come to the earldom ill prepared, and he needed all the knowledge that you already have, my lord. I felt challenged again, and needed.'' He cleared his throat again. ''As it happens, I'm quite devoted to my Lady Faircastle. Perhaps I ought to tell you that she is—''

''Devil take Lady Faircastle,'' Grey said sulkily. ''No disrespect intended, of course, but one can't help feeling a trifle dismal hearing about the happy household you are part of now. How can I blame you for choosing this over sitting about at Hartford House wondering if I'd make it back alive?''

''Now, now, my lord, don't get yourself into a taking. It's my opinion that you are upset about coming back to find that things had changed in your absence. None of us like change. I'll tell you frankly that I was frightened to death about my new life here, but it's all turned out for the best, I think. And, I daresay that a change of manservants will do you good as well. After your experience in France, I should imagine that you feel as if you're beginning to live all over again.''

Grey saw that arguing would only make Speed feel more uneasy, so he managed a weak smile. ''How unutterably tiresome it will be to spend my first days home interviewing valets. But I wish you well, old man, and want you to know that if you should ever need me . . .''

''May I echo those sentiments, my lord?'' Speed clasped

his former employer's outstreched hand. "And, I may be able to put you in the way of a manservant. It so happens that my son, Jasper, has decided to leave farming and take up his father's profession."

This sounded ominous to Grey, but he assured Speed that he would be pleased to speak to his son. "I ought to be on my way, then, before Lord Faircastle returns and discovers that I invaded his home and attempted to steal back my valet."

As they walked toward the library door, the old man was breathing easier. "My lord, I hope you'll not take offense if I say that I was pleased when her ladyship ran away. She was never *my* idea of a bride for you . . ."

"So you mentioned, as I recall," Grey said, with soft irony. "I should have listened to you. Which reminds me, there was something else I meant to ask you tonight."

"I am at your disposal, my lord."

"Speed, I know I can confide in you and depend upon your discretion. Today, when I opened my, uh . . . wife's jewel box, I discovered that all the family heirlooms were gone. I had hoped that you might tell me you had put them away."

Speed's frown deepened the lines on either side of his mouth. "I fear, my lord, that I can give you no such reassurance. Who would have guessed that she could have been as brazen as *that*?"

"Only I could have guessed," Grey said grimly, "and I chose to ignore the signs of character that she flaunted before me. Perhaps I deserve to be punished for my poor judgment, but I do not intend to deprive my entire line as a result of my folly."

The manservant attempted to sound a more positive note. "Well, it's all done with now, and you can get on with your life."

"I mean to do that very thing, Speed." He opened the door to the passageway, which was filled with golden candlelight. "I'm on my way to visit Miss Hamlyn in an effort to make amends to her for the shoddy way I treated her when I married Mrs. Burke. I must have lost my senses to have tossed her aside for that—"

"High-flying shrew?" a feminine voice supplied gently.

Grey froze, his eyes seeking the owner of the voice, his heart pounding in his chest. Slowly he turned his head and saw Alycia Hamlyn standing a short distance away. Her rich dark hair was dressed simply, her blue eyes were bright, and her loose robe of celery green silk covered a belly swollen with child. Diamonds glinted at her throat, ears, and on her wedding finger.

Clive Speed forgot his place and rushed to the aid of the dazed-looking Grey. "My lord, may I present to you the Countess of Faircastle."

"Hello, Grey," Alycia said softly, extending her hand. "How very pleased you must be to be home."

Chapter Ten

April 1–2, 1814

"PLEASED TO BE HOME?" GREY REPEATED AS HIS mind whirled crazily, attempting to make sense of the present situation. Once again, Speed had tried to warn him, and he had interrupted with another barrage of self-absorbed prattle. "Pleased to be alive, my lady, but rather more confused to be home. Nothing is quite as I expected."

"Life rarely is, so I'm told." In spite of herself, Alycia felt her heart go out to him. "You must call me Alycia, you know. We're old friends."

Speed made unobtrusive good-byes and disappeared, leaving them alone in the vast hallway lined with flickering oil lamps.

"I suppose I shouldn't be surprised," Grey said harshly, "but I am. I'd hoped—"

"That I would still be waiting for you, as I did during the first two years you were away? Waiting even after you turned away from the love I offered and took another as your wife?" She paused to calm the bittersweet throb in her voice, then continued more softly, "If I believed that you had truly loved me and simply made a mistake when you wed Mrs. Burke, I might have waited. However, I forced myself to be honest for the first time. You are a hard man, Grey, and have grown harder as you've aged, I think. That does not diminish your many outstanding qualities, but I finally had to face the fact that you were never going to offer me the tender romance I longed for." They were walking slowly toward the front door

110

as Alycia spoke. "I used to fool myself, thinking that our next meeting would be the occasion on which you would reveal your gentler, loving side. Sad to say, that day never did come."

Memories flooded back to him of their romps in bed, the sound of Alycia's laughter, her knack for having everything just as he liked it, from the soap in his bath to the way his meat was cooked. And he remembered feeling her gaze and turning to look into her great, sad eyes so filled with longing. Sometimes Grey had wished that she'd forgotten the soap or botched his dinner, and toward the end, the sight of her hungry gaze had made him want to bolt. There was no use denying the truth now that he wished it were different. Looking at her now, big with Faircastle's child and rosy with contentment, Grey realized that there was no more point in defending himself to Alycia than there had been in trying to lure Speed back to his side.

"I suppose I was a fool, and may be yet," he said ruefully.

Tears sparkled in her eyes. "You never understood that I needed more from you than even the house and security you were afraid to give me. After your marriage, I resolved to change my life. I did not want to end like the many aging 'fashionable impures'—entertaining old titled gentlemen who continue to keep them in style. Edward offered me not only security, but love." A smile faltered on her pretty mouth. "You see, I really had no choice."

"That's quite plain." He put his hand on the door handle. "I wish you happy, Alycia."

"Thank you. I hope, with all my heart, that you will find peace now, Grey. So much has changed for you—and how sorry I am about David's death! Such a shock to us all. But, knowing you as I do, I have no doubt that you will cope brilliantly with the challenges ahead. I shall keep you in my prayers." It was all Alycia could do to refrain from inquiring about the scar on his hand and reaching out to touch the silver hairs that had not been there when last they'd met. She longed to urge him to take care of his health but knew she must not. It was no longer her place. Perhaps it never had been.

Grey bent to kiss Alycia's hand so that she wouldn't see his face. Then, stepping into the starry London night, he added, "I'll be grateful for your prayers, my lady. I've a notion that you're a good deal nearer the ear of God than I."

"Was your dinner with Mr. Murray *very* grand?" Adrienne Beauvisage demanded as she perched on the edge of her cousin's bed. "You must tell me everything!"

"I'm afraid there really isn't very much to tell that would interest you," Natalya replied a trifle apologetically. "Mr. Murray and one of his associates named Laurence Poole took me to dine at the Clarendon Hotel in Bond Street, which I was curious to see since that is where Grey—that is, Mr. St. James—would have had me stay had I not encountered you in Piccadilly. The chef's name is Jacquiers, and Mr. Murray told me that he was a refugee from the revolution in France. We had an excellent meal, cooked in the French style, and Mr. Murray and Mr. Poole flattered me excessively. They made a gift to me of a presentation copy of my book."

Adrienne rushed to retrieve it from the side table near the door, her long, lustrous hair flying out behind her. Watching her, Natalya was poingantly reminded of the girl-child she had known at Château du Soleil, the innocent her parents held still in their memories. Wonderingly Adrienne ran her fingers over the handsome volume of *My Lady's Heart*, bound in morocco and stamped in gold.

"How very peculiar it is to think that my own cousin is an *author*," she mused. "Will you be celebrated like Lord Byron—or Miss Jane Austen? How I adored *Pride and Prejudice*! I have heard that she is not very pretty, though, and cares nothing for society. She lives very quietly in Hampshire and comes to London to visit her brother very infrequently. Only think, cousin, how easily you might eclipse her!"

"I assure you that I have no such ambitions, Adrienne," Natalya protested, with perhaps more vehemence than was called for. In truth, she was discovering that the prospect of becoming the toast of London, if only for a few days, was not altogether distasteful to her, and she wondered at such vain impulses.

"Will you be *very* rich?" asked Adrienne.

"Haven't you been taught that such questions are entirely inappropriate, cousin?" Natalya smiled to soften the gentle rebuke.

Adrienne grimaced. "I beg your pardon, Talya, but I couldn't help myself. I hoped that one was allowed to breach etiquette with one's relatives."

Natalya laughed. "So one should. No, I doubt that I'll be very rich, but I do believe that I may have independent means. Mr. Murray says that my book has earned nearly a hundred pounds for me in the month since its publication. I'll own I am very excited. And, he has presented me with a handsome payment in advance for the novel I am currently writing."

After absorbing this with wide eyes, Adrienne remarked, "Mrs. Sykes says that Mr. Murray offered Byron a thousand pounds for *Giaour* and *The Bride of Abydos* last year."

"Truly?" she laughed. "Tactless child! But then, Byron is at the pinnacle, isn't he? I hardly think I ought to aspire to such heights." She paused, then added wryly, "At any rate, not just yet, hmm?"

"I didn't care for either *Giaour* or *The Bride of Abydos*," Adrienne confided, "though I didn't say so in company for fear of being shunned. I found them both to be quite nonsensical and barbarous. I daresay I shall like *your* book a thousand times better, no matter how little Mr. Murray paid for it."

"Your loyalty is touching, dear cousin," Natalya replied, trying not to betray her amusement. "Now, I wish that you would tell me about Miss Harrington's Seminary for the Daughters of Gentlemen. How are you progressing with your studies? And how does Miss Harrington feel about your not living at school any longer? I must say, I find it queer that she would condone such an arrangement without first receiving Uncle Nicky's approval."

Adrienne squirmed on the bed. "There simply wasn't time to write Papa and Maman and wait for a reply that might never arrive. You must be able to see that my life here with Mrs. Sykes is *far* superior to my dreary existence at Miss Harrington's Seminary.'' Her expression at the mention of her school conveyed her distaste.

"I still do not understand why Miss Harrington allowed you to leave. Do you continue to attend school in the daytime?''

"When it is convenient," Adrienne replied vaguely. "Oh, all right, I shall tell you the truth, but you must promise not to scold me.''

"No such thing" exclaimed Natalya. "Now, kindly enlighten me.''

Her young cousin began to twist a long strand of hair round and round her finger as she said reluctantly, "When Papa sent me the latest payment to give Miss Harrington, I kept it. I told Miss Harrington that the war had drastically reduced my father's circumstances and he could no longer afford to keep me at her seminary. Mrs. Sykes spoke to Miss Harrington personally and assured her that I would have the best of care here, as would Venetia, and the deed was done.''

Barely concealing her horror, Natalya inquired, "And Uncle Nicky's money? What has become of it?''

"Why, I gave it to Mrs. Sykes, of course. It was very little to offer in return for her tremendously unselfish generosity. How much she has taught me! And the routs and assemblies, even at this time of year, have been too thrilling for words! Can you imagine how it will be when the Season begins in earnest? When Papa sends more money, Mrs. Sykes promises that I shall have gowns worthy of a princess.'' Adrienne's lovely, innocent face was flushed with excitement. "Already I have gained the notice of a handsome baron, one of the Carlton House set. Mrs. Sykes assures me that I'll have a dozen proposals of marriage to choose among before the spring is out.'' She put a hand out toward her cousin. "Is it not wonderful? You really ought to stay on, Talya. I know that you're rather past the age most men consider marriageable, but you haven't lost your looks yet, and if you become celebrated for your book, your age might be overlooked. Mrs. Sykes would be a great help. She's quite knowledgeable about such matters.''

Natalya took her cousin's outstretched hand, smiling in spite of herself. ''That's very charitable of you, cousin, but I'm not in search of a husband, and if I were, I would not enlist the aid of Mrs. Sykes.''

''Is your heart set on that dashing viscount who brought you here?''

''No!'' she cried, then took a breath to recover. ''Let us return to the subject of *you* and your present situation. I can see that you are quite carried away by all that has happened, and I appreciate your feelings. However, I cannot help being concerned, particularly about the fact that Uncle Nicky and Lisette are completely uninformed about all this.''

''Don't say you mean to *tell* them?'' wailed Adrienne, squeezing Natalya's hand to the point of pain. ''Papa is so old-fashioned, he would spoil everything! Oh, Talya, if you see to it that I'm sent back to that horrid seminary for young ladies, I shall simply wither away and *die*!''

''I highly doubt that,'' her cousin replied. ''Now there's no need to predict doom, Adrienne. No one shall lock you in a dungeon. I simply want to remind you that you are only seventeen and still under the protection of your parents, and you have deceived them. Uncle Nicky would throttle me if he learned I had been a party to this. I realize that at your age you believe you are a woman, but I can assure you that you are not. You're a Beauvisage through and through, impetuous and eager for adventure, but—''

Adrienne pulled her hand away and mimicked, ''But, but, but! I vow, cousin, you are sounding like a proper spinster! You may be younger than Mrs. Sykes, but her attitudes are far more enlightened. If I'd known that you meant to spoil everything, I never would have begged you to stay with us, or confided in you. I thought that you cared for me!''

''I do care, dearest, more than you know,'' Natalya replied, sighing. Obviously there was no way to resolve this situation in one evening, and it would do no good to upset Adrienne further. ''Pray don't be angry with me. I only worry because I love you. Perhaps I am being overanxious. Let us enjoy our time together and not speak of this again for a day or two.''

''Mrs. Sykes was going to invite you to accompany us to a

rout tomorrow evening,'' Adrienne muttered, ''but perhaps you are above such amusements.''

''On the contrary, I would like it immensely.'' Natalya gave her a winning smile and opened her arms. ''Do give me a hug, puss, and let us cry peace.'' The cousins embraced, and Adrienne retired for the night, faintly reassured.

Alone in her ornate crimson-and-gold bedchamber, Natalya stood and stared about her in distaste. There was a quality to the furnishings in her room that she feared was rather vulgar, and unfortunately the rest of Mrs. Sykes's house was decorated in much the same manner. The style was a bit too grand to be in good taste and only added to Natalya's vague sense of unease regarding Adrienne's situation. Pacing restlessly to the window, she drew back the velvet drapery and looked down on the cobbled street. Hacks and carriages clattered by under the streetlamps and starlight, and she wondered who the passengers were and where they were bound. Suddenly Grey St. James pushed past her concerns about Adrienne and Mrs. Sykes to fill her thoughts. Where was he tonight? Natalya wondered. Dancing at a fashionable rout? Gaming with old friends? More likely he was in the arms of a lover, she thought, and her heart tightened. Certainly he must be far too occupied to spare a thought for her. . . .

The ethereal, fair-haired figure looking down from the window above bore an uncanny resemblance to Natalya, Grey thought as his chaise jolted over the cobbles en route to White's Club for men. Odd that his mind would play such a trick; odder still that he would think of her at all in the midst of the chaos this day had brought to his life.

By God, he was thirsty! Upon reaching White's, he meant to drink himself into oblivion. With luck, he'd encounter an old crony or two with whom he could exchange any number of impersonal stories about the war. He'd be happy to ramble on about Boney or Wellington or the regent. Even listening to the latest round of rumors about the hapless Princess Caroline would be preferable to talking about himself. Men were fa-

mous for superficial conversation, and White's was just the
place for it.

There was little activity in the old club's celebrated bow
window tonight. Brummell was not there, and Grey noticed
as he entered the club that the dandies who were languishing
in that place of honor were not only unknown to him, but
shockingly young. When Raggett, the proprietor, came forward to welcome him home, Grey immediately accepted his
offer of champagne. He then retired to the card room and
blended into the crowd, idly watching the men who stooped
over the green baize tables, intent on their games of whist,
faro, and hazard. Many of them would drink far too much,
become increasingly fuddled, and remain until dawn, usually
parting with sums of money they could ill afford to lose. But
gentlemen remained stoic in the face of disaster just as they
hid their joy on the rare occasions when fortune smiled upon
them.

Grey had switched to brandy and was beginning to feel
pleasantly numb when a hand suddenly clapped him soundly
on the back. Fearing that he was about to behold one of his
father's boisterous old cronies, Grey looked over as coolly as
he was able.

"I say, old chap! What a shock! When did you get back,
and why haven't you sent word round to me?" The speaker
was a tall, emaciated-looking fellow with dark curly hair, sharp
cheekbones, twinkling blue eyes topped by peaked brows, and
a toothy, genuine smile.

Grey was flooded with relief and surprisingly strong emotion. "Gib! What the devil are you doing in London? Thought
you were still with the Fifty-second Regiment in the Pyre-
nees!" He was grinning like a schoolboy. "I only just got
back today. How *good* it is to see you, old fellow. You are so
welcome a sight that I almost believe you must be an illusion!"

The Honorable Osgood Gibson smiled broadly. "I've been
home since January. Wounded in the battle for Bayonne. It
was a bayonet wound in my left thigh, and has nearly healed
now, but 'twas enough to render me quite useless for several
weeks. Now, of course, it appears that I may not have to return

to my regiment.'' He shook his head in wonder. ''I daresay you're the last person I expected to bump into here tonight!''

''God knows I was overdue for a pleasant surprise,'' Grey rejoined, with a trace of irony. ''You know, I've been in prison at Mont St. Michel this past year. Aged me ten years, I'll wager, but I thought it was better than being dead—until I arrived home today and discovered that most of my old life here had changed beyond salvaging.'' He smiled caustically, then the two men exchanged a brief, abbreviated embrace of the sort that was acceptable between brothers and the closest of friends.

''Steady on,'' Gib admonished himself. ''Nearly spilled my champagne!'' He didn't know how to reply to Grey's speech. ''Looks as if you've adopted my cure for disappointment. I see you're into the brandy and doubtless half-sprung in the bargain.''

''Not quite yet; I've only just arrived. But I intend to be *more* than half-sprung before this night's out,'' Grey replied grimly.

''Can't say as I blame you, old boy. You've come home to a devil of a coil. Must admit that I was dead shocked when I heard from Alvaney that your bride had run off. I thought that Francesca was a jolly enough girl at the wedding—certainly a beauty. Who'd've thought she'd turn out to be such a—a—''

''High-flying shrew?'' Grey supplied.

Gib glanced at him in surprise. ''Not quite the term I'd've chosen, but it'll do. Come on, then, let's go and find a corner. We've a good deal to discuss.''

They appropriated a decanter of brandy and settled onto two blue brocade wing chairs in a quiet, dimly lit corner of the club. Deducing that his friend wanted to forget himself for a time, Gib regaled him with tales of the war on land, and they exchanged theories about Napoléon's current situation and rumors of his deteriorating mental state. Then they turned to news of their old school friends and the latest romantic entanglements in London Society. These topics took up the better part of an hour, by which time the brandy was having the desired effect on Grey. Finally he brought himself to talk a bit about his year in prison, his escape, and the visit he had paid to Château du Soleil. Gib listened spellbound to the story of Grey and Natalya posing as husband and wife to flee across France from Autueil.

"Traveling with a girl must have been quite diverting, particularly given your year of enforced celibacy," Gib remarked. "Was she pretty?"

"Yes, quite extraordinary, actually. You'll be shocked to hear it, I know, but romance was the farthest thing from my mind this past week." Amusement flickered briefly in his eyes. "Well, almost the farthest. Miss Beauvisage is not the sort of woman one trifles with, however. She's six-and-twenty, and an author of some sort. Murray's published a book she wrote."

"Really! Murray's all the rage, you know. Publishes Byron and Scott, and since the success of *Pride and Prejudice*, it looks as if Miss Austen will take her manuscripts to him as well." Gib struggled to loosen his uncomfortably high cravat, which was beginning to feel like a noose around his neck. "It speaks well for your Miss Beauvisage if John Murray liked her book well enough to publish it. Six-and-twenty, you say? Too bad. If she were rather newer goods, she'd probably be quite the star of the Season. Have you put her up at Hartford House?"

"No, Miss Beauvisage is staying with . . . friends." Grey found that he hadn't the energy to launch into that story, much as he would have liked to hear Gib's opinion of Mrs. Sykes. "And, she won't be around for the Season. She wants above all things to sail to America, and I've promised to help her find a way."

"You sound as if you aren't particularly keen on that task."

Grey looked up to see the honest concern in his friend's eyes and felt a barrier give way inside himself. "I fear that I'm deep in a trough of self-pity, old man. Time stood still for me while I was away, and I was foolish enough to suppose that the clock had stopped in London as well. I can't say that I'm broken-hearted over the loss of Francesca, but it was a bit of a shock, and I'm angry, too. You see, she took Mother's jewels when she ran . . . family pieces that were generations old. I mean to retrieve them somehow." He paused, and Gib nodded soberly. "Then I discovered that Speed had left Hartford House. You are perhaps the only person who might understand what a blow that was. I made up my mind to persuade him to come back, and then I was going to see Alycia. I'd missed her, and regretted the way I handled the . . . situation between us. So"—Grey took a long drink of brandy—"I went first to Faircastle House to find Speed. I discovered that he did not want to be persuaded . . . and then, as I was leaving, I encountered Alycia."

"Good God," murmured Gib, "you *have* had a hellish day. So sorry! If I'd seen you first, I could have told you. Didn't your father prepare you?"

Grey laughed harshly. "A foolish question, and well you know it! I had to pry the news about Francesca out of him. You know how he despises conversations about *people*."

"Yes, yes, of course." Gib looked away and cleared his throat.

"But now I've seen you and am reassured that at least one old friend is still by my side. I'm of a mind to immerse myself in a life of dissipation for a bit." Arching an eyebrow, he grinned rakishly. "What do you say, Gib? Let's drink and game and wench until the past years are merely a blur in our minds, hmm? We'll have first pick of the lovely and talented cyprians before the war ends and London is flooded with our comrades-in-arms."

Gib squirmed a bit as he recognized the wicked gleam in Grey's eyes. "Well, that certainly sounds tempting, and I hate to dash cold water on your enthusiasm, but I don't quite know if I'll be able to participate fully in your plans for debauchery. That is to say—and I hope you'll be pleased for me old man . . ." He paused, drawing on his cheroot. "I'm thinking of getting married."

"Are you roasting me?" Grey demanded. "Has everyone gone mad? What's brought on all this sobriety and commitment?"

"Well, we ain't as young as we once were, are we? Matter of fact, I happened to speak to Lady Faircastle on this very subject at one of the Lady Jersey's assemblies last week . . .

and asked her advice. She said just what I have. I'm not putting it well; the brandy's muddled my brain. But what I mean is that we agreed that life's going by. I don't see myself dallying with ladybirds when I'm bald and fat like Prinny. I'd like a wife now, and babies.''

"Good God,'' Grey said in a leaden voice, and sank back in his chair, looking more dismal than ever.

"I suppose you might say I've begun courting Lady Mary Stewart—but nothing's been said.'' Gib hastened to reassure him. "I mean, I'm still quite free, old fellow! No reason I can see why you and I shouldn't enjoy a night out for old times' sake. After all, we have a great deal to celebrate, and you need cheering up. I propose that tomorrow night we go together to a rout I've been invited to. I gather that it should be a most interesting mix, with not a few cyprians among the females. The champagne will flow like water, and all our old cronies should be present.'' Gib was heartened to see Grey straighten slightly. "What do you say then, old chap? Shall we venture forth?''

Grey couldn't help smiling. "I should be delighted.''

Chapter Eleven

April 2, 1814

"OH, GOD, LET ME ALONE," GREY MUMBLED INTO his pillow as a blinding shaft of sunlight pierced the gloom of his bedchamber. Dimly, as he lay facedown on the great Gothic bed, it occurred to him that he had forgotten to close the bed's curtains the night before. Hardly surprising, since he didn't remember *going* to bed, but in a tiny corner of his mind a stubborn voice whispered that *Speed* wouldn't have forgotten. How good Speed had been when Grey had arrived home in his cups. The very soul of restraint. Not a word of reproach had ever passed his lips, and he looked after St. James in such a way that the entire ordeal became almost bearable. Later, perhaps, the manservant might impart an oblique observation regarding the wisdom of men who knew their limits, but such remarks were made with the utmost tact. Speed never belabored a point.

"I'm frightfully sorry, my lord." It was Dimbleby, standing at the window, holding the drapery edge like a pickpocket caught in the act. "I thought that perhaps a bit of light might rouse you . . . gradually."

"Why in the bloody hell must I be roused at all?" growled Grey. He peered at the butler through narrowed eyes. "What's the time?"

"Half past ten, my lord. I wouldn't have disturbed you but there is a fellow belowstairs who insists that he's here to interview for the position of your manservant. I'd've simply turned him away if not for his family connections." Dimbleby took tiny, halting steps toward the bed as he spoke. "He says his name is Jasper Speed, son of none other than our very own Clive. The younger Mr. Speed assures me that his father arranged for this interview, and that you agreed."

Grey felt as if his head were in a vise. "Give him a mug of ale and a mutton chop and bid him wait."

"I should be happy to oblige, my lord, but the young man has already been here nearly three hours. He has consumed a full breakfast—*and* the mug of ale and mutton chop you suggest."

He had no more strength to argue. If the caller were anyone but Speed's son, he'd simply have pleaded illness and sent him away. "Give me a moment to wash and put something on. You may bring young Speed to me in a quarter hour, Dimbleby, and warn him that I shan't be particularly well turned out."

"Yes, my lord." The aged butler wore a crooked smile of relief. "I'll send a kitchen maid up with coffee and—"

"Nothing else, Dimbleby." Tentatively Grey sat up with a groan and swung his legs over the side of the bed. "The mere notion of food repulses me at the moment."

"Naturally, my lord." The old man nodded with grave understanding and backed out of the bedchamber, closing the door behind him. Once in the passageway, he leaned against the wall and gave vent to a long-suffering sigh. "As if we didn't have enough to contend with, now his lordship has become an out-and-out rakehell," he muttered under his breath. "I'll be fit for bedlam if this goes on!"

"So, you're Jasper Speed," Grey said, observing the young man with hooded eyes. Clad only in a forest green silk dressing gown, he lounged on a wing chair, his bare legs stretched out and crossed at the ankles. "Do sit down."

Jasper Speed took the chair opposite his potential employer and pretended as if nothing were amiss. However, although his expression was pleasantly implacable, he was, in truth, quite shocked. His father had told him that the viscount had been something of a libertine, but he was, after all, an officer in His Majesty's Navy and recently returned from the continent. He had rather expected to meet a handsomely dressed nobleman with military bearing. Certainly he had never imagined that Viscount Altburne would interview him in his bedchamber, half-naked and looking positively dissolute. His silver-flecked hair was tousled, he was unshaven, and the smudges under his eyes contrasted sharply with his pale skin. Speed repressed a sigh of distaste. Did he really want to be in the employ of such a man?

"You'll pardon me, I hope, for not rising, but I've a devil of a headache," Grey said in a voice that was edged with boredom. "I had a rather late night."

"Of course, my lord."

"Would you care for coffee?" He gestured toward the silver pot on the low table between them.

"No, I don't care for coffee, my lord. Thank you."

"Ah, yes, I gather that you ate and drank your fill belowstairs."

Without much interest, Grey raised his eyes and took a good look at the son of his beloved Speed. The young man was short like his father, but the resemblance ended there, for Jasper was stocky and strong, his snub-nosed face reddened by sun and wind. His most distinctive feature, however, was the surprising flame-orange color of his curly hair. Grey thought idly that he had never seen a less likely candidate for the position of valet.

"Sorry to have kept you waiting, but I wasn't aware that we had an appointment, and to be honest, even if I had been aware, it probably wouldn't have mattered on a morning like this." Grey drank from his own cup, then added, "I'm afraid I'm not feeling quite the thing today."

"If you'll pardon me for saying so, my lord, that is quite apparent." Jasper decided to indulge his fondness for speaking his mind, rather hoping that the viscount would take offense and send him away.

"Indeed?" Grey's brows rose slightly as he felt a flicker of interest. For some unknown reason, he knew an urge to be candid. "The fact is, Mr. Speed, that my homecoming, my return to my life here in London, has not been the happy occasion that I had anticipated. In truth, most of the circumstances of my past are now severely altered. I feel a bit . . . lost.''

"As do I, my lord." Jasper was moved by Grey's honesty, and suddenly he saw beyond the dissipated, cynical rake seated on the chair across from him. This man, for all his gifts and rank and advantages, needed him. "Don't know if my father told you or not, but I lost my wife not long ago. Polly died in childbirth, and my baby boy a day later." Only the slight thickening of his voice betrayed his pain. "I found that I couldn't stay on alone on our farm, and that's why I've come to London and taken up my father's work. It's a new life I'm seeking, and I know all about being lost."

Grey felt a twinge of shame for his own self-pity. "Then, perhaps we're well suited, hmm?" he said softly. "I've no idea what the future holds for me. I don't even know if I'll stay in this house. If you don't mind that sort of uncertainty, I'd be pleased if you would accept the position of my valet."

Soberly Jasper replied, "I'd be honored to accept, my lord. I know I have a great deal to learn, but I shall do my utmost to fill the void left by my father."

I must be mad, Grey thought, trading the best valet in London for a young, green farmer. Aloud, he said, "Would you mind if I call you Speed, as I did your father? It would be vaguely comforting to have at least that much continuity in my life."

"I would be honored, my lord." Jasper Speed stood and took command of the situation. "You'll be wanting a bath now, and a shave. I'll see to it immediately, my lord. The day is wasting away before us!"

The Earl of Hartford was standing in the middle of the long, elegant drawing room staring at a painting on the red damask-covered wall. He may have noticed the entrance of his son, but a long minute passed before the old man favored Grey with a portion of his attention.

"Oh, there you are," he said absently. "Just having a look at this painting I've purchased. *Frosty Morning*, it's called.

This young fellow Turner is all the rage, you know, but I have my doubts.''

Grey walked over and stood a polite distance from his father, noticing as he did so that this room, which had seemed so grand in his youth, was beginning to look a trifle shabby. In truth, he had begun to have the same uneasy feeling about much of Hartford House.

Although his opinion of the painting had not been solicited, the conversation seemed to require a response. Grey copied his father's pose, laying a finger against his cheek as they stood side by side, staring. The rural scene was deceptively simple: a barren brown landscape featuring a couple of horses, a wagon, and drably clad farmers. A few leafless tree branches stood out crookedly against a luminous, golden-peach dawn sky, and in the foreground the dark earth sparkled with hoarfrost. ''I find it quite stunning, sir. Turner has an absolute genius for light. Look at that sky! And a gift for details like that frost on the ground.'' He paused. ''However, it might look better in the library. This room is rather overpowering.''

The earl snorted. ''I'd've preferred Turner's *Battle of Trafalgar*, but Palmerston got that one.''

Grey could sense that his father was about to make an excuse and leave, but he spoke first. ''Could you spare me a few minutes of your time, sir?''

''Are you in trouble?'' Hartford asked as they seated themselves on the ancient Jacobean-style chairs near the arched window overlooking Grosvenor Square. ''I perceive that you were out most of last night. You haven't gambled away Briar Hill, I hope? What a bother it would be to get it back.''

''No, Father, I'm in no trouble.'' Grey smiled slightly in an effort to diffuse the tightness in his chest. ''Is it so terribly annoying to have me at home again?''

The earl arched one white brow and said mildly, ''My dear boy, I trust I should not betray such an emotion even if I felt it.''

Grey's smile reached his eyes. ''No, I trust not.''

''Have you plans? I gather that you won't be returning to the continent. The *on-dit* is that the Bourbons will be back in power by summer, and I shouldn't wonder that you've had enough of military life.''

''Actually, sir, I haven't thought much beyond some of the more immediate matters on my agenda. I want to see my horse. It's been two years since I've ridden Anton, and I thought that this afternoon I would—''

His lordship cleared his throat. ''I do wish that Dimbleby had relieved me of a few of these unpleasant announcements. This is not a role I relish.'' Hartford turned to examine Turner's painting then and said, ''Your wife sold Anton. I had no part in it, nor did I know until a fortnight later.''

''What?'' Grey went pale with fury. ''Why the devil did she do a bloody thing like that?''

His father yawned. ''Must we have another scene? I believe that she took a dislike to the horse, but it doubtless had more to do with the price she got. You'd really have to ask her yourself, my boy. In any event, the deed is done, and I do have an engagement at two o'clock, so—''

''I have only one or two questions more. I shan't keep you above ten minutes.'' Grey sat forward. Only the silver glint in his eyes betrayed the anger he was feeling. ''I had hoped I wouldn't have to come to you about this, Father, but it seems I have no choice. Mother's jewels are no longer in Francesca's jewel box. I've asked Dimbleby and Speed, but they know nothing. Is there a chance that you put them away?''

''My dear boy, why would I do such a thing?'' the earl replied, apparently untroubled by the implications of Grey's words.

''I didn't think that you had,'' his son admitted dryly, ''but I had to ask. I cannot tell you how furious it makes me to think that she has disappeared with the jewels that have been in our family for generations and that *must* be passed down to the next Countess of Hartford! Somehow I must contrive to recover them.''

''A noble plan,'' the earl remarked. ''Now, if there's nothing else—''

Grey cut in swiftly. ''Have you news of my ship, Father, or has that been sold as well?''

"No, not at all," Hartford said, with a thin smile. "Why would you think so? I saw the *Wild Rover* myself just last week, and I can assure you that it has been well cared for in your absence. Your *friend*, that hideous fellow Fedbusk, has been looking after it for you. I cannot fault him there."

"She's seaworthy then?"

"Apparently. Are you planning a sea voyage?" Hartford asked, a hopeful note creeping into his voice.

"I doubt it, but I've promised to help someone get to America, and the *Wild Rover* may be the only way to do it. I'll go and have a look at her now and consider my options."

"Then don't let me keep you, my boy." The earl stood up, visibly relieved. "You mustn't waste another minute here on *my* account."

Grey laughed in spite of himself as they walked toward the library door. "How thoughtful you are, Father . . ."

"I gave the driver the address. It's rather a distance," Gib said as he sat down opposite Grey in the carriage and folded his long legs into the most comfortable position possible. "I say, old fellow, you're looking much better! Those evening clothes are devilishly flattering."

They bumped over the cobbles as the light, four-wheeled post chaise gained speed. "Are they?" Grey said, relaxing against the soft leather upholstery. He glanced down at his white stockings, black knee breeches, black cutaway coat, and the starched perfection of his cravat. "They're looser than they were two years ago. I'll have to pay Weston a visit and order an entire new wardrobe. What a bore!"

Gib shook his head emphatically. "The weight will return in no time now that you're home, and until then, the ladies will be crowding round you, old chap. Byron has made pale, brooding men all the rage. You'll be a tremendous hit, I can promise you."

"You're too kind," Grey said with pointed irony.

Undaunted, his friend pressed on. "Now, tell me what's been happening. Have you any news more encouraging than yesterday's?"

"Not particularly. I have a new valet. It's Speed's son, Jasper, who until very recently was a farmer. He knows very little about his new trade, but he makes up for it by ordering me about."

"Well," Gib said brightly. "That sounds . . . amusing!"

Grey cocked a dubious brow at him. "Indeed. I also spoke with my father again and learned that my erstwhile wife sold Anton."

This drew a look of horror from his friend. "Old man, I *am* sorry! What a beastly thing to do! Anton was a veritable prince among horses."

"It's no use flying into a rage over something that is long past fixing, but it is more fuel for the fire I'm building at the feet of Francesca's memory." Grey's expression darkened further. "Also, Father knows nothing about Mother's jewels, so it's certain that Francesca has them. If I knew where she could be found . . ."

"As a matter of fact . . ." Gib cleared his throat uneasily. "I have reservations about telling you this, St. James, for fear you'll do something quite mad, but on the other hand, I do feel bound, as your friend—"

"Speak, Gib!" Grey commanded, a muscle flexing in his jaw.

"I discussed the situation of your . . . uh, wife with my own father today, and he told me that he heard a rumor that she's in America, in the city of Philadelphia. As you might imagine, Francesca has been short of funds from time to time since she ran away, and has been forced to contact her father. Of course Carsbury isn't known for keeping his own counsel. Still, it is only a rumor, and may have been muddled in the retelling. Remember, too, that even if it *is* true, she may very well have moved on by this time." The burning, faraway look in his friend's eyes brought Gib to the brink of panic. "For God's sake, old chap, you must be realistic! To dash off to America with no more than this would be pure foolishness. My advice is to wait until you have more definite knowledge of her whereabouts. Proceed with caution for once in your life. After all, you're getting older, and—"

Looking bored, Grey held up his hand. "My dear Gib, you're running on like a dowager. I take your point."

"All right, I'll say nothing more about it . . . for the moment." He sat back against the seat and tried to relax, watching shadows from the post chaise's flickering lamps play across the chiseled face of his friend. At length he spoke again, in a gentler tone. "Do you know, old fellow, I realized later last night that I neglected to offer condolences on the death of your brother. It's been so long since David was lost, I suppose I forgot that I hadn't seen you since. I am sorry. It's been a bloody war."

Grey's thoughts were far away, but he tried to bring them back. "To be honest, I don't believe I've quite taken it in myself."

"One has a tendency to pretend that the person who has died is simply away, in cases like this. That he'll be coming home later on," Gib said carefully.

"Yes. Quite." Grey nodded, sighing. He had no desire to delve into his feelings about David's death—or life, for that matter.

As the post chaise drew up before a large, brightly lit house on Russell Square, Gib asked, "How is your father dealing with his loss?"

"I've no idea, really." As a footman opened the door and he climbed out of the post chaise, Grey glanced back over his shoulder and added, "The subject of David hasn't come up."

"It's simply dazzling," Natalya said sincerely. "There is no other word to describe it."

"How kind you are, Miss Beauvisage. We are very fortunate to have you among us in London," replied the tall, elegant Mrs. Lynchford. She was the hostess of this fabulous rout and at least thirty years younger than the host, who was apparently a duke since everyone addressed him as "Your Grace." Natalya had met many people in the half hour since she, Adrienne, Venetia, and Mrs. Sykes had arrived at this mansion in Russell Square, but very few of them appeared to be married . . . at least to each other. Now, a woman wearing a feathered headdress and a virtually transparent muslin gown was waving to Mrs. Lynchford.

"I must speak to dear Fanny Smithfield," Mrs. Lynchford said, smiling. "You'll excuse me? Have some champagne, my dear. It will put you at ease."

She plucked a crystal goblet of golden liquid from a passing tray and gave it to Natalya before disappearing into the crowd. Natalya sighed, then decided to follow her hostess's advice and sipped the champagne. She would have been grateful if something as simple as a beverage could put her at ease. She peered intently into the mass of guests, searching for Adrienne.

Natalya had been in many beautiful homes in her lifetime, but none had been quite as dazzling as this one, just as she had said to Mrs. Lynchford. However, several other adjectives came to mind as well, gaudy, ostentatious, and decadent among them. Apparently the entire third floor of the duke's home had given over to this ballroom, which boasted an ornate domed ceiling covered with paintings of cherubs and dreamy-looking women in various states of undress. Mrs. Sykes had pronounced it "very romantic; quite divine!" The ceiling and its supporting pillars were further ornamented with tiered chandeliers fringed in gold and carved scrolls, fruit, urns, and other gilded decorations. The chairs that ranged along the walls were gilded as well, and there were more paintings than Natalya had ever seen. The nearest one featured a centaur carrying off a naked woman.

"Hello, beauty," a low male voice murmured from behind her.

Natalya turned to discover a rather portly gentleman at least twice her age standing so near that she could have, had she been so inclined, counted the tiny spider veins blossoming on his cheeks and nose. "Have we met, sir?" she inquired politely.

"A thousand times." He smiled then, bloodshot eyes crinkling. "In my dreams, beauty. A thousand times in my dreams."

She noticed that his words were a trifle slurred, so that *dreams* became *dreamsh*. Because of the incredible crush of people, it was impossible for Natalya to offer an excuse and slip away from this old lecher, so she was forced to stall for time. "It's exceedingly warm in here, don't you think?"

"Only where you are, beauty," the gentleman replied.

Nearby, another, younger man was watching the exchange between Natalya and her admirer. Sir Christian Laidlaw was an accomplished rake whose style was admired for its subtlety. He had seen Natalya enter with Mrs. Sykes and instantly fallen under her spell. He was certain that she was the most enchantingly glorious woman he had ever seen and immediately undertook to learn her name from the woman he assumed was her patroness. Even the conditions Mrs. Sykes placed on an introduction to Natalya did not daunt him. Now, after working his way through the crowd to stand near her, Laidlaw decided that she was even more beautiful than he'd originally surmised. She was a vision of springtime in peach muslin over ivory silk, a tantalizing suggestion of her breasts peeking above the bodice. The high-waisted gown skimmed the curves of her body, hinting at the delights hidden beneath rather than advertising all like so many of the "fashionable impures" present here tonight. Natalya wore no plumes or jewels in her hair; instead, she had woven sprays of tiny wildflowers through the cloud of burnished curls surrounding the Grecian knot atop her head. There were simple pearls in her ears and round her creamy throat. Laidlaw thought this a wise choice, for no amount of costly ornamentation could have competed with that utterly exquisite face.

Sir Christian meant to have her, but first he would have to get rid of Lord Pondsmarsh. As usual, the old fool was deep in his cups and lusting after a woman beyond his reach, not unlike most of the other men present tonight. Nearly all of them had wives, as did Laidlaw and Pondsmarsh, but wives played little part in their lives beyond providing a veneer of respectability when the occasion demanded. These were days when self-indulgence, eccentric narcissism, and frankly scandalous behavior were commonplace.

"Excuse me, my dear Pondsmarsh, are you well?" Laidlaw slipped past the couple nearest him to hover over the aging marquis. "You don't look at all the thing. Perhaps you ought to take a spot of air."

Natalya looked up gratefully as her admirer snuffled in surprise. "Well?" his lordship echoed. "Of coursh I'm well. Never felt better in my life."

Laidlaw gave Natalya a knowing smile. "Allow me to introduce myself, Miss Beauvisage. I am Sir Christian Laidlaw, and I am honored to stand before so celebrated a lady. All of London desires to meet the lovely author of *My Lady's Heart*."

A delicate flush spread over Natalya's cheeks. "You exaggerate shockingly, Sir Christian, but I am flattered," she replied. "Perhaps you can help me. I need to seek out my cousin; I did not mean to become separated from her. The crowd is so dense that I cannot penetrate by myself, but—"

Laidlaw waved a pale hand, dismissing such a notion. "You must not spoil your own evening with such worries, Miss Beauvisage. I met your cousin just a few moments ago, and I can assure you that she is safe in the care of Mrs. Sykes."

This did not set Natalya's mind at rest, but she restrained from comment. At least she had been rescued from Lord Pondsmarsh's slurring attentions. And this Sir Christian Laidlow—tall, slim, blond, and impeccably turned out—was not only attractive, but appeared to be reasonably sober. At his urging she accepted a fresh glass of champagne and drank it down.

"There, you see?" said Sir Christian, with a pleased smile. "Nothing like champagne to make one forget one's cares, what? Have another."

Trapped in the hot, decadent splendor, surrounded by high-pitched laughter and pinned beneath the hungry admiration of two noblemen, Natlaya seemed to have little choice. Perhaps reality might be more tolerable if it were a trifle blurred. Holding out her hand, she accepted the glass from Sir Christian.

"You're very kind," she murmured.

"My dear," Laidlaw replied, thinking that she looked absolutely succulent, "I can assure you that the pleasure is mine. . . ."

Chapter Twelve

April 2–3, 1814

IT WAS NEARLY MIDNIGHT, DINNER WOULD NOT BE served for three hours, and Grey began to feel bored even before entering the ballroom where the rout was in progress. Covering his mouth with a gloved hand, he yawned.

Gib paused in the doorway and glanced over at his friend. "Look here, Grey, perhaps I ought to remind you that this was *your* notion of a rousing good time. Observe: There, spread before us, is the cream of London's demimonde. Dozens— nay, *hundreds* of beautiful cyprians all waiting to take the place of your dear Alycia, waiting to help you forget the trials of the past years in the most delightful ways possi—"

"Dear old Gib, you're in danger of becoming a prattlebox," Grey murmured. "Must you lecture me at every turn?"

The Honorable Osgood Gibson positively bristled. "I say, there's no need to be unpleasant!"

They both took glasses of champagne, drained them, and took seconds from the same tray. "Devilish hot in here," Grey remarked. "Where's the duchess?"

"In Kent, no doubt, with her grandchildren. Roundwellen only installs her here these days when there is some sort of state occasion, if you take my meaning."

Nodding, Grey stifled another yawn and leisurely surveyed the packed ballroom from the safety of the crowd's edge. As Gib had asserted, there were indeed a great many lovely young ladies. There were also many dandies much younger than he, all strutting like peacocks in exaggeratedly narrow-waisted coats, tight trousers, and impossibly high collarpoints shooting up over their flawlessly tied cravats. Holding canes or quizzing-glasses in one hand and hooking the fingers of the other in their waistcoat pockets, every one of them assumed a nearly identical *dégagé* attitude. With an inward start of surprise, Grey realized that he no longer belonged in their ranks.

In the not-so-distant past, it had been important to him to meet certain standards, to pass muster with people like Beau Brummell. Now, all that seemed . . . rather frivolous, an amusement of his youth. Looking at the simpering young dandies and eager girls, some of whom appeared to be scarcely out of the schoolroom, Grey suddenly felt much older than he had even during the time he'd spent in London two years ago.

"Do you know, Gib," he said ruefully, "I feel rather like one of those old reprobates I used to mock—those aging noblemen who come to slightly decadent routs like this one and lick their lips as they survey the newest crop of demireps."

"Nonsense, old chap! You're only thirty-six."

Grey's eyes met Gib's and his brows rose meaningfully. "Exactly so."

He reached for another glass of champagne as the thought occurred to him that he no longer cared for this sort of life. Quickly he drank before his mind could proceed to the point of wondering what all this meant regarding his future.

Fortunately distraction appeared in the form of Mrs. Sykes. Grey saw her standing not far away, also on the edge of the crowd. Next to her was the flaxen-haired, rosy-cheeked Venetia Hedgecoe. They were conversing with a young nobleman whom Grey recognized but could not place. Deeper in the crush, he spied Adrienne Beauvisage, looking more beautiful than he remembered, her chestnut curls drawn back from her lively, glowing face. So young! How could Mrs. Sykes have brought her into this den of sin? Adrienne wore a simple, virginal-looking gown of white muslin, but the effect was spoiled by the sight of the man paying her court. Viscount Pryce was one of the most notorious members of the Carlton House set, a truly infamous libertine.

Distractedly Grey rubbed the scar on the back of his hand through the glove that covered it. "Gib, do you know anything about Mrs. Sykes? What is she about with those girls she's taken in?"

"*There's* a tale," Gib said, with relish. "After your father broke with Mrs. Sykes, she apparently decided that her chances of finding another . . . sponsor, were growing slim. After all, even Lord Hartford didn't really *keep* her, as you're well aware. So, Mrs. Sykes shifted boats and became what she calls a 'patroness.' She brings girls into her home, grooms them, I suppose you'd call it, then introduces them into the demimonde. Here's the kicker: She charges what she terms a 'presentation fee.' Every man who wants to meet one of her girls has to pay for the privilege, and apparently there are additional charges if Mrs. Sykes decides to let matters progress to their natural conclusion."

"How do you know all this?" Grey asked, his throat suddenly dry.

"Oh, it's common knowledge at the clubs," Gib answered gaily. "I know all sorts of fellows who've paid that presentation fee, and Valbourne made one of her girls his mistress last year. Keeps her in lovely rooms near Covent Garden. Incredible, hmm?"

"Yes. *Quite*." His mind was racing while his eyes raked the crowd for Natalya. Was it possible. . . ? "Gib, have there been many girls? I mean—"

"Under Mrs. Sykes's wing, so to speak? Gad, yes! A dozen or so, at different times, of course. Rumor has it that she now has two new ones, but I haven't had a chance to see them for myself because I've been occupied with Mary." He looked at Grey and blinked. "Perhaps you're right. We *are* getting old."

"You'll have to excuse me for a short while, old chap," Grey said. "There's a matter I must attend to."

"Certainly. Go right ahead. More than enough people here to keep me occupied."

Grey went straight to Mrs. Sykes, who looked up in surprise to find him looming over her, his face stormy. A smile faltered on her lips.

"What an unexpected pleasure this is, my lord. I didn't see you before, but then that's hardly unusual given the number of guests. Are you well, my lord? I do hope so. My dear Natalya speaks so kindly of you, and I'm—"

"Is she here?" he cut in, eyes narrowing.

"Natalya? Miss Beauvisage?" Mrs. Sykes laughed nervously and put up a hand to adjust the peacock feathers that swept upward from her coiled hair. "Yes, yes, indeed she is. I must assure you, my lord, that it was entirely her own idea. I mean—"

"That I won't have to pay a presentation fee to speak with her?"

"Ha, ha, ha! How amusing you are, my lord! My, such a wit. Wherever did you get such a notion as that?" She was growing increasingly pale behind her painted cheeks.

"I'll deal with you later regarding the younger Miss Beauvisage and"—he glanced down at the round-eyed, confused Venetia—" this young lady. First, however, I'll thank you to direct me to Natalya."

Mrs. Sykes was on the verge of proclaiming her innocence, but the stare Grey suddenly leveled at her cut her dead. The smile wilted on her red mouth. "She's back there somewhere," she told him sourly. "Near the painting of the centaur, last time I looked."

Without another word, Grey started into the sea of jostling, laughing people. Others had tried to move around the ballroom without success, but the energy surrounding Grey's tall, broad-shouldered body seemed to precede him, and the crowd parted before him. The air was warm and heavy with the odors of perfume and champagne. The women's gossamer-thin muslin gowns were slipping off their plump shoulders to afford glimpses of the rouged tips of their breasts, while the men had begun to perspire in earnest, as much from lust and drink as the heat. Grey moved through them without acknowledging either the greetings of acquaintances or the curious, admiring gazes of the women. His eyes were shot with silver as they sought Natalya.

Had only a day passed since their parting in Piccadilly? So

much had happened, it seemed much longer, and deep inside Grey felt a pang of deprivation. He missed her. He never should have let her go with that woman, despite the invitation of her young cousin. He had promised her uncle that he would guard her, that he would not desert her in London, and now she was lost in this rakehell's paradise of sin. . . .

Grey glimpsed the tall figure of Lord Byron first, standing not far from the painting of the wicked-looking centaur carrying a naked woman. He was staring through his quizzing-glass at something, eyebrows lifted with interest. Grey looked to the left to see what it was and discovered that the object of Byron's scrutiny was Natalya—or, more precisely, her bosom. Grey's heart clenched as he took in the sight of her sparkling eyes, flushed cheeks, and gay smile.

Natalya was laughing—and drinking champagne!

Worse, she appeared to be surrounded by drooling men. Bryon was on the edge of the circle, and there was that old fool Pondsmarsh, and right in front of Natalya stood Sir Christian Laidlaw, looking more like a fox than ever. As the crowd parted to let Grey through, he saw Laidlaw take Natalya's slim hand and kiss her palm lingeringly.

"Excuse me," Grey said coldly, reaching over to remove Natalya's hand from the grasp of her would-be ravisher.

"Grey!" she exclaimed, startled. "What's the matter?" Dear God, how handsome he looked, and how dangerous. He was considerably taller than most of the other guests and looked more powerful despite his leanness. Most impressive of all, however, was his proud head: the mane of black hair with gleaming strands of silver, slashing brows over stormy gray eyes, sculpted nose and cheekbones, and the hard set of his mouth and jaw.

"You are coming with me," he told her, his voice ominously low.

Sir Christian was looking on with growing annoyance. "See here, Altburne, Miss Beauvisage isn't going anywhere with you! I'm afraid you'll have to wait your turn."

"I'll thank you to remove your hand from my arm, Laidlaw, and step aside."

"I'll do no such thing!" Rivulets of perspiration marred the
layer of powder on his face. "I suggest that you take this up
with Mrs. Sykes, Altburne. Not to put too fine a point on it,
but I *paid* for Miss Beauvisage's company."

"What?" cried Natalya, her confusion mounting.

"I'm afraid you'll have to ask Mrs. Sykes for a *refund*,"
Grey told Sir Christian in acid tones. "You see, Miss Beauvisage is not for sale."

He pulled her along after him then, and the crowd parted
again. Behind them Laidlaw was shouting, "I ought to call
you out for this, Altburne! You'll hear from my second!"

Grey never looked back. Natalya thought she heard him
mutter, "Terrifying," in a sarcastic undertone. Her wrist
chafed beneath his grip, but she was too conscious of the hundreds of silent, curious faces to protest. As they neared the
edge of the crowd, Grey paused to confront Mrs. Sykes.

"I suggest that you pry Adrienne Beauvisage and her friend
away from their admirers and have your carriage brought
round, Mrs. Sykes. I will take Natalya home and wait for you
there so that we may discuss this matter more . . . fully."

There was a menacing note in his voice and a steely glint
in his eyes that told her all would be worse if she argued. So
Mrs. Sykes gave him a short nod full of resentment and turned
away.

Grey found Gib still standing near the door holding yet another glass of champagne. "By Jupiter, old chap, whatever are
you on about? Looks as if you've been making a tremendous
scene," Gib exclaimed.

"Never mind. I'll explain later. I have to leave now." Grey
glanced back at Natalya, who appeared to be seething with
anger. "Shall I come back for you?"

Gib blinked. "Hardly necessary, is it? Someone'll bring me
along. Come by tomorrow."

Mrs. Lynchford appeared then, looking distraught. "My
lord, is anything the matter?"

He gave her a tight smile. "I fear that Miss Beauvisage and
I must cry off for dinner tonight, Mrs. Lynchford, but I rather
doubt whether we'll be missed."

Moments later, Natalya found herself being pulled behind him down the magnificent marble staircases, her senses swimming. Servants stared as they passed, and a footman handed Grey his cape and Natalya her mantelet when they reached the front door. Because of the line of richly garbed footmen who stood in the entry hall, Natalya kept quiet as they waited for Grey's post chaise to be brought round. The deep rose staining her cheeks and the flash of her turquoise eyes were the only indications of the storm building behind her silence.

When the post chaise arrived, Grey reached for her arm, and she pulled away. "I am quite capable, sir," she said, and strode past him into the night air.

Once inside the light carriage, Natalya moved sharply away when Grey seated himself beside her. Their eyes met in the shadows and sparks seemed to fly.

"I have never been more humiliated in my life," she pronounced as the post chaise began the journey to Bennett Street.

"I should think not," Grey returned coolly. "You reek of champagne."

"I am referring, sir, to *your* conduct!" Her voice rose.

"Indeed? Perhaps more might be gained by examining your own. Or are you now in the habit of attending cyprians' balls and encouraging the attentions of lascivious men who care only to imagine how you might look in their beds?"

Her emotions ran riot and she seemed powerless to control them. "I only went to that ball because Adrienne invited me, and I have been trying to learn more about the life she is leading! Do you imagine that I know anything of cyprians outside of Greek literature?"

"You would appear to be a quick study, my dear," Grey said cynically.

"You had no right to interfere," she cried. "I am not a child!"

"That is evident, I assure you." His gaze dropped meaningfully to her breasts. He wanted to tell her that it had driven him crazy to see Byron undressing her in his mind, to watch her laugh up at Laidlaw, seeming to encourage his lust. But he could say none of these things.

Natalya blushed under his regard. "You are a bigger cad than all of them! What a hypocrite you are, coming to that rout like a randy stallion and then forcing *me* to leave because you saw that I was enjoying myself. I am a grown woman, *my lord*, and I do *not* need or desire your *protection*."

"Exactly what do you need and desire, my beautiful little hellion?" Grey asked softly. "Perhaps I can supply it in Laidlaw's stead."

Suddenly she was conscious of his nearness in an entirely different way. She knew she ought to slap him but found that she could neither move nor speak. In the tense silence, Natalya was certain he must hear the pounding of her heart. We've both had too much champagne, she thought dizzily, and he thinks I'm . . . experienced . . . or something.

Lucid thought ended when his gloved forefinger touched her chin, tilting it up. "You really are—so beautiful," Grey said, and it sounded as if the words burned his throat. Softly his mouth grazed hers, and the feeling was so exquisite, beyond all her memories or imaginings, that tears sprang to her eyes. She leaned forward instinctively, and then Grey took her in his arms and her lips parted. She tasted sweetly of champagne, but also of a kind of innocence that he had nearly forgotten. Her response was passionate and guileless all at once; utterly enchanting to him. Dimly it occurred to Grey that they both had been locked up far too long, he in his prison and she in her château. Then he, too, stopped thinking.

He bent her back against the velvet seat of the post chaise and ran his mouth down the soft length of her neck. When Natalya gave a low moan, he pulled off his right glove with his teeth and touched her. First his fingers traced the softness of her throat, then wandered lower, curving around the warm fullness of a breast. Strong currents of arousal washed over him full force, and he nearly bit his lip in an effort to contain them. The heat was rising quickly in his loins.

Natalya ran her fingers through his thick hair as they kissed again, his tongue stroking hers. She loved the taste of him, the heady clean male scent of him, the strength and size of his body against her own. His hand was moving lower, over the lush curve of her hip, across the softness of her belly. Natalya gasped when he touched the throbbing place between her legs through the silk and muslin of her gown.

"Dear God, how magnificently you are made," he whispered hoarsely. "Natalya, you are made for love."

Suddenly she was frightened. What was she doing? "Grey, please—"

He drew back immediately. Reality struck him like a splash of icy water and he sat up, raking a hand through his hair. "I beg your pardon." His eyes met hers in the wavering shadows as he endeavored to forget the dull throb in his groin. "It seems you were right about me after all. I am no better than those other men."

As the post chaise drew up before Mrs. Sykes's house on Bennett Street, Natalya realized that her hands were trembling. She balled them into fists and said, "That's the reason I prefer to write about men rather than deal with the actual flesh-and-blood variety. In the real world, you are all far too predictable. Rather boring, actually." Was her voice shaking, too? Privately she realized that she was responsible in part for what had occurred between them, but she could not admit that to Grey. "I propose that we put this . . . incident behind us. After all, I'll soon be gone and we shall never see each other again." Her tone became businesslike. "At the moment there is another matter to deal with. You see, I am very worried about my cousin. You must explain to me what it is you have learned about Mrs. Sykes, and then we must see to it that Adrienne is removed from the clutches of that woman and returned to Miss Harrington's Seminary."

As he helped her out of the carriage, Grey smiled wryly at the back of her head with its froth of honey curls. Had she called him *boring*? Aloud he said, "We'd better work fast, then, my sweet. You are sailing for America in two days—and I'm going with you."

Chapter Thirteen

April 3–4, 1814

"YOU ARE GOING WITH ME?" NATALYA ECHOED IN disbelief. She recovered herself quickly and began walking toward Mrs. Sykes's house, laughing as if amused. "I can assure you, Mr. St. James, that such drastic measures are unnecessary. I am perfectly capable—"

"I know, I know," he sighed, matching her pace. "I believe I may have memorized your speech about just how capable you are. Unfortunately there's no getting around this. You are going to have to endure my company for a few more weeks, I fear, because we will be sailing to America on board my schooner, the *Wild Rover*."

"Is there no other way for me to travel?"

Grey shrugged. "Britain is at war with America, so there is a certain amount of risk involved in any sea voyage between the two countries. I feel responsible for your safety, whether that pleases you or not." He paused. "I also have some personal reasons of my own for making this journey, not the least of which is a desire to be at sea again. The *Rover* has scarcely left the river Thames in four years."

"This is *not* the plan I expected," Natalya declared.

"Cheer up, my dear. It won't last forever. I'll be out of your life before spring wanes." With that, he lifted the knocker on the front door just as a hack drew up with Mrs. Sykes, Adrienne, and Venetia Hedgecoe inside.

"I nearly forgot," Natalya whispered. "We couldn't have

143

gotten in. She has no live-in servants. She only hires them when someone is coming to visit—for appearances, you understand.''

Looking extremely vexed, Mrs. Sykes charged up the footpath, the two girls in tow. Adrienne's curls were disheveled, and when she nearly bumped into Grey, he could smell the champagne on her.

''You had better have some very good reasons for causing such mayhem on this of all nights, my lord,'' Mrs. Sykes barked as she turned the key in the lock.

''Oh, I think my behavior was justified,'' he replied, with heavy irony. ''I'll be interested to learn if you can justify your own conduct.''

She led the way into a dark, narrow parlor and set about lighting several candelabra on pedestals entwined with garlands. Temporarily diverted, Grey looked around the room in fascination. The windows were hung with drapes of crimson brocade embellished with golden tassels, and there was a Turkey carpet on the floor that exemplified the worst taste of its kind. He was further intrigued by the furniture, which consisted of green-striped couches with crocodile legs, lyre-back chairs, tables inlaid with marble and covered with dubious objets d'art, and footstools on lion legs, also glossily striped.

''Perhaps your lordship is unfamiliar with the current styles,'' Mrs. Sykes said defensively, noting his expression.

''That's true,'' he replied. ''I had no opportunity to become acquainted with crocodile-legged couches during my year in prison.'' A smile played briefly about the corners of his mouth.

''It's an Egyptian influence,'' the older woman proclaimed, slurring the words slightly. Then she turned to her charges. ''Girls, you may leave us.''

''No,'' Grey said, his expression hardening. ''I prefer that the young ladies remain. Let us sit down.''

Natalya was surprised to discover that she enjoyed the sense that Grey was deftly in command of the situation, just as he had been that harrowing night in St. Malo. For some reason, his confident manner was reassuring rather than irritating. Ever since she had first arrived at this house the previous day, she had been trying to puzzle out a solution to her cousin's obviously unacceptable situation. Now she was grateful to be able to turn the matter over to Grey St. James.

Mrs. Sykes began to protest that he had no right to give orders in *her* home, but the steely ice of his stare silenced her. She perched on the edge of a lyre-backed chair, peacock feathers slightly askew and her painted lips smeared, while the young ladies seated themselves on one of the squat crocodile-legged couches. Adrienne wore an expression that mingled defiance with grudging admiration for the rakish nobleman so clearly in charge of the situation. Venetia, flushed and dizzy from too much champagne, looked frightened. Natalya sat next to her cousin and endeavored to appear as serious and adult as possible.

"First of all," Grey said coldly, "I have to say that I have rarely encountered a matter more shocking than this. Mrs. Sykes, I know that you have not only removed these girls from the safety of their school without their parents' knowledge, but you have proceeded to sell introductions to them among the demimonde, setting the stage for them to become involved in illicit love affairs. Because of you, their lives and reputations could have been ruined . . . and your only motive was financial gain. You may cover these goings-on with a veneer of false respectability, but this arrangement makes you no better than the madam of a bordello."

Mrs. Sykes gasped in horror, and the girls went white.

Grey continued, "You grew overbold because these young ladies were completely innocent, without any notion of what was truly behind your supposed kindness. Perhaps you even convinced yourself that you were doing them a favor? Was that your motive tonight for selling introductions to *Natalya*?"

Though she was shaking visibly, Mrs. Sykes drew herself up. "Authoress or no, she's been on the vine far too long, and I only thought to help her a bit by bringing her along to the duke's rout, where she could mingle with men. They all know that my girls are beautiful, well mannered, and—"

"You speak of them as if they were your merchandise," Grey cut in harshly. "Adrienne and Miss Hedgecoe are still young enough to have parents who are responsible for them and make decisions for their well-being. If Nicholai Beauvisage knew what you were up to with his daughter, he'd have you tossed in prison!''

''But, my lord!'' she cried shrilly.

''I have neither the time nor the inclination to argue this matter further,'' he said, looking out the window. His face was even more forbidding in profile. Slowly he drew off his gloves and turned back to capture Mrs. Sykes's fearful gaze. ''Tomorrow morning, Adrienne Beauvisage and Miss Hedgecoe will return to . . . uh . . . .''

''Miss Harrington's Seminary for the Daughters of Gentlemen,'' Natalya supplied, biting back a smile.

''Exactly. I cannot imagine how that title could have slipped my mind.'' He gave her a grin that flashed for an instant before he schooled his features into an expression of dangerous intent, and addressed Mrs. Sykes. ''I will have a carriage sent round at eleven o'clock to collect them and all their possessions, and I will personally escort them back into Miss Harrington's care.''

''But,'' Venetia whispered fearfully, ''we have no money to pay Miss Harrington, and if I were to explain to Papa . . .'' She dissolved into hiccupping tears.

Grey crossed the parlor and patted her golden curls. ''I shall take care of this matter for the remainder of your term, Miss Hedgecoe. Your parents need not learn of this—if you make me a solemn vow *not* to engage in folly of this sort again as long as you rely upon your parents for financial support and moral guidance. Do we have an agreement?''

Venetia nodded madly through her tears. Grey looked at Adrienne, who watched silently and now gave him a rather more sulky nod.

''It really wasn't necessary for you to interfere, my lord,'' she murmured.

Natalya spoke up, outraged. ''Adrienne Beauvisage, you ought to be ashamed of yourself! If Uncle Nicky had seen you tonight, he would have tied you up and carried you back to

France forever. You should be grateful to Mr. St. James for extricating you from this monstrous coil.''

''And what would Uncle Nicky have said if he had seen *you* at the rout tonight?'' Adrienne couldn't resist asking.

''That is not the issue,'' her cousin cried. ''I was looking after you!''

''Really?'' Adrienne's voice dripped sarcasm.

''That's enough,'' Grey cut in roughly. ''I suggest that you young ladies retire for the night and pray that you are spared what could be the extremely ill aftereffects of the champagne you drank. Be grateful that you've been saved from untimely ravishment at the hands of one of your admirers. You could well have found yourselves in a strange bed on the morrow rather than safely returned to school, where girls of your age and breeding belong.''

''You seem to be quite an expert on the subject of ravishing innocent maidens,'' Adrienne said petulantly, but dropped her eyes in the face of his stormy glare.

Natalya, shocked by her young cousin's behavior, exclaimed, ''Yes, let us go up to bed! I for one am very grateful for Mr. St. James's help tonight. I only hope that it's the champagne that has made you so unforgivably insolent, Adrienne.'' As she led the two girls from the parlor, she looked back to find Grey staring at her.

''I will see *you* tomorrow, too,'' Grey said. ''I haven't changed my mind.''

Natalya gave him a bleak smile. ''I feared as much. . . .''

''Why did that horrid man have to bring you to London and take it upon himself to meddle in *my* life? He may be handsomer than Byron, but he's odiously arrogant!'' Adrienne wailed as she tossed a muslin chemise into her hastily packed trunk. ''I was having such fun!''

Natalya stood in front of the bedroom windows that overlooked Bennett Street. Sunlight haloed her upswept honey-gold curls and white-and-lemon-striped gown, but the look on her face was far from angelic. ''Adrienne Beauvisage, I am shocked by your attitude! What would your mother say if she could hear you? Certainly I can understand that you might be led astray by the more adult pleasures of London, particularly since you have spent most of your life at Château du Soleil, but you must have enough sense to see that Mrs. Sykes had introduced you to a darker world that would have meant your ruin.''

''You're just too cowardly to seize life with both hands, Tałya. You might as well have been locked up at Miss Harrington's Seminary yourself all these years for all the living you've done.'' Adrienne tossed a velvet spencer atop the pile of garments in the trunk and then collapsed onto a chair as if exhausted by her labors. ''Why, I'll wager that if a real man, with hot blood and warm lips, tried to *kiss* you, you'd run away like a frightened fawn!''

Maddeningly Natalya felt herself flush, and then sneeze. ''You shouldn't speak of such things, Adrienne.''

''Why not? Because it's true? How can you *write* about love and passion if you've never experienced it yourself? Honestly, Talya, I begin to fear that you'll die a maiden, untouched and unawakened!''

''I may not want to marry, but that does not mean—'' Natalya broke off hastily. ''You're far too precocious, cousin, and far too naughty. It will do no good to taunt and upset me simply because you cannot have your own way. Mr. St. James will be here shortly, and I will be able to leave for America with peace of mind knowing that you are safely back in school.'' She bent down next to Adrienne's chair, then sneezed again into a lawn handkerchief. ''Goodness, I do hope I didn't contract an illness at that horrid rout. Now, don't sulk, Adrienne. You should enjoy your youth while it lasts, and dream of the time when you will be properly presented in society. By then your parents should be able to travel here to be with you during your first Season. Be patient, my dear.''

Her cousin gave her a gentler smile and leaned forward to kiss her cheek. ''All right, I'll try to behave. I am sorry if I've been a brat to you. I know you love me and have been worried about me.'' She sighed. ''It's just that I do so enjoy having *fun*, and there's none of that at Miss Harrington's Seminary.''

Natalya smoothed back her cousin's chestnut curls. "You're a Beauvisage through and through, but hopefully you'll gain a measure of judgment as you grow older. And, the time will pass. Maman always says that pleasure postponed is pleasure enhanced."

A gleam of mischief appeared in Adrienne's green eyes. "And how long do you intend to postpone *your* pleasure, dear cousin?"

"Egad, what a day *this* has been!" Grey St. James expostulated. "I thought I'd never see those girls safely back in the care of Miss Harrington. The Beauvisage girl forgot to pack all her slippers and we had to go back, and then her trunk came open when we unloaded it at the school. The little vixen had the nerve to smile, as if she were enjoying my efforts to hold my temper. God go with the man who dares to wed *her*!"

Gib sipped his friend's excellent brandy and gazed around the darkened bedchamber. There was a great deal of activity going on, particularly in Grey's dressing room, where Jasper Speed was packing for his master's voyage to America and a succession of young housemaids were bustling in and out with freshly laundered and pressed clothing. Grey and Gib sat on the two chairs near the bedchamber's windows, drinking brandy as if to cushion themselves from the hubbub.

"So, you're really going?" Gib murmured.

"I'm afraid so." Grey gave him a weary smile and loosened his cravat. "I spent the early morning on board the *Rover*, conferring with Fedbusk and assuring myself that all the preparations could be made in time to set sail tomorrow. I can't see that I've missed anything. I've even enlisted Dimbleby's assistance in finding a ladies' maid for Miss Beauvisage. We're going to nip one of the housekeeper's best maids. Mrs. Thistle won't like it, but she won't know until the girl is gone." He used the candle on the table between them to light a cheroot and closed his eyes. "It's been a devil of a day. In fact, my life seems to have been one long ordeal ever since I arrived back in London. Quite the opposite of what I expected. . . ."

Gib's face looked longer than ever as he pursed his lips and

studied his gaunt-looking friend. It seemed that all this talk of
trunks coming open and meetings with Fedbusk and plots to
steal the Earl of Hartford's kitchen maid was merely a diversion from the real issue.

"Old chap, you don't really expect to find Francesca in
Philadelphia, do you?" he asked softly.

Grey's hooded eyes opened a fraction. "To be perfectly
honest, I haven't considered the matter at length. I simply
know that I must make the effort before I can put the past to
rest."

"I realize that it's none of my affair, but I can't help wondering how much this sudden journey has to do with that stun-
ner you forcibly removed from the rout last night."

"Miss Beauvisage and I do not get on at all, if that's what
you're hinting at," Grey replied in carefully even tones, closing his eyes again. "She's a thorn in my side, and the only
way I can rid myself of her honorably is to fulfill my obligation
and deliver her to her home in Philadelphia. And there's no
time to waste. You saw what happened when I left her alone
for one day here in London."

Gib thought there was more to it than that, but he refrained
from saying so. "You are coming back, though?" he asked
suddenly. "From America, I mean."

Drawing on his cheroot, St. James gave him a charming
smile. "Why would I not? What would possibly keep me there
once I've relieved myself of the prickly burden of Natalya
Beauvisage and made my inquiries about Francesca?" What
Grey didn't say, and could scarcely bear to think, was that
there was little left in London to return to. In his present state
of mind, it was easier to sail away to America than remain in
England and fumble with the pieces of a new life.

Dimbleby appeared in the doorway. "His lordship has returned from the theater, Lord Grey, and is preparing to retire
for the night."

"Thank you, Dimbleby. I'll go to him now and make my
farewells." Grey drank down the remainder of his brandy,
stubbed out his cheroot in a candy dish, and stood up. "Don't

mean to toss you out, Gib, but it's long past midnight and I have an appointment at dawn."

Gib struggled awkwardly to his feet and embraced his friend, surprised to feel the sudden sting of tears. "I'll miss you, old fellow. Godspeed."

"No cause for sadness, Gib. I'll be back before you know it, and I've no doubt that you'll be far too involved in this business of courtship and betrothal and God knows what else to notice my absence. Take care of yourself . . . and thank you." He patted his friend's shoulder. "If not for you, I would have felt positively unloved and abandoned these past days."

The words were spoken in a light-hearted tone, but Osgood Gibson recognized the undercurrent of emotion in Grey's voice. They walked into the hallway together and parted at the stairway as Grey went on to his father's suite of rooms at the other end of the house. Gib raised his hand in a last farewell, wondering at the vagaries of fate that had dealt his comrade such an unfriendly hand of late. The future was even more uncertain, but as Gib descended Hartford House's splendid staircase, he hoped that Grey would find a measure of joy and fulfillment in the adventures that stretched before him.

"Ah, there you are, dear boy," the Earl of Hartford remarked, with his usual air of mild regret, when he saw his son standing in the doorway to his bedchamber. Chester, the earl's manservant, was helping him out of his old-fashioned cutaway coat, and Grey saw that his father looked thinner and more frail without it. "I thought perhaps you'd left."

Grey blinked. "Left?"

"Gone off to one of those house parties in the country or whatever it is young people do these days to amuse themselves," his lordship replied, waving a hand. He turned to his manservant and said querulously, "Go to bed, Chester! You hover like an old woman!"

Chester, who was accustomed to such abuse after thirty years in the earl's employ, merely bowed and left the room, closing the door behind him. Grey thought that his father appeared extremely fatigued, wavering slightly as he struggled with the buttons on his waistcoat.

"Father, I know that it's late, but could you spare me a moment of your time? Perhaps we could sit down."

The earl eased himself onto his favorite wing chair, clutching the arms, and waited as Grey perched on the edge of the mammoth Tudor bed.

"I've been to see that Kean fellow perform," Hartford remarked. "I'm not at all certain what the fuss is about."

"Edmund Kean? They say he's brilliant." Grey sighed and pushed aside the frayed bedhangings of blue velvet that brushed against him. Every time he tried to converse with his father, he felt as if there were an impenetrable wall of glass between them. "Father, I'm sailing tomorrow to America on the *Wild Rover*."

"Yes, yes, I suppose so," the earl replied. "Doubtless it is dull for you here. I find it dull myself."

"That's not precisely why I'm going. I have an obligation to fulfill; I've promised to deliver the daughter of your friend Alexandre Beauvisage to Philadelphia."

The old man's ice blue eyes warmed for an instant. "Beauvisage? Such a long time ago. I suppose he must be dead by now."

"Actually I don't think so—" Grey broke off, seeing that the earl wasn't listening. "Father, is there anything that I can do for you before I go?"

"Do? Do? Whatever can you mean?" He waved his thin hand dismissingly. "I manage very well on my own, dear boy, and you must do as you please. I shall miss you, of course."

A heavy sigh swelled in Grey's chest as he stood and held out his hand to the earl. "Good-bye, then, Father."

Hartford gazed longingly toward his bed. "Good-bye, dear boy. Do visit me when you are next in London."

Chapter Fourteen

April 15–19, 1814

NATALYA AWOKE TO A STRANGE ASSORTMENT OF sounds. Gradually she recognized the high-pitched squawk of sea gulls, the slap of waves against creaking oak, and the clatter of footsteps above her. She looked around groggily to find herself tucked into a cozy bunk built into the corner of a teak-paneled cabin that smelled faintly of lemon oil. Sunlight streamed through a narrow transom overhead. There was a writing desk against the far bulkhead, a Windsor chair, and braced shelves lined with books. After noting that her trunk was within reach, she nestled into the softness of down-filled linen pillows and closed her eyes again.

"Miss Beauvisage?" a timid voice spoke a short time later.

Her lids were so heavy that she could scarcely open them. "Yes?"

A plump, rosy-cheeked girl with curly brown hair swayed in the doorway, trying to keep her balance as the ship rolled and the contents of the tray she held nearly slid off. "You're awake!" Hurriedly the girl staggered over and pulled down the folding table built in next to the bunk. With a sigh of relief, she set the tray on it. The edges of the table were ridged upward to prevent objects from falling off. "I'll never get used to this ship," the girl cried. "I'm forever bashing into walls, falling down, and dropping things."

Natalya felt light-headed. Should she know this person? Vaguely it seemed that she did, but—

153

"How are you feeling?" The girl straightened her mobcap, then reached for a steaming mug of tea. "Doesn't this smell grand? It'll be so much easier to get you to take a bit of nourishment now that you're truly awake. Mind you don't nod off again, Miss Natalya. Not until you've had some tea and a bit of soup and fruit." She plumped the pillows behind Natalya and boosted her up against them.

"I'm afraid . . . I'm not quite certain . . ."

"Oh mistress, you've been very, very ill. Do you remember me? Charlotte Timkins? His lordship brought me along as your new maid when we sailed from London, but you were feeling poorly that very first morning, sniffling and all. You insisted you'd only caught a bit of a chill and wanted to stay up on deck, but his lordship would have none of that and sent you below to lie down."

"Yes . . ." Natalya nodded, sipping the tea laced with lemon and honey. "I do remember now. I felt very warm, and dizzy, and I lay down here . . ."

"And you've scarcely moved since. I've managed to get a bit of tea or soup down you, and kept you in clean nightgowns, and we've all just prayed for your fever to break. Oh, there were moments when you opened your eyes and spoke, but it was all nonsense. Just between us, you called for his lordship on more than one occasion. Since I knew it was all just dream talk, I didn't see any point in disturbing him."

"This soup is delicious. I'm simply famished!" Natalya sat up straighter, noticing that she wore a soft lawn nightgown edged with Belgian lace that had been a gift from her aunt Lisette. Her hair was twisted into a relatively neat braid that hung over her shoulder and down over her right breast. "I must look a sight!" She turned the bowl to get the last drops of soup onto her spoon. "I do hope that you haven't let anyone else in here, Charlotte."

"Lord Altburne tried to come in, but I made him peek from the doorway, just so he could see that you were breathing and such," Charlotte confessed. "I mean, Mr. St. James. He says he wants no part of titles, but it's difficult to change."

"Charlotte," Natalya said between spoonfuls of custard, "how long have I been ill?"

"Oh, ten days, I'd wager, mistress. I never really feared that you wouldn't recover, for I've nursed people who have died and I know the look when death is near, but you were frightfully ill."

"Ten days!" Natalya murmured, stunned. "Have we been at sea all this time?"

"Yes'm. His lordsh—I mean, Mr. St. James has a lovely, trim ship and the wind's been with us. There was a squall two days ago that frightened me badly, but he brought us through it splendidly." Smiles wreathed her plump face.

"Why, we might be halfway to Philadelphia! How could I have missed so much? Charlotte, where have you been sleeping? Has it been very awful for you, the only woman among so many men?" Questions raced through her mind, and she heard herself exclaiming them aloud. "Is there more food? Who has been cooking it?"

The young maid patted her mistress's pale hand. "Yes, I believe that we may be more than half the way to America, Miss Natalya, as long as some ship doesn't take it into its mind to attack us. The captain's managed to outwit them all so far. I'll own I've never seen a more magnificent man than Mr. St. James. I like that word, don't you? *Magnificent.*"

"Well, I rather think that it tends to denote royalty or a true work of art or something of that sort," Natalya replied dryly, "and Mr. St. James does seem to fall rather short in my opinion."

Charlotte shrugged philosophically. "Each to his own taste, as my mum would say. To answer your other questions, I've been sleeping in a hammock that fastens to those hooks." She pointed to large brass hooks attached to beams in the cabin's far corner. "I had to be nearby at all times. As for all the men, I don't mind them a bit. It's a small crew, and they're nice boys—all except for Mr. Fedbusk, who is rather unpleasant and full of himself. Acts as if it's *his* ship when the captain's not about, but as I understand it, Fedbusk oversaw the *Wild Rover* while Mr. St. James was off at war, so—"

"Is there more food?" Natalya interrupted. Every dish on her tray was scraped clean and she was ravenous.

"Indeed, mistress. How good it is to see you eat! There's a proper cook on board, name of George, and I know he'll be delighted to fix you anything your heart desires."

"Anything at all would be welcome. Do you think you might ask him?"

"Right away! But it will have to be food that will go down gently, and not too much all at once."

"Whatever you think is best, Charlotte," Natalya said, with a smile. "I am indebted to you for caring for me so diligently these past days. I may well owe you my life."

The girl blushed with pleasure. "It was an honor, Mistress Natalya. I'll go and speak to George now, and you just rest." Charlotte took the tray and stumbled right and left as she crossed the cabin, nearly losing the dishes again. Then, with a bright smile of parting, she went out into the gangway and managed to pull the door closed behind her.

The weather was exquisite. Clouds as soft and light as stretched cotton drifted across a cornflower-blue sky, while the *Wild Rover* sliced through the Atlantic Ocean, her sails filled with a warm west wind. The *Rover* was light, with sharp, clean lines, made for speed and beauty. After his years aboard giant ships of war, it was pure joy for Grey to stand on this polished deck and bask in the sunlight as they sailed nearly effortlessly toward America. He felt freer and happier than he had in a very long time, except for the constant worry in the back of his mind about Natalya Beauvisage. After their first day at sea, when it had become clear that she was afflicted with something far more serious than a simple cold, he had nearly turned back. Charlotte Timkins had persuaded him that she had nursed many through similar illnesses, having learned the duties of a sickmaid from her mother. It did seem that Natalya was now out of danger, but—

"Captain?"

He turned from the polished rail to find Charlotte weaving before him. Putting out a hand to steady her, he immediately inquired about Natalya's condition. "She's not worse, is she? Dear God, if anything were to happen to her, I'd never forgive myself!"

Charlotte blinked at this sudden exclamation of apparent emotion. "Rest easy, sir. Didn't I tell you that I would see her through? I could tell in the night that Miss Natalya was better by her breathing. The cough had gone and her brow was much cooler. Now she is awake and alert for the first time, sir. Hungry as a horse, she is, and in fine spirits!"

"I'm going below to see her," Grey said immediately.

Charlotte caught his sleeve as he started past her. "Oh, no, sir, that wouldn't be proper."

"The devil take propriety," he shot back angrily. "You've kept me from her these last ten days, and I abided by your rules, but no more."

Fedbusk, a wiry, balding, sun-weathered man, had been standing nearby and looked on with interest as St. James stalked across the deck toward the companionway leading to the cabins. Only a few years older than Grey, he had grown up as a stable boy for the Earl of Hartford, son of the head coachman. It had been he who had taught Grey to ride and fish and had imparted the secrets of mating. Because the earl disapproved so strongly of their friendship, Grey had clung to it even more stubbornly, installing Fedbusk as his first officer when he purchased the *Wild Rover*. Now, as Fedbusk watched St. James disappear belowdeck, he scratched his head and chuckled. "Wonder what that's all about," he murmured.

Charlotte's mouth puckered and she hurried after the captain, determined to chaperone her mistress.

Grey opened the door to Natalya's cabin silently and looked inside, afraid that he would find her a ghostly shadow of her former self. But his first glimpse flooded him with relief. Natalya looked like an angel lying against the snowy pillows. Her molten-honey braid flowed down over the front of a prim white nightgown edged with lace, and he could see that there was color in her fine-boned cheeks.

When he approached the bunk and whispered her name, Natalya opened her eyes and nearly gasped aloud. "Grey?"

A disarming smile lit his face. "The same, my sweet."

Her aqua eyes were huge with surprise. "How . . . *well* you look!"

It was an understatement of epic proportions, for Grey had been transformed during his ten days at sea. A few of his lost pounds had returned before they left London, but the remainder had been added quickly on board the *Rover*. George had delighted in cooking his captain's favorite dishes, and the brisk salt air had completely restored Grey's appetite. The sun and outdoor activity had done the rest, and now the man who stood before Natalya was utterly magnificent, just as Charlotte had said.

His ebony hair with its gleaming strands of silver was windswept, framing a bronzed face with the same rakishly familiar features she recognized . . . yet somehow his brows seemed to arch more recklessly, his smile seemed whiter, his jawline stronger. And there was an added light in his steely eyes. Grey's physique was now truly powerful. He wore a loose white linen shirt, open halfway to his waist to reveal the soft mat of black hair covering his tanned chest. The shirt was tucked into fawn breeches that clung to the long muscles of his thighs and disappeared into topboots. Natalya could feel the aura of male potency surrounding him.

"I *am* feeling more myself again, thank you," he said, with a grin. "But it is your health that concerns me at the moment. Charlotte tells me that you are better?"

"I never really knew I was ill," she confessed. When he reached out to take her hand, Natalya felt herself flush. "It's all a blur to me, from the time I came on board ship in London until this morning. I knew I wasn't feeling well, even the day we took Adrienne and Venetia back to school, but I thought I had simply caught a chill."

When Grey perched on the edge of the bunk, still holding her hand, Charlotte made her presence known in the doorway by clearing her throat. Instantly his head turned and he gave her a piercing glance. "Leave us."

The girl pressed her lips together. "I'll just fetch Mistress Natalya's tray from the galley, then, and be back in a trice."

There was an undercurrent of amusement in Grey's voice as he remarked, "It would seem that I have chosen, completely by chance, the two least submissive servants in all of London for your maid and my valet."

"I should think that Charlotte would be eager for a respite now that I am feeling better. She must be quite bored by the sight of me."

"She fears that I will try to take advantage of you in your weakened state," Grey whispered, with mock gravity. "Obviously she does not understand our relationship."

"No. Obviously not," Natalya replied in a small voice, feeling vaguely alarmed by her response to his physical presence. "I will have to inform her of the facts on that score."

"Yes. Tell her that you are merely tolerating my company until we reach Philadelphia." There was a glint of mischief in his eyes.

"Yes, and I'll explain that you are only taking me there out of obligation."

They nodded together, solemnly. After a moment's silence, during which Natalya felt her cheeks growing pinker as she hungered to experience his intoxicating embrace, she said, "Now that I am so much better, I believe I'll resume work on my book. My manuscript is packed in my trunk. I have missed writing, and it seems to be the perfect way to pass the remainder of our voyage."

Charlotte entered with another tray, and Grey stood up, releasing Natalya's hand. "A splendid idea, Miss Beauvisage. There's nothing like romance at sea, especially from the safe distance afforded by fantasy, hmm? I'll have Speed bring you pens and paper." He watched as Charlotte settled the tray onto her mistress's lap, neatly catching the dish of pudding that slid off one side. "I perceive that Charlotte's sea legs are a cause for concern," he observed wryly, replacing it. "We'll have one of the crew give you lessons, all right, Charlotte? In the meantime, keep a close eye on Miss Beauvisage. She's a tempting morsel on a shipful of ravening men, and there's no telling who might try to sneak a taste!''

For four days Natalya remained obediently in her bunk and allowed Charlotte to nurse her back to health. She napped, ate, and wrote her book on a lap desk that Grey's valet brought with a supply of quills, ink, and paper.

Soon, however, she began to grow restless. The plot of her story was fraught with drama and romance, but instead of distracting her, it only intensified her boredom. On the fourth afternoon, Grey poked his head into Natalya's cabin and found her biting the end of her quill and scowling at the sheets of paper scattered across the bunk.

''Would you care for an apple?'' he inquired affably.

Her heart skipped at the sight of him, and when he came over to sit down beside her, she could smell the freshness of the sun and sea breeze on him. Was it possible that she had once been held in those arms, kissed by those lips, touched by his strong hands? . . .

''Are you all right?'' he asked, brow furrowing.

''Yes—yes, of course!''

''You were shivering for a moment. Shall I get you another quilt?''

''No, I'm fine. And you have the apple. Charlotte has just removed my luncheon tray and I couldn't eat another bite.'' Dragging her eyes from his face, Natalya gestured at the papers on her lap. ''I'm just struggling with the next scene in my book. I can't decide quite how to do it.''

''Will you tell me the plot of your novel, or is it a secret?''

She peered at him from under her thick lashes, wondering if he would laugh. ''Well, my heroine, Eloise, has been sent to an Italian convent by her father because he fears that she will be seduced by Charles, the charming but mysterious hero, who appears to be penniless but is actually a duke. Eloise's father means to keep her pure until he can find a wealthy husband for her—''

''But, of course, the forces of passion conspire to thwart

Father's plans?'' Grey supplied. "I take it that Eloise is a heroine of the hot-blooded, reckless variety?''

Natalya nodded, looking down and straightening the pages of her manuscript. Suddenly she heard Adrienne's voice in her mind, taunting, *How can you write about love and passion if you've never experienced it yourself? I begin to fear that you'll die a maiden, untouched and unawakened!*

Noting the flush that crept into her cheeks, Grey refrained from inquiring himself about Natalya's source of knowledge regarding romantic relations between men and women. Again he reminded himself that she *was* twenty-six years old; she had to have some experience in her past. They were silent for a moment, and Grey's eyes strayed to the curves of her breasts, soft and full under the fine cotton of her nightgown. The sharp response in his loins alarmed him and he nearly reached for her.

"I ought to leave you,'' he said abruptly, standing up, "before Charlotte returns and accuses me of prurient intentions. I'm certain, given your fertile imagination, that you will be able to overcome this temporary barrier in your story. How fortunate you are to be able to make up stories of love rather than live them out. It must be much more satisfying to be able to control the outcome.''

Natalya was confused by his tone. Was he mocking her, or did she detect a note of bitterness behind his light words? She watched him cross the cabin with a strong, graceful stride, admiring the set of his wide shoulders and the lean lines of his hips. Grey paused in the doorway, then turned back with a kind smile. "You mustn't allow Charlotte to keep you prisoner down here. If you feel well enough, venture up on deck. The sunshine would doubtless do you good, and I'll see to it that the crew behaves.''

Natalya beamed like a little girl who had been promised an unexpected treat. "Thank you!''

Charlotte appeared then, wearing an expression of flustered alarm as she squeezed past Grey in the narrow doorway. He bit into his apple, glanced back over one broad shoulder to give Natalya a brief wink, and then he was gone.

Chapter Fifteen

THE SUNSHINE WAS WARM ON NATALYA'S FACE AS she reclined on the captain's chair, which was bolted to the quarterdeck. Her curls were pinned up in artful disarray, she wore a simple gown of yellow-sprigged muslin, and her slippered feet were propped on a coil of rope supplied by one of the high-spirited crew. *Pride and Prejudice*, the latest novel by Jane Austen, lay open on her lap. Natalya would read for a few minutes, pause to bask in the sunlight with her eyes closed, sip from her glass of wine, chat with one of the crew or Grey if he happened to be near, then repeat the sequence of events again. It was bliss.

There was an infectious frivolity about these days, she mused. The men were in excellent spirits, singing and joking as they handled the ropes and climbed the tall, raking spars, all of them seeming to enjoy the presence of a beautiful woman on their ship. Only Fedbusk and Charlotte were openly disapproving of Natalya's conduct, but she would not let their censorious looks spoil her fun. When the sea spray showered her with a fine, fresh mist and she watched Grey St. James laughing with his crew, she felt as if she were in the midst of a magical, light-hearted dream under the sun.

"You're looking very happy, minx," Grey remarked as he hunkered down next to her chair, his grin a flash of white against the golden brown of his face.

"And you're looking very piratical, Captain," she parried

162

lightly. Then she met his eyes, her own aquamarine like the ocean, and said sincerely, "I am enjoying myself immensely, you know. Sometimes I think I must still be ill, and all of this is a feverish hallucination. It seems too wonderful to be real."

He could have said the same thing about her, but he only smiled with secret amusement. Natalya appeared to be completely unaware of her enchanting good looks, which added all the more to her appeal. Her hair shone in the sunlight, begging for his touch, her skin had warmed to a peachy-gold hue, and dimples winked on either side of her inviting lips. Grey tried not to look below her neck, tried to block his response to the lush curves of her breasts and hips outlined against her muslin chemise frock. There were moments, though, when he suddenly imagined Natalya lying naked across silky sheets, her body warm and golden in a haze of candlelight, and the effort to banish such thoughts made his head ache.

"Ah, here is Speed with a picnic, and not a moment too soon," he said cryptically, rising to take the tray from his manservant. Speed had been suffering from seasickness for most of the voyage, and thus had little energy to spare fussing over his master, much to Grey's relief. "You're green as pea soup, Speed. I suggest that you get into bed and stay there until we dock in Philadelphia."

The young man looked queasier at the mention of pea soup. "Well, if you're certain you won't be needing me, sir, I may just have a short lie-down—"

"And do not stir until I summon you!" Grey thundered. "That's an order!"

"Yes, sir." With a grateful smile, Speed took his leave.

Natalya was already attacking the food, tearing a hunk from the loaf of dark, warm, crusty bread and spreading it with butter. "I'm prodigiously hungry," she confessed.

He poured more red wine into her cup and broke bread for himself, pairing it with Wensleydale cheese and a slice of smoked trout. It was a pleasure to see Natalya eat with such relish, and he watched her in silence for a minute before taking a sip of wine and remarking:

"Your nose will be sunburned if you aren't careful."

She gave him an impudent smile. "You sound just like Charlotte. Every day she tries to block the door and persuade me to remain in my cabin like a proper lady. When that fails, she produces a cottage bonnet and attempts to force it onto my head!" Natalya began to giggle. "I fear that Charlotte is quite out of patience with me. She was a good deal happier when I was insensible, I suspect, and she had to feed and dress me like a baby."

Grey watched her savor a bite of trout. "Are your high spirits due to the fact that you'll soon be home again? You must be counting the minutes until we reach Philadelphia."

"Well . . ." Her smile faded behind a cloud of mixed emotions. "To be perfectly honest with you, I'm trying not to think about it very much. Look what happened to the high expectations you had en route to London. I know that my life will be more complicated. I haven't had to deal with parents for a very long time, and as much as I adore Maman and Papa, I'm sure that they will have ideas of their own about the course of my future." She gazed off across the shimmering blue ocean. "I doubt that we'll be in agreement."

"Parents and children rarely are," Grey replied neutrally.

"I'm not the conventional child, though, am I? I'm perilously close to spinsterhood, some would say, and I've no intention of marrying . . . especially not to satisfy a lot of silly conventions. Maman and Papa will doubtless allow me to chart my own course with a minimum of interference, but then there are other relatives, and old friends . . ."

"You have some challenges ahead, but I have a feeling that you'll meet them unflinchingly." Grey gave her an encouraging smile that melted her heart. "My guess is that you were ready for some challenges, and that's why you wanted to return to Philadelphia."

Natalya was touched by his insight. "I know that I want to write, and I want to be with my family in America again, but—"

"If you imagine that you can avoid men, Natalya, you are deluding yourself." Grey got to his feet and bent to rub the stiffness from his lean-muscled thighs. "Every man who sees you will yearn to have you."

She blushed deeply before his bold stare. "But, I'm so *old*!"

Grey gave a bark of wicked laughter. "How can you call yourself a writer and be so inept at choosing words? I for one have no desire for thin, insipid girls just out of the schoolroom. My taste runs to *women*. Nay, my sweet, you are not old, but ripe and luscious. Never let anyone convince you otherwise."

For the next three days, Natalya felt flushed and restless. She was plagued by shocking, carnal thoughts that gave her no peace. Sometimes, while she was dozing on the *Rover*'s quarterdeck, her nipples would begin to tingle or she would experience a hot, congested feeling between her legs. Opening her eyes, she would sometimes discover Grey St. James staring at her, his eyes like molten silver. Other times, her body's physical responses were the result of her own imaginings, and this both alarmed and excited her. She began to dream of taking mad risks, of doing something that would be impossible once she arrived at her parents' house and Grey sailed back to England.

The closer they got to Philadelphia, the more intense her fantasies became. She had never been with a man before, so she wasn't certain if her imaginings were accurate, but when she watched the play of muscles in Grey's body as he moved, when she felt the caress of his voice and the heat of his stare, and when she caught a whiff of his scent, Natalya knew enough.

She tried to write a romantic scene between Eloise and Charles and felt consumed by her own desires. The memory of Adrienne's words taunted her. If she didn't seek fulfillment now, would the opportunity be lost forever?

At dusk on the afternoon of the twenty-fifth, when Grey brushed past her on the companionway and casually mentioned that they might see land on the morrow, Natalya made up her mind.

"I surely don't like the way you've been looking these past few days, mistress," Charlotte declared as she fastened her hammock to the brass hooks. Stumbling with each roll of the ship, she had to take several minutes just to accomplish the one task. "You've been flushed and your eyes are so bright."

"Charlotte, dear, I'm *happy*! I assure you that I've never felt better in my life." Natalya hummed to herself as she poured wine into cups.

"Well, I don't like it. You may think you're happy, but you look more like delirious to me. Insisting on a bath, and washing your hair—it wasn't good sense, but you're too naughty to pay me any mind. Now, just get into bed and I'll tuck you up nice and snug."

"How can you call me naughty, Charlotte? Have some wine with me and let us cry peace." Natalya held out a cup to the girl with an ingratiating smile. "You're overwrought, and it will help you sleep."

Charlotte pursed her lips. "If I drink this, will you behave yourself and go to bed?"

"I promise."

Soon the cabin was dark and Charlotte's hammock was swinging gently, matching the rhythm of her snores. Moonlight streamed through the transom over Natalya, who was having a hard time containing either her mirth or her excitement. Charlotte had been absolutely right to accuse her mistress of being naughty, for Natalya had put a dose of laudanum in her maid's wine. The last thing she wanted was Charlotte Timkins waking up later on and staggering around the ship in search of her mistress.

Natalya already knew that Fedbusk had the night watch, and she had been fortunate enough to overhear Grey telling his first officer that he was retiring early to read since the sea was so peaceful. Now she lay in her bunk for what seemed an eternity, waiting until there were no more sounds of movement on the lower deck. The moon above told her that midnight was at hand when she crept at last out of her bunk. Clad only in her thin nightgown, she tiptoed across the cabin, stepped into the lantern-lit gangway, and turned in the direction of Grey St. James's quarters.

* * *

Grey closed the volume of *René* that Natalya had given him at Château du Soleil and placed it on the table next to his bed. The cabin boy had changed the sheets earlier that morning, and they felt wonderfully sensuous against his clean bare legs. He was about to blow out the candle and slide down into bed when there came a faint tap at his cabin door.

"Yes?" Had Fedbusk run into difficulty after all? Had another ship been sighted?

The door opened and, to Grey's utter astonishment, Natalya Beauvisage entered. He blinked, certain he was seeing things, for the woman who stood on the threshold was the embodiment of his most forbidden dreams. Haloed by the lantern light from the gangway, her body was clearly visible through her transparent nightgown. Grey drank in the sight of soft curves and hollows, long slim legs, and the shadow where they met. . . .

For a long moment he was paralyzed, but at last he found his voice. "Is—is there something wrong?" he said hoarsely. "Have you need of me?"

Natalya gave him a radiant smile and closed the door. "Yes, I have need of you." Slowly she walked toward the bed, her luxuriant hair swirling about her shoulders like liquid honey. "Grey, I want you to make love to me."

His black brows flew up as he bit back a grin. "Is that so? Dar God, Natalya, I do love your flair for drama! You are the most original woman I have ever known!"

She stopped, frowning. "Don't you dare laugh at me, Grey St. James!"

"Laugh? I?" His eyes danced with mischief, but he struggled for an expression of gravity. "It is just that you have taken me by surprise. I must own that, given our past history, this was the last thing I expected you to do." He reached out for her hand. "I imagined that you were counting the minutes until you could bid me farewell forever in Philadelphia, but it seems that I, foolish male that I am, have misread your feelings."

"Are you teasing me?" she demanded, trying to read his irresistibly handsome face in the candlelight. "You must *know* that I am not here to do anything so ridiculous as pledge my love for you or any nonsense of that sort."

"Natalya, darling, my state of undress prevents me from coming to you, so I suggest that you sit down right here"— Grey patted the edge of his bed in the manner of a cat coaxing a canary— "and tell me just exactly what has been happening in that fascinating mind of yours that led you to plot my seduction."

"I have *not* been plotting your *seduction*," she cried in tones of outrage.

"Shh, sweeting." He placed a lean finger over his lips in a way that maddened her. "You'll wake the crew. Now, come and sit down."

Feeling increasingly foolish, Natalya did as he bade her, perching on the edge of his beautifully carved walnut bed. Grey sat next to her, the covers drawn up over his hips, his wide, strong chest nut brown against the snowy pillows. She felt a change in the cadence of her heart, and her palms grew moist as he looked at her, waiting patiently and trying not to smile.

"You're spoiling it all, you know, making me explain!" she burst out in a furious whisper. "This was not the way it was supposed to happen. I came here because I want to become a . . . woman, in the true sense. I mean—"

"I think I know what you mean," he said dryly.

"This seemed the perfect opportunity. I felt that I should have this experience for the sake of my art, and—"

"I like that," Grey interjected, nodding.

"And since I don't intend to marry, I began to doubt whether I would ever have another opportunity after I reach Philadelphia. I'm not one of those women who could have love affairs, and they sound like such a bother, don't you think?"

"Well, there wouldn't be any question of *this* being a love affair, would there? Once we reach Philadelphia, you'll be rid of me . . . and no one would know about tonight, hmm? You're a very practical woman, Natalya."

His gray eyes were roaming over her body as he spoke, and she began to feel quite warm. "I didn't mean to be practical," she protested. "I thought that we would share an interlude of—of . . ."

"Passion? Ah, yes, I understand now. You'd invented a scene of high drama and reckless desire in your mind, and I'm not playing my part very well, am I? Do you want to go back out and come in again?"

His attitude of subtle, ironic amusement was more than Natalya could bear. Her composure gave way completely and she began to cry. "No," she burbled, "I don't want to come in again!"

Grey was instantly contrite. He had reveled in his own enjoyment of her with no thought for her feelings. "I'm sorry, darling. I've been a cad to tease you." Gathering her into his arms, he felt her tears moisten his shoulder.

"Yes"—she nodded emphatically—"you are . . . a very bad, bad . . ." Her voice trailed off as she became suddenly, acutely aware of the warm, strong arms that held her and the crisp chest hair that tickled her cheek. His smell was impossibly wonderful, a mixture of soap, fresh air, cheroot smoke, and his own male essence. "I thought that you—you wanted me," she confessed in a small voice.

"God help me," he said, now utterly serious, "but I do." The desire Grey felt was excruciating. He buried his face in her glossy, fragrant hair and drew a ragged breath. Then his mouth found hers, burning Natalya's soft, sweet, full lips, and her slim arms rounded his shoulders. Grey could feel the pounding of her heart, while the pressure of her breasts drove him mad.

Reaching down, he drew back the covers. "I want to see you," he whispered, kissing the tiny contours of her ear.

Each touch of Grey's lips and hands sent showers of hot sparks over her nerves; it was as if he had put a spell on her, and she was utterly powerless to resist. Dimly Natalya thought that *passion* was a most inadequate word for this storm of sensation that was building between their two bodies.

Staring into her great turquoise eyes, Grey slipped the nightgown over her head. He eased her back against the pillows, then gave his hungry gaze free rein. Natalya was the incarnation of his fantasies, just as he'd suspected that night in the library of Château du Soleil. Her body was soft and creamy, her breasts full and firm with exquisite pink nipples. Her waist was small, but the curves of her hips and derriere were lush, and there was an adorable triangle of burnished gold curls where her elegant legs met. Natalya Beauvisage was delectably made . . . a feast of womanhood.

Finally his eyes returned to her face. Her hair was splayed over his pillows and there were rosy smudges across her cheekbones. She was watching him with a mixture of apprehension and thrilled daring. Grey ran his fingers lightly from her throat to the gentle curve of her belly, watching her shiver in response.

"You are the most extravagantly beautiful woman I've ever seen," he said.

Natalya's blush deepened, but she smiled. "I had no idea. Thank you for saying so."

It was stunning for Grey to think that she was still chaste at twenty-six, that no other man had reaped the pleasures of her body before this night. "You're certain about this? I feel as if I don't deserve—"

"Grey, I want to do this. I am very . . . attracted to you." She wanted to tell him that she found him physically magnificent, too, but couldn't find the words. The mere sight of him kneeling beside her in the candlelight was almost unbearably stirring. "May I touch you?"

"Oh—by all means." He looked heavenward, his voice a raspy whisper. "Feel free."

Natalya turned on her side, rising up on an elbow, and reached out with her right hand. She felt the texture of Grey's hair, the roughness of his cheek and the chiseled line of his jaw. How brilliant God had been to devise such differences between men and women! Her soft fingers wandered down his corded neck and over the breadth of his shoulder. Brown, taut skin covered the steely muscles of his arms and chest, and she loved the crisp black hair that curled from the base of his throat across the expanse of his chest and then tapered into a thin line down his hard, ridged belly. Grey reached out to grasp her wrist before she could venture lower. Natalya hadn't dared look before, but now she stared in fearful fascination.

"Oh, my," she whispered involuntarily. She had only seen this part of the male anatomy on statues and little boys. She understood that desire caused it to grow but had never imagined—

Her curious gaze heightened Grey's arousal past any point he'd known before. Her eyes seemed to scorch his tumescent manhood, and he lay down beside Natalya feeling as if he were venturing into highly dangerous territory. She came eagerly into his arms, pressing herself against the length of his body, running her hands over his muscular back. They kissed for long minutes before he turned her onto the pillows. His mouth traveled over the graceful curve of her throat, then lower. When Grey kneaded her breasts, the aching, tingling sensations intensified in her loins, and when he took one of her nipples in his mouth, she moaned aloud.

"Oh, please."

He caressed Natalya's back, her bottom, the tender insides of her thighs, all the while sucking gently at her pink nipples until she began to arch her hips against him. His lean-muscled thigh pressed gently between her legs and he could feel how wet and swollen she was. When he met her eyes again, a sudden rush of emotion surged up to join the cresting wave of his desire. Her response was so guileless and free, her body so soft and sweet fitted to his. When they kissed, more than passion flared between them.

Natalya was touching his buttocks, then one hand stole around and came in contact with his throbbing member. He flinched.

"You mustn't touch me; I can't bear it," he groaned.

"Unfair." She giggled softly, taking it in her hand. "How very big you are!"

"All for you, my shockingly incorrigible darling," Grey muttered through clenched teeth.

"Will it fit?" Natalya was panting now as he rubbed against her. A core of hot, maddening sensation was concentrated there, and she felt as if she were about to explode, pausing, almost—

When Grey came slowly into her, the delicious aching heightened further. The feeling of him inside her, hard and hot and pulsing, was indescribable. Gently he pushed past the barrier of her maidenhood, and Natalya gasped at the sensation of fullness when he drove in to the hilt. Instinctively her hips arched to meet his thrusts. She looked up at Grey's face, splendid in the flickering candlelight. Tendons stood out in his neck, and she was pausing again, pushing against him, yearning for the release that came suddenly in shuddering, warm, euphoric waves that radiated from their fused bodies.

Feeling her contractions, Grey surrendered to his own burningly powerful climax. Damp with perspiration, their hearts thudding in unison, they shared a breathless kiss. Still joined, Grey curved a hand around her bottom and turned her with him on his side.

Natalya felt suddenly shy. "Thank you."

"Whatever for?" He reached out to smooth disheveled curls from her brow.

"You've made me a woman."

White teeth flashed as Grey laughed. "I believe, without conceit, that I can claim to be something of an expert on the subject of women . . . in the sense you mean." He ran an appreciative hand down the length of her body. "Darling Natalya, you were a woman long before tonight. You just needed the chance to prove it."

Smiling, she snuggled against his chest and murmured primly, "It's kind of you to say so." A moment later, Natalya was sound asleep.

PART THREE

Small is the worth
    Of beauty from the light retir'd;
Bid her come forth,
    Suffer herself to be desir'd,
And not blush so to be admir'd.

EDMUND WALLER
(1606–1687)

Chapter Sixteen

Philadelphia, Pennsylvania
April 27–28, 1814

THE CASEMENT WAS OPEN JUST ENOUGH TO ALLOW the warm, sunny breeze to float into the upstairs library, tease the curtains, and coax Caroline Beauvisage to put down her book. Curled on the window seat, her stockinged feet tucked beneath her, Caro gazed out over Belle Maison's vast, vividly green grounds. Diamond-shaped beds of tulips, daffodils, and hyacinths were jewel bright in the spring sunshine. Leaf buds were bursting open on the tree branches near her window, and the birds were trilling sweetly.

"Maman? Am I disturbing you?"

Caro turned to discover her youngest child, Kristin, framed in the sunlit doorway. Shining blue-black curls escaped the Grecian knot high atop her head to frame her arrestingly beautiful face. Physically Kristin was the image of her father, right down to the dark turquoise hue of her black-lashed eyes. Taller than her mother or older sister, she had a willowy figure and small, firm breasts, set off today by a simple powder blue chemise frock. At twenty-one, Kristin Beauvisage was said to be the fantasy of every eligible bachelor within Philadelphia and its environs.

Holding out her arms to her daughter, Caro smiled. "You could never disturb me, love. What is it?"

"Hollis Gladstone has asked to escort me to the theater again," Kristin said in plaintive tones as she crossed the Persian carpet and kissed her mother's cheek. "I have invented excuses three times in reply to his invitations, hoping that he would give up, but instead he only becomes more determined. This morning, when I encountered Hollis on Market Street and he asked me again, I told him that I would have to consult my engagement diary. He's calling at four o'clock to receive my answer.''

Caro moved over to make room for Kristin and patted the cushion next to her. "Why are you so set against the idea of attending the theater with the man? It's hardly a proposal of marriage.'' Wrapping an arm around her daughter, she added, "And who is this Hollis Gladstone? The endless procession of ardent men who march through your life makes it difficult to remember. . . .''

Rolling her eyes, Kristin replied, "He works at Girard's bank, and is quite a favorite of Stephen Girard's. Don't you remember, Maman, when Hollis attached himself to us at that showing of Thomas Sully's portraits a few weeks ago?''

"Oh, yes!'' Caro's memory produced the unremarkable face of a serious young man, sandy-haired and rather rumpled, with a physique that could be kindly described as cuddly. "Mr. Gladstone has nice eyes, doesn't he? They are green, if memory serves. I found him quite agreeable. Do I know his mother?''

"Hollis's parents died in a carriage accident when he was eighteen. They were Quaker, and although he has become an Episcopalian, he still behaves like a Quaker much of the time.''

"There's nothing wrong with Quakers, Kristin,'' her mother said firmly. She tucked an errant curl into the silken bandeau that secured her hair, a warm honey hue now softened with strands of white. "Quakers are fine people. How sad for Hollis to lose his parents when he is still so young. Is he all alone?''

"No, he lives with an aunt, I think.'' Kristin yawned. "There's really no point in this conversation, Maman. Hollis is nice enough, but certainly not my idea of a suitor. I was hoping that you would help me think of a gentle way to discourage him.''

Caro smiled with loving forbearance. "It occurs to me that you have never told me what you *are* looking for in a suitor.

Since you have made and broken two engagements thus far, perhaps this is a subject that ought to be explored.''

"You are being very difficult, Maman,'' Kristin complained, pressing her rosy lips together. "If I knew exactly what sort of man I wanted to marry, I wouldn't have gotten engaged to John or Malcolm, would I? Obviously I haven't found the right person, but I do know that he won't be like Hollis Gladstone.'' She gazed out the window and sighed. "He'll be handsome, like Papa, and strong and smart and able to laugh in the face of danger. He'll be rich and have beautiful things, and he'll pamper me—''

"Good heavens,'' Caro interrupted, "with a list of requirements like that, you'll never leave home! Kristin, it seems to me that you are setting standards no mortal man can meet. You're not buying a horse, you know. We all have flaws; they are the basis of our humanity.''

"Papa is human. If I can find a man like Papa, he'll be perfect enough to satisfy me,'' Kristin insisted, twisting the sapphire ring that sparkled on her right hand.

Losing patience, Caro replied, "I can most definitely assure you that your father is very human and *imperfect*! He's stubborn and volatile and—'' She broke off suddenly when she saw Kristin staring at the doorway. Turning, Caro discovered that her husband was standing there. "Alec! I didn't think that you had returned from town yet.''

A wry smile curved his handsome mouth. "Don't allow my presence to interrupt your catalog of my character defects, dearest wife. I find this highly enlightening.''

"Maman didn't mean any of that, Papa,'' Kristin said. "She was just trying to convince me to settle for a husband less wonderful than you.'' She looked at Caro with wide eyes. "Can I help it if I've been raised by parents whose own love story is indescribably romantic? Can you blame me for wanting no less for myself?''

"Darling, all I ask is that you listen to your heart rather than relying on a list of standards you've concocted. Give each young man a fair chance.'' Caro patted her daughter's soft cheek. "Will you do that for me?''

"Certainly, Maman." Kristin gave her a bright smile, then rose to meet her father and kiss his cheek. "I'll leave you two now. I must think of what I'm going to say to Hollis Gladstone when he arrives."

"Perhaps you could *accept* his invitation," Caro called after her departing daughter.

"I'll consider it," she replied before disappearing down the corridor.

Alexandre Beauvisage went to his wife, who rose and stepped thankfully into his arms. "Oh, Alec, whoever said that it was easier to raise daughters than sons was surely mistaken. Étienne has always known his own mind and moved with assurance through the stages of his life, while his sisters . . ."

"Also know their own minds, but are thwarted by a society that rewards subservience in women." He kissed Caro's brow and moved toward his Chippendale desk to look through some papers. "I can hardly blame Natalya for going to Europe to extend her years of independence, nor can I blame Kristin for changing her mind about marriage more than once. As long as she remains in this house, she is free to be and do as she pleases."

Caro followed him, perching on the edge of the desk. For a moment she regarded her husband, thinking how well the years had treated him. Alec was past sixty, but he remained fit and handsome. His black hair had gone white, but it was very striking, accentuating his bronzed face and gleaming turquoise eyes. Caro realized she was as vulnerable now to his physical appeal as she had been thirty years ago. Could she have followed the advice she gave Kristin? she wondered. Would she love Alec differently if he were bald and paunchy?

"It's a shame that Kristin cannot pursue other goals, the way men can," Caro said to her husband, "and as her sister has done with her writing. She loves to ride and garden, but those are hardly occupations. You know, Alec, she is very aware of the power of her beauty, and these flirtations she conducts with men are her chief source of amusement. She is twenty-one years old. This cannot go on forever."

He put aside his papers and slipped a hand caressingly around his wife's waist. "Kristin's situation will resolve itself in time, and all your worrying will not speed up that process. Try to be patient and trust her."

"She wants to find a man like you." Caro smiled into his eyes. "A magnificent knight on a charger who will carry her off on an eternal love affair. There has only been one man like you, and I worry that she will spend her life searching for someone who doesn't exist."

"My darling, your bias is most flattering." He cupped her cheek in his hand and rubbed a fingertip over the pattern of delicate lines at the corner of her eye. "Your vision of me is colored by love, and when Kristin finds the man God has created to be her mate, she will feel that *he* is the most extraordinary human being alive and that she is the luckiest woman."

"I hope you are right." Caro sighed and kissed his palm. "Have you any word of the Raveneaus? I've been thinking of them so much today."

"I saw Lion Hampshire at the Junto Club," Alec replied. "He said that André and Devon Raveneau decided to go to England, just as we hoped. They and their daughter should set sail any day now."

"How I wish that we could go, too!" Caro exclaimed suddenly. "I even thought of asking you. I haven't said very much, but I've been missing Natalya terribly lately. I try not to think about it, but April is always the worst month for me because it was in April that she left six years ago. I never dreamed that she would stay away so long."

"Darling, you know that the war has been to blame. She *couldn't* come home."

Caro couldn't hold back the tears that brimmed over her lashes. "I *miss* her, Alec. When I allow myself to think of her, I miss her so much that I ache. No mother should be separated from her child for so many years. I cannot even read the book that she has written! If we went to England, we might be able to get to France. Wouldn't you adore seeing Nicky and Lisette, too?"

Alec sighed and rubbed his jaw. "Let us wait a bit and see

how the war progresses. Perhaps something will be resolved before autumn, and then I'll reconsider.'' He gathered his wife in his arms, tipping up her chin to kiss her salty cheeks and then her sweet, full lips. "I understand what you are feeling. I miss Natalya, too. This house hasn't been the same since she left. . . .''

The scene on the wharf in Philadelphia was one of pandemonium. After the relative calm of the sea voyage, Natalya felt rather overwhelmed by the sights and sounds of sailors arguing on the docks, trunks being carried on board and off, and women bidding good-bye to men in uniform. The cool morning air carried the scents of fish, tar, hemp, and fried pastries.

"How does it feel to be home?''

She turned to find Grey St. James standing behind her, drawing on a pair of doeskin gloves. His hair shone in the early sunlight and ruffled back from his strong face like the feathers of a raven. For the first time in weeks, he wore a high collar and a cravat, flawlessly tied and white against his deeply tanned skin. A pearl silk waistcoat, gray frock coat, white trousers, and gleaming black boots all fit his powerful body like a second skin. Natalya suppressed an urge to sigh.

"It feels . . . rather odd,'' she answered, returning her gaze to the waterfront and the neat red brick city beyond. "Everything looks different, but I suppose it hasn't really changed. I'm very used to Europe. Philadelphia seems so . . . new!''

Charlotte Timkins and Jasper Speed came up behind them then, and Grey said, "If everyone is ready, we'll go ashore now. Fedbusk has hired a carriage for us.'' He gestured toward the simple post chaise on the street beyond the wharf. Its driver tipped his hat at them.

Natalya had been steeling herself to say good-bye to Grey. Indeed, she had only been able to endure the past two days—and the ever-present memories of her brazen invasion of his bed—by telling herself that once they reached Philadelphia, they would part forever. Grey would keep her secret, she believed, and even if he did not, he would soon be thousands of miles away in London. Yet for all the blushing she did whenever she thought about what had passed between them, she had no regrets. In fact, it was rather exciting to think that she was returning to Philadelphia with a *past*.

Natalya had dressed that morning with the ''farewell scene'' in mind. A demure gown of white muslin and a spotless white lawn tucker, both trimmed with heather-rose ribbons, lent her an air of unimpeachable dignity. She also wore a high-crowned, chip-straw bonnet that covered most of her curls and effectively shaded her face. Assessing her reflection in the cabin's tiny mirror, she had practiced the calm, sophisticated, yet poignant words of parting she would speak when Grey took her hand for the last time.

''Excuse me,'' she now heard herself saying instead, ''but there is no reason for you to accompany me any farther, Grey. We can simply bid one another adieu here. I know that you have much more important matters to attend to, and I am perfectly capable of traveling the short distance to my parents' home unescorted.''

''I won't hear of it,'' he said firmly. ''All the arrangements are made. Surely you don't imagine that I would abandon you on the waterfront after all we've endured to come this far? I owe it to your uncle to see that you are safely returned to your parents.''

She felt uncontrollably flustered. ''But—really, there is no need—I mean, I insist!''

''No, *I* insist,'' Grey countered in steely tones. He then turned away, giving orders for Natalya's trunks and boxes to be transferred to the waiting post chaise.

Natalya saw that it was useless to argue with him. Jasper Speed was already guiding her down the gangway while the *Wild Rover*'s crew gathered at the rail to call out their farewells. On the wharf, Natalya turned to look back at the ship, her cheeks dimpled and pink with pleasure as she waved to the men. Grey came down the gangway then and caught her elbow.

''They'll miss you, but Fedbusk won't,'' he remarked. ''He contends that it's bad luck to have a woman on board, not to mention the fact that you've transformed his disciplined crew into a mob of slobbering idiots.''

Was that a note of admiration in his voice? A compliment hidden in his words? ''Nonsense,'' she declared, slightly perplexed. ''The crew were all perfect gentlemen.''

''With the possible exception of their captain?''

Natalya glanced up in surprise but found that Grey was staring straight ahead, his expression only mildly sardonic. Then he was handing her into the carriage, next to Charlotte, while he and Jasper took the seats facing them. Inexplicably Natalya found herself staring at the long muscles in Grey's thighs and then at the lean, dark hands resting lightly upon them. She knew what the rest of his body looked like and remembered every hard curve; she could even close her eyes and recall the texture of the crisp black hair on his thighs and calves. She had touched him, caressed him, kissed his wonderful hands—palms, fingers, even the scar he had refused to discuss. . . .

''Natalya?''

Her eyes flew up to meet his silvery gaze and she felt her cheeks burning. ''Yes?''

''You'll have to tell the driver the name of your parents' estate. Did you say that it was north of Philadelphia?''

Natalya knew only that she had to separate herself from Grey St. James in order to regain her peace of mind, and the sooner the better. ''There's no need to go all that way. My grandmother lives near here, on Third Street, between Spruce and Willing's Alley. I'd really rather stop there first. My grandfather died last year and I am anxious to see dear Grandmama.'' Seeing Grey's doubtful expression, she tried another tack. ''Also, it is Sunday. My family will doubtless be at church, and invariably they go to Grandmama's afterward. I can return to Belle Maison with them.''

Grey acceded with a shrug and gave the driver the address. As the carriage pulled away from the waterfront and into the pretty, orderly part of Philadelphia known as Society Hill, all its occupants were temporarily distracted by the new sights. The brick footpaths were teeming with people on their way to or from church. Many were Quakers, garbed in plain black and white, while others wore gowns and suits that would have blended perfectly in London society. Natalya felt a rush of pride as she surveyed the fine Georgian and Federal brick homes that lined the wide, poplar-shaded streets. She had nearly forgotten how neat Philadelphia was, its streets and squares laid out at exact right angles, completely unlike the winding mazes of Paris and London.

She felt odd, disjointed somehow, as she spotted familiar places that had been forgotten over the past six years. She scanned people's faces, wondering if she'd known them as children. They passed the Drinker House on Pine Street, and then Natalya glimpsed St. Peter's Episcopal Church on the corner of Third Street. They were turning north, but she leaned out the window, staring at the magnificent brick church she had attended for services nearly every Sunday for the first twenty years of her life.

Parishioners were gathered in clusters outside while others strolled away toward home. Church must be over, Natalya thought, and her heart began to pound at the thought of meeting her family. Would they all be at Grandmama's, as she had predicted? Suddenly the dear faces of her relatives filled her mind and she felt like a little girl again as she imagined embracing her parents.

Her grandparents' home came into view on the left side of Third Street, completely and reassuringly unchanged. The other occupants of the post chaise were forgotten as they drew up in front.

"This is the Beauvisage home," the driver said.

Grey paid him and asked him to wait, impressed by the simple grandeur of the three-story Georgian mansion with its white shutters. There were white marble keystones above each window and a fanlight over the front door, which was supported by Doric columns on either side.

Natalya stepped out onto the footpath without a word, walked up to the house, and knocked at the paneled door. Grey followed after telling Speed and Charlotte to wait in the carriage. He stayed a few steps behind Natalya as she waited for the door to open. Remembering his own homecoming, he half expected someone she didn't know to appear and tell her that the house had changed hands.

"Yes?" The door swung back to reveal an exquisite, tiny old woman. Her white hair was pinned up neatly, and she wore an older-style gown of dark blue silk edged with white pleated lace. Pearls and diamonds sparkled at her throat and ears, and she wore a large diamond ring on her wedding finger. Her expression was alert and gracious; behind tiny golden spectacles, emerald green eyes twinkled, then widened. Grey, expecting a servant, was taken by surprise.

"Grandmama . . ." Natalya whispered the name in a voice thick with tears. "It is I, Talya. I am home."

"I thought I was dreaming," the old woman murmured. Her arms opened, and her granddaughter rushed into them, weeping. "How I have missed you, dearest!"

"Oh, Grandmama, when I heard about Grandpapa I thought my heart would break, and I wanted more than anything in the world to come home and be with you. I am so sorry!"

Antonia Beauvisage drew back, gazing at Natalya's face and smiling. "It was time for Jean-Philippe to go, my dear, and we were prepared to be parted. Your grandpapa was nearly ninety. It was becoming difficult for him to walk, and there was so much that he could no longer enjoy in life. He is with God now, and I have no regrets." She paused. "Your mother and father and sister are in the garden. We've just come from church. I hope Caro doesn't faint when she sees you; do you know, just this morning she told me that she misses you so much, she has been trying to persuade your father to take her to Europe. You must go to her—but first tell me how you have accomplished this miracle! These days sea travel is far too perilous for a young woman traveling alone."

Suddenly Natalya remembered Grey. "Uncle Nicky enlisted the aid of an Englishman who had been a French prisoner of war to help me leave France. Grandmama, I would like you to meet Grey St. James, who brought me to London and then on to Philadelphia." She gestured for Grey to come forward, conscious of her grandmother's curious gaze.

Grey bowed over the old woman's tiny hand and kissed it. "It is a great honor to meet you, Mrs. Beauvisage."

"How can we thank you, sir, for delivering our beloved Talya to us? This is truly a day for celebration."

Natalya interceded. "I hope you'll excuse Mr. St. James, Grandmama. He only wanted to be certain that I had safely reached my family, and now there must be far more important matters for him to attend to."

"Oh, but Natalya's parents will want to meet you, sir," Antonia protested.

"I have no pressing business," he replied lightly. "I am at your disposal, my dear Mrs. Beauvisage."

Natalya gave him a dark look, which he pretended not to notice. Just a few more minutes, she told herself. Still, she didn't want him to meet any more of her family; she didn't want Grey to seep into the new life she was beginning today. It would be easier to keep what the two of them had done together in a separate compartment in her heart if the people she loved in Philadelphia knew nothing about him except his name and what *she* chose to divulge.

"Mr. St. James is ever the gentleman, Grandmama, but we must not detain him for more than a few minutes," she said in a sweet voice. "His carriage is waiting outside, and there must be a great deal for him to do before his ship sails back to England."

"I plan to remain in Philadelphia for a short time," Grey interposed. "My crew needs a rest and so do I." He turned his back to Natalya's shocked stare and offered Antonia his arm. "Lead on to the garden, dear lady."

Antonia glanced back at her granddaughter. "Let us go ahead of you so that I can soften the shock."

Given her turmoil over Grey's refusal to exit her life, Natalya did an admirable job of overlooking his glaring presence in the midst of her long-awaited family reunion. She stood inside the glass doors that led outside and watched as Grandmama and Grey approached the distant figures of her parents and sister. The garden behind the Beauvisage home was part of a large enclave shared by several mansions. There were flagstone walkways lined with ribbon grass, sculpted boxwood hedges, and clusters of daffodils dancing above borders of grape hyacinths. Alec, Caro, and Kristin were standing near one of the brick walls, apparently surveying a new piece of statuary.

Natalya's heart began to hammer when she saw her mother and father turn toward the house as Grandmama approached. How well and wonderful they looked! A few words were spoken, then Antonia glanced back and nodded to her. She pushed open the door and stepped into the April sunlight, tears blurring her vision. It was as if she were five again, running to her parents after Étienne teased her or she took a tumble.

"Natalya!" Familiar arms were holding her fast, and she smelled the soft, fresh clover scent of her mother. They were the same size, and their tears mingled as they kissed; then Caro drew back for a long look. "I cannot believe it! It really is *you*! My dear, you'll never know how we've missed you!"

"Maman . . ." She smiled into her mother's warm golden-brown eyes. "I missed you, too. I had to come home!"

Then Alec was reaching for her, cradling her against him as he had all her life. "Darling Talya," he murmured. "Welcome home."

"Oh, Papa . . ." Tears of joy ran down her cheeks, and he produced a handkerchief.

"Your grandmother tells us that this man St. James brought you all the way from France," Alec said, glancing back toward Grey. "I owe him a proper thank-you."

Kristin appeared then, and Natalya's eyes widened in surprise when she discovered that her little sister was now taller than she. "Look at you, Krissie—you're a woman!" They hugged, and then she stepped back for another look. "And so beautiful! My goodness, you were still in the schoolroom when I left!"

Resplendent in her new morning gown of blue-and-white-striped muslin, its hem fetchingly ruffled, Kristin twirled in the sunlight. "Do you really think I look pretty? As pretty as the women in France and London?"

"Oh, certainly!" Natalya smiled with fond indulgence.

"Now, when are you and Malcom getting married? I hope I'm not too late for the wedding."

Kristin made a moué. "I've broken the engagement, Talya. I want to be certain that, when I marry, I shall never regret it."

"That sounds very . . . prudent." She glanced toward their mother, who lifted her brows for an instant. "We have so much to talk about. I cannot tell you how anxious I am to see Belle Maison again, to have everything just as it was—" Natalya broke off when Grey and her father came up beside them.

Kristin was staring appreciatively at the Englishman. "I don't believe we've met, sir," she murmured.

"This is Grey St. James, Kristin," Alec said. "He is responsible for delivering your sister home from France, and, of course, we owe him a great debt of gratitude. Caro, I've asked Grey to come back with us for Natalya's welcome-home supper. I thought it would be a splendid opportunity for all of us to become better acquainted."

"By all means," Caro agreed, with a radiant smile.

"Oh, yes!" Kristin exclaimed.

Natalya stared in horror and said frantically, "But I'm certain Mr. St. James has better things to do and is probably too polite to say so. Really, Papa, you must not put him in so awkward a position. He's quite bored with this entire business, and—"

"Miss Beauvisage," Grey said coolly, "you couldn't be more wrong. I can think of nothing I would enjoy more than a day with your family, and I am delighted to accept this invitation. Unless, that is, *you* have some objection to my presence?"

Everyone's eyes were fixed on her. Blushing, trying to conceal her fury, Natalya managed to smile. "I? Object? How silly!"

Chapter Seventeen

April 28, 1814

"My lord?" Charlotte Timkins inquired hopefully as the hired post chaise turned off Germantown Road.

Grey sat across from her and Speed, his gaze fixed on the verdant spring countryside. Now, his eyes flicked back to the young woman and he murmured, "I have asked you to call me Mr. St. James, Charlotte."

"I beg your pardon, sir." Recognizing that his attention was already wavering, she plunged onward. "Mr. St. James, what if my mistress no longer needs me when she gets to her parents' house? What if there is a family retainer she would prefer to have wait upon her? What if—"

"Enough, my dear Miss Timkins," Grey cut in, holding up a hand. "Let us wait and see rather than expect the worst. And then, if your fears should come to pass, you will simply remain in my employ . . . and eventually return to England with me, if you so choose."

"You aren't going back immediately?"

Grey shook his head, staring out at the chestnut trees that lined the drive leading to Belle Maison. Daffodils grew wild, like yellow stars sprinkled amid the lush green grass. "My plans are tentative at this time." He glanced back at Charlotte, aware of her curiosity. "And I must ask that you refrain from discussing my plans, or lack of same, with Miss Beauvisage. Do I make myself clear?"

Charlotte widened her blue eyes. "Aye, I suppose that you do, sir."

"Thank you."

"Mum's the word," Jasper Speed chimed in.

"Exactly."

The carriage ahead of them began to slow, and Grey caught his first glimpse of Belle Maison, Natalya's girlhood home. The large house was a beautiful example of Georgian architecture. Constructed of red brick, it was square and solid, shaded by huge elm trees and generously framed by sweeping lawns and exquisite beds of tulips. Fourteen perfect, many-paned windows, all with pure white casements, marched across the front of the house, surrounding a magnificent white front door with brass fittings. The Beauvisage carriage stopped right in front of the patterned brick walkway that led to the house's entrance. Grey watched, pensive for a moment, as Natalya stepped giddily onto the path and turned in slow circles, her fingers pressed to her lips in silent wonder. Alec stopped beside her, and she looked up at him, eyes bright with tears.

"Oh, Papa, it seems like a dream. I don't think I realized how desperately I've longed for home . . . until now."

Arm in arm they went into the house while Grey, Speed, and Charlotte disembarked from their post chaise. Caro was waiting for them while Kristin lingered nearby, staring at Grey.

"I can't tell you how pleased we are that you could join us," Caro said sincerely, taking Grey's arm. "I'm going to have Pierre, our butler, send someone to take these two lovely people out to our kitchen for a good, hot meal . . . and a nap if that would be desirable. Meanwhile, we'll sort out who is staying and who is going. . . ." She continued to chatter on as they reached the front door, at which point a wizened little old man appeared. "Mr. St. James," she said, "I should like to present Pierre DuBois, who is our major domo and generally in charge of running our home."

"Bonjour, monsieur!" Pierre greeted him, dark eyes twinkling with interest. "This is a happy day! Life has been a trifle dull here of late, I must confess—indeed, I had been deliberating on a way to enliven this household. But you, sir, have relieved me of that burden by returning Miss Natalya to the fold.''

Grey was charmed to see that Pierre wore an old-fashioned suit, not unlike the one he himself had donned to elude Auteuil and Poujouly during his and Natalya's flight from St. Briac. Pierre's coat and breeches were mustard-yellow satin, his buckled shoes sported two-inch heels, and his powdered wig was set off by a long waistcoat of gold-and-red brocade. Never had Grey encountered a butler like this in England! Before he could reply to the old man's speech, Natalya had come between them to hug Pierre, who blushed with delight.

"Pierre, when did you come back to Belle Maison? Did Maman write to me and have I forgotten?'' She half turned to explain to Grey, "Pierre was Papa's valet for years, and before that he sailed with my grandpapa on his pirate ship, didn't you, Pierre? Then, when he married Hyla Flowers, who helped Aunt Lisette run her coffeehouse, they took it over together when Lisette and Nicholai went to live in France. That was twenty years ago, when I was just a little girl, but I remember very well how sad we all were when you left Belle Maison, Pierre! You used to sneak me treats from the kitchen and let me choose flowers for my very own. . . .''

"You were a dimpled little peach blossom as a child, ma-demoiselle, and remain so as a woman,'' Pierre said effusively. "It's a great pleasure to welcome you home. I have been back in your parents' employ nearly two years now, and Hyla is here, too, overseeing the kitchen. We're not as young as we used to be, you know, and the unceasing activity in the coffeehouse became tiring. Do you remember James String-fellow, the barman?'' When Natalya nodded, Pierre said, "Stringfellow and his wife, Nancy, purchased the coffeehouse from us. Their two sons are nearly grown, and I think they were ready for new challenges.''

"How lovely that everything has worked out so neatly,'' she exclaimed, noticing out of the corner of her eye that Kristin had managed to place herself in front of Grey.

"Mr. St. James, all this family gossip must be fearfully dull to you,'' Natalya's sister said, brushing back a stray ebony curl from her cheek. ''Would you like me to show you around?''

He smiled carefully. ''I'm not bored in the least, but it's kind of you to offer, Miss Beauvisage, and I would very much like to see more of your home.''

''That's an excellent idea, Krissie,'' Natalya approved, her voice sounding hollow. Obviously her sister was rapidly becoming starry-eyed over the handsome Englishman, and it bothered her to see Kristin trying to improve the acquaintance. But she reminded herself once again that Grey would soon be gone and that she ought to put him out of her mind and enjoy her homecoming.

For his part, Grey was fascinated by Natalya's family and their home. The style of Belle Maison was very different from that of grand homes in either England or France. It was much simpler, and yet the house possessed an appealing elegance and warmth that London mansions lacked.

The entry hall was laid with a diagonal pattern of bricks, and the paneled walls were lovely with their plain coat of ivory paint. There was no gilding or marble to be found in Belle Maison. Kristin led the way through a graceful arch with double doors that brought them into the stair hall. Two spacious, lovely parlors opened off of each side of the stair hall, and Grey wandered into the north parlor on his own.

''Is your mother responsible for the design of these rooms?'' he asked. ''Did she choose the furnishings?''

''For the most part, no, I think not,'' Kristin replied, walking over to stand beside him. She could scarcely believe that he was real, so potent was his attraction. Grey St. James looked exactly as she imagined her father must have thirty years ago. ''Maman found Belle Maison so beautiful when she first came here that she has always striven to keep it much the same. This was Papa's house, you know. He told me when I was a little girl that our home had been orphaned during the Revolution. A battle was fought in the village of Germantown, and the owner of this house was killed accidentally. His family fled, leaving nearly all their possessions.''

''An ideal situation for a single man,'' Grey remarked, ''particularly if he approved of the previous owner's tastes!''

"Well, Maman has tried to make gradual changes, adding pieces and replacing worn items over the years. I'm sure it must be grander now than when Papa first acquired it." Kristin's long-lashed gaze touched upon paneled walls painted a soft, pale green, a graceful wing chair beautifully embroidered with crewelwork, a Chippendale settee upholstered in rose damask, and the stunningly patterned English rug that covered the wide boards of the floor. "It's the taste we Beauvisages all cling to, particularly in the midst of the current rush to adopt the Federal fashion. Maman says that the style of our home is timeless, but to me it is . . . reassuring." She turned her head a fraction so that she was looking directly into Grey's eyes. "If you truly want to return to England, you shouldn't remain here long, Mr. St. James. I believe that my family and our home are under an enchanted spell, and no one who is here for any length of time ever wants to leave. We've all been blessed with extraordinary happiness and good fortune as long as we are under this roof. . . ."

Laughing, Grey walked away from her, over to the fifteen-paned glass doors that opened onto the lawns and gardens behind Belle Maison. "You are amusing yourself at my expense, aren't you, Miss Beauvisage? You know, I come from England, not Ireland. We don't put much stock in leprechauns and faeries back in London." His gaze swept appreciatively over the impeccably sculpted beds of tulips divided by mossy brick footpaths. "In any event, your theory doesn't quite fit Natalya, does it? She's been happy—and healthy—thousands of miles away from Belle Maison. Your brother's left, too, hasn't he?" He glanced back at her, gently arching a black brow. "Your tale of a golden aura hovering over this house sounds to me like an excuse for *you* to linger on here with Maman and Papa, long after most of your school friends have married and established homes of their own."

Kristin swept past him, her back straight, leading the way into the back hallway. "I shan't dignify such outrageous effrontery with a response, except to say that I am unmarried by choice, Mr. St. James. I am unashamed of the happiness I own here, and until I meet the perfect man, I see no reason to leave.''

Grey smiled to himself as he followed her past the winding back stairway that opened off the servants' entrance to the house. He reflected that there was nothing like a bit of badinage with a Beauvisage female to get one's blood flowing. ''I must apologize. I was completely at fault and had no right to speak to you on such familiar terms. The only defense I can offer is that I have grown used to teasing your sister, though you mustn't tell her I've confessed to it.''

Kristin whirled around in front of the entrance to a small plant-filled, glass conservatory. Struck by the unmistakably fond undercurrents in his voice when he spoke of Natalya, she said, ''I was under the impression that the two of you didn't deal together very well?''

''That was true, some of the time.'' The silvery glint of a smile crept into Grey's eyes. ''There were also . . . enjoyable moments.''

''I can hardly wait to hear all the details . . . of your travels,'' Kristin said, watching him.

''I doubt whether your sister will care to dwell on that subject.'' As they reached the dining room, Grey gestured toward the doorway. ''After you.''

Realizing that no more bits of gossip would be forthcoming, Kristin returned to her role as guide. Her tour of the dining room and south parlor were matter-of-fact. She pointed out a corner cabinet filled with pieces of china and keepsakes from Beauvisage voyages and the travels of her parents abroad. The rooms themselves were tasteful and charming, decorated with creamy walls, rugs in shades of cranberry, blue, ivory, and tan, and more Queen Anne and Chippendale pieces that had been lovingly cared for. Over the fireplace, faced with Delft tiles, hung a portrait of Alexandre and Caroline Beauvisage. Kristin paused with Grey to gaze up at the large painting, which was an excellent likeness of her parents.

''That was painted twenty years ago, not long after my birth,'' she said. ''Charles Willson Peale was the artist. No doubt he is virtually unknown in Europe, but Philadelphia holds him in high esteem, and he has sired or taught a whole clan of other Peales. Also, he has a museum in the city filled with animals that have been stuffed and placed in re-creations of their natural habitats. There are tigers, exotic birds, snakes, a mongoose, and the skeletons of two prehistoric mastodons, which Mr. Peale excavated and assembled himself. He's seventy-three now and as active as ever.''

"Indeed?'' Grey tried to think of a suitable response. ''You obviously must believe that we Britons are sadly lacking in education, but I can assure you that I have heard of Charles Willson Peale. However, although I was familiar with his work as an artist, I must confess that I was ignorant of the mongoose and the mastodons.'' He smiled suddenly, his teeth white against the bronze of his face. ''I have always heard that America is quite different from England or France or anywhere I am used to. A friend told me that Americans have been able to invent themselves and their country, making up all sorts of new rules. So far, I am thoroughly charmed by all I have seen and heard, from this wonderful house to your tale of Peale's distinctly original museum!''

Kristin began to feel a bit dizzy. Had Grey St. James no defects? She was learning that not only was he the picture of strength and healthy, virile good looks, but he was also intelligent and apparently wealthy, witty and charming, *and* appreciative of new experiences. "I have one more surprise for you in this parlor before we go upstairs,'' she said, walking over to open a door that was barely noticeable in the paneled wall. ''This is our whispering closet, apparently built into the house during the Revolution, or when the British lived here after the former owners ran off.''

Grey joined her, leaning into the empty closet to watch as she found the secret opening in the back wall. As the panel opened, he ducked his head under the low threshold and discovered three different passageways. One led farther along the parlor wall, over to the south side of the house, he guessed. ''I gather that this was a hiding place for eavesdroppers,'' he remarked.

"It's been used as a refuge for those in danger as well,''

Kristin replied, nodding, and stepped past him into the closet. Lit only by the sunlight that spilled into the parlor, it appeared dim and dingy, and it smelled of damp earth and must. "You're probably wondering where the tunnel goes that leads underground."

"Rather," he agreed dryly.

"It passes under the gardens and then forks. One side leads to the kitchen building and the other connects with the little cottage where my great-grandmother once lived. And this"—Kristin took a few steps around a corner in the tunnel, gesturing toward a narrow, curving stone staircase that went upward—"goes upstairs. I find it all rather frightening, but when we were children, Étienne and Talya and our cousins played in these passageways a great deal. I was the baby, and always afraid that I would be left behind or a spider would touch me or something else equally horrific."

As they returned to the spacious parlor, Grey shook his head in wonderment. "I thought that only we British went in for hidden doors and secret passageways. All through my boyhood, I felt cheated because none of our residences possessed one. This is indeed quite a home."

Moments later, as he followed Kristin up the sweeping curve of the staircase, Grey decided that Belle Maison was exactly the right size: large enough for dignity and spaciousness, small enough for comfort and modesty. It was the ideal home— impressive without being overwhelming, elegant without the least affectation. England could learn a great deal about living well from her rebellious offspring.

Upstairs, their tour was more abbreviated. Grey did little more than poke his head in doorways and nod as Kristin pointed out each of the welcoming bedrooms. Most had window seats built in below recessed windows, and he found this a charming touch. The elder Beauvisages shared a large bedchamber decorated in blue and white with Chinese red accents; next to it was a small sun-drenched morning room with freshly painted lemon-yellow walls and a circular Aubusson carpet. In passing, Grey glimpsed a lovely bedroom done in ivory and moss green with a Sheraton field bed as its centerpiece, and then Kristin pointed out her own room, which was rose and pale blue.

Voices drifted out to them from a room at the back of the house. "We ought to join the others," Kristin said, opening the door. "I suppose I should warn you that Belle Maison is quite famous for its library."

Grey let out his breath appreciatively as they entered a magnificent room that spanned the width of the second floor. There were two other entrances at the middle and far end of the library, and all the walls were lined from floor to ceiling with handsomely bound books. Alec Beauvisage's desk was across the room from where Grey and Kristin stood, and Natalya and her parents were seated on a settee and wing chairs grouped before the mahogany-framed fireplace in the center of the library.

"Ah, here you are at last!" Caro called cheerfully. "We've just poured a glass of sherry, and Rose announced that we shall dine in half an hour. Do come and join us."

As Grey and Kristin took matching flame-stitched wing chairs, Natalya murmured, "I thought perhaps you two had gotten lost."

Kristin laughed, glancing at Grey under her lashes. "Have we been terribly long?"

"I've been admiring your home," Grey interjected, speaking to Alec and Caro. He sat back in his chair and stretched out his long legs, appearing to be very much at ease and oblivious to Natalya's suspicious looks and Kristin's smitten gaze. "I like it immensely."

"It's kind of you to say so," Caro rejoined. "We love Belle Maison."

"It does seem to have a character all its own," Alec agreed. "Sometimes I feel that the house is as alive as we are."

Distracted, Natalya sipped her sherry and beamed. "It really is wonderful to be back. I've missed all of you—and Belle Maison—more than I realized."

"I still cannot believe it," her mother said, reaching over to clasp her hand. "It's like a dream."

Looking at Grey, Kristin murmured, "It certainly is. . . ."

* * *

Dinner was exceedingly festive. Natalya brightened when Caro seated Grey next to Alec and placed Kristin at the opposite end. If Grey St. James had to intrude on her family reunion, she would rather he befriend her father than further intoxicate her sister.

Hyla DuBois and her staff had labored in the kitchen behind the house to create a magnificent meal on short notice: clam-and-mushroom bisque, sour milk biscuits with sweet butter, duckling with apple stuffing, codfish cakes, mashed carrots and parsnips, and young greens with bacon dressing. Natalya and Grey were both famished and ate far too much. Natalya happily answered questions about Nicholai and Lisette, discussed the publication of *My Lady's Heart*, and divulged selected details of her sojourn with Adrienne in London. Alec, along with the others, wanted to hear all about Napoléon's downfall and Grey's other experiences in the war. Finally Natalya and Grey took turns describing their flight from France and voyage across the Atlantic.

"I cannot express the gratitude my wife and I feel for all you have done to help Natalya return to America," Alec said at last, pushing his plate away with a satisfied sigh.

"Natalya aided in my escape from France," Grey replied. "I might well have failed without her assistance, and failure would have meant death. What I have done to repay her is really very little." He gave Natalya a wry smile, his gray eyes twinkling with secrets. "Actually I've quite enjoyed myself. Your daughter is highly . . . original!"

Her cheeks flaming, Natalya wished with all her heart that he would go away. She picked up her fork and aimed it at her plate—only to discover that there wasn't a bite of food left on it. "Goodness! I've been a monstrous glutton, haven't I?" Her voice was loud with false gaiety. "I have an excuse, though. Hyla is the best cook in the world, and besides, it's been six years since I've eaten real American food. Lisette still prepares some of her old recipes from the coffeehouse, but somehow they taste different in France."

Grey helped himself to the rest of the greens with bacon

dressing. "For my part, I can attest that this is quite possibly the best meal I have ever had. Is this the sort of thing everyone in Philadelphia eats?"

"Everyone who can afford good food," Alec said.

"Then I may never leave!" Grey laughed with a trace of mischief, enjoying himself as he witnessed the flush that rose again in Natalya's cheeks.

"I am suddenly very tired," she announced. "It must be all the excitement. Krissie, why don't you come upstairs and help me unpack? I want to hear all about your suitors. And Maman, you must come, too, and tell me the news of Étienne. When is he coming home from that horrid war, and what of his wife and baby?"

Caro watched in surprise as her daughter stood up. "But, Talya, there's rhubarb tapioca for dessert. It was always your favorite."

"Oh, Maman, I simply couldn't eat another bite. Tell Hyla I'll have mine for breakfast, won't you?" Natalya came around the table, held out her hand to Grey, and said, "You must think me incredibly rude, making such an abrupt exit, but I really am too exhausted to sit up a moment longer. I have already told you how grateful I am to you for bringing me all this way, and I wish you all the best in your new life in England." She forced a smile but avoided his keen silver eyes. "Good-bye, Grey. I know I've been a trial to you at times, but these past weeks have been memorable, and you were a gift from Heaven. Have a safe journey home, and I hope that you'll think of me with a smile from time to time."

Coolly he arched his eyebrows, all too aware of their audience. Standing to face her, he lifted Natalya's hand to his mouth and kissed it. It pleased him to feel her involuntary shiver. "Good night, Natalya."

She waited for him to make a farewell speech, but none was forthcoming. Blushing again, she pulled her hand free and stepped backward, nearly landing in her father's lap, then turned toward the doorway. "Krissie, are you coming with me?"

Reluctantly Kristin rose from the table. She was beginning

to feel foolish for having flirted openly with the Englishman since he was apparently leaving on the morrow, so she mustered her dignity and exchanged pleasant words of parting with him. He leaned across the table to clasp her hand, smiling as he thanked her for the tour of Belle Maison.

"I'll be up momentarily," Caro called as the sisters left the dining room. Then, turning to the men, she said, "I have a notion that the two of you would enjoy some time alone to chat. I'll have dessert and port served, then go upstairs and tuck my daughter into bed."

"I'll come up to kiss her good night after a bit," Alec said, squeezing his wife's hand. "Don't look so puzzled, *chérie*. It's her first night home and she's bound to be restless and preoccupied."

"You're right, of course." Caro gave him a grateful smile. "I ought to bid you good-bye, Mr. St. James, and thank you once more for all you've done. If we can ever repay you, do not hesitate to call upon us."

After Grey offered more words of appreciation for her hospitality, Caro went upstairs, and he found himself alone with Alec Beauvisage. Crystal dishes of tapioca were served and port was poured from a cut-glass decanter.

"Are you really sailing tomorrow?" Alec asked, raising his glass. "Talya keeps insisting on it, but I haven't heard a word of confirmation from you."

"Actually"—Grey sipped his port, smiling slowly,—"no. I have a few matters to attend to in Philadelphia before I return to England. Your daughter would prefer that I make myself scarce, but since I cannot accommodate her wishes, I thought it might be better for the moment to not comment on my plans in her presence."

Alec couldn't bring himself to ask why Natalya was so anxious that Grey return to England. Instead he said, "Won't you tell me more about yourself and your family? I've spent some time in London, and your name seems familiar somehow."

"Actually, sir, I believe you know my father, the Earl of Hartford," Grey replied.

Alec registered astonished delight. "Of course! You're

Hartford's elder son, aren't you? I'd simply forgotten that St. James was his family name. My God, now I am indebted to both of you, for Hartford spared my life in 1781, during the battle of Yorktown. . . ." His gaze wandered as memories returned, then he looked back at Grey, smiling. "Your father must be very proud of you. Is he well?"

"Quite, sir. He's not a warm man, but I suppose that he enjoys life after a fashion. And he's had his share of sorrows. My mother died in childbirth when I was ten, and then my brother David was killed in the battle of Salamanca two years ago."

"Lord, what a terrible blow for a father—and for you. I cannot imagine what it would do to me if our Étienne were lost in this war." Alec sighed. "Hartford was full of life and fun when I knew him. He'd had a few whiskies the night he caught me spying on Cornwallis. He started asking me questions about myself and we became friends. I gave him my word to leave quietly, and so he let me go."

Grey blinked, trying to imagine his father in the scene Beauvisage had described. "He has always spoken kindly of you, sir, and has been pleased to receive your letters."

Nodding thoughtfully, Alec sipped his port for a moment before asking, "Can you discuss your business in Philadelphia, or is it private? If I can assist you in any way . . ."

"It's a long story," Grey said lightly. "I'd rather not divulge all the details, but I can say that I am searching for someone who may have recently arrived in Philadelphia. Have you by chance met a beautiful Englishwoman, somewhat haughty, I should think, with auburn hair and green eyes? Her name is Francesca and . . . she is in possession of some property that belongs to my family. I hope to find her and reclaim these lost items before I return to England."

"I see. . . ." Alec digested this information with interest. "I cannot recall meeting such a woman, but I can ask Caro, and—"

"Please, sir, do not," Grey said curtly. "I must ask that this conversation remain between us for the time being. If

Francesca should hear of my presence in Philadelphia before I discover her whereabouts . . ."

"I may know someone who can help you. Before Lisette married my brother, she inherited Hahn's Coffeehouse from her father. The coffeehouse has long been one of Philadelphia's most popular meeting places. It is now owned by James Stringfellow, her old friend and the barman there for many years. He's an Englishman and a wonderful fellow who keeps his ears open and is always aware of the latest news. If anyone has word of the woman you seek, it would be Stringfellow, and he can be trusted to keep your secrets." Alec grinned. "If he knows that you're a friend of Lisette's, he'll do anything for you."

Grey, who had been listening intently, returned his host's grin. "Thank you, sir. I have a feeling that I shall be able to make good use of that information."

"You will need a place to stay," Alec decided, "and I have just the solution. Nicholai's house on Spruce Street is large and comfortable, and we have kept it for the use of visiting relatives. I insist that you make yourself at home there for as long as you care to stay."

Their eyes met, and Grey realized that he had a friend who offered the sort of camaraderie he had always longed to share with his own father. A genuine smile lit his face as he replied, "I appreciate your generous offer and accept with gratitude."

"It's the least we can do for you. We'll loan you a carriage, and one of our drivers will deliver you and your manservant tonight, then your things can be sent over from the ship in the morning." Alec paused to take a spoonful of tapioca. "I confess that I've missed my son since the war took him away, and my father's death this past year has left me lonely. I like you, Grey, and I hope to spend more time with you. I'd like to show you our shipyards, and I could take you to my club. . . ."

"Your kindness renders me speechless, sir."

"Nonsense." He grinned. "And for God's sake call me Alec! I'm not in my dotage yet."

"I'd be honored, Alec," he said, smiling back, thinking that this family was like a fantasy in comparison with his own.

"I ought to go out to the kitchen and inform Speed, my valet, of our plans. Oh, and I should ask you about Charlotte Timkins, Natalya's maid these past weeks. She came with us from the ship, just in case."

"Naturally, if she chooses to remain here, she is welcome," Alec said immediately. He rose to his feet and held out his hand to Grey. "I shall bid you good night, then. Pierre will arrange for your carriage. Perhaps I'll drop by to visit you in a day or two, to make certain there's nothing you need."

"I'll look forward to it, Alec."

Beauvisage walked Grey to the back door, pointing out the brightly lit kitchen building behind the house, then he started up the servants' stairs to visit his elder daughter.

Alone at last, her family's good-night kisses still warm on her cheeks, Natalya lay in the Sheraton field bed and gazed up at the moonlit snowflake pattern in the net canopy that curved above her. This had been her mother's room when she had first come to Belle Maison as Alec's ward more than thirty years ago. Growing up, Natalya had shared the rose-and-blue bedroom with Kristin, but now she was sleeping here. She had always loved this room, most especially the beautiful field bed with its arched canopy frame draped in hand-tied snowflakes. She had spent many a daylight hour lying here on her back and dreaming.

Smiling contentedly, Natalya burrowed deeper into the soft linens and quilts covering her. Even the faint jasmine smell of her home was poignantly familiar, evoking memories of her childhood when her mother held her close. It felt so safe to be back at last. The dangers of her journey, the risks and confusion of her relationship with Grey, were behind her. The future, complete with the challenges of adjusting to life in Philadelphia and meeting old and new friends, could still be held at arm's length. For now, she could be her mother's and father's daughter again, tucked snugly into her favorite bed at Belle Maison.

What was that sound? She sat up in bed, hands clasped over her breasts, staring at the paneled wall. She heard another tap and then a click. Before she could cry out for her father, part of the wall slid back and Grey St. James stepped out into a shaft of moonlight. Her first thought was that he looked like a dangerous pirate, bent on ravishing a defenseless maiden.

Dusting off his hands, Grey arched a brow at her and remarked, ''I thought I ought to drop by to bid you a proper good night. You didn't really think that you could fob me off with that feeble, wooden scene in the dining room, did you?'' His grin flashed in the shadows. ''My dear Natalya, your penchant for underestimating me will one day prove your downfall.''

As he approached the bed, Natalya opened her mouth to scream, but the only sound that emerged was a tiny squeak.

Chapter Eighteen

April 28–29, 1814

"WHAT—? HOW IN THE WORLD—?" NATALYA managed to whisper as Grey reached the side of her bed and loomed above her.

"I was in the kitchen, rousting out Speed, but he had torn his jacket and your outrageous cook, Hyla, insisted on mending it for him. While I waited, I decided to explore the passageways Kristin showed me earlier." His tone was maddeningly conversational. "When I reached the top of the hidden stairway, I saw that there was no light under your door, nor did I hear voices. Knowing you were alone, I decided to bid you good night on *my* terms."

"How did you know which bedchamber would be mine?"

"Instinct," he replied enigmatically.

When he sat down next to her, Natalya's heart began to race in earnest. "I can call my father, you know."

Grey laughed softly. He had removed his jacket, and his shirt was luminously white in the moonlight, causing his chest and shoulders to look exceedingly broad and powerful. "My dear Natalya, I thought that this sort of visit was perfectly acceptable to you. Did you not burst into *my* bedchamber and awaken *me* just a few nights ago?"

Her cheeks burned with mingled anger and humiliation. "Cad! Why will you not go away and leave me in peace? What happened on board the *Rover* was a unique and isolated inci-

dent, certainly not a common practice on my part! Everything
is different now—''

"According to whom?'' Grey cut in coolly, his gaze sweeping over her. "I think it only fair to warn you, my sweet, that
the world operates a trifle differently outside of your castle
tower in France. Others may not care to have you direct them
thither and yon across the stage of life, nor will they bend to
the rules that you make and then alter according to the per-
mutations of your moods.''

"There is no need for you to concern yourself with my
moods or character defects, sir,'' she hissed. "I thought that
I would never see you again after we docked this morning. I
am home now, with my family, and I would like to put you in
the past.''

"There you go again, attempting to manipulate others according to your desires. Just because you have decided what I
must do does not mean that I will comply.'' His soft voice cut
the shadows like a knife. "Far from it.'' Reaching out, Grey
grasped her wrist, caressing the fragile pulse point below the
palm. He gazed at her in admiration. How ravishing she looked
in her thin lawn bedgown, her honey-hued tresses swirling
about her shoulders, lustrous in the starlight.

"Unhand me,'' Natalya whispered, "or I'll scream.''

"And you call yourself an author,'' he murmured, amused.
"Can you not invent a more original threat?'' One arm encircled her waist, and in the next instant she was against him, her
breasts branding his chest through the fine material of his shirt.
"You did me a disservice with that tepid farewell in the dining
room tonight, Natalya. Did you honestly imagine that you
could dispose of me so easily?''

She was furious, yet giddy with desire. Everything about
Grey stimulated and aroused her, from his clean male scent to
the way he held her. Though gently sensual, his hands and
arms were as unyielding as bands of steel. "Let me go,'' she
protested weakly.

Grey responded by kissing her. Helplessly Natalya submitted to his demanding mouth, parting her own lips to allow the
thrilling invasion of his tongue. Lying across his lap, she felt

molded to him somehow, as if the curves of her body had been
made to fit against his lean-muscled hips and chest. Grey tasted
so good to her, and the way he kissed her fired her senses.
One of his hands caressed her back, lingering on the curve of
her hip and then wandering upward to graze the edge of her
breast. Just as a whimper rose in her throat, Grey released her.

"That, at least, was *honest*," he said grimly, and lifted her
away from him. Natalya huddled against her pillows, watching
as he walked over to the open panel in the wall and then glanced
back over his shoulder. "Good night, Miss Beauvisage . . .
until we meet again."

There were smudges of exhaustion under Natalya's eyes
when she appeared in the upstairs morning room to breakfast
with her sister. The sun was shining brightly, birds were singing, and Kristin wore a bored expression as she stared out the
window.

"Good morning," Natalya offered from the doorway.

"Where have you been? I've eaten two buns with honey
while waiting for you! I'll be as fat as Hyla if you sleep this
late every morning." Picking up the Chinese porcelain cof-
feepot, she filled both cups and spooned sugar into her own.
"You're looking rather pale. Don't you feel well?"

Upon waking and discovering the time, Natalya had dressed
hurriedly in a Circassian wrapper and then paused before the
mirror to brush her hair and draw it back with a pink ribbon.
As she did so, she noticed that she looked haggard, as if she
hadn't slept at all. "I've just arrived home after a very long
journey, Krissie," she said, with a wan smile, sipping her
coffee gratefully. "It may be a day or two before I am quite
myself."

"I didn't mean to be short with you, Talya. Indeed, I am
overjoyed that you've come home. As much as I adore Maman
and Papa, and am able to confide in them, I do get lonely. It
will be wonderful to have a sister again." Kristin reached out
to squeeze her hand.

"How difficult it is for me to realize that you are actually
twenty-one! If I should forget and treat you as if you're a child

from time to time, you must reprimand me immediately."
Feeling more cheerful, Natalya cut a raisin-studded hot cross
bun in half and took a bite. "You must know that you are
terribly beautiful, Krissie. What a charming gown that is! You
will have to take me to your dressmaker."

"And I am eager to see all the lovely clothes you brought
from France. The lace on your wrapper is exquisite! I do love
fine things."

"I'm afraid that I was unable to bring very many gowns
with me," Natalya replied absently. After another sip of coffee, she asked, "Is this love of fine things one of the reasons
you haven't married? Are you looking for a rich husband?"

"What a question!" Kristin exclaimed, with a laugh. "What
of *you*? But, never mind, I'll be frank and answer. I think that
the reason I haven't married is that I am searching for a man
who can excite me for a lifetime, and I haven't yet found him."
Her dark turquoise eyes were dreamy as she stared out over
the meadows surrounding Belle Maison. "Don't you think I
was right to break off my engagements rather than marry
someone I didn't truly love? I'll admit, I do long for a grand
home and beautiful clothes, but I long even more for a great
love, like the one Maman and Papa have." She looked back
at her sister, eyes twinkling. "There's nothing between you
and Grey St. James, is there?"

Taken aback, Natalya nearly choked. "Heavens, no! Certainly not! Why would you ask such a question?"

"Because I find him *exceedingly* attractive. I confess that I
dreamed about him last night. . . ."

"But, Krissie, he's gone back to England, or at least he's
preparing to sail. Besides—"

"Haven't you heard?" Kristin interrupted gaily. "Mr. St.
James is staying on in Philadelphia. He told Papa he has busi-
ness to attend to. I vow, I can't recall feeling more elated than
I did this morning when Maman told me."

"I—I can't believe it," Natalya gasped, trying not to betray
her outrage and panic. "How can this be?"

"Wait, there's more," her sister announced, enjoying the
drama. "He's moving into Uncle Nicky's old house on Spruce

Street. That affords me a perfect opportunity to become better acquainted with him!''

Growing paler by the moment, Natalya asked, ''How did this happen? How could he have had the effrontery to install himself in one of *our* homes?''

''Why, it was Papa's idea! Apparently they got along splendidly last night after you and Maman and I retired. Papa sounds as if he'd like to adopt Mr. St. James.'' Since Natalya's only response was an openmouthed stare, Kristin continued merrily, ''It's a shame that you are so tired today. I was going to ask you if you would like to come with me to town in a little while. We could visit Grandmama and the dressmaker, and then I thought it would be a splendid idea to drop in at the house on Spruce Street and offer assistance to Mr. St. James in getting settled. Maman thought that he might be able to use someone from our kitchen until he can find a cook.''

''No!'' cried her sister. ''I have no desire to see Grey St. James again, and the very last thing I care to do on my first full day home is visit *him*!''

Kristin gave her a quizzical look. ''I do wish you would tell me what it is about the man that bothers you so. All of us like him tremendously. This isn't a case of unrequited love, is it, Talya? Did he reject you because you're rather . . . well, past the first bloom of youth?''

Horrified, she exclaimed, ''Absolutely not! That's the silliest thing I've ever heard! And, for the record, I am not *bothered* by Mr. St. James. I feel, rather, that our association is part of the past, and I have more than enough to occupy me in reestablishing my life here.''

Kristin shrugged and stood up. ''Well, then, I'll go alone. Perhaps you and I can take a walk in the garden later this afternoon. I do want to hear all about Paris and London.'' She kissed her sister's cheek and started toward the door.

Torn by confused frustration, Natalya saw that she had no choice. Even worse than seeing Grey again would be an afternoon spent here wondering what he was doing with Kristin. Besides, she was bursting with the need to give the arrogant Mr. St. James an angry dressing-down.

"Wait!" she called, and, putting on a smile, went to join Kristin in the doorway. "I've changed my mind. I *do* want to see Grandmama, and I badly need to visit the dressmaker, so I'll come with you after all."

Returning to her bedchamber, Natalya opened the door and was surprised to discover that the brass bathtub she remembered from her youth had been placed in front of the fireplace. A servant was bent over it, pouring in steaming water. Why did the generous curves of the maid's bottom look so familiar? Natalya wondered.

"Good morning," she said politely.

"Oh, my Lord!" Startled, the girl whirled around, backed up against the tub, and barely recovered her balance in time to save herself from tumbling into the hot water. Mobcap askew, she clutched the pitcher against her generous bosom and laughed nervously. "Nearly jumped out of my skin, didn't I, Mistress Natalya? I wasn't expecting you yet."

"Charlotte?" She stared in disbelief. "What are you doing here?"

"Why, I'm your maid, ma'am." Her smile faded when Natalya made no response. "Didn't you want me?" she asked worriedly. "When Mr. St. James came back to the kitchen last night to tell me that I was to stay at the behest of your father, I was overjoyed! I already love America and this house and all your family, and I supposed that it was your wish that I remain as your ladies' maid. If not . . ."

"No, no, it's not that I don't want you." Natalya crossed the room to pat Charlotte's arm and smile into her brown eyes. "I have simply been so preoccupied since we arrived that I forgot to ask about you, and apparently Papa made these arrangements after I went to bed last night. I never dreamed that you'd want to remain in America, Charlotte, but I'm pleased that you do."

Reassured, Charlotte helped her mistress into the scented water and then left to finish unpacking. Since the dressing room that adjoined Natalya's bedchamber belonged to her

mother, she would share again with Kristin, who had generously set her own maid to work clearing space for her sister.

Alone at last in the hot, soothing bath, Natalya tried to make
sense of the chaos her life had so quickly become since the
Wild Rover had docked the previous morning. Perhaps this
was just more of the same tangle that had begun with Grey St.
James back at Château du Soleil? She had submitted to his will
many times during their journey from France to America,
partly because she'd secretly enjoyed doing so and partly because she'd been certain that her life would be her own again
once they reached Philadelphia. She pondered Grey's incendiary appearance in her bedchamber the night before and
Kristin's shocking news that he was not only *staying* in Philadelphia, but installed in a Beauvisage house. Finally, she reflected upon her reaction to the continuing presence of
Charlotte Timkins. She felt mean-spirited for wishing secretly
that Charlotte were not there, but the simple fact was that
the girl reminded her of Grey and their sea voyage, especially
the one night that she now longed to forget.

Was this all a game Grey was playing at her expense? She
had been brimming with plans for the life she would shape
upon returning to Philadelphia, and now all she could think
about was that infuriating Englishman. Rinsing the soap from
her neck and shoulders, Natalya resolved to confront Grey and
settle the matter once and for all. And this time she would
neither bend to his will nor allow him to have the last word!

Drawing on a pair of kid gloves, Natalya walked into the
dining room, where her parents were sitting down to a lunch
of cold chicken, perfect crimson strawberries, and corn bread
with honey.

Caro's face glowed at the sight of her daughter. ''Darling! How lovely you look! Do come and join us. I was
just about to ask Pierre if you had made an appearance yet
today.''

Clad in the blue-sprigged, silk-sashed gown of white muslin
that she had worn during the ride from Dover to London,
Natalya did indeed look lovely, if a trifle pale. Her hair was

drawn up in a soft Grecian knot, honey-hued tendrils framing her delicate yet sensual features. Smiling, she went to the table and kissed both her parents before taking a chair.

"Have some strawberries," Alec said, spooning a few onto a dessert plate and placing it before her. "Hyla's very proud of them. She has a little hothouse behind the kitchen now and gives us all sorts of exotic fruits and vegetables year-round."

"She is very eager to see you, Talya," Caro added.

"Goodness, how you both stare at me!" Natalya laughed, blushing. "Have I a spot on my chin?"

"It's still difficult to realize that you are truly here," her mother replied.

"And that you have grown so beautiful," added Alec. "You were a girl when you left, and now you have returned to us a woman. I might add, without an ounce of paternal bias, that you are one of those rare women who grows more beautiful with the passing years. I must brace myself for a veritable onslaught of suitors!"

"Don't be silly, Papa. I'm twenty-six, in case you've forgotten. Hardly marriageable." Cheerfully she ate a strawberry, closing her eyes with rapture. "Oh, heaven! How utterly delicious! . . . Why are you two looking so concerned? Do you imagine that I *want* a husband? Just the opposite. I am perfectly content to write my books, socialize with friends, and enjoy the company of my family." As the tall case clock near the doorway struck twelve, Natalya inched her chair away from the table. "I really hate to leave you so abruptly, but Krissie has convinced me to come with her to the dressmaker, and we thought we'd visit Grandmama for tea. Do you mind terribly? You know, Grey and I were forced to travel so lightly that I was unable to bring most of my gowns, so it is imperative that I have new ones made."

"Oh, Talya, must you go *today*?" Caroline could not suppress her disappointment. "Your father and I were so looking forward to spending the afternoon with you, and so many of the staff have been waiting to greet you. We haven't even had a look at your book yet, and we wanted to take you out behind the garden to your great-grandmother's cottage—"

"We thought it might serve as a study for you," Alec said. "A quiet place where you could write your books."

Flushing guiltily, Natalya hastened to apologize. "This is truly not the way I planned to spend my first day at home, but I can't go around in the same two or three crumpled gowns, can I? I'd love to see the cottage again, and using it as a study is a wonderful idea. It's so generous and thoughtful of you to offer it! . . . " She reached over to pat her mother's hand. "Pray do not be unhappy with me. I promise that once these other matters have been resolved, I shall be able to relax and enjoy my homecoming."

"I could accompany you," Caro murmured.

"Nonsense, Maman. Why should you suffer the boredom of my fittings?" Unable to meet her mother's eyes, Natalya busied herself with donning the blue spencer she'd carried in with her. Then, just before she rose from the table, she glanced at Alec and said in an offhand tone, "Oh, Papa, I heard that you invited Grey to live at the house on Spruce Street. I'll own that I was rather surprised to hear that he was not returning to England, and to discover that you and he had become so friendly in such a short space of time."

"I like St. James very much," he replied frankly. "I don't often take to people so readily, but I sensed immediately that he was a man of character. Of course you know that, since he was good enough to bring you all the way from Nicky's door to our own. I couldn't have been more pleased by his decision to remain in Philadelphia for the time being, and I look forward to improving our acquaintance."

Feeling rather ill, Natalya tried to smile. "How . . . nice."

Kristin appeared at that moment to announce that they would be terribly late if they didn't leave immediately, so both girls kissed their parents and hurried out the front door.

For a long moment Caro and Alec were silent, then their eyes met.

"I wonder what our little girl is up to this time?" he murmured, arching a white brow.

"Why do I doubt that it has little to do with an overpowering need for new gowns?" Caro replied. Pensively she drizzled honey over a wedge of corn bread and added, ''She's behaving very oddly. We may not have seen her for six years, but I know my daughter. . . .''

''Less than twenty-four hours have elapsed since she arrived in Philadelphia,'' Alec exclaimed. ''How could she have become embroiled in a drama so quickly?''

''I think Grandmama may have a gentleman friend,'' Kristin said. She and Natalya had just settled back into their carriage after being turned away by their grandmother. She hadn't time for tea that afternoon, she'd explained, because of a pressing engagement she could not break. The girls had hinted that they could remain at the house on Third Street and partake of refreshments without her, but Antonia had been firm, if apologetic. It was a most inconvenient day, she'd sighed, shooing them gently out the door.

''Grandmama?'' Natalya echoed, incredulous. ''But she's past eighty! And it's been less than a year since Grandpapa's death. What you suggest is . . . unthinkable!''

''Is it? She's been awfully secretive lately, and why did she make us leave?''

''I don't know. Why did she?''

Kristin's voice dropped conspiratorially. ''Because her gentleman friend was about to arrive and she didn't want us to see him.''

''Ridiculous! If Grandmama is behaving oddly, it is probably because she's becoming a trifle eccentric in her old age.''

Kristin shook her head. ''She's as alert as ever, and still very much a woman, Talya. Don't underestimate her.'' Looking out the carriage window as they turned onto Spruce Street, she gasped suddenly and drew back against the seat. ''Oh, dear, I think he saw me!''

''Who?'' Natalya asked in surprise.

''Hollis Gladstone. He's determined to court me whether I desire it or not.'' Kristin made an exasperated face. ''I just caught a glimpse of him, turning west at the corner, but now I'll wager that he's following us.''

The carriage drew up in front of a three-story red brick

house with Georgian window frames and shutters and a Colonial doorway complemented by two columns and an arch. Natalya had always adored this house; it was here that Nicholai Beauvisage had lived when he and Lisette fell in love. It galled her now to think that Grey St. James was making himself at home inside.

As the driver assisted the two young ladies out of the carriage, a pleasant-looking man hurried toward them on the brick footpath. Clad in a rather old-fashioned suit of brown broadcloth, his cravat slightly askew, he had the look of an amiable bear. When Kristin smiled politely, he grinned with unabashed pleasure.

"Hello, Hollis," she said, smoothing her exquisite pale lavender walking dress. "I don't believe you know my sister, Natalya. She is a published authoress, you know, and has just returned home after six years in France."

He turned to smile at Natalya. "It's a pleasure to meet you, Miss Beauvisage. Kristin has told me a great deal about you, and I don't doubt that your return to Philadelphia is cause for much celebration by your family." His tone was friendly and his green eyes were warm, but as soon as the amenities were dispensed with, he returned his attention to Kristin. "I was just about to summon my carriage to drive to Belle Maison, Kristin. Had you forgotten our plans?"

"Plans?" she repeated.

"Why, yes! When I visited you on Saturday and you were unable to attend the theater with me that evening, you promised to dine with me tonight instead."

"Oh, of course! No, no, I hadn't forgotten." He was so ardent that her heart went out to him.

"Then you must have come into town to spare me the journey out to Belle Maison. How thoughtful you are, Kristin, and how fortuitous that we are able to begin our time together early. My aunt Felicia has just arrived from Williamsburg, and begged me to bring you for tea at the Man Full of Trouble Inn. Her own daughter died recently, so I have been trying to cheer her up a bit, and meeting you would surely do so."

Kristin's lips parted as she groped for an excuse, then conscience quickly overcame her more selfish instincts. "I would be delighted to take tea with your aunt and do whatever I can to improve her spirits, but first—"

"I can look after this matter on my own," Natalya assured her quickly. "After all, we were only paying a courtesy call on Mr. St. James. I'll inquire after his comfort, offer a servant or two if needed, and be on my way. You go along with Mr. Gladstone and have that tea we missed at Grandmama's." Silently Natalya gave thanks for Hollis Gladstone's timely appearance, for she had been worried that she might not be able to speak to Grey alone. Certainly what she had to say to him was not fit to be overheard by her sister.

Presently matters were sorted out, and Natalya bade the couple good-bye and walked alone up the steps to the front door. Lifting the knocker, she fantasized that an old family retainer would answer and tell her that Grey St. James had decided not to remain in Philadelphia after all.

The door swung open to reveal a startlingly familiar face, followed by a gravelly cockney voice inquiring, "Can I help you, mum?"

"Fedbusk?" Natalya blinked at the sight of the weathered, balding sailor clad incongruously in a black frock coat, knee breeches, and a white cravat.

"The same, mum." He eyed her knowingly. "Here to see the cap'n?"

"Why—why, yes, I am." In struggling to regain her composure, Natalya was relieved to discover that her sense of humor had not deserted her entirely. Fedbusk gotten up as a butler was definitely cause for amusement. "Is Mr. St. James available?"

"Follow, me, mum." He turned and walked with a rolling, seaman's gait through the entry hall that led to the beautiful house's most impressive feature, a stunning elliptical stairway that soared and curved unsupported up three floors. Trailing after Fedbusk down the long central corridor, Natalya peeked into familiar rooms and noticed that most of the holland covers had been removed from the elegant furnishings. She expected to find Grey in her uncle Nicky's study, but Fedbusk passed that and continued on into the kitchen. "Miss Beauvisage to see you, sir," he announced loudly.

The cozy, whitewashed kitchen was dominated by a large, open fireplace, a hundred-year-old Welsh dresser lined with Bristol delft china, copper pots that hung from the ceiling, and a scrubbed worktable in the middle of the room. A beautiful woman with skin the color of café au lait stood next to the table writing on a long piece of paper. Swallowing, Natalya finally allowed her gaze to rest on Grey St. James.

The sight of him made her heart leap, for he had never looked more devastatingly handsome. Clad in a simple white shirt and biscuit breeches, and perched casually on a rough-hewn stool, his booted feet propped on a rung, he was the embodiment of male virility in repose. His skin was deeply tanned, his black hair was windblown, and his eyes glinted silver as they met hers.

"Ah, Miss Beauvisage," he murmured, a hint of mirth in his voice. "What a surprise to find *you* here. How thoughtful you are to pay us a call of welcome. I'm *deeply* gratified."

Natalya smiled sweetly, fighting a powerful urge to choke him. "Knowing your fondness for surprise visits, sir, I could not resist the temptation to bestow one upon you. Moreover, there are certain matters we should discuss. . . ."

"Indeed?" His brows flicked upward. "I wonder what those might be. . . ."

Chapter Nineteen

April 29, 1814

GREY STOOD UP, SMILING, AND GESTURED TOWARD the woman on the other side of the table. "Natalya, you must meet the gracious lady who has agreed to be my cook. This is Laviolet Pritchard. Laviolet, allow me to present Natalya Beauvisage."

"A pleasure, mam'selle," Laviolet said in a lilting French accent. "I believe I know your *grandmère*. I've helped cook for her parties. She is a woman of great beauty and character."

"I agree," Natalya said warmly. "It's good to meet you, Laviolet." She looked at Grey with curiosity. "How did you find a cook so quickly?"

"Speed discovered her when he went to the market this morning. Laviolet came to Philadelphia from Santo Domingo, during the slave revolts twenty years ago, and married a cabinetmaker. It seems that her last employer died recently, and Speed heard her mention that she was seeking a new position." He grinned. "Fate is kind to me, don't you agree?"

"You do have the devil's own luck," Natalya replied, with a touch of irony.

"Laviolet insists on knowing all my tastes in food, hence the notes she is making." Grey couldn't resist the opportunity to further annoy Natalya. "I fear that she will spoil me so outrageously that I may never leave Philadelphia. . . ."

"You may be too fat to fit through the doorway," Natalya

agreed mildly, nodding. "Would it be possible for you to spare me a few minutes of your precious time?"

Watching them with a mixture of curiosity and amusement, Laviolet waved a slim hand at Grey. "I have a great deal to occupy me for the moment, m'sieur. Perhaps you would allow me to prepare a proper tea for you and your guest?"

He nodded, brightening. "Splendid! Might I have some oysters as well?"

"It's not the usual custom to combine oysters with tea, but for you I shall make an exception," she answered. "Where may I serve you?"

Grey pondered this. It seemed likely that Natalya would find cause to raise her voice at some time during their conversation, and he preferred that they not be overheard. "We'll be in the upstairs sitting room, Laviolet. Have Speed carry the tray; he's accustomed to physical exertion," he told her, eyes twinkling.

Then, taking hold of Natalya's elbow, he guided her out of the kitchen. They had proceeded only a little way down the corridor when she whispered loudly, "Why are you taking me *upstairs*? I hardly think—"

"This is precisely the reason," Grey cut in. "You seem to have so little control over your temper that I thought I would spare you the further embarrassment of servants' gossip. Perhaps if we conduct this interview on another floor, we can avoid sharing its contents with the entire household."

Cheeks burning, Natalya realized that he was dominating the situation once again. As they started up the flying staircase, she said, "You have settled very quickly into your role of master here; so quickly that one might imagine this house belonged to *you*! Lest you forget, sir, you are here through the benevolence of the Beauvisage family, and—"

"If I don't behave myself you'll have me tossed out on my ear?"

"Kindly refrain from mocking me!"

"I'll be happy to, if you will likewise refrain from adopting the manner of a toplofty dowager speaking to an insolent gamekeeper." Grey tightened his grip on her elbow when she tried to pull away from him. "For heaven's sake, relax. I won't gobble you up the moment we're alone."

Remembering what had occurred between them on her bed the night before, Natalya shot him a murderous look. "Past experience has taught me that you are capable of nearly any transgression."

He shrugged lightly and chuckled. "Well, perhaps where *you* are concerned . . ."

They had reached the top of the stairs, and Natalya paused for a moment to look down. "How I adored this staircase when I was a child. First I would stand at the bottom and look up, wondering how it could not collapse when someone ascended. I used to worry that it would do so while I was on it. Then Papa told me that it was called a flying staircase, and that because of some magic means it needed no support. He took me up and down, up and down, until I had conquered my fears."

"How old were you?" Grey asked softly.

"Oh . . . four, I suppose. It's one of my earliest memories."

"This is a wonderful house, but then the Beauvisage family seems to have an affinity for them. I really am grateful to be staying here, you know, and I would be desolate if you tossed me out on my ear."

Disarmed by his honesty, Natalya turned away from the carved banister and started toward the sitting room. "Well, it's all academic, isn't it? I couldn't have you put out even if I wanted to. It was Papa who gave you leave to occupy the house, so this is between the two of you. From the sound of it, you've charmed him mightily."

"Do I detect a note of disapproval in your voice?" Grey followed her into the cozy sitting room, which was filled with bookcases, luminous watercolors of gardens painted by Lisette Beauvisage, a pair of blue-and-gold-striped sofas that faced each other on a Kuba rug, and two brocade wing chairs. The glass double doors at the back of the room opened onto a white-pillared porch from which steps descended to the walled garden below. Natalya walked over to look outside for a moment before taking a seat on one of the sofas. To her dismay,

Grey chose to sit next to her. "Tell me the truth now," he pressed. "Why are you *really* so annoyed by my presence? Is it because we've made love?"

Her long-lashed aqua eyes were wide as she turned to face him. "I must ask you not to speak of that night again, sir!"

"To anyone else, or to you? I certainly haven't told anyone if that's what's worrying you, nor shall I." Grey began to fold back his cuffs as he continued, "Rather warm up here, isn't it? Perhaps it's just the sunshine. Ah, I can see by your expression that you're in no mood to discuss the weather." He grinned slightly in spite of himself. "My darling minx—"

"Don't call me that!"

"What's become of the charming free spirit who wore her hair loose in the breeze, sitting on the quarterdeck of the *Rover*? Or, more to the point, where is the passionate *minx* who came to my bed just a few short nights ago and insisted that I make love to her? Are you not the woman who reveled in the beauty of her own naked body and—"

"Enough!" An errant curl brushed Natalya's burning cheek as she leaned forward and clapped her hand over his mouth. "That was in the past, and I don't wish to discuss it ever again!"

Grey removed her hand firmly. "The past is part of you, my sweet; everything you have ever done or felt or yearned for is part of you now. The pleasure and awakening you felt that night were real. You were honest about it then. What has changed?"

"Everything," she hissed. "The only reason I was able to do something so *reckless* as that—"

"Excuse me, sir," Jasper Speed interjected from the doorway. "Your tea?"

Natalya blushed furiously as the stocky, redheaded manservant placed the tray on the table before them. "Good day, Miss Beauvisage," he said, with a smile. "I hope you are well?"

"Yes, Speed," she replied through gritted teeth. "How do you find Philadelphia?"

"Highly interesting, miss. Do you take milk?"

"We'll pour our own," Grey said, already squeezing lemon

juice over the closest oyster on the plate. "Did you have any luck with your errand, Speed?"

"Possibly, sir."

Grey looked up, silver eyes agleam. "I'll speak to you later, then."

"Yes, sir. I'll be downstairs."

He was gone then, and Natalya poured tea for them both while Grey savored an oyster. There was also a little plate of cakes, and one of sliced apples. After a moment Grey looked over at her expectantly and said, "Well, do go on. You were saying that you only behaved so recklessly—"

"I remember!" Natalya's color was high and her hands shook slightly as she stirred milk into her tea. "You know, I really haven't the slightest desire to continue this conversation."

"But I do." There was an undercurrent of steel in his calm voice. "You behave as if I have done you some terrible wrong, as if the mere sight of me is cause for the most unrelenting aggravation, and I believe that I deserve an explanation."

"Fine; then you shall have one." Taking a deep breath, Natalya continued, "I hope that I do not have to repeat all the reasons I originally cited for coming to your cabin. I wanted to have . . . that experience, and since I don't plan to marry, you seemed a logical person to . . . have it with." She could feel the blood rising to her cheeks again and rushed ahead. "I thought we were about to part! If I'd known that you would stay in Philadelphia—"

"Ah, I thought so," he interjected curtly. "That very night, when I suggested that you wanted me because you believed you'd never see me again, you protested that your motive was passion, not practicality. How would you feel if a man did the same thing to you—seduced you, shared your bed, and then hoped to be rid of you forever?"

She stared at him in shock. How had he managed to twist everything so that she was being painted as a cold-hearted harlot? "That's not fair! You know I'm not like that!"

"I know you're confused," Grey remarked laconically, leaning forward to spear another oyster.

"If I'm confused, it's *your* doing!" Despite her fury, Natalya was struck by the endearing way his mouth puckered slightly as he savored the oyster's tangy blend of salt water and lemon. She fought an urge to smile. "You misled me, Grey. What I—we—did was crazy. I allowed myself to—to—"

"You needn't search for proper-sounding words," he said imperturbably. "I remember what you did."

She tried to ignore him. "I did it because I wanted to, but also because I thought it would be safe, that it wouldn't haunt me. I wasn't being callous. You implied that you were going to deliver me to Philadelphia and return to England."

"I said that I would be out of your life before spring waned," Grey corrected her. "We're only at the brink of May, my dear."

Jumping up, Natalya began to pace in front of the ornate glass doors. "Is this a game you are playing? Do you enjoy watching me squirm?"

He shrugged. "I may enjoy watching you come to grips with the fact that you cannot control other people, least of all me. You had everything worked out, planned down to the details of our lovemaking and the farewell speech that you would deliver to me on the dock." Draining his teacup, he returned it to its saucer and added, "I fear I don't do very well with other people's plans."

"You're enjoying this, aren't you?" Natalya cried. "Was it so horrid for me to plan and dream what my life would be like once I returned to Philadelphia? I almost wonder if you are doing your best to disrupt my homecoming because your own, in London, was fraught with disappointment!"

Grey rose with casual grace and crossed to stand before her. "You don't know the first thing about it." The silvery flame in his eyes betrayed him as he grasped her hands in his and said, "Futhermore, I hate to puncture your bubble of self-importance, but I have legitimate business to attend to here." His grip tightened slightly. "If you seriously believed that you could come here today and browbeat me into leaving, you were sadly mistaken. I am *not* a character in one of your bloody books. You cannot write me out of this or any other scene until I am damned well ready to go."

Natalya's heart seemed to stop as she absorbed the raw passion in his voice; she was paralyzed. In the next instant, the sound of her own heartbeat seemed to fill her body. Her palms were moist, and when she looked into Grey's eyes it was as if she'd stepped off a precipice. What was happening?

"In any case . . ." Slowly he drew her near until their bodies touched, all the while holding her gaze. "You don't want me to leave. You thrive on my presence, whether you can admit it or not."

A tide of conflicting emotions surged up to torment her. Could his words be true? She ached and knew not why. Her senses were dizzy with Grey; coherent thought was impossible. When his hands moved to gather her into his embrace, she made a low sound of protest and tried to struggle. Grey tipped her chin up, and she saw the heat and will and something elusive in his silvery eyes.

"Yield to me, Natalya," he said in a voice so rich with texture that it was like a caress.

She gasped with pleasure when he began to kiss her, his mouth leisurely yet insistent as it worked its magic. Her spencer had come open to reveal the fine muslin beneath, and her breasts strained against Grey's chest. With a will of their own, her arms rounded his neck and her lips parted so that her tongue could find his. Natalya could feel the muscles in his thighs through the gauzy fabric of her gown. His body was like a drug, infusing her with a heady, sweet helplessness. Tears pricked her eyes when Grey bent her backward, his lips traveling down her neck, burning as they tasted the curves of her throat and breasts. A muffled voice in the back of her mind scolded her, but she was powerless to heed it. Bewildered but deliriously happy, she sank her fingers into his gleaming raven hair and pressed him closer.

Through the muslin bodice, Grey felt her nipples harden in response to the touch of his hands and lips. Christ, he thought, she is almost more than mortal man can realize. Everything about her was utterly, glowingly exquisite; a lush feast for his senses. And, most tantalizing of all, was the formidable spirit and mind inside Natalya's glorious body. He kissed her bare shoulder, then the soft baby curls along her hairline. Soon her tawny gold hair would be loose, and he would bury his face in it, inhaling its fragrance.

Without a word, he swung her off the floor and up into his arms. As he carried her into the bedroom, Natalya thought giddily that it must be wonderful to be a man, a strong, reckless man like Grey who could take whatever he wanted. She knew she shouldn't let him take *her*, but she was unwilling to deny herself this joy.

Natalya had been in this bedchamber many times in the past, but it seemed different now that Grey was in residence. His trunk sat on the Persian carpet, his neckcloth was draped over the back of a chair, his brandy winked from the mantel, and his books were stacked on the Chippendale lowboy next to the bed. The spacious forest green and beige room was dominated by a Hepplewhite tall post bed with a deep feather tick covered by soft sheets and quilts. Grey deposited Natalya on the edge of the bed and smiled at her.

"You look like Satan himself," she remarked, without displeasure.

"At sea you compared me to a pirate. I must be gaining depravity in your estimation!" He grinned at her, teeth flashing white, as his eyes roamed from her loosened curls to the radiant glow on her face to the creamy expanse of her neck and shoulders. "You, my darling, look like a goddess."

Natalya watched, her heart racing, as he pulled off his boots. It struck her again how much he had changed since they'd left England. He'd always been strikingly attractive . . . compelling, certainly. But now, with his bronzed skin and rugged, healthy vitality, he was irresistible. If he had looked like this when he'd come to Château du Soleil, she thought, Uncle Nicky would never have put me in his care!

"Turn around," Grey murmured as he leaned against the bed, flicking open the buttons of his shirt. When Natalya gave him a quick glance and then obeyed, he massaged the tension from her neck with lean, strong fingers. Then, as he felt her relax, he bent to press feather-soft kisses at her nape before drawing the pins from her hair. Long, luxuriant curls spilled down her back, and Grey ran his fingers through the shining, rippling mass, lightly touching her brow and temples as he did so. Her skin was like satin, her hair like spun silk.

Natalya swam in a sea of blissful sensation, tingling from head to toe under Grey's skilled hands. Finally, as his fingers strayed to the tiny fastenings of her gown, she became aware of the heat blossoming between her legs. The blue-sprigged gown opened to reveal her slim back, and she waited for his touch. A moment passed, accompanied by the rustle of clothes, then Grey ran a fingertip down her spine, and she let out her breath in a gasping sigh.

"Beautiful," he whispered, his mouth trailing fire over her shoulder. He slid the gown forward, caressing her as he pulled the short, puffed sleeves down over her hands. When his chest with its crisp mat of black hair skimmed her back, Natalya knew that he was naked. Her head dropped back against his shoulder, and their eyes met for an instant before Grey reached up to cup her breasts. His touch was firmer now, and she welcomed it, feeling her breasts swell against his hands, the nipples taut and tingling between his fingertips.

"Grey," she breathed, arching as her arousal intensified.

"Mmm." He scorched her neck with kisses and shifted so that she could feel him, throbbingly erect, against the small of her back.

"I want to touch you." Natalya's voice was low and rich, like a stranger's . . . a woman's.

He turned her into the quilts then and removed the rest of her clothes. Natalya's hair flowed over the sheets, a mane of honey on the dusk-tinted bed, and the sight of her delectable body was almost more than he could bear.

Reaching up, Natalya ran her hands over the soft hair on his chest, memorizing each muscle and ridge. Since the night on the *Rover*, she had tried to erase her memories of Grey's body and the chiseled splendor of his face, but they had broken through in her dreams. Now, touching his warm, golden brown skin, she smiled, surrendering to the fates that drew them together. Her hand grazed his manhood and she whispered, "Please, kiss me."

"With pleasure," he replied, smiling. He lay over her, one knee between her thighs, and kissed her long and deeply. As their tongues caressed, he could feel Natalya's moistness against him. He longed to plunge inside her and find release but held himself back. Their passion mounted as he branded her with his mouth and fingers, exploring her throat, lingering over her breasts, nipping gently at her sides, the softness of her belly, her tender inner thighs.

Natalya moaned with pleasure and moved her hips against him. Slowly, brazenly, he kissed her there, and *there*, but stopped before she could realize what he'd dared. Her eyes opened when his face returned to her view. Wrapping her arms around Grey's tapering back, she kissed him with shameless ardor, thrusting rhythmically against the skilled fingers that had slipped down to touch her intimately. Burning, she cried aloud as release came at last in crashing waves of exquisite sensation.

Grey pushed into her then, savoring the feel of her contractions. Natalya was riding a fierce tide of rapture, and the fusion of their bodies only took her higher. She loved the raw abandon of Grey's face above her, the rasp of his hair-roughened thighs against her own satiny flanks, the pounding of their hips as he thrust deep inside her again and again. When both of them were covered with a sheen of perspiration, Grey reached his own fiery, heart-stopping climax. Shuddering, he lowered himself with unsteady hands and rested against the fragrant tumble of Natalya's hair.

"Christ, I can barely speak," he managed to mutter after a time. "How do you feel?"

"Shall I tell you the truth?"

It was relief to detect a piquant note in her voice. "By all means."

"I'm actually quite splendid."

"Good. That's how you ought to feel." Gathering his strength, he rose on an elbow and gazed down at her beautiful, flushed face. "You're looking splendid, too. Very womanly."

Natalya put out a hand and touched his hair, fingering the silver strands among the ebony. "I wonder what it all means . . . and yet I'm afraid to wonder."

Grey gave her a rueful smile. "I think I'd rather not know at the moment." Dropping back against the pillows, he gazed up at the canopy and tried to clear his mind of everything—past, future . . . everything but the feel of this one, satisfying moment.

Natalya told herself it didn't matter, and yet there came an ache around her heart, and her sense of ebullience faded. Pulling up the soft sheets and quilts, she lay back beside Grey and thought how little she really knew of herself and her own hidden needs. Why had she succumbed to him . . . with such reckless joy? An hour ago she wouldn't have believed that they could be lying together in the burnished rose twilight, Grey's long fingers idly caressing the curve of her breast. It was frightening not to know what would happen next, for she clearly had less control over herself—and much less over *him*— than she had previously thought. Turning her head slightly, she stole a glance up at Grey. His hair ruffled and his features relaxed, he appeared disarmingly boyish, and she felt a mutinous weakness steal over her. What did it *mean*?

A knock came at the door then, rousing them from their separate reveries. Startled, Grey sat up, then glanced down at Natalya and laid a finger over her parted lips. "What is it?" he called.

"It's me, sir—Fedbusk," the unlikely butler whispered loudly. "I seen her with me own eyes! 'Twas my lady! Just now, on the street, sir!"

Grey's eyes sharpened, and Natalya saw the muscles in his arms flex unconsciously. She could almost feel his thoughts. "I'll be down in a moment, Fedbusk, and we'll discuss it then."

"That's not all, sir," Fedbusk persisted, clearing his throat. "There's a man downstairs name of Beauvisage. Says he's lookin' for his daughter!"

Natalya, whose heart was already thundering in panic and confusion, gave a little cry and pressed the covers closer to her body. "Papa?" she moaned. "Good God!"

Chapter Twenty

April 29–30, 1814

"I DON'T MEAN TO BE RUDE, RUSHING YOU AT A time like this, but I'm afraid you'll have to get dressed immediately," Grey told Natalya after he had sent Fedbusk belowstairs with orders to offer Mr. Beauvisage a glass of Madeira.

She was already throwing back the covers and scrambling off the bed, oblivious of her own nakedness. "Where's my gown? And my chemise? Oh, Lord, look at them! It looks as if I've worn them to bed!" In the process of shaking the wrinkles out of her muslin gown, Natalya colored prettily as she realized what she'd said. Grey had already pulled on his own shirt and trousers, and now he paused to help her dress, fastening the back of her gown with amazing speed.

"My hair," she hissed, catching sight of her cascading amber curls in the looking glass. Near tears, she searched frantically through the bedclothes for her hair pins. "How could Papa be *here*? Could this be a jest on Fedbusk's part?"

"Wishful thinking, my dear. Here are your slippers. I'll go downstairs and distract your father until you have made yourself presentable. I'll tell him that you are looking for a book you loaned me." Grey paused before his shaving stand mirror to rake a hand through his hair, which fell obligingly into place, then he looked back and flashed a daring grin. "Cheer up, minx. Think of this as an adventure that you'll laugh about later."

Watching him go, Natalya felt more like sobbing than laughing. Her father would surely guess; he'd see it in her eyes, and nothing would ever be the same. However, after finding a silver-backed brush and arranging her hair carefully, hope began to blossom in her breast. Her gown looked almost presentable, particularly after she had donned her blue spencer and buttoned it primly. As an afterthought, she grabbed the copy of *René* she had given Grey in France and hurried down the elliptical staircase.

Grey was entertaining his guest in his ground-floor study. It was a cozy room, decorated for Nicholai Beauvisage in shades of terra-cotta and gold. One whole wall was a mosaic of handsomely bound books, and Natalya discovered her father and Grey sitting before the freshly laid fire on matching wing chairs. When she appeared in the doorway, a spot of color on each cheek, they rose to greet her.

"Talya," Alec said, opening his arms, "what a surprise to find you here! I stopped on a whim to ask Mr. St. James if he'd care to join me for supper at my club."

Grateful for the shelter of his embrace, Natalya replied, "I originally drove here with Kristin because Grandmama was too busy for us and Krissie wanted to see if there was anything Mr. St. James might need. Outside, we encountered a Mr. Gladstone, who took Kristin off, so I was forced to visit alone." Emboldened, she looked up to give her father a smile. "I was just upstairs in the sitting room when you arrived, looking for this." She held up the book, then backed away to take the chair that Grey had drawn up for her. "It's *René*, a particular favorite of mine. I've been missing it *intensely*."

Alec smiled amiably, but his turquoise eyes were keen as they rested first on his daughter and then on Grey. "It was thoughtful of you to look in on our guest," he said to Natalya, pausing to sip his Madeira. "I'll admit that I am pleased to see the two of you getting along. Perhaps it was my imagination, but yesterday I could have sworn that there was little love lost between you."

"I owe Mr. St. James my very life, Papa," she replied politely. "He can always count me among his friends."

Grey bit back a grin, amused by her credible performance. Then, as Natalya and her father chatted on about inconsequentials, Fedbusk's words returned to haunt him. *'Twas my lady,* he'd said. And that could only mean one person: Francesca. Grey felt an odd thrill, not unlike the anticipation one experienced on the eve of battle. And at that moment all he wanted was to be left alone to puzzle out his next move. The drama with Natalya and her father seemed dull by comparison, and he began to edge the conversation toward their departure.

"Now that you're here, sir, Natalya won't have to travel home unaccompanied after dark," he remarked at length.

"That's true." Beauvisage nodded. "Unless you *would* care to dine at my club. . . ."

"I fear I'll have to cry off tonight. I find that I'm overweary. The sea voyage is catching up with me, I suppose."

Alec looked at his daughter and smiled. "In that case, I'll ask you another time. I must admit that I welcome the chance to have Talya all to myself for a little while." He finished his wine and set the glass on a Pembroke side table. "We have six years' worth of conversation to replenish."

Soon Natalya found herself standing next to her father in the front doorway, bidding Grey good night. His face was unreadable as he shook Alec's hand, then clasped her own. Did he squeeze it just that way to remind her of what they'd shared in the bedchamber upstairs? A moment later her father was guiding her to the carriage. When he walked away to tell her own driver that she would be traveling back to Belle Maison with him, Natalya looked toward the doorway. She wanted a last glimpse of Grey, but he had already disappeared inside. Unaccountably, Fedbusk's curious announcement echoed in her mind.

I seen her! he'd hissed. Grey had known exactly what Fedbusk meant; his entire body had tensed instantly. Now she realized that Grey had rushed them out of the house so that he could interrogate his butler thoroughly.

'Twas my lady! Just now, on the street! Fedbusk's hoarse words stirred up clouds of confusion, curiosity, and a sharper emotion she couldn't name. Grey had told her that he had

business to take care of in Philadelphia. Instinctively Natalya knew that the mystery woman Fedbusk had sighted was the real reason the Englishman had remained in America.

Fedbusk sat awkwardly on the molten-gold brocade wing chair and cast a sidelong glance at Jasper Speed. When Speed smiled back from his own chair by the fire, the crotchety first mate grunted and looked away, scratching his balding, sunburned head. Both men rose quickly as Gray entered with three glasses in his hand.

"Sorry to keep you waiting. Laviolet insisted that I taste the shrimp concoction she's preparing for dinner. It's nothing like English food, which delights me enormously." He splashed brandy into the glasses and handed one to each man. "I'm eager to hear from both of you, but I'll ask Speed to speak first since he garnered his information earlier in the day."

"I want to know," Fedbusk growled, downing his brandy, "why you send *him* out into the streets and keep me imprisoned in this house all got up in this queer costume!" He reached down and yanked at one sagging white stocking. "I'm the one who knew Lady Altburne, and I should be the one looking for her 'stead of answering the door and bowing to a lot of bleedin' Colonials!"

Slowly Grey arched a black eyebrow. "Old chap, we've been all through this, haven't we? Francesca might recognize you if you were to encounter her on the street, and that simply wouldn't do. I agree that it would be much more efficient to send you on this mission, but I cannot afford to take the risk." He poured brandy for himself, then took the shield-backed chair recently vacated by Natalya. "Now then—"

"A mighty queer arrangement if you ask me," Fedbusk interjected sulkily. Speed stared at him, astonished that the older man would continue to argue with their employer.

"Have you finished?" Grey's tone was cool, but his eyes were sharp as silver rapiers.

"I suppose so. Just don't expect me to put up with this humdudgeon forever. I understand that you want to find my lady Francesca, and I'm all for it, but when I'm strutting about this house all day trussed up like a turkey I begin thinkin' about *myself*, and I can tell you—''

"I'd rather you didn't, if you don't mind." Grey's voice silenced his childhood friend. "Now then, Speed, perhaps you can bring us up to date on your activities today. I gather that you learned something?"

"Yes, sir." Speed squirmed restlessly and took a sip of brandy. Obviously spying didn't sit too well with him. "After I returned from the market with Mrs. Pritchard, I set out for Hahn's Coffeehouse as you recommended. There I made the acquaintance of Mr. Stringfellow, the proprietor. Upon learning that I was newly arrived from England myself, he served me personally and later joined me for a mug of ale. I told him that I worked for you, sir, and that you had recently visited Lisette Beauvisage, who used to own the coffeehouse, in France. As you suspected, this had quite a rousing effect on Mr. Stringfellow, who . . ."

Fedbusk yawned loudly and hunched down on his chair as if contemplating a nap. Grey gave him a menacing look but said to Speed, "Perhaps you can give me these details later and proceed to the actual information you received regarding my wife."

"Yes, sir. Once I felt certain that Mr. Stringfellow could be trusted, I mentioned that you were looking for an English-woman whom you believed to be in Philadelphia. I then received his promise not to speak of this matter to anyone else and proceeded to describe Lady Altburne. He said that he did indeed know such a woman, though by a different name. She has a small, elegant house nearby on Pine Street, is active in society, and portrays herself as a widow. Mr. Stringfellow said that this woman calls herself Frances Wellbeloved."

Grey, who had been listening intently, now gave a shout of laughter. "Does she indeed? Hilarious. Now then, Fedbusk, it's your turn."

The crusty seaman jerked his head up as if regaining consciousness. "Eh? Oh, yes. Not much to tell, except that I was sitting in the dining room, resting my achin' feet, when I saw an open carriage pass. 'Twas my lady, sir, clear as day, and more beautiful than ever, which doubtless means that she's more evil as well. I knew what she was the first time I clapped eyes on her before your wedding, but you'd have none of *my* advice—''

"For God's sake, Fedbusk, get on with it!"

"Nothing else to say, is there? She's here, in Philadelphia, and now *you* have to decide what you're going to do about it!"

Caro knocked softly on the dressing room door that connected with Natalya's bedchamber. "Darling? I just wanted to say good night."

"Come in, Maman."

She entered to find her daughter clad in a loose muslin nightgown and sitting in the middle of the field bed, its curved canopy arching toward the shadowed ceiling. Sheets of paper covered with writing were scattered before her across the bed. Oil lamps, lit on each bedside table, afforded the only light.

"It's very late, Talya," Caro exclaimed, crossing the room. "What are you doing?"

"It's part of the manuscript for my new book, Maman. I must begin writing again tomorrow, and I'm trying to return inside the heart and soul of my story." She smiled at her mother, then looked back at the paper in her hand. "But first I must close a door on my own life if I am to do my best writing, and that's rather difficult."

"I should think so—you just arrived home." Caro's tone was slightly injured. "Do you mean to isolate yourself?"

"That would be ideal," Natalya admitted. "It was lovely of you and Papa to offer me Great-Grandmère's cottage, and I can scarcely wait until morning to explore it."

Caro perched on the edge of the bed and reached out to stroke Natalya's brow and the shining honey-hued curls that cascaded around her shoulders. "My darling, you look like a little girl. It's difficult for me to realize that you are a grown woman of twenty-six who is perfectly capable of ordering her own life. If I am unable to resist giving you advice, you must scold me."

"And then you would stop?" Natalya looked up, her rich aqua eyes twinkling.

"Probably not," Caro admitted, laughing.

"Do you know, I said nearly the same thing to Krissie this morning, so I understand your feelings. It's very hard for me to think of *her* as a grown woman."

"Well, I'm not entirely certain that she is one yet, but that's another subject." They were silent for a few moments, then Caro said, "Your outing in the city must have done you good, or else it put you off such excursions. This morning you were far too preoccupied to think of Grandmère's cottage or your books."

"I confess I am still preoccupied," Natalya said, with a bittersweet smile, "but sometimes I welcome the escape writing affords. It takes me out of myself."

"I had rather hoped that you would postpone writing for a while and simply enjoy your homecoming. It's spring, and there are so many old friends who will be eager to see you and doubtless give parties to celebrate your accomplishments. Philadelphia may boast many authors, but precious few of them are women."

"Maman, I recognize that gleam in your eye! Your thoughts have been running to a match for me, haven't they."

Caro laughed at her daughter's teasing, yet a disquieting feeling persisted within her. "I simply want you to enjoy yourself, darling Talya. I want you to be happy."

"Then you must let me write, Maman. Right now it's what I need most." A strange, confusing wave of emotion swept over her, and tears pricked her eyes. It wouldn't do for her mother to see and wonder, so Natalya looked back down at her papers. The words written there were a blur.

"I will leave you, then, if you promise to go to sleep soon. You need your rest, Talya."

"Yes, Maman," she replied, with an obedient smile, and leaned forward to hug her mother. "I love you. Kiss Papa for me."

"I'll be happy to." Caro held her close. "I love you, too, darling, and I am so happy that you have returned to us."

* * *

"I keep telling myself that Talya is twenty-six and does not need a mother to watch over her, but there is something in her eyes that arouses all my maternal instincts." Caro lay back against her pillows, watching Alec shed his robe and climb naked into bed beside her. "Do you think that I am being foolish?"

"Of course not, *chérie*." He turned toward her and rose on an elbow to gaze down at her beloved and beautiful face. How many nights had they lain together thus, discussing the events of their lives in the quiet of nighttime, holding and caressing each other, whether it led to lovemaking or not? It was Alec's favorite hour of the day; the renewal of intimacy between them. "I admit that I have concerns of my own regarding Natalya, but I fear that there is little we can do and say beyond reminding each other that she is fully an adult and must be allowed to live her own life as she sees fit."

Caro groaned and ran her hand over the familiar terrain of Alec's chest, lingering unconsciously over the places she knew were most sensitive. "She seems so *subdued*, and says she wants to shut herself up in Grandmère's cottage and return to writing."

"I know. She told me during the drive home tonight." Alec's own fingers found their way to Caro. He stroked her throat and neck, then gently massaged away the worry lines on her face. "You know, Talya was very preoccupied most of the way from Philadelphia. When I mentioned it, offhandedly, she laughed and said that she was thinking about the new gowns she'd ordered." Alec snorted softly in half-amused disbelief. "Does she take me for a stranger? Then, almost immediately, she began talking about her writing, and there was such relief in her voice, as if she'd forgotten that escape could be so simple."

"You always were a master in the art of deduction," Caro murmured, closing her eyes and savoring his touch.

"Not always; I think I learned it as a means of survival after I became a husband and a father. People rarely say what they really mean, and sometimes they don't know themselves. I love you and our children too much to listen to you only with my ears." He chuckled and kissed her. "I've had to develop previously undiscovered senses!"

"Perhaps you learned about that from me, love."

"And what did your instincts tell you when you visited our daughter just now? Did she actually *say* anything meaningful, about Grey St. James, perhaps?"

"Perish the thought. His name was never mentioned." Caro felt Alec recline against the pillows and snuggled into the crook of his shoulder, where he held her close. "You know, I've been thinking about something you said earlier. Didn't you tell me that Talya and Grey were upstairs when you arrived, looking for a book she'd loaned him, and that she remained there for quite a while after he joined you—until her search was successful?"

"That's right," he said drowsily, leaning over with his free hand to put out the light. "Talya said it was a favorite book, *René*, and she'd been quite lost without it."

"But, Alec," Caro persisted, looking up to search his face in the shadows, "she had no book when you two came home. She must have left it behind . . . and hasn't said a word about her error. Don't you find that *odd* in light of earlier events?"

"Yes, but we can worry and deduce all night long and it won't change a damned thing." Alec turned on his side and enfolded his wife in his arms, kissing the nape of her neck. "Go to sleep, *chérie*. Talya's not a child. Hard as it is, you'll have to accept that. . . ."

When at last her eyes began to sting with fatigue, Natalya blew out the lamps and crawled under the covers. Certain that sleep was moments away, she surrendered, lying back against the snowy pillows and carefully arranging her blankets.

She closed her eyes, then opened them. Moonlight streamed into her room through parted draperies, illuminating the neat stack of papers she had placed on a chair. She turned away toward the wall, but when her face pressed close to the mane of loose hair fanned across her pillow, she caught a faint whiff of Grey in her own silky curls. Her heart quickened and tightened, and tears rose in her throat. *Why am I feeling this way?* she cried inwardly. *It was nothing, nothing but a pleasurable romp with an immensely attractive man. It's not as if I want him to declare his love and beg for my hand in marriage! Why, I would have to break his heart, for such a match could never work.*

Guilt. Natalya settled on that weighty word, deciding that guilt must be to blame for her churning emotions. She had grown up watching her parents' love affair, and somehow the physical act by itself, without love, seemed wrong. Actually she'd always believed that there could be no pleasure or meaningful passion in the physical act without love, but that certainly wasn't true. . . . Did that mean that she was immoral? Or did it mean—

His face filled her mind, and she recalled the sound of his voice, the tender intimacy of his touch, his demanding kiss, the heat of his body moving against her own.

Think about the book! Natalya ordered herself, but for the first time, she could not envision her characters. In the tower room at Château du Soleil they had acted out all her own suppressed fantasies, more alive than she felt herself to be. Had Eloise and Charles died the afternoon Grey St. James appeared in the courtyard?

Blinking back tears, Natalya vowed to resurrect them on the morrow. It was as if she had lost the key to a secret door, but there had to be a way to get back inside. There *had* to be a way. . . .

PART FOUR

To be wise and love,
Exceeds man's might.
SHAKESPEARE

Chapter Twenty-one

May 1–3, 1814

FRANCESCA ST. JAMES, THE VISCOUNTESS ALT-burne, rose from her elegant *bonheur-du-jour*. The delicate ladies' writing table, veneered in tulipwood and mounted with Sevres porcelain plaques, had been imported from France and was her latest acquisition for the residence she had recently rented in Philadelphia. The tall, narrow town house on Pine Street was owned by a congressman who had since moved with the capital to Washington, leaving much of his furniture behind. This served Francesca's purposes, since she had come to New York, and now to Philadelphia, ill equipped to furnish an entire house.

"I am frightfully restless," she said, crossing the long parlor to gaze out at the courtyard garden. A few tulips were blooming, but they didn't appear to be very healthy.

"Dearest, why not sit down beside me and allow me to rub your beautiful feet?" The man seated on the rose silk-upholstered settee put down his newspaper and gazed at her expectantly. Although not yet thirty-five years of age, he looked much older. His thinning hair had gone prematurely gray, and he had lost considerable weight since his affair with Francesca had commenced two years ago. At social gatherings, he replaced his gold-rimmed spectacles with a quizzing-glass and styled his hair with Macassar Oil, à la Byron. It was enough to fascinate the American women, but he could rarely elicit such interest from Francesca anymore.

She wandered over and sat down beside him but did not remove her kid slipper and offer him her slim foot. "I can't think why I am so restless," she complained again.

"Why don't we ring for some of those raisin cakes you adore?" When Francesca shook her head, pouting slightly, he sighed. Dear God, but she was beautiful! Each time he saw her he experienced the same thrill he'd felt the first time, when he'd returned to London after she'd become Grey's wife. Her slanting green eyes, porcelain skin, shining auburn hair, and full mouth had driven him insane then, and continued to do so. His passion for Francesca had overpowered all else, including duty to family and country. Not that he'd *wanted* to continue on in that terrifying war, but now, as fear began to creep over him that he might lose his love, he told himself that he'd thrown everything away for her. He'd deserted Wellington's army during the battle of Salamanca, risking capture, disgrace, and death to return and take her away from England and her marriage to the absent Viscount Altburne. He'd even given up his own name to go into hiding with her! At first it had all been a wild, reckless adventure; they'd thrived on their own misbehavior and reveled in the illicit passion of their love affair. However, after nearly two years . . .

"I find that something very odd has been happening to me," Francesca said suddenly. "I've been dreaming about Grey."

For a moment his heart caught, but then he saw that her expression reflected uneasiness and fear rather than longing. "Do you know, it's curious that you should say that. He's been in my mind, too. Yesterday afternoon, when I was walking toward the bootmaker's shop, I saw a man turn the corner a distance ahead of me who bore a chilling resemblance to Grey. I knew that I was being ridiculous, but I quickened my pace and followed him. However, when I rounded the corner myself, he had disappeared. You'll doubtless laugh at me for imagining that such a thing was even remotely possible, but—"

"Which corner was it?" she broke in.

"I beg your pardon?" He turned to find Francesca holding one hand over the low bodice of her cream sarcenet gown, pressing her fingers against her heart. Her catlike eyes were wide open and brilliantly green against the pallor of her face. "Do you mean you want to know which street corner the man turned?" he asked as a sense of foreboding stole over his own body. "I haven't the foggiest notion, dearest. Philadelphia is still a maze to me."

She gripped his hands, her own damp with panic. "What if he's here?"

"In Philadelphia?" He laughed hollowly. "Impossible! Dearest, you are getting yourself in a taking over a *dream* and a man who simply happened to resemble Grey. It's all coincidence, I assure you!"

"Perhaps." Francesca calmed herself, staring thoughtfully into space. After a time she said in an even voice, "It's all well and good to reassure ourselves that Grey could not be anywhere else but in France, but we know better than most that people are not always where others assume them to be. We mustn't underestimate him; he's extremely shrewd and determined when the situation demands. I want to take extra precautions." Her voice turned colder. "You'll have to take rooms of your own, David. If Grey is in Philadelphia, he'll find me, and it wouldn't do for him to discover his late brother in my bed. . . ."

"It was good of you to see me so late at night, Mr. Stringfellow," Grey said to the engaging white-haired Englishman as they seated themselves in front of the hearth in the coffeehouse's keeping room. "I know that you must be tired."

"Call me Stringfellow. Everyone does." The older man crossed his nimble legs and grinned. "And I don't mind the hour. It always takes me a while to slow down after the coffeehouse empties at night. I run about from dawn to midnight, and when I get into bed I feel like a clock that's been overwound." Pausing, Stringfellow drank thirstily from his mug of ale. "I understand that you've seen our dear Lisette."

"I have indeed. She and her family took me in after I escaped from one of Napoléon's prisons. I was half-starved and running from two of Boney's thugs, so their hospitality was

keenly appreciated.'' Feeling increasingly at ease, Grey
stretched out his booted legs and propped them on a low stool.
"Mrs. Beauvisage is delightful, and I cannot imagine that she
ever looked more beautiful. She reminded me of a yellow rose
in full bloom.'' He paused, searching his memory. ''Our meal
was delicious, completed by an apple tart that she said was
made from a recipe she used to make here. It's obvious that
she has fond memories of this place.''

Stringfellow inquired after the rest of the Beauvisage family,
and Grey obliged by giving detailed reports. "In truth, Adrienne is a little spitfire,'' he said in closing. ''The man who
falls in love with her will have his hands full.''

"Ah, just like her lovely mother! How I long to see them
all. As soon as this bloody war is over, I'm going to take
Nancy, my wife, abroad. We've never gone because of the
children, or because we couldn't leave the coffeehouse, but
life's short, hmm? Can't afford to put it off forever. . . .''
Stringfellow stared into the dying fire for a long minute, lost
in thought, then turned back to Grey with bright, dark eyes.
"Now then, how can I help you?''

"You already have, my good fellow. You gave my manservant, Jasper Speed, a great deal of important information regarding the woman you know as Francesca Wellbeloved. I
have merely come to ask a few more questions. You're the
only one who can tell me anything at all, and I feel that I can
trust you.''

"Alexandre Beauvisage stopped here yesterday and encouraged me to assist you in any way I could. He said that you
brought his daughter Natalya safely home all the way from
France.'' Stringfellow appeared to drift again, remarking, ''I
should like very much to see her again. Has anyone told you
how perfectly gorgeous she was as a child? Hair like silken
honey and those huge blue eyes. Never seen eyes that color
before or since. Like the sea. . . . She had lovely skin as well.
Her mother was another beauty. Used to pop in here with
Natalya years ago, after Lisette went to France. Lisette asked
her to look in on us, I suppose. In any event, little Natalya
would take center stage and have everyone in the keeping room

looking at her. She'd flash her dimples at us, say charming things—get us all laughing—and insist on helping Hyla with the cooking, standing on a stool and waving a wooden spoon about like the conductor of an orchestra. I used to say that she'd be on the stage one day, but I understand that she's become an authoress. Is she still a feast for the eyes?''

Grey realized that he'd been leaning forward in the bow-back chair, listening in fascination. "What? Oh—yes. Yes, she is. And she still loves drama. Natalya is . . . a most unusual woman.''

"Ah, how I appreciate a beautiful woman with an agile mind,'' Stringfellow declared. "This Francesca you are looking for is a beauty as well, so it's no wonder I heard about her almost immediately after she came to Philadelphia. Are you going to tell me what the connection is between you, and what she's done to bring you all this way in search of her?''

Grey met Stringfellow's frank gaze, his own eyes momentarily uncertain. "I must ask for your word that—''

"No one will even suspect that I've met you, sir,'' he interjected, looking a trifle offended. "Anyone in this city will tell you that I am a man of impeccable honor.''

"I did not mean to suggest otherwise, I assure you.'' Grey sighed. Setting down his empty tankard, he began to tell his story. "Francesca Wellbeloved is, in reality, Francesca St. James—my wife. We married two years ago, shortly after we met during one of my leaves from the Royal Navy. My father is an earl, and as the elder son, I am a viscount. It was an advantageous match for Francesca, and I—I wasn't quite sane. I thought I'd probably die in the war, and it seemed like the thing to do; try for an heir and all that.'' He arched an eyebrow and shrugged slightly. "And, as you said, she's beautiful—in a way that creates another sort of insanity in susceptible men. Francesca also possesses the agile mind you spoke of, but precious few other redeeming qualities. As it turns out, she's selfish, spoiled, sly, and dishonest. After I escaped from prison last month and returned to London, I discovered that she'd run away not long after our wedding. There were rumors that she'd fled to America with another man, which I was inclined to believe, and the latest gossip indicated that she'd written her father that she was leaving New York to take up residence in Philadelphia. Natalya needed to come here in any case, so I brought her myself. I want to find Francesca and confront her. I don't think I can get on with my life until the book is closed on our marriage.''

Stringfellow's brows, like tufts of white fur, bobbed up and down as he pondered this information. ''I say, that *is* quite a tale! But there's more, isn't there?''

Grey gave him a grudging smile. ''Your wits are no match for mine, Stringfellow. Yes, there's more. I discovered that Francesca took my mother's jewels when she left London. My father loaned them to her when we were married, but they wouldn't have rightfully passed to us until I assumed the earldom. Quite honestly, I consider titles a bore, but I do place some value on family possessions. Aside from the fact that these pieces are priceless, they are to remain in trust, passed down through the generations from one Countess of Hartford to the next. What Francesca did, stealing them, was unconscionable.'' His eyes flashed with suppressed anger. ''I mean to return my mother's jewels to Hartford House.''

''Here, here!'' Stringfellow set down his tankard and applauded. ''A noble cause indeed! I'll do whatever I can to help, but I must confess that I don't have much information to offer. I've seen the lady, and I've heard her name, which I told your man Speed. She's taken a house on Pine Street and hired servants. I know one or two of them, if that will help you. I believe that she's passing herself off as a widow, but I have heard rumors about a man. My wife mentioned seeing her in a bookshop with some fellow, but Nancy thought he looked a trifle drab. Gray hair and spectacles, she said, and they appeared to be having a tiff in the manner of people who know each other well.''

''Interesting,'' Grey remarked, sifting Stringfellow's revelations.

''We could doubtless gather information from her staff, and it would be easy enough for you to appear at her door and confront her.''

"No, I'd prefer to be more creative." When he smiled, his teeth flashed in the shadowy firelight. "I'm not a vindictive man, but I do believe that she ought to suffer a bit. I wouldn't mind giving her a scare; turn up next to her in a crowd and see the horror in her eyes."

"Wouldn't it be jolly if she fainted!" Stringfellow laughed, joining into the spirit of Grey's plans.

"Indeed," he agreed dryly. "I'd enjoy it immensely. I would like to toy with her a bit before I close in. Perhaps I won't even mention the jewels at first. I might play the role of heartbroken husband. . . ."

"How can we arrange such a scene?" asked the older man.

"I wonder if there isn't a way to organize a party—"

"A party for *Natalya Beauvisage*!" Stringfellow broke in. "Wouldn't that be a brilliant stroke? She's only just returned, and everyone is reading her book and longing to see her, but she's scarcely set foot in the city. It's the perfect solution." In his excitement, he jumped up and paced back and forth in the darkened keeping room. "Who would host such a party? It must be a great hostess, whose invitation your wife would be certain to accept, and it must also be someone who knows the Beauvisage family well. And, someone I know well enough to approach. I'll have to persuade her to have the party, and also make her understand that she must invite both you and Francesca Wellbeloved—"

"And the man with the gray hair and spectacles, if possible," Grey chimed in, laughing.

"I have it!" Stringfellow shouted triumphantly. "I'll ask Meagan Hampshire."

"Who's that?"

"She's the wife of Lion Hampshire, a senator, and an old friend of Caro and Alec Beauvisage's. The Hampshires just happen to be staying at their country house south of town these past few weeks, and I believe they intend to remain until June. Mrs. Hampshire is a treasure. I know I can depend upon her." Stringfellow stopped in front of Grey and announced, beaming, "By jove, I'm brilliant—if I do say so myself!"

* * *

Hyla Flowers DuBois peeled potatoes so fast that it made Natalya feel vaguely dizzy to watch her. The old woman was a marvel. She was fat now—there was no other word to describe her enormous bulk—but continued to paint her mouth and cheeks, and she liked to pin some decoration in her coarse gray hair. Today she wore a bunch of small, waxen cherries next to the coil of hair atop her head. Years ago, during the Revolution, Hyla had earned her way in the world as a prostitute, but hard living had put an end to that career. Instead she'd come to work at the coffeehouse, overseeing the chaos in the public room. Fifteen years later, when Lisette left, Hyla and Pierre married and Hyla took over the kitchen chores: by that time her feet hurt too much to labor in the keeping room from dawn to dark. In contrast with the rigors of the coffeehouse, cooking for the Beauvisage family at Belle Maison was child's play.

"I've a chore for you, sweetheart," Hyla said to Natalya. "It's unlucky to peel potatoes while someone's watching, so here's something to keep your eyes and hands busy." She handed Natalya several bunches of rhubarb, a knife, and a bowl. "Just cut the tender parts into little pieces."

"Are you going to make a pie?" Natalya asked hopefully.

"Shall I? I'd thought about a cobbler. . . ." Hyla feigned indecision.

"Oh, no, please, a pie!"

"All right, then, a pie." She pinched the girl's soft, rosy cheek. "For you, sweetheart."

Natalya hitched her rush stool closer to the worktable, sitting in the middle of a warm sunbeam. Her curls, caught back in a wide aqua ribbon, were burnished with gold dust. Hyla stood for a moment, knife and potato in hand, looking at the middle Beauvisage child. Dressed in a soft, simple gown of white muslin trimmed with aqua ribbons and inserts of Belgian lace, she was truly exquisite. Her skin was creamy, her mouth full and sensual, her eyes alert and curious.

Feeling the older woman's stare, Natalya looked up. "Is anything wrong, Hyla?"

"Mercy, no! I was just thinking how *beautiful* you are,

sweetheart. You're all soft and curvy and golden, like a ripe peach. Why haven't you gotten married?''

''Well,'' Natalya replied candidly, ''I think there's more than one reason, but the main one is that I want to be independent, and now that I've had success with my writing, I can be. I'd prefer not to answer to anyone, especially a husband. I know that Papa doesn't order Maman about, but most men do.'' She gave a philosophical shrug. ''I know myself well enough to know that such an arrangement would never do for me. I couldn't tolerate being dominated. . . .''

Hyla pondered these revelations, smiling. ''I know exactly what you mean, love. Do you know, I was fifty years old before I married Pierre. I always wanted to be on my own, too, but I came to realize that a lady has to make compromises. I never wanted to admit that I liked having a man take care of me, and yet it's true. And, I take care of him, too. The trick is to find a man who can dominate without seeming to, so's you'll find yourself enjoying it.'' She smiled broadly. ''There's no shame in admitting you need what a good man can offer. In fact, there's a sort of joy you feel deep inside; it has to do with accepting womanhood, I think. I finally learned that, and I'll wager that you will, too.''

When Natalya left the keeping room and wandered through the gardens to her great-grandmother's cottage, she found herself remembering the thrill she'd known when Grey had taken charge. She reflected on the night they'd escaped from the inn in St. Malo . . . the way he'd all but physically removed her from the cyprians' ball in London . . . his commanding resolution of the situation with Adrienne—even their most recent confrontation at the Spruce Street house, when she had intended to bully him into leaving Philadelphia and had ended up in his bed, eagerly returning his kisses. Natalya had to admit that Hyla might be right—an instinctive part of her did enjoy Grey's confident assurance, even when it meant yielding to his strength. The notion that this might be normal was almost revolutionary to her.

Shallow flagstone steps marked the entrance to the cottage, which seemed adrift in narcissus of every variety. Danielle

Beauvisage had lived nearly seventy-five years in France before retiring to Philadelphia after the death of her husband and taking up residence here on the grounds of Belle Maison. Natalya had been only four when her great-grandmother died, but she felt as if she knew her intimately, for her spirit was everywhere in and around the cottage. All her favorite flowers and herbs were planted in the tiny garden, which Alec maintained in her memory. The snug cottage was filled with Great-Grandmère's needlework on chairs, cushions, tablecloths, and bed linens, and her paintings of the garden and her loved ones lined the walls. It was a place where Natalya felt at home. Certainly she would be able to create here, she told herself each day.

The morning after her encounter with Grey in the Spruce Street house, Natalya had risen at dawn and come out to the cottage. She'd hated to disturb the familiar furnishings but had moved one drop-leaf table in front of the sitting room window and chosen an inviting wing chair to go with it. Then, during the next two days, she had found herself occupied with many tasks that had little to do with writing. She'd spent hours poring over the French books that had belonged to her great-grandmother, telling herself that one might provide needed inspiration. She'd written a letter to Nicholai, Lisette, and James, then one to Adrienne. She'd cut yellow, peach, and white narcissus and placed them in vases throughout the cottage. And she'd stared out the windows, searching for diversions.

Natalya had sworn that today would be different, but when she sat down at the table and took quill in hand, Eloise and Charles eluded her again. Hyla's words kept intruding in her mind, followed by scattered memories of Grey St. James. She'd half expected him to turn up these past three days, if only to taunt her, but there was no sign of him. Was he occupying himself with the woman Fedbusk had sighted on the street?

Voices drifted from the garden through the open window, and Natalya looked up to see Kristin and Hollis Gladstone strolling among the beds of tulips. Kristin was a vision in a green-sprigged morning gown, while Hollis looked slightly ill at ease in a dark blue coat and buff trousers. Watching them, Natalya wondered why he persisted in courting Kristin when she clearly wasn't interested. And then she wondered why, if Krissie wasn't interested, she didn't simply say so.

Hollis's bearlike shape and tousled hair appealed to Natalya's tender heart. He was speaking earnestly to Kristin, gesturing with his large hands, apparently to no avail. Kristin smiled, touched his arm, and then walked away toward the house, pausing once to look back and wave good-bye. Hollis continued to stand amid the bright beds of tulips, looking lost.

"Mr. Gladstone?" Natalya called impulsively through the window. "Will you join me for tea?"

She went out to meet him, guiding him back to the cottage, and busied herself for several minutes preparing tea while he wandered around the parlor and sitting room. His expression was both puzzled and bereft. When they were settled at last on the walnut settee, Natalya came straight to the point.

"Mr. Gladstone, I do not mean to pry, but I cannot help noticing that you do not appear to be pleased with the progress of your association with my sister. If there is anything I can do to help, I assure you that I would be happy to do so."

He gazed at her through his spectacles with bewildered green eyes. "I confess that I am in love with your sister, Miss Beauvisage, and haven't even enough pride remaining to hide that fact. I have tried everything, including getting myself up in these fashionable clothes, which she seems to admire on other men."

"They look very nice," Natalya said politely.

He grimaced and shook his head. "I may not be skilled at tying a cravat, but my regard for your sister is sincere, and I feel that we would balance each other's temperaments well. Kristin can be a trifle impractical, even hotheaded, which I say with great fondness. I cannot help but think that marriage to a stable sort of man, like me, would suit her better than a passionate love match—which would doubtless prove far too . . . incendiary. Furthermore, I do not consider myself to be boring. In ordinary circumstances, I am a cheerful sort who enjoys life to the fullest. I like to laugh, to read, to learn, and to explore the world beyond the confines of Philadelphia.'' Hollis paused for breath and ran a hand through his sandy hair. ''I am affectionate and loving. I know that I am not handsome like some of Kristin's other suitors, but I have an open heart. I would take care of her, work hard to provide nice things for her, and show her that I cherish her each and every day.''

''An open heart is the most valuable asset any man can claim,'' Natalya said, with feeling, liking him more and more. ''Mr. Gladstone, I think that you should alter your approach in courting my sister. I sense that you *are* passionate, and you must show her that. Don't follow her like a puppy, begging for her time. Stand up for yourself! Let Kristin see that you are a confident man who has pride. I believe that she longs to be swept off her feet. Show her that you have taken a firm hold on the reins of your involvement with her, and then woo her with strength and tenderness.'' She gave him a glowing smile. ''I agree with you, Mr. Gladstone. I think that you may be the perfect mate for Krissie, and I've a notion she'll come around to the same conclusion if you follow my advice.''

Hollis sat up straighter as a gleam of hope crept into his eyes. ''You're a writer of novels, aren't you? I suppose that makes you something of an expert on the subject of romance.''

''I don't know about that,'' Natalya replied, blushing as she thought of her own tangled private life. ''Perhaps I'm learning. And, I *am* Kristin's sister, which qualifies me as something of an expert on her, I suppose.''

Finishing his tea, he put the cup and saucer aside and stood up. ''I believe I'll keep my distance from Kristin for a while. Who knows? Perhaps she'll miss me just a little. And then, when we meet again, I shall do my best to put your advice into practice.'' He walked with Natalya to the cottage door. Standing on the flagstone step, he took her hand and smiled in a way that she found surprisingly winning. ''You have given me hope, Miss Beauvisage. I am more grateful for your time than you will ever know.''

''It was a pleasure, Mr. Gladstone,'' she said sincerely. ''May I add that you should smile like that more often? I think that you are handsomer than you realize.''

Natalya watched him stride purposefully toward the stables, then wandered back inside and sat down to finish her tea. All the things she had said to Hollis Gladstone came back to her, and she realized how closely they resembled Hyla's advice to *her*. Again, Natalya wondered what had become of Grey. What was he doing at that moment; whom was he with? The fleeting thought that he might have suddenly decided to return to England after all sent an unexpected chill through her body. Realizing that Grey had, almost against her will, become a stimulating, vital part of her life, Natalya decided that the time had come for her to examine her feelings honestly. Running from them only heightened the ache in her heart. . . .

Chapter Twenty-two

May 6, 1814

MADAME HENRICÔT, A FRENCH ÉMIGRÉ WHO HAD parlayed her skills as a seamstress into a highly successful career catering to Philadelphia's elite, had just delivered Natalya's new wardrobe. Alone in her bedchamber, Natalya gazed upon the delightful array of gowns for morning and evening and walking, the cashmere shawls, spencers, riding habits, and undergarments of fine soft muslin that were spread over her bed and chairs. Tomorrow her mother was taking her into the city to purchase new bonnets, shoes, parasols, and reticules to match Madame Henricôt's creations, but Natalya felt little enthusiasm for the project.

Wandering down the corridor, she discovered Caro curled on her favorite window seat in the library. A fine rain misted the glass panes behind her, and *My Lady's Heart* was open on her lap. Natalya paused in the doorway, smiling. How young her mother looked today—like a girl, really, in her gown of white muslin delicately trimmed in gold. Her amber curls were pinned loosely atop her head, and stray tendrils accentuated her lovely profile and the line of her neck. At her feet lay a long-stemmed pink tulip, resting innocently against the dove gray cushion that lined the window seat.

"Hello, Maman," Natalya greeted her softly.

"Darling!" Immediately Caro closed the book and got to her feet. "Have you been trying on your new gowns?"

"A few," she lied. They sat down together on the flame-stitched chairs facing the fireplace.

"I must tell you that, in my completely unbiased opinion, *My Lady's Heart* is sheer delight," Caro pronounced, beaming at her daughter. "I find it every bit as well written as *Pride and Prejudice*, and not nearly as slow. What a talent you have for dialogue! I'm sure you inherited it from me."

Natalya laughed, glad to be cajoled out of her bleak mood. "Oh, Maman, how silly you are!"

"On the contrary, I'm completely serious," she replied, trying not to smile. "And if anyone is qualified to judge, it is I. The scene that I am reading now is so exciting! Katherine is just about to walk into Justin's study and find him with that schemer Yvette. Will she faint at the sight of them together?"

Horrified, Natalya replied, "Maman, my heroines *never* faint!"

Alec's voice drifted to them from the hallway, followed momentarily by his appearance on the library's threshold. Next to him stood a petite, winsomely beautiful woman with black curls caught up under a straw Victoria hat, its crown turned up in front. She wore a long-sleeved gown of thin jaconet muslin over a lavender slip, the color of which accented her large violet eyes. Natalya thought that their guest looked familiar but could not place her until Caroline exclaimed:

"Meagan Hampshire! I didn't know that you and Lion were still in Philadelphia." She hurried across the library to embrace her smiling friend. "If I had known, I would have brought Natalya round to see you at Hampshire House. Is it possible that only a month has passed since we all dined together and I told you and Devon Raveneau that Talya was far away in France? Even then she was on her way home to us! How long has it been since you've seen her?"

"Years," Meagan replied as Caro caught her hand and led her toward Natalya. "I encountered James Stringfellow in town, and he told me the happy news. I couldn't be more delighted for you all!"

"I remember you very well, Mrs. Hampshire," Natalya said, extending her hand. "When I was a child, Maman took me to Hampshire House to see your three babies after their christening. I thought I was very important, touching the babies of a senator, even though I wasn't entirely certain what a senator *was*!''

Amid the ensuing laughter, Alec said, ''I'll have refreshments sent up and then return to join you.'' None of the women noticed when he disappeared.

''Since the nation's capital was moved from Philadelphia to Washington, our visits here have been far too scarce and brief to suit me,'' Meagan said as they sat down on wing chairs. ''How difficult it is to realize that our children have all grown! The war has stolen Ben and Michael, but Susan is with us. Wait until you see her, Natalya! She's quite the coquette, yet I have reason to believe that Susie may be falling in love at last. I have such dreams for her wedding!''

''I know what you mean,'' Caro said, with a wry smile. ''My own wedding was such a hurried affair that I long to give my daughters more. Yet Kristin cannot find a man she judges worthy, and Talya seems set against the notion of marriage altogether.''

Natalya felt obliged to reply, though her usual arguments sounded hollow somehow. ''I simply want to remain an individual, and that is difficult to do in a marriage. In our society, women can enjoy freer exercise of mind and fancy in a single life. That may be unfair, but I fear it is true. As long as I am able to retain financial independence, why should I restrict myself in a marriage?''

Caro and Meagan looked at each other for a long moment, their delicate brows lifted slightly. Taking a breath, Meagan said, ''I suppose that makes a good deal of sense, in theory, but love rarely heeds philosophy. When you meet the man who challenges your mind, arouses your senses, and treats you with respect and justice, all the theories in the world won't matter.''

Caro smiled and nodded. ''Well said, Meagan.''

''Of course, it will not be easy for you to meet such a man if you stay hidden here at Belle Maison—''

''I am writing a book!'' Natalya protested.

''Very admirable, I'm sure, but there must be more to a

balanced life. I would like to do my part to welcome you back to America, so Lion and I would like to give a party in your honor. Would that please you?'' Meagan's tone was firm yet kind. ''I thought it would be lovely to have the party in the afternoon. Our gardens at Hampshire House are glorious this month, and Bramble, our cook, is already planning the food. Even Stringfellow has offered his services, so you simply must agree!''

''How kind you are, Meagan,'' Caro exclaimed, her face aglow with pleasure. Turning to her daughter, she said, ''It would be a wonderful opportunity for you to meet people your own age.''

''You mean men, don't you, Maman?'' Natalya smiled in spite of herself. ''But, of course I'll agree. It is very generous of you and Senator Hampshire to go to so much trouble for me.''

''Good!'' Meagan clapped her hands triumphantly. ''I must confess that I am happier than you can imagine to have a reason for a real party. I miss our friends here. It was a stroke of good fortune that we had to come north to meet with Devon and Andre Raveneau when they came from Connecticut last month, otherwise I should never have been able to shake Lion loose from Washington. Now, we've lingered on to enjoy the spring, and this party for Natalya will be a perfect way to crown our weeks in Philadelphia. How *pleased* I am!''

Alec appeared then, carrying a silver tray laden with blown-glass tumblers etched with a tulip pattern. The glasses were filled with iced lemonade, and Hyla had sent along a plate of freshly baked molasses applesauce cookies. Kristin followed her father into the library, sipping from her own tumbler of lemonade, and pulled up a chair to join the group in front of the fireplace.

''Isn't it a divine afternoon in spite of the showers?'' she asked. ''Mrs. Hampshire is giving a party and we shall have a full week to dream about it. I wonder if I should have a new gown made?''

''How did you know about the party?'' Natalya inquired, a

bit put out that her sister had begun making plans before she had even agreed to the affair.

"Papa and I spoke to Mrs. Hampshire downstairs. Aren't you thrilled? Oh, Talya, wait until you see Susan Hampshire! She's one of my dearest friends—even though she does steal away half my beaus!" Glancing at Meagan, she hastened to add, "Not that she means to. It's just that Susie is the most captivating creature. I fear that Grey St. James will take one look at her and fall desperately in love."

Meagan leaned forward at the mention of Grey. "I am looking forward to meeting this man myself. I do hope he accepts our invitation. I have heard that he is devastatingly handsome."

"He looks much like Papa did when he was young," Kristin agreed. "And he's utterly charming and witty, in that very attractive, dry sort of way."

"Well, I wouldn't count on St. James making an appearance," Alec interjected. "I've yet to pry him out of the Spruce Street house. He always has a glib reason not to come out with me, but it still seems damned odd." He shrugged, adding, "It's almost as if he's hiding, but for what purpose I cannot imagine."

Natalya, who had been dying for days to ask her father if he had news of Grey, turned these words over in her mind, then set them aside to examine later at length. At the moment, Kristin's future was more important. "Mrs. Hampshire," she said, turning toward Meagan, "I do hope that you will invite Kristin's friend, Hollis Gladstone. He is surely one of the finest men in Philadelphia."

Kristin gave her a quizzical look. "I wasn't aware that you and Hollis were well acquainted."

"We've become friends, and I like him enormously," she replied, meeting Kristin's stare.

"Hollis Gladstone, did you say?" Meagan put in, oblivious to the tension between the two sisters. "I'll certainly add him to our list, and anyone else you would like to invite."

"That's very kind; thank you," Natalya said, with a polite smile, watching her sibling out of the corner of her eye.

"It's getting rather warm in here. I believe I'll go and sort through my gowns," Kristin announced, and rose gracefully from her chair. "My intuition tells me that Grey St. James *will* come to the Hampshires' party, and I intend to be prepared!"

She bade Meagan a polite good afternoon and had just reached the doorway when a fuming Natalya hurried after her. From the hallway, Natalya's raised voice carried clearly back to the three older adults seated in the library.

"Krissie, don't be a dolt! He's only a man under his looks, and a complicated one at that. He's jaded and hard—and far too old for you! Besides, it's only been lately that he's looked like this. When I first met him, he was pale and thin from prison, and this burst of renewed vigor he's enjoying probably won't last."

Kristin continued on to her bedchamber, out of earshot of their parents and Meagan Hampshire. Once there, she whirled on her sister, eyes flashing. "You told me that I should scold you if you tried to give me advice, so consider this a scold! I'm a grown woman, Talya, not a child." She looked away, out the window, and as her thoughts turned to Grey St. James, her voice softened. "I find it vastly romantic that he was pale and wan after being locked away from the world by that monster Napoléon. And to think that he's recovered so quickly and so splendidly . . . " Kristin sighed. "Oh, Talya, can you imagine making love with such a man? I vow, I could risk ruining my reputation for such an experience. . . ."

Francesca lay next to David in her ornately curtained bed and thought back to the nights and days she had spent in Grey's arms. The pillow that cradled her head was redolent of her special scent and David's perspiration, and he snored gently while she stared up at the canopy. In a few moments she would have to awaken him and send him back to his rooms on Water Street, but for now she relished the opportunity to wander through her secret memories.

The dreams she'd been having about Grey both disturbed and excited her. Bored now with David and their scandalous affair, she found herself having second thoughts about the husband she'd abandoned so carelessly. Grey might be a cold-blooded libertine who could never worship her the way his brother did, but she had ever been prone to discontent, wanting what she did not possess. After Grey had returned to France, she had moped for weeks, desperately lonely, starved for attention, and certain that the war would leave her a widow. When David had appeared on the scene, his unrestrained infatuation had been just the entertainment she'd hungered for. Grey had never betrayed the least weakness where she was concerned, and it had galled her. Running away with David after his desertion in battle had been both a grand, thrilling adventure and a secret source of pleasure as she'd imagined the pain Grey's pride would suffer when he came home to find her gone. Part of her had wished he, and all of London, could know the identity of her lover. Then he'd be sorry for not loving her.

Was he dead? she wondered now. Or would he be returning soon to London? Remembering the tempestuous nature of their lovemaking, if it could be called that, Francesca began to grow warm all over. He had been like a panther in bed, powerful, wild, and tireless. There had been no tenderness between them, only a struggle for fulfillment and control. She had been able to fool all the other men, fool them into believing she was a goddess. Before Grey, *she* had always been the one to withhold love, knowing that men thrived on challenge and would remain smitten only as long as she held her heart just out of reach. Grey had been the only one who refused to play her game, who seemed to know what she was really like, and this had maddened her. Now, however, she longed for a challenge of her own. What if she hadn't given up so quickly? Perhaps, after Grey came back from the war, he would have surrendered to her eventually.

Meanwhile, she'd still be a viscountess. The frosty Earl of Hartford could not live forever, and when he died Grey would inherit his title and all the Hartford estates and material possessions.

David made a gurgling sound in his sleep, and Francesca

glanced over at him with disdain. She really couldn't bear him anymore. Although he had been an amusing enough companion over the past two years, he now bored her to tears. She found that she was tired of making all the decisions; she longed to be taken care of. Unfortunately David had neither prospects nor ambition.

Moving him out of her house and into rooms of his own had been the first step in easing him out of her life completely. When she made her debut in Philadelphia society, she wanted to be unencumbered. Sometimes she fantasized about abandoning David without an explanation, returning to England, and winning Grey back. If David turned up one day, she doubted he'd want to tell anyone where and with whom he'd been. However, it would be far wiser and safer, she realized, to marry a rich Philadelphian and settle down as a faintly decadent member of American society. Even with the war on, there were plenty of wealthy men in this area. But first she had to meet them.

Carefully she slipped out of bed and drew on a Chinese silk wrapper. The soft, cool fabric moved sensuously against her flesh as she carried a candlestick across the room to her dressing table. Glancing back at the bed to make certain that David still slept, she opened the middle drawer and withdrew a key that was hidden under the drawer's false bottom. A profusion of ribbons and lace threatened to spill out of the deeper drawer Francesca now opened on the opposite side of the dressing table. She sorted through the tangled ribbons and took out the carved box below, opening it with the key. Her eyes gleamed at the sight of the Hartford jewels, which Francesca considered her possessions. She'd had to sell a ring and a sapphire pin in New York, but the rest of the collection was intact. The jewels were her security and her calling card into Philadelphia society.

On top of a priceless ruby-and-diamond necklace lay a small parchment note, folded over, its waxen seal broken. Francesca opened it and read again:

Senator and Mrs. Lion Hampshire request the pleasure of your company at a garden party in honor of Miss Natalya

Beauvisage, author of *My Lady's Heart*. We hope that you
will join us at Hampshire House at two o'clock on the fifteenth of May, 1814.

Francesca had heard of the Hampshires but had no idea how
they knew of her. She had seen the volume in question displayed in bookshops around Society Hill but was certain she
had never met its author. Still, she had wasted little time ques-
tioning the invitation. Unbeknownst to David, she would go
to this garden party, outshine the guest of honor with ease,
and launch herself into Philadelphia's best circles. With a bit
of luck and finesse, she might be married before the leaves
turned in autumn. . . .

"Of *course* I'm going to Talya's party!" Antonia Beauvisage exclaimed as she sidled toward the front door, hoping that
her daughter-in-law and granddaughter would follow her lead.
"I wouldn't miss it for the world."

Natalya glanced at her mother, wondering if she, too, felt
that Grandmama was behaving strangely. She'd been flustered
when they appeared at her door with two baskets of strawberries, chatted with them distractedly while stealing peeks at the
tall case clock, and now she was edging them right out of the
house.

"I hope our unexpected visit hasn't been an inconvenience,
Grandmama," Natalya said a trifle stiffly. "I'm to blame, you
know. It's just that ever since I've come home I've hoped to
spend more time with you."

"Oh, my little love, I have wanted to spend more time with
you, too," Antonia declared, embracing her granddaughter.
"And a visit from you could never inconvenience me! I fear,
though, that even little old women like me need a little privacy
from time to time in order to sort out their lives. If I seem
preoccupied, you must remember that it has no bearing at all
on the love I feel for you, Talya."

Caro smiled at her mother-in-law and took Natalya's hand.
"Have I told you how beautiful you are looking, Antonia? I

have always loved that gown on you, and I vow that there are roses in your cheeks.''

''Thank you, darling!'' She kissed Caro's cheek and opened the front door. ''Now then, you two should be on your way if you are going to deliver that basket of strawberries to Mr. St. James. It was kind of you to bring so many berries to me, but I could never eat them all. Much better to give the other basket to him.''

''I've been wanting to see how he's doing,'' Caro agreed, ''and this gives us a perfect excuse to stop by. Take care of yourself, Antonia, and we'll see you at the garden party.''

When Caro and her daughter were in the carriage and Antonia had shut the front door, Natalya said, ''I am worried about Grandmama. She's behaving very oddly.''

''What nonsense,'' Caro replied, laughing. ''She has never looked better.''

''But this is the second time since my return that she has refused to allow a proper visit. Do you think she wants to be alone because she is still feeling melancholy about Grandpapa's death? If so, I can understand—''

''No, I don't think she is sitting in a darkened room and weeping for Jean-Philippe, nor would he want her to. My hope is that your grandmother is beginning to live again.''

Natalya brushed a loose curl back from her temple. ''Krissie suspects that Grandmama may have a *beau*. Can you imagine?''

''Yes, frankly, I can,'' her mother said gently.

''Maman! Why that's almost''— she groped for the right word—''blasphemy!''

''How absurd. Your grandmother is a woman, not a saint.''

''But, even if it *were* true, why would she hide it from us?'' Natalya felt numb with disbelief.

''Perhaps because she is afraid some of us might not be happy for her,'' Caro replied, her tone faintly accusatory. ''In any event, she is free to do as she chooses, and to tell us only as much as she cares to, in her own time. Meanwhile, it is getting late and we must hurry to Spruce Street.'' She gave instructions to the coachman and they were on their way.

Sinking back against the upholstered seat, Natalya tried to

subdue the flood of emotions that overwhelmed her. Normally she would have been brooding about her grandmother, but the prospect of seeing Grey within minutes overrode everything else. As the coach clattered over the cobbles, past sturdy brick houses that seemed to glow in the gathering twilight, Natalya tried to decide how she would behave and what she would say to Grey St. James.

"Here we are," Caro said almost immediately.

Rodney, the coachman, helped them down, and as they approached the front door Natalya whispered, "I ought to warn you—Grey's butler is rather . . . unique."

"Is he?" her mother replied, brown eyes twinkling. "That sounds promising."

They had to knock twice before Fedbusk threw open the door. His cravat was tied in a style that had no name, and his black breeches sagged. "M'I help you?"

"It is I, Fedbusk—Natalya Beauvisage," she said, smiling in spite of the nervous drumming of her heart. "This is my mother, Mrs. Alexandre Beauvisage. Is Mr. St. James in?"

Fedbusk nodded at Caro, then cleared his throat loudly, as if considering his answer with care. "Aye, the master's in . . . but I think he might be busy."

"Perhaps you could tell him that we are here, and have brought him a basket of strawberries from Belle Maison," Caro suggested, bestowing one of her most charming smiles upon the unwitting Fedbusk. "We merely wanted to pay our respects, and would not keep Mr. St. James above a few minutes."

The grizzled butler turned pink under his sunburn and very nearly smiled himself. "Well, mum . . . I suppose I could tell him that."

"We'll wait in the parlor," Natalya said firmly, setting the basket of strawberries on a carved Pembroke table.

As they crossed the entrance hall and watched Fedbusk mount the flying staircase, Caro murmured, "I do adore this house. Sometimes I would almost prefer living here to Belle Maison if only for the pleasure of going up and down the stairs all day long."

"Maman, you don't mean that," Natalya replied automatically. They entered the parlor and seated themselves on the chair-back settee that Caro had ordered from Ephraim Haines in 1807. Over the next few minutes Natalya managed to chat with her mother about the furniture, but her mind was running frantically upstairs after Fedbusk. Was Grey there? Would he come down to greet them? It seemed an eternity since she had said good-bye and left this house in the company of her father. Her feelings about Grey had undergone changes since that night, and it seemed reasonable to assume that his may have, too. Was that why he hadn't come to Belle Maison? Was he avoiding her? Did he regret what had passed between them? Or was he occupied with the mysterious woman Fedbusk had sighted on the street?

Questions and fears danced together in Natalya's imagination, while a flush stained her cheeks. She wished there were a mirror; did she look pretty? When she and her mother had departed from Belle Maison, there had been no thought of seeing Grey, and in consequence she had worn a simple gown of ecru muslin with gold ribbons. Perhaps it did not suit her. Was her hair mussed? What if—

"Well, what a pleasant surprise." Grey spoke from the doorway, and Natalya's heart leaped in response. He looked stunningly handsome as he crossed the parlor, the long muscles of his thighs flexing under his buff-colored trousers. His linen shirt was snow white, his cravat impeccably tied in the mathematical, and he wore a waistcoat of dark blue velvet that set off his silver-gray eyes and black hair.

"Mrs. Beauvisage," he said, bending over Caro's hand, "I am sorry that you had to seek me out. It is I who should have paid a call upon you before today."

"You must call me Caro, for we do not bother with such formalities in our family." Dimples winked at him when she smiled. "Talya and I have simply brought you a basket of strawberries and our regards. And I wanted to see for myself that you were comfortable here. If you need *anything*, you have only to ask."

"Strawberries! I love them better than anything. You and

your family make me feel completely at home in Philadelphia, Caro, and I appreciate your kindness more than you know.'' He drew up a chair, sat down, and looked at Natalya. ''Can I offer you ladies some refreshment? Lemonade, perhaps? Or—strawberries?''

Natalya was dismayed by her own shyness. She felt exactly as she had at fourteen, when she had been certain she was in love with Nathan Raveneau during a family visit to Pettipauge, Connecticut. She longed to search Grey's eyes for some sign of his feelings but could not summon the courage to meet his gaze. It seemed impossible that they had once been so close, quarreling across France, kissing in the back of a carriage in London, laughing over a picnic lunch on the *Rover*'s quarterdeck, and lying together naked, touching, kissing, making love. . . .

''Talya?'' Caro nudged her gently. ''I said that it's time for us to go. Hyla will have dinner prepared, and your father will begin to worry if we don't start for Germantown now.''

''Oh—yes!'' Blushing, she glanced up and found that Grey was looking at her, his eyes unreadable. ''It's nice to see you again . . . Grey.''

He gave her his hand, careful to keep his touch light as she rose from the settee. ''I'm sorry that you two have to rush off, but I do understand.''

As they walked into the entrance hall, Caro inquired, ''Will we see you at the Hampshires' party on Saturday?''

''I wouldn't miss it for the world,'' Grey assured her. His gaze wandered to Natalya, who was walking in front of him, and he had to stop himself from reaching out to brush a rebellious curl from her brow. She gave him only a fleeting glance as good-byes were exchanged, and then he was alone again.

Grey returned to the parlor, staring pensively through the parted curtains as a young coachman helped Natalya and her mother into the handsome carriage. Staying in this house was driving him mad, but he knew that he had no choice, just as he had no choice regarding Natalya Beauvisage. He had to keep her at arm's length, both physically and mentally, until the matter with Francesca was resolved. Again he reminded himself that he was still a married man, and nothing must interfere with his revenge against his wife. . . .

Chapter Twenty-three

May 15, 1814

NATALYA STARED AT HERSELF IN THE QUEEN ANNE looking glass that hung on her bedroom wall. Her chemise-style gown, the loveliest of Madame Henricôt's creations, was fashioned of thin peach jaconet muslin over a champagne-tinted taffeta slip. The bodice was daringly décolleté, and the sleeves puffed out at the shoulders, then fit close to her arms, covering the backs of her hands with two buttons undone. Straw-colored kid slippers peeked out from under the gown's lace-edged hem, and there were matching gloves on the bed next to a peach-and-champagne-striped parasol.

"Maman, are you certain I look all right?" Natalya inquired of Caro, who stood in the dressing room door.

"You are exquisite, love," she confirmed. "Your great-grandmère's choker is an ideal finishing touch. She would be so happy if she could see you today."

Natalya touched the pearl choker that encircled her graceful neck. Its rosy-peach cameo centerpiece coordinated perfectly with her gown. "I adore it. Thank you for letting me wear it."

Caroline walked over and slipped an arm around her daughter's waist. She wore a simple, elegant gown of pale yellow muslin with primrose accents, and in the old, slightly hazy looking glass they appeared more like sisters than mother and daughter. "The choker is a gift, Talya, from Papa and me and your great-grandmère. She would want you to have it."

268

"Oh, Maman," she whispered, her eyes misting. "You are too good to me."

"You're my daughter and I love you." Caro fussed a little with the champagne satin ribbons that wound through Natalya's artfully loose, upswept curls. "I want you to be happy . . . today of all days. You know that I couldn't be prouder that you are using your talent to write, but I hope that you won't pursue the dreams in your novels at the expense of your own."

Natalya's mind and heart were full of Grey and the knowledge that she would see him today at the garden party. Lying awake during the night, she had realized that she was badly in need of advice, and now she took a deep breath and prepared to confide in her mother.

"Caro?" It was Alec, clad only in dark blue kerseymere trousers and a pleated white shirt. He stood on the threshold to the dressing rooms, a neckcloth in each hand. "Aren't you coming back? I can't remember which cravat I'd decided to wear."

His wife laughed girlishly and shook her head. "Is this the same man who would not allow a woman to touch his clothes when I met him?"

Grinning at Natalya, Alec countered, "It's a plot, you know. A clandestine plot among wives! Somehow, we gullible husbands are hoodwinked into believing that we can no longer match colors or trust ourselves to know if a coat hangs properly once we've taken marriage vows. Before we realize what has happened, we've dismissed our valets because we don't want them poking about the bedchamber at odd hours, and we find ourselves depending shamelessly on our wives when we have to get dressed. It's a source of secret embarrassment to grown men, I can assure you!"

Still laughing, Caroline took Alec's arm to lead him back into the dressing room. He gave his daughter a wink in parting. "You're a vision, Talya," he called before disappearing. "It's clear that I'll have to spend the afternoon protecting you from frothing would-be suitors!"

"Thank you, Papa," Natalya replied, with a giggle. Then,

gathering her gloves and parasol, she went across the hall to see if her sister had finished dressing. She wanted to put in a good word for Hollis Gladstone before they left for Hampshire House.

Meanwhile, Caro helped Alec choose a cravat and watched him tie it, her eyes pensive. He brushed back his white hair, slipped on a waistcoat of gold-and-blue figured silk, then sat before his shaving stand and drew her down on his lap. "Where have you gone, *chérie*?" he murmured. "Your thoughts are miles away."

"Years, actually," Caro amended, with a catch in her voice. "I was thinking back to the weeks after I first came here, not even knowing who I really was. I see myself in our darling Talya and remember when I slept in her field bed and dreamed of you across the walls. Oh, Alec, how quickly the years have sped away from us!" She gazed into his turquoise eyes and touched the face that was so dear to her. "It seems such a short while since I used to visit darling Grandmère in her cottage. How she loved to surprise us by appearing through the secret passageways." A tear slipped down Caro's cheek, and Alec kissed it away, holding her securely in his arms. "I remember our first Christmas, when you declared your love for me at last. What good times we had, dancing in the garden under the moonlight, ice-skating on the Delaware River, riding our horses over the meadows in the spring . . ."

"Darling Caro, we still do those things!"

"Yes, but there is something special about experiencing such things when you are young . . . and falling in love. The years pass so quickly. How can it be that we have been together more than thirty years, that our son is now a father, and our daughters past twenty?" Her voice throbbed with emotion. "I want to tell Talya that she cannot afford to put her own needs and dreams aside, waiting for the day to come when she is better able to confront them. Each day is a precious gift that must be embraced, even if it holds challenges that are difficult to face!"

"Ah, Caro, how I love you," her husband murmured, kissing her. "As for Talya, take heart. Perhaps today will be the day our child summons the courage to embrace her life. You don't need to tell her; she's watched you do that very thing since the moment of her birth.''

"You always say just the right thing. . . ."

"Do I?" He brightened. "That's encouraging. I fear I'm too old to change even if you insisted on it.''

Caro rested her cheek against his. "I love you just as you are, Alec. Besides, you will never be old.''

He was chuckling when two female voices chorused from the hallway, "Maman! Papa! It's time to leave for Hampshire House!''

Laughing, Lion Hampshire reached out to grasp the back of his wife's gown as she rushed past him. "Slow down, fondling. You don't want to look *harried* when you greet your guests!" He glanced over at Stringfellow, who was carrying a tray of miniature almond cheesecakes toward one of the garden tables. "I love that word '*harried*,' don't you? Splendid word.''

Nodding thoughtfully, Stringfellow replied, "Splendid indeed, sir. May I add that it's a pleasure to hear it used in conversation?''

Meagan turned to face her husband, arms akimbo and violet eyes twinkling. "Have you two been into the Madeira? No, I see that you are teasing me. Well, that's all well and good, but you must promise not to carry on this way in front of our guests.''

Although he had recently celebrated his fifty-eighth birthday, Senator Lion Hampshire looked and felt much younger. There were silver strands in his golden hair and lines etched in his tanned face, but he remained a remarkably attractive man. His eyes glinted now with desire as they swept over Meagan. Her gown was reminiscent of the one she'd worn twenty-five years ago to President Washington's inauguration in New York. Fashioned of cream silk overlaid with gauzy lilac muslin, it was cut low to display the upper curves of her breasts, which were further accentuated by a silk ribbon marking the gown's high waist. Around her neck she wore the necklace of three exquisite amethysts he had given her after their triplets were born, and sprays of lilac had been woven into her ebony curls.

"You grow more beautiful with each new day," Lion told her softly.

Meagan knew he meant it and glowed in response. "You are looking very handsome yourself, Senator, but don't let it go to your head!"

It was nearly one o'clock and there wasn't time to worry further; the guests would soon be arriving. Gazing around the garden and into the spacious parlor, Meagan smiled. The parlor in particular was always a source of pride to her. White-and-dove-gray paneled walls complemented the bloodred moreen chairs and draperies, while the blue, gray, and cranberry Kuba rug and brass accent pieces harmonized perfectly to complete the effect. Today, the garden doors were thrown open, more chairs had been added around the parlor, and Meagan herself had labored over the floral arrangements: fragrant clusters of lilacs, red and white tulips, peonies, hyacinths, and purple anemones. A trio of soberly clad musicians sat near the garden doors with their harpsichord, flute, and violin, quietly tuning their instruments, and in the far corner of the parlor reposed a handsome cherrywood desk. Meagan planned to have Natalya sit there and inscribe the copies of *My Lady's Heart* that Mr. Thomas had promised to bring from his Chestnut Street bookshop.

The garden was in full spring bloom. Pink and white dogwood and apple tree blossoms scented the air, mingling with the sweet fragrance of violet wisteria that cascaded over the arbor wall. The gardens near the house were rather formal, with neat boxwood hedges surrounding beds of tulips and roses just beginning to bud. Here, Meagan and Bramble, the Hampshires' ancient, dour cook, had arranged tables with embroidered cloths. Bramble and Nancy Stringfellow had labored all week over the food, most of which now covered the tables in gay profusion. There was a beautifully carved Virginia ham, iced oysters garnished with lemon and horseradish, a smoked turkey, and a huge Chinese bowl filled with spiced shrimp.

Accompanying the meats were dishes of Carolina red rice, succotash, sliced carrots, and sweet-and-sour red cabbage. Another table was arrayed with neatly sliced loaves of all types of bread: rye, Anadama, raisin, potato, Sally Lunn, and Boston brown bread. Accompanying the breads were dishes of sweet butter, honey, and an assortment of Bramble's famous preserves.

"Lion," Meagan scolded when she saw him reach for a slice of raisin bread, "you'll spoil the symmetry!"

He gave her a look that suggested she was carrying things too far and began to eat the bread. "I'm hungry, sweeting. Show your husband some mercy."

Smiling indulgently, Meagan surveyed the other tables. Fresh fruit, including grapes, strawberries, segmented oranges, pomegranates, and wedges of melon, were colorfully arranged on platters. There were bowls of nuts and tiny iced cakes topped with candied violets. One entire table was devoted to desserts, including a Williamsburg orange cake, blueberry betty, concord grape trifle garnished with almonds and frosted grapes, cocoa cake, and the almond cheesecakes.

Stringfellow had arranged the beverages on a table in a sheltered corner of the garden near the wisteria arbor. Bottles of sherry, madeira, and other wines stood behind pitchers of iced ciders and tea and one large bowl of champagne punch with raspberries. Meagan had provided him with a chair, and he was now at his station, feet propped on a large rock.

Bramble wore one of the black, old-fashioned gowns she had owned since working for William and Anne Bingham twenty-five years ago at their legendary Mansion House in Society Hill. No one knew the cook's exact age, but it had seemed to Meagan that she was excessively old when they first met in 1789.

Meagan had come to Philadelphia from Virginia after her parents died and she had been informed that she would live with her fusty aunt Agatha. Instead she had chosen to masquerade as a ladies' maid to her friend, Priscilla, who had arranged to travel to Philadelphia to marry Lion Hampshire. Priscilla and Meagan had stayed with the Binghams', then the

city's richest and most socially prominent citizens. A great
many changes had taken place since then. Meagan and Lion
had fallen in love and married, Bramble had come to work for
them, and Priscilla had died in childbirth at nineteen after
marrying another man. The government had moved its capital
from Philadelphia to Washington in 1800, uprooting the
Hampshire family and many others. Yet Meagan knew that
she would see familiar faces today, and despite the changes
wrought by time and progress, Philadelphia herself was much
the same.

"Your guests be coming," Bramble muttered to Meagan.
Although the old cook was bent and appeared frail, she refused to give in to age, working as she always had and eschew-
ing rest.

"Bramble, why don't you sit down?" Meagan urged as she
started toward the parlor. The cook's only response was a snort
of disgust.

Nancy Stringfellow had already welcomed the Beauvisage
family, and now Lion and Meagan met them in the parlor.
Even though a year or more might pass between visits, their
friendship remained warm and constant. Greetings were exchanged all around, compliments were given and received,
and then Lion stepped to the foot of the Chinese Chippendale
staircase and called his daughter.

A door upstairs burst open and Susan Hampshire hurried
down the steps, pausing midway to strike a pose for the benefit
of her father. "Well?" She rested a hand on one hip and tilted
her chin upward. "What do you think?"

Lion smiled up at her, delighted as always by his daughter's
style. She was a lovely creature, with hair the color of sunshine
and eyes of ocean blue. Petite, winsome, and headstrong—
like her mother, Lion reflected wryly—she looked deceptively
angelic today in a simple gown of white muslin accented with
daffodil-yellow ribbons. "You are a picture of springtime,"
he told her, holding out his hand.

Susie fairly ran down the remaining steps and kissed her
father's cheek. "Thank you, Papa. Another perfect compliment!"

She then hurried over to greet Kristin Beauvisage, who was a vision in a lace-edged chemise-gown tinted the color of pink rosebuds. Krissie's raven hair had been wound into a high Grecian knot that emphasized the classic beauty of her face and graceful neck, and her thick-lashed eyes seemed more vividly turquoise than ever. "I vow, Kristin," Susan exclaimed, "I shall never attend another party with you. I labor for hours striving for mere *prettiness*, and then I encounter *you*! It's so discouraging!"

These complaints were belied by the affectionate sparkle in Susie's eyes. She turned to kiss her mother, chatted with Caro and Alec, and fussed over Natalya, whose book she had read and adored. Finally, as other guests began to arrive, Meagan pried the guest of honor away from her daughter.

"Many people wrote to me, in response to our invitation, to ask if you might inscribe copies of *My Lady's Heart* during the party," Meagan said, leading Natalya toward the corner desk. "Mr. Thomas has agreed to bring his entire stock—ah, there he is now!" She waved to the diminutive, balding gentleman who was entering the parlor followed by a clerk loaded with books.

As she greeted Mr. Thomas, whose bookshop was one of many she had frequented with her parents since childhood, Natalya knew a vague sense of discomfort. Would people think her vain and self-important if they found her holding court at her own desk in the Hampshires' parlor? On the other hand, it might be fun to bask in her own accomplishment, which was, after all, unique and considerable. As Mr. Thomas's clerk stacked copies of *My Lady's Heart* on the mahogany Queen Anne desk, Natalya felt herself respond to the drama inherent in the situation. People were already looking at her and the books, and she felt special.

"I hope you don't mind that I made these arrangements without consulting you," Meagan said, touching Natalya's arm. "I couldn't imagine that you'd object, though. How often do any of us receive recognition for our talents? If you're going to be famous, you may as well wade in and enjoy it!"

"I'll do my best," Natalya agreed, with a game smile.

Moments later she was sitting at the desk, inscribing books to old friends and people she pretended to remember. Mr. Thomas conducted his business discreetly, merely making note of each person who selected a book so that he could present his bill later, in less conspicuous surroundings.

The line that quickly formed was made up mainly of friends of the Beauvisage family who were anxious to offer congratulations and anecdotes related to some event from her childhood that proved her talent had been evident all along. Natalya knew the old society families: the Willings, Powels, Shippens, Biddles, Penns, Chews, Wistars, and Wisters. She recognized her parents' friends, and most of their children as well, for they had been at school together and later attended the select dancing assemblies that often served to launch young ladies into society and, in some cases, act as a breeding ground for stiff and proper marriages. The dancing assemblies had been part of the reason Natalya had fled Philadelphia for Europe; rigid, suffocating affairs, they had left her resentful and determined to escape. The course charted for her as a daughter of wealth and society had nothing in common with the life she envisioned for herself. Perhaps she wasn't happier than the couples who had married, produced babies, and now spent their time at country homes and city clubs, but at least she had been able to pursue her dreams in her own way. . . .

Natalya found that she was quite entertained by these chats with old friends. It was fun to learn which suitor had been chosen and how many children had since been born, but after a while she noticed that more and more unattached men were standing near the back of the line. Emboldened after a glass or two of Madeira, they were eyeing her with appreciative curiosity.

"I'm an old friend of your grandmother's, and I watched you grow up in church," an elderly woman was saying as she presented her book for Natalya to inscribe. "I bought this myself last week, and I read it to find out what all the fuss was about. It's apparent that you have talent, child, but I must say that I was shocked by your references to . . . pleasures of the flesh. I cannot imagine what your family must think!"

"You would have to ask them that question yourself, Mrs. Armstrong," Natalya replied politely after signing her name under a brief, personalized inscription. "However, I do feel that no one should read my book simply because they know me. You see, I must write to please myself and those who appreciate this type of novel. If this is not the sort of book you generally prefer, there is no reason why an acquaintance with the author would change your opinion. In fact, I daresay we are often more critical of artists and writers whom we know because they are more human to us. Don't you agree?" She gave her a charming smile and returned the book to its owner.

"Well, I suppose there is some sense in that. . . ."

"I'm so pleased that you came today, and I hope that you'll have a wonderful time. Isn't it a lovely afternoon?"

"Splendid, my dear. Thank you." Mrs. Armstrong wandered off, wearing a rather bemused smile.

Next in line were Raphael and Rembrandt Peale, sons of the great painter Charles Willson Peale. They were more than a decade older than Natalya, but she had danced with them at assemblies and loved to visit the stimulating Peale home, which was always filled with children, inventions, stuffed animals being prepared for exhibit in the elder Peale's museum, and paintings by members of the family in various stages of completion. Now, after animatedly discussing *My Lady's Heart* with her and exchanging information and news, Raphael and Rembrandt drew a younger man forward.

"This is Thomas Sully," Rembrandt informed her. "He came to Philadelphia just four years ago, while you were in France. He's studied with Gilbert Stuart in Boston, and with our own Benjamin West in London."

"I've heard of you, Mr. Sully," exclaimed Natalya, extending her hand. "You're the portrait painter whom everyone is talking about. Papa has mentioned having me sit for you, if you can fit me into your schedule."

"I like your father very much," he said, with a smile. "And it would be a great honor to paint a woman as beautiful as you."

At that moment Grey St. James was just entering the parlor,

blocked from Natalya's view by the Peale brothers and Thomas
Sully. Meagan came forward to greet him and introduce herself.

"I'm so pleased that you could attend, Mr. St. James. Everyone is talking about the dashing Englishman who brought
Natalya safely home, but few have met you save our dear
Stringfellow." Noticing that his silvery eyes were surveying
the crowd as she spoke, Meagan added, "You'll doubtless
want to speak to Natalya, but she is rather occupied at the
moment, inscribing books for her many admirers. It's so exciting to have a woman author in Philadelphia!"

One side of Grey's mouth turned up in a grim smile. "And
who better to play such a role than Natalya Beauvisage?"

"I beg your pardon?" Meagan replied, momentarily nonplussed. Was that a note of sarcasm in his voice? An incurable
matchmaker, she had been intensely curious to meet the man
who had aroused such strong reactions from the Beauvisage
ladies. She had heard rumors of Grey's chiseled good looks,
which had led her to imagine various possibilities for the relationship between him and Natalya. How romantic it would
be if he had fallen in love with Natalya at sea and remained in
Philadelphia to woo her! Now, as Meagan watched him observe Natalya laughing with Thomas Sully and the Messrs.
Peale, she wondered at his caustic retort. Was he being un-
kind—or did he perhaps care more than he would admit? . . .

"Miss Beauvisage has a flair for the dramatic," Grey explained. "And, she is beautiful. A much more satisfactory
candidate for the role of female author than a timid, plain
bluestocking, don't you agree?" He had softened the edge in
his voice with an effort, just as he had forced back the unnerving surge of jealousy that had come over him at the sight of
Natalya holding court. Grey could not allow his feelings for her
to interfere with today's real business.

"Point taken, Mr. St. James." Meagan nodded. "Won't
you come out to the garden? My husband is eager to meet you,
and all the refreshments are there."

Natalya saw him then as he walked with Meagan Hampshire
toward the garden doors, seemingly oblivious to her place of

honor at the party. Her eyes devoured him, taking in every detail from his proud bronzed profile to the polished toes of his black boots. He wore a smoke-colored frock coat that fit perfectly against his broad shoulders and tapering back, a white shirt with high collarpoints and an expertly tied cravat, a Prussian blue and dove gray waistcoat, and snug pantaloons so pale a shade of gray that they were almost white. Natalya's heart began to ache with longing to speak to him, to touch his strong hand, to feel the heat of his smile . . .

"Natalya?"

It was Rembrandt Peale, looking expectantly toward the book she had been inscribing for him. "I'm sorry!" she exclaimed. "I just saw—an old friend, and was momentarily distracted." She finished writing her name as Raphael smiled and murmured:

"A fortunate man indeed—and, by the look in your eyes, considerably more than a friend!"

Natalya felt a maddening blush spread over her cheeks and glanced involuntarily toward the garden door. Grey had disappeared into the crush outside, where she knew Krissie was waiting eagerly. Where was Hollis Gladstone? Suddenly she had no heart for the task at hand; but people continued to gather around the desk, peering at her as if she were somehow different from them simply because her name was engraved on the spine of a book.

"You look as if you'd like to join your party," Thomas Sully said kindly.

"Perhaps I shall, in a few minutes," she said. "It was a pleasure meeting you, Mr. Sully."

"I hope to see you again soon," he replied, moving away from the desk.

"Father is out there somewhere," Raphael told her. "He has no patience with queues like this, but I know he's eager to see you. No doubt you'll find him near the Madeira!"

"I'll join you shortly in the garden," Natalya called in parting, then looked up with a smile to greet the next person in line. Standing before her was a woman, a very beautiful, slender woman with sparkling green eyes that slanted upward exotically. Her glossy auburn hair was braided into a crown high on her head, and she was blessed with elegant cheekbones and sensuously full lips.

"So, you are Philadelphia's celebrated new author," the woman said, her voice rich with a cultured English accent. "How charming. I've decided not to purchase a book, for I never read novels, but I did want to meet you." She held out a slim, pale hand. "My name is Francesca Wellbeloved."

Inexplicably a chill ran down Natalya's back as she took the woman's hand. Even though she was certain they had never met, Natalya felt an eerie foreboding, as though somehow their fortunes, their very lives, would be inextricably bound together—or had been for some time . . .

Chapter Twenty-four

 May 15, 1814

IN THE HAMPSHIRES' GARDEN, KRISTIN BIDED HER time, watching Grey converse with Lion Hampshire, his booted foot propped on a stone bench in the midst of a secluded drift of daffodils, violets, and ribbon grass. On his knee he balanced a blue-and-white china plate and partook of shrimp and rye bread as they talked. Everything he did looked appealingly effortless to Kristin.

When a stout man in a brown suit waved to Lion, he excused himself, and Kristin seized her opportunity. Grey remained at the bench but appeared distinctly preoccupied, gazing over the crowd, when she approached.

"Good afternoon, Mr. St. James," Kristin greeted him. "You're looking very . . . *well* today."

"Oh—good afternoon, Miss Beauvisage." He seemed not to notice the coquettish smile she bestowed upon him, nor did he think to return her compliment. A lacy willow branch partially concealed Grey's face as he continued to sort through the crush of guests with his eyes.

Kristin tried again. "I had hoped that you might visit us at Belle Maison earlier this month."

"Ah, well—I've been busy." He gave her the briefest glance, accompanied by a distracted smile. "Settling into a new city can take up a great deal of time."

This was not going at all the way Kristin had envisioned through all the days and nights leading up to the party. In fact, she had imagined that Grey would approach *her*, overwhelmed by her beauty and a desire to be near her. Now she suppressed an urge to pull on his sleeve in an effort to gain his attention. Instead she drained her glass of champagne and inquired recklessly, "How do you like my gown? You're the only man here who hasn't given me a compliment."

"Perhaps that's just as well," he replied, with cool irony. "Another flattering word might inflate your vanity to unbecoming proportions, and we wouldn't want that, would we? Now then, if you don't mind, Miss Beauvisage, there is another matter to which I must attend. . . ."

Her cheeks burned and tears stung her eyes as she turned away from Grey, mumbling, "Excuse me, sir. I can see I've misjudged you."

Near the garden doors, Natalya stood with Hollis Gladstone. Freed at last from her station behind the Queen Anne desk, she had rushed to seize his arm and guide him into battle. "There, you see? She is with Grey St. James over behind the willow tree. Hollis, he is a wicked man in his dealings with ladies, and Krissie has no sense of such things. You must go over there and *assert* yourself."

"Good Lord, how beautiful she is," he murmured.

"Yes, she's beautiful, and you understand her as no one else ever can. For her own good, you must make her see that *you* are the man she needs." She gave him a little shove just as Kristin appeared again on the edge of the crowd, blinking back tears.

Hollis took a deep breath, squared his shoulders, and strode toward his ladylove. "Kristin," he said in forceful tones, "I've had enough of this nonsense. It's time that you and I had a serious talk!"

He tucked her hand through his arm just at the moment her step had begun to falter. As he led her away from the house toward a grove of blossoming dogwood trees, Kristin found that his rumpled, bearlike presence was oddly comforting and warmly familiar. She liked the way he was taking charge while still gazing at her with adoration in his sage-green eyes. "Yes, Hollis." She leaned her head against his shoulder for a moment as they walked. "I believe you're right. I'm ready to listen to you now."

Natalya, meanwhile, remained in the doorway to the parlor, trying to decide what to do. Francesca Wellbeloved slipped past her, murmuring, "Pardon me," en route to the table of refreshments manned by James Stringfellow. Grey remained on the other side of the garden, still shielded by the willow tree. Like her sister, Natalya had imagined quite a different scene for her meeting with Grey today. She could not understand why he hadn't come up to greet her when she'd been surrounded by men at her desk in the Hampshires' parlor. Perhaps, she thought, he hadn't wanted to intrude—or even better, perhaps he'd been jealous! Still, she wanted him to come to her. Now, as fashionably garbed guests milled around her, Natalya stared at his distant figure. When she caught his eye, a spark of hope flared in her heart, then died as he glanced away. Suddenly she remembered how he had accused her of snubbing *him* when they'd quarreled at the Spruce Street house, and Natalya's disappointment was supplanted by anger. How dare he ignore her? Balling her hands into fists, she started toward him—then stopped when someone touched her back.

"Talya?"

She turned to see her grandmother, tiny and radiant in a gown of pale green watered silk. Emeralds and diamonds sparkled at her throat, and soft green plumes adorned her white hair. "Grandmama! How lovely you look! I'm so *glad* that you were able to come today."

"My darling girl, I am exceedingly proud of you! Your wonderful, witty book is all anyone can talk about, and I must be forgiven for claiming some credit for its author." Antonia embraced her, laughing lightly, then looked back at a slim, balding man of medium height who stood behind her. "Barton, step forward and greet my granddaughter. I know that you have met before, but that was years ago and memories need refreshing from time to time."

Natalya knew immediately what was afoot between Barton Saunders and her beloved grandmother; there was no mistaking the light in Antonia's emerald green eyes, nor the answering warmth in Barton's smile. As they chattered politely Natalya felt numb, horrified to see her grandmother looking at another man the way she had looked at Jean-Philippe. It was even more horrifying to see this *person* touch Antonia's back and gaze lovingly into her eyes. Furthermore, Barton Saunders was nothing like her grandfather—he was an American by birth, quite possibly *younger* than Antonia, and his looks were altogether unprepossessing. What right had he to lay claim to the affections of so extraordinary a woman, a woman who had given all of herself for more than sixty years in marriage to an equally extraordinary man! Poor Grandpapa, Natalya thought dimly. What would *he* say if he could see his loyal bride now?

She realized that there was something inherently wrong with the case she was building, but she couldn't help herself. It was a mistake to judge Antonia Beauvisage by a set of standards entirely different from that which she would impose on any other woman, but surely that was the way of the world with grandmothers. As a child, Natalya had placed Antonia on a pedestal, *with* Jean-Philippe, and she didn't know how to change that now. . . .

Grey had very nearly let down his guard and gone to Natalya when he saw her in the garden, so intense was his longing to be near her. During the past weeks of his self-imposed confinement, he had found himself daydreaming about her more often than he cared to admit—remembering the radiance of her smiles, the feel of her skin, the sound of her laughter. . . . Then, just as he'd made up his mind to go to her, he'd caught sight of Stringfellow waving from his post at the refreshments table.

Francesca . . . She had turned in profile, her auburn curls gleaming in the sunlight as she drank most of a glass of champagne. A cold chill swept over Grey, followed immediately by a surge of energy. His hands made fists of steel as he recognized the necklace and earrings she wore; they made up the parure his great-grandmother had received as a wedding gift. Grey heard a voice whisper, "Bitch," and realized that it was his own.

Silently, with the power and purpose of a stalking panther, he made his way through the crowd. Francesca had turned back to Stringfellow to have her glass refilled when Grey came up behind her and clamped lean fingers around her arm.

"I beg your par—" she began to protest, glancing back in annoyance. Her voice died the moment she saw Grey, and she feared her heart might stop, too. Yet even as the blood drained from her face, she began to marshal her wits. This was just one more scene in the game, she told herself, and it was imperative that she be the victor.

"Surprised to see me?" he murmured harshly.

Forcing herself to meet his deadly silver gaze, she smiled. "A trifle shocked, I'll own, but not surprised. How are you, Grey? I gather that you came safely through the war after all. Knowing your penchant for danger, I did not expect to see you again."

"Spare me your polite inquiries after my health, and especially your analysis of my character," Grey ground out.

Stringfellow was watching them with concern. "Sir?" he said in hushed tones, leaning across the bowl of champagne punch. "Might I remind you again of the summerhouse beyond the garden? If you and the lady would prefer to converse freely—"

"A splendid idea." His grip tightened on Francesca's arm as he said with heavy irony, "Come along, *Mrs. Wellbeloved*. I feel certain that you are even less eager to create a scene than I. The scene itself may be unavoidable, but an audience is not."

She did not protest as he led her deeper into the garden, where the brick footpaths gave way to flagstone steps cut into a gentle hill. Here the garden was wilder, denser, and even more lovely. Honey locust trees mingled with weeping willows, under which grew a profusion of moss-pink roses, daffodils, pansies, delphinium, and larkspur. In the distance, sheltered by giant elm trees, stood the small hexagonal building that had served as a schoolroom for young Benjamin, Michael, and Susan Hampshire.

Upon reaching the summerhouse, Grey opened the door

and swept his arm before him in a gesture of mock gallantry. "After you."

Francesca entered, disengaged her arm from Grey's hold, and seated herself gracefully on one of the upholstered benches that followed the window-lined walls. She was glad for the walk and the time it had given her to formulate her plan of attack. Obviously Grey was expecting a spectacular confrontation. He would demand the Hartford jewels as well as divorce, and leave her with nothing. If she fought back in kind, he would surely win.

"It was very thoughtful of you to seek solitude for us," Francesca said in a quiet voice. "I could not have let my feelings show if we had been forced to talk in that crowd."

Caught slightly off-guard, he stared at her with narrowed eyes. "If indeed you do have feelings, they are of no consequence to me, Francesca. What is of consequence is your abandonment of our marriage and the theft of my mother's jewels."

"Theft?" She laughed shakily. "That's putting it rather strongly, isn't it, darling?" Grey had crossed to stand over her, and she found that she was thrilled by the angry strength of his presence. Her nipples grew taut as she looked up at him and continued, "But, you must let me explain all. I realize that it must be tempting to paint me as a villainess in this piece, but—"

"Damn you! Do you imagine that you can *charm* me into complaisance?" he demanded, holding himself in check with an effort. "You are fortunate that I have not put my hands around your beautiful neck and choked you to death, for that is exactly what I long to do! And, speaking of necks, give over my mother's necklace and earrings."

Francesca blanched but obeyed docilely. After handing him the priceless earrings, she stood and presented her back to him. "You'll have to work the clasp, darling. You know I'm hopeless with such things."

"For God's sake, stop calling me darling," he shot back through clenched teeth. When he touched her neck, the sudden, sighing intake of her breath sickened him. The clasp was unfastened in a trice, and he dropped all three pieces of the parure in his coat pocket.

"Do you know, it's quite amazing, but I am not curious as to how you found me," she said softly. "I knew that you would somehow, if you lived."

Grey gave her a chilling smile. "Fascinating."

Francesca sat down again and assumed an earnest expression. "Now, then, Grey, you must hear me out. You owe me at least the few minutes it will take to tell my story. I realize that what I've done must appear altogether inexplicable—"

"Not at all. The explanation is simple. You are selfish, cold-blooded, and spoiled, and I was a fool to marry you." His manner grew dangerously calm as he continued, "Perhaps I shouldn't fault you for recognizing the truth about the farce we were engaged in, for I surely would have done so myself in time. However, I do condemn you for leaving me when I was not even present to discuss the matter, leaving me without word of your whereabouts, still tied to you by wedding vows and unable to loose those legal bonds."

"But, Grey, I *loved* you!" She turned green eyes up to him, bright with pain. "Have you forgotten all that we shared during those . . . private moments? No, don't answer; I can see that you mean to pretend that there was ever naught between us, and I suppose I cannot blame you. But, it was different for me. I was afraid to let my feelings show after our wedding because you were so cavalier about the entire business."

"What the devil are you going on about?" Grey broke in impatiently, pushing open a window to let in some air. "Do you take me for one of those drooling puppies who believe whatever you tell them, despite the obvious facts? Not that it signifies in the least, but you ran off mere weeks after our wedding! Damned odd behavior for a wife in love, wouldn't you agree?"

Francesca stretched out her hand and touched his for an instant, thrilling to the warmth of his bronzed skin, remembering his intoxicating scent and the heady rapture of his kisses. "You doubtless won't believe me, but I left *because* I loved you so. I was frightened, Grey! Desperately frightened that you would be killed in the war, and even more afraid that, if you did come home to me, you would break my heart. I had never known such powerful longing before, and—''

''I'm afraid you'll have to do much better than that, my dear,'' he drawled sardonically.

She began to weep, burying her face in her hands. ''I knew that you would be this way—that I would be better off striking back in kind than telling the truth!''

Standing in the middle of the summerhouse, Grey cast his eyes heavenward. ''I shudder to think what you imagine you can gain from these histrionics, Francesca, but you would be wise to take a different tack. You know me very little if you believe I can be manipulated.''

Experience had taught Francesca that all men could be manipulated, and in any case, she had no other option save surrender, and that did not occur to her. Shakily she rose to her feet and threw herself against him, sobbing. ''My darling! Can you not feel the sincerity of my pain? Have you not the smallest piece of love for me hiding in a corner of your heart?''

The Francesca he had known in London had been sly, keen-witted, wildly passionate, and self-absorbed. Grey had never known her to display a single tender emotion, and he was taken aback by these tearful pleas. He had expected defiance, even threats and lies, but never this! Clasping her shoulders, he was about to put her away from him when a movement outside the summerhouse caught his eye.

''Good God,'' he muttered. There, amid a profusion of orange and yellow daylilies, stood Natalya. Her beautiful eyes were wide with confusion and disbelief. Just before she turned to flee, Francesca lifted her head from Grey's chest and looked back, recognizing Natalya Beauvisage . . . and understanding instantly that she was her rival.

Grey St. James walked toward the little cottage behind the gardens of Belle Maison. The mansion was dark and silent, but candlelight illuminated the cottage windows, beckoning to him. It was nearly one o'clock in the morning, and he realized that anyone seeing him wandering about would, perhaps rightly, think him mad. Tonight, however, his cool head and ready wit had deserted him, replaced by emotions that burned too hot to touch, much less examine. Sleep was impossible, and a force Grey didn't understand had drawn him on horseback through the starlit night. Without choosing a destination, he'd found himself at Belle Maison.

It seemed as if an eternity had passed since he had come away from the Hampshires' garden party. By the time he and Francesca returned to the house, most of the guests had departed, and Natalya had been surrounded by young women in the parlor, laughing gaily. It was obvious to Grey that she was hiding from him behind the barricade of females, and he was oddly grateful. He didn't know what to say to her then.

He still didn't know, but he felt compelled to say something now that he was here at this impossible hour. Dear God, what a coil his life had become in one short day! The situation with Francesca gave him precious little peace, for he couldn't fathom what she was about. In an effort to gain some control over the matter, he had closeted himself in his library earlier that evening and written to her, coldly demanding the return of all the Hartford jewels and informing her that he would seek to have their marriage dissolved immediately upon his return to England. Speed, warming to his role in the drama, had dressed in black to deliver the missive, impressively sealed by Grey's signet ring. He hardly expected Francesca to obey his commands without protest, but the action had allowed him to put that particular problem aside for the moment.

Grey's body ached with fatigue as he listened to the calls of the night birds and smelled the fragrant spring flowers. A horse stirred and snorted in the nearby stables, while shredded clouds floated past the moon. Grey paused on the mossy brick footpath, inhaling the cool air and wondering what the devil he was doing. Somehow he had learned that Natalya was using this cottage as her writing study, but that certainly did not mean she slept there as well. And, even if she did, what explanation could he give for disturbing her in the middle of the night?

Then, as if in answer to his questions, a white-clad figure

moved past the candlelit window, pausing to open it a few inches. Grey almost imagined that he beheld a ghost as a breeze stirred the loose white gown and tumbled honey curls of Natalya Beauvisage.

She saw him but did not move. Her heart raced with a sweet, reckless joy as she drank in the familiar lines of his lean, shadowed body, the ebony gleam of his hair, and the white glow of his shirt in the moonlight. How could one human being, even in the form of a vision, be the source of both acute heartache and immeasurable happiness?

Today, after leaving the Hampshires' party, Natalya had wanted to get into her bed, draw the covers over her head, and remain there, asleep preferably, until her pain eased. Knowing that such behavior would alert her entire family to her humiliating, helpless passion for Grey St. James, she had chosen instead to take refuge in the cottage, explaining that the party had given her several inspiring ideas for her book that must be recorded without delay.

"I must be seeing things," she whispered now. "Seeing things and going quite mad. . . ."

The apparition walked slowly toward the cottage, and she went to open the door. "You are doubtless wondering what I am doing here," Grey said, with self-directed irony.

"You're *real*!"

"Unfortunately, yes. Are you?" When she nodded, he smiled. "Perhaps we're having the same dream, for that would make more sense than the two of us meeting like this in the middle of the night. Will you let me in?"

The air, scented with the wisteria that plunged over the cottage roof, seemed imbued with magic as well. "What sort of dream would this be if I did not?" Natalya answered, stepping back so that he might pass. "I am curious to discover how it will end."

"To be frank, so am I." Spying a decanter of brandy on a table in the parlor, he went over and removed the stopper. "Do you mind if I help myself?"

"No." She stared at his profile, which was irresistibly burnished by the glow of a dozen candles. "In fact, I believe I ought to join you."

When Grey had splashed brandy into two crystal tumblers, he joined her on the settee. "I hope you have a more plausible reason for being here at this uncivilized hour than I do." His voice still held a note of satiric disbelief, as if part of him were watching the scene from a distance.

Natalya's first sip of brandy gave her courage, but she tread carefully. "I was writing."

"Is it your custom to write when the rest of the world sleeps?"

"No," she answered simply, "but I was in no mood for sleep. What of you? Is it *your* custom to wander my family's garden, miles from your own in Philadelphia, after we have all gone to bed?" She imitated him by arching a delicate brow.

Grey grinned in spite of himself. "Ah, minx, you have the devil's own wits. No, it is not my custom; in truth, I am not quite certain what brought me here tonight."

"Are you not?"

A silence fell between them, broken finally by Grey. "This area is one where I have seldom strayed. . . ."

"What area is that?" she prodded, with feigned confusion, watching the way his long fingers tightened around the glass.

He glared at her. "I mean, the area of—the realm in which—" He broke off, sighing harshly. "God knows what I'm trying to say, because I'll be damned if *I* do! I've no business even speaking of this to you given the complicated circumstances of my life—and the fact that I've really no idea what it means, or where it's going, or—"

"Grey . . . are you talking about your feelings for me?" Natalya felt oddly serene in the face of his agitation.

"See here!" he cried accusingly. "I don't think we ought to be discussing this at all. All my life, I've been taught to act and think, not feel. Quite honestly, I'm not even certain what a feeling is when I'm having one, so I've learned to avoid the blasted things entirely." He stood up. "I'd better go."

"Oh, no, you don't!" Warmed by the brandy and this glimpse of vulnerability, Natalya caught Grey's hand and pulled him back down on the settee. "I seem to recall another conversation not so long ago, in your upstairs sitting room on Spruce Street, when you accused *me* of running from my feelings. You implied that I was callous because I had tried to pretend there was nothing between us, and although I now remember that no discussion was made of *your* feelings, you did maneuver me quite neatly into bed." Pausing to sip her brandy, she grinned at him. "This time, you owe *me* an explanation, sir—many explanations, in fact. You may as well resign yourself to providing them. No doubt you'll be able to sleep again after our little talk."

Grey stood up, looking pained, and went to fetch the decanter of brandy. Pouring more into his glass, he returned to the settee and put it on the low table in front of them, securely within reach. "You can be a merciless vixen, Natalya."

A warm, dizzying euphoria filled her body. "Perhaps," she teased, "and yet . . ."

"If you imagine that I'm going to say I'm in love with you, you're mad!" he shouted. "Love! What the devil is *love*?"

"I can see that you are upset," Natalya soothed. "Let's put the subject of love aside for the moment and come back to it later. Besides, I'd really rather hear about Francesca Wellbeloved. Who is she, and what is her role in your life?"

"You just had to ask that, didn't you? You'll wish you hadn't when you hear the answer." His tone was scorching.

"But, Grey," she said gently, "I have to hear it, just as you have to say it, or we can never move forward."

"Damn you!" He heard his voice as from a distance, and it was like a stranger's. "Francesca is my *wife*!"

Chapter Twenty-five

🌸 *May 16, 1814*

"FRANCESCA WELLBELOVED IS YOUR WIFE?" Natalya echoed in a small voice, pressing a hand over her aching heart. "You must be jesting!"

"Would that I were, my dear," Grey replied ruefully. Seeing that she had begun to tremble in her thin lawn nightgown, he retrieved a blanket of Irish wool from a nearby chair, wrapped it around her body, and put her brandy glass in her hand. "I do hope you're not planning to faint."

She sat up straighter, eyes sparkling. "I'll have you know that I *never* faint!"

"Of course not." He gave her a fond smile. "I apologize for suggesting that you might."

"Apology accepted. Now then, I suppose that you'd better tell me everything." She shook her head and sighed. "Really, Grey, how could you be married to such a woman? What possessed you?"

"Satan, I presume," he answered dryly. "Actually there were several reasons why I married Francesca, but in retrospect none of them seem very good."

Bundled in the blanket and curled up on her side of the settee, Natalya nudged him with her toe. "Well?"

He shot her a dark look but continued, "Two years ago, I had a few weeks' leave from the war and was in a reckless mood, drinking quite heavily, which didn't help my judgment. I began to think that I would probably be killed in France, and it occurred to me that I should marry at long last and perhaps leave an heir behind. As it was, everyone had been on at me forever to take a wife, and I was bored to death with mamas pushing their daughters at me . . . .''

"It must have been *awfully* trying to be so popular," Natalya remarked, with mock sympathy.

Grey's free hand moved down to squeeze her foot, then stayed there, resting lightly against her. "My family is another story entirely, and perhaps I'll tell you one day, but the fact is that my home bore no resemblance whatsoever to yours. My father is . . . aloof, and my mother died before I was old enough to be influenced by her. When I met Francesca, who was newly widowed and as reckless as I, Father encouraged the match. She had a rather handsome dowry, which he needed to pay some gambling debts."

"It sounds very romantic," Natalya observed mildly. She found that, in spite of Grey's cataclysmic news, she felt happy. They had crossed a line; there was a new bond between them, even if no words of love had been spoken. Grey was confiding in her, and she knew the reason why—even if he did not. She also found herself divining a great deal from his spare description of his upbringing, storing away each fact to be pondered later. "So, you married Francesca because it amused you and your father needed to pay his gambling debts. What happened next? Were you ever happy with her?"

"The happiness issue rather begs the point, because I was scarcely with her." Grey sipped his brandy with a bemused smile. "The little time we were together before I returned to my ship was more in the nature of a brief affair. I . . . ah— released a certain amount of passion in Francesca's company, but there was no tenderness between us. Quite frankly, I don't think either of us knew the meaning of the word."

He had begun idly to stroke her foot through the blanket, and the radiance in Natalya's breast intensified. Still, she couldn't help asking, "Was that what I saw in the summer-house today? Passion?"

"God, no!" His brows lowered over stormy eyes. "Nothing of the kind."

"Then tell me, Grey," she pleaded. "Why did you never speak of a wife? Why is she here, rather than in London, and why is her name different from yours? Was my need to return to Philadelphia just an excuse for you to come in search of her?" Natalya gazed at him in the candle glow, utterly mesmerized by his presence, by the sight of his face and the feel of his body close to hers.

Their eyes met, and Grey did not look away. He'd already looked away from her once too often and was beginning to realize that it was hopeless. "Francesca ran away several weeks after I returned to the war. I heard rumors but wasn't certain, which was the reason for my preoccupied state of mind during our journey back to London. I can't say that I was sorry when I learned the truth, but men do get caught in traps of pride." He laughed with grim humor. "I may not have wanted her, yet it stung to discover that she had left first. Rumor had it that she had flown with another man, but I still don't know about that. Perhaps it's over. At any rate, I doubtless would have sought a divorce and let it go, but I discovered that she had taken all the Hartford jewels, which would have passed to her when I inherited the earldom. I couldn't rest until I made an effort to find her and retrieve what belonged to my family."

"I don't blame you," Natalya agreed, shocked.

"Through a friend, I heard that Francesca was in America and had written of plans to travel to Philadelphia." Grey paused, staring into Natalya's eyes. "To be perfectly honest, I don't know if you gave me an excuse to pursue her, or if she gave me an excuse to bring you home. Probably my motives overlapped."

Even as her heart began to sing, Natalya started to fit together other pieces of the puzzle. "Ever since Fedbusk saw Francesca on the street, you've been plotting to confront her, haven't you? Did you have anything to do with the party today?"

Grey nodded. "Stringfellow helped me arrange circumstances that would bring the two of us together. It was crucial that I surprise her, away from her home, so that she couldn't have me put out or hide behind a locked door."

"Odious man!" Without thinking, she leaned over and cuffed his arm. "You have used me repeatedly to further your own ends! Stringfellow persuaded Meagan Hampshire to have that party, didn't he? It wasn't to celebrate my success, it was merely a means to an end for you!"

He caught her raised arms and pulled her down across his lap. "For God's sake, don't take on as though this had all been arranged to humiliate you personally! Why must you assume that there was only one motive for the party? Meagan Hampshire knew nothing of me or Francesca. The celebration was planned in *your* honor, and you deserved it! Next you'll accuse me of hiring all those young swains who swarmed around you while you were holding court in the parlor." The instant the words were out, he longed to call them back. Natalya ceased struggling for an instant, and a triumphant light shone in her eyes.

"Aha! You were jealous!"

"What manner of conversation *is* this? You are as erratic as—as—"

"I know." Waves of contentment washed over her as she lay passively in his strong embrace. "I'm behaving like a woman in love."

Grey looked stricken. "Dear God—"

"I said I'm behaving like a woman in love, not that I *am* a woman in love," she teased him, giggling softly.

Even though it was sheer magic to cradle her against him, Grey panicked when she taunted him with that word. Every male impulse in his body cried out to kiss her delicious mouth, to caress the tantalizing curves that awaited him under the gossamer nightgown; yet to do so would bring him even closer to that terrifying emotion. . . .

"Now you must end my suspense and tell me what happened between you and Francesca today," Natalya said, interrupting his thoughts. She nestled contentedly in the lean-muscled circle of Grey's arms as if it were the most natural place in the world for her to be.

He looked down at her expressive face and smiled in spite of himself. "You're a minx."

"So you have said. Proceed."

"Francesca is up to something . . . I just haven't quite decided what it is. She's extremely shrewd. I had expected her to respond in kind when I confronted her, to refuse to give up the jewels she wore, to be cold and threatening. However, she wept and insisted she loved me, then spun a nonsensical explanation for leaving our marriage. She handed over my mother's jewels without a word, and was crying and begging for my forgiveness when you appeared outside the summerhouse."

"She wants to reconcile," Natalya said, feeling distinctly uneasy. "She realizes that she made a gigantic mistake, and now she wants to be your wife again."

Grey stroked her honey-gold hair and stared off into the distance. "Humdudgeon, as our own Fedbusk is wont to say. I'm not fit for marriage, especially with a woman like Francesca. No, it's not love she's after. I'll wager her agenda is much more devious."

Trying to block out his statement about marriage, Natalya murmured, "What is going to happen now? . . ."

He shrugged. "If I have my way, I'll recover the rest of the Hartford jewels, then sail home to England and obtain a divorce. I wrote to Francesca tonight and said exactly that."

"Do you think she'll accede to your wishes?"

"I intend that she shall," he replied tersely, propping his booted feet on the low table.

Natalya felt less certain, but for the moment she was satisfied. Yawning, she snuggled against Grey's broad chest, feeling the crisp hair through the fabric of his shirt. It might be true that he had made no mention of her in his plans, but he had shared much with her tonight, and in her heart she knew a sense of peace.

"Rest assured, Grey, I'll help you," she whispered as her eyes closed and sleep drew her under.

Looking down at her exquisite, winsome face, Grey gently brushed a stray curl off her brow and sighed. "That's what I'm afraid of," he said in an ironic undertone. Holding her thus and watching her sleep felt dismayingly natural to him. At

length he cuddled her closer, enjoying the lush warmth of her
body in a way that was only partly carnal, and wondered what
the devil was happening to him. In the midst of his rumina-
tions, a surge of fatigue made his eyes feel heavy and he let
them close. Perhaps a short nap would revive him for the ride
back to Philadelphia. . . .

The blushing dawn roused Caro from a night of fitful dozing. When she opened her eyes, she discovered that her husband was already awake beside her.

"You look like a little girl," he said affectionately, kissing
her tumbled curls.

As if their bedtime conversation had not been interrupted
by several hours' sleep, Caro said, without preamble, "Perhaps
you ought to go out to the cottage and see if she's all right."

"How can we be certain she didn't come to her own bed
during the night?"

"Because we would have heard her, and well you know it,
for parents listen quite efficiently in their sleep. Do not look
at me as if I am an overanxious mother, Alec! All last evening
you tried to convince me that my worries about Talya's mood
and behavior were groundless, but I *know* her, and I have
instincts about such things. Something is bothering her."

"*Chérie*, it is scarcely dawn. No doubt she is sleeping.
Would you have me disturb her at this hour?" Alec ran a hand
through his thick white hair and sank back against the pillows.
"I think that we are both guilty of making far too much of this
situation."

Caro tried a gentler approach. "What harm could there be
in you going quietly through the passageway and opening the
panel at the cottage? Talya would not even notice unless she
were awake herself. You can peek in to see that she is safe,
then come back to reassure me and we can doze awhile longer
and . . . *rest* together in the sunshine." She gave him a bla-
tantly suggestive smile and caressed his chest with her fingertips. "Will you not do this one small thing for me?"

"You are incorrigible, do you know that?" Alec shook his
head as if exasperated, then caught his wife in his arms and

kissed her deeply. "It *has* been a while since we lingered in bed." His brows rose as he considered the possibilities. "All right, wench, don't move. I shall return in mere minutes."

Caro beamed as she watched her husband rise from the bed and shrug into his black silk dressing gown. When he paused in the doorway to look back, she was already pulling off her nightgown, and he quickened his step.

It had been months since he had been in the passageway and tunnel that connected the main house with his grandmother's cottage, and he took a candle from Natalya's bedchamber to help light the way. Pierre saw to it that the servants regularly swept away the cobwebs, so Alec reached the other end unscathed for the most part. There before him was a thin panel, and he knew a pang of nostalgia for the many times he had visited Grandmère in just this way. It still seemed odd to realize that he would not find her in the cottage, perched on the brocade settee, drinking sherry and embroidering.

Very softly, Alec touched the spring that opened the panel and slid it over a mere inch or two. A ray of light pierced the gloom of his hiding place, and then he saw them. Grey was seated across the parlor on the settee, fully clothed, his feet propped on a low table. Natalya lay curled in a blanket beside him, her upper body cradled against his chest. She looked like an angel, her hair flowing over Grey's thighs. Alec was suddenly reminded of the first time he had seen Caro, lying unconscious on a carpet of autumn leaves. Disguised as a boy, she had been wearing a hat, and when he had lifted her in his arms and pulled off the hat, the most beautiful honey-colored hair he had ever seen had spilled out. Had he loved her even then?

The road to love and happiness had been a long one, but each step had been necessary. Natalya and Grey must be allowed to travel the path that destiny had designed for them, at their own pace, without interference. Silently closing the panel, Alec started back through the tunnel toward the house.

"Good Lord," said Grey when he opened his eyes, "it's morning."

Clinging to him, Natalya made a sound of protest. "Kiss me," she begged, unwilling to acknowledge the reality of daylight.

He stared at her for a moment, touched his mouth to her upturned lips, then lifted her away from him. "I must go. How could we explain this to your family? As it is, I'll have to sneak around the stables and pray the servants don't recognize me." He stood up, rubbing his eyes. "I feel like the devil himself."

"Must you be so testy?"

Standing at the window, he drew back the Belgian lace curtains and peered out at the sunlit garden. "Egad but it's bright! And there goes Pierre DuBois."

Natalya frowned and rose from the settee, still holding the blanket around her body. "Grey—"

"I must go, before he comes out of the kitchen." He tucked in his shirt, ran a hand through his tousled hair, and turned to find Natalya standing right behind him. "And you'd be wise not to make too much of this, minx."

"I don't know what you mean," she replied. "We didn't do any more than fall asleep together, did we?"

Though he would never admit it, that was precisely the problem. When there was lust involved, it was easier to explain away other emotional lapses and forms of intimacy, but Grey had no such excuse for the bond he and Natalya had forged last night. "Don't be difficult, Natalya. You know perfectly well what I mean. Just because I discussed a few things with you—"

"After wandering past my cottage window at one o'clock in the morning, purely by chance," she interjected.

Grey's eyes narrowed. "You are the most trying little vixen I have ever known! I merely wish to point out that you'll save yourself heartache if you don't make more of this past night than was actually there."

"Never have you made a more ridiculously *male* statement! It's quite apparent that you don't know yourself what you mean, but I can assure you that I do." Looking adorable wrapped in the blanket that trailed behind her, Natalya flung open the cottage door. "Although you may be confused, sir, I am not. Ride safely. I shall see you later!"

When Grey was gone, Natalya used the tunnel to return to her own bedchamber. Climbing the hidden stairway, she realized that she could conceivably get into her own bed and behave as if she'd been there all night. It was still early, after all; no one would be the wiser. Humming softly to herself, she touched the spring that opened the panel . . . and beheld her father sitting on a moss-green chair in front of the fireplace. He wore a black dressing gown and looked as if he had just come from bed.

"Ah, there you are, child," he said genially. "Do come in and join me. Would you care for tea?" He gestured toward the china teapot, cups, and a fresh plate of croissants drizzled with icing.

Natalya's throat was dry as she closed the secret panel and glanced self-consciously at the lawn nightgown that revealed a faint outline of her lovely body. "Let me slip on a wrapper, Papa, and I shall be glad to join you." She found one of her own in Caro's dressing room and fumbled with the sleeves, her mind whirling. He knew! A man had spent the night with her, and even though no real scandal had taken place, Natalya still felt nervous. She thought back to the other time her father had appeared at the worst possible moment, when she had been in Grey's bed, still basking in the afterglow of their coupling. Had he known then as well?

Alec had never been an overprotective father, but the young men who had courted Natalya before she went to France had quaked at the sight of him. He had never raged at her, yet her respect for his authority remained fully intact. When she felt he'd caught her at something, it didn't seem to matter how old she was. . . .

As Natalya crossed the bedchamber and took the chair Alec had drawn close to his, he handed her a cup of tea and said, "I've been talking to your mother, and I think it would be a good idea for the two of us to go away for a while. It's been rather a long time since we've visited her farm in Connecticut.

Although it's being looked after, as you know, we do like to go up ourselves from time to time.''

"I remember that you used to take Maman away to the farm every spring when we were growing up," Natalya said softly.

Alec grinned. "In those days, it was a good excuse to have her to myself."

She sipped her tea, feeling her cheeks grow warm. "Papa . . . what is really behind this? Why were you waiting for me, and why do you think you and Maman should go away at this particular time?"

"I have to keep reminding myself that you are a woman," he told her gently. "You've lived away from people, except for Nicky and his family, for a long time, and I believe that you are now discovering that there are more important aspects of your life than books and dreams. I know that a relationship has begun between you and Grey—"

"Papa, last night we didn't—"

He held up his hand. "No, don't explain. You don't have to explain to me, and I don't expect you to discuss your personal life with us unless you choose to, or you need our help. If you were younger or I felt differently about St. James, I might be more tempted to interfere, but my instincts tell me that I can trust him, ultimately, and I have great faith in the strength and wisdom of your heart, *ma fille*." He leaned back in his chair and gazed at her lovingly. "It is difficult for parents to stand by and watch their children explore life. Your maman has an even harder time than I, for she wants so much to help you find happiness. That's why I feel we should leave you alone for a while. It's a decision I've made as much for our sakes as yours. We won't have to decide whether to meddle or not, day in and day out, if we aren't here." Patting her hand, Alec added, "And you deserve some privacy. You're a grown woman."

"Oh, Papa." Natalya's heart swelled with love and her eyes brimmed with tears. "You really do trust me. . . ." Weeping in earnest, she came over to him and sat on his lap, her face buried against the familiar expanse of his chest. "No girl has ever had a better father. I love you so!"

"And I love you, my darling daughter." He stroked her hair and held her as he had when she was a little golden-haired child with huge aqua eyes. "Be patient with Grey, up to a point, for he is the sort of man who may be afraid to yield to love. With a woman like you, there can be no half measures, and that can seem daunting. I held out far too long before I surrendered to loving your mother." He sighed at the memory. "If you should need us, you need only send word, and if you crave advice, you must go to your grandmama. She is very wise in the ways of love."

"I shall, Papa." Natalya sat up and smiled at him. "It is a very exciting and happy and terrifying time for me. I really don't know how it will all turn out."

"It will turn out as it should," he assured her.

"Does Maman know—about Grey and me?"

"She suspects, and it is driving her mad!" Alec chuckled, his expression transformed as he thought of his wife. "Her maternal instincts are working at a furious pace. She worries about you and wants to help, and, of course, it is because she loves you so."

"I am so fortunate to have the parents I do." Natalya kissed his cheek and added, "And especially to have so brilliant a father!"

"Ever since you were a baby, you have had a gift for flattering me at the right moment, *chérie*." Alec laughed and set her on her feet. "I won't keep you any longer. Your maman and I must pack, and you doubtless have plans of your own."

Natalya picked up a croissant, took an inelegantly large bite, and grinned at him. "As a matter of fact, I *do*. . . ."

PART FIVE

Did ye not hear it?—No; 'twas but the wind,
Or the car rattling o'er the stony street;
On with the dance! let joy be unconfined;
No sleep till morn, when Youth and Pleasure meet
To chase the glowing Hours with flying feet.

LORD BYRON
(1788–1824)

Chapter Twenty-six

May 16–17, 1814

"WHAT IS THE MEANING OF THIS?" DAVID ST. JAMES held up a note penned in Francesca's flowery script. "And where have you been these past few days?"

Reclining on a daybed of red japanned beech that featured silver and gilt decoration and cushions of white silk, Francesca gazed serenely out her bedroom window. Despite her expression of studied gravity, she looked as flawless as a Greek goddess. Her shining auburn curls were caught up loosely, falling over the gold ribbon she wore high on her forehead, and her lips were artfully painted a deep red. Her gown was of the thinnest muslin, revealing rouged nipples beneath the low neckline, and a golden armlet set with an emerald circled the soft, creamy flesh above her elbow.

"Hello, David," she said softly. "Won't you sit down? It was very good of you to come."

"Whatever's the matter? Has someone died?" He perched on the low end of the daybed, crossed his legs, and withdrew a priceless Sevres snuffbox. Delicately inhaling a pinch, he regarded her with mild curiosity.

"I've seen Grey," Francesca announced in ominous tones.

"Indeed?" He raised his eyebrows. "Did he come to you in a dream or did you glimpse his profile from a passing carriage?"

"How dare you mock me at such a moment? I tell you, your brother is *here*, in Philadelphia, just as I feared! And, he knew that I was here. He trapped me in an inane garden party that was given for some overweening spinster who has managed to write a book." Francesca paused to gauge her lover's reaction and was pleased to note that his face had gone white as death. "Ah, I see that you believe me. Grey is out for blood, my dear. He forced me to hand over the parure of rubies that I was wearing, and demands that I return *all* the jewels. David, you know that you have as much right to those jewels as Grey does—more, if justice were served. Why should he have *everything* of value simply because of an accident of nature? He'll have the title, and Hartford House, and Briar Hill, and—"

"Francesca, we've been over this a thousand times. You know I agree that we should keep the bloody gems, so kindly refrain from wasting my time shrieking about them!" David's hands were knotted into fists as he stalked to the cellaret, there to pour himself a generous brandy.

"I was *not* shrieking," Francesca said icily. "Kindly beg my pardon."

He tossed down the brandy, poured another, and returned to the daybed. Clasping her slim, outstretched hand, he murmured, "Forgive me, dearest. This has been a rude shock, to say the least."

"Forgiveness granted, darling. Now do sit down and let us discuss this calmly."

David did as she bade, pushing back his spectacles with trembling fingers. "You must tell me all. What is Grey doing here, of all places? He hasn't any idea that I'm—"

"Alive? Coupling with his wife?" Her lips curved in a feline smile. "No, he hasn't the foggiest notion. He must have come back to London and heard that I'd written Papa of my intention to visit here. No one knows that you weren't killed at Salamanca, and no one knows that it was you who spirited me out of England, so how could Grey know?"

"As far as I'm concerned, anything is possible. He's never been quite human," David said darkly.

"Don't talk nonsense. What you and I must do is work together to ensure his speedy return to England."

"God's eyes, Francesca, how do you intend to do that? And what part could I possibly play? 'Twould be wiser for me to lock myself in a store room until he's gone—or flee Philadelphia altogether!" David had begun to perspire. "He'd kill me if he discovered what I've really been about these past two years. If he knew that I'd deserted the regiment, faked my own death, disgraced our family name, stolen his wife *and* our mother's jewels—"

"Stop it!" If it hadn't required an effort on her part, Francesca would have leaned over and slapped him. "First of all, even if Grey were to pass you on the street, I doubt he would recognize you. In case you weren't aware of it, you've changed drastically, my dear. Now then, try to compose yourself and listen to me."

David gulped the rest of his brandy and stared at her, glassy-eyed. "I'm listening."

"I have reason to believe that there is more to Grey's sojourn in Philadelphia than his quest to bring me to justice. I don't know all the details, but I'll find them out somehow." She stared out the window again, pondering that problem, then continued, "What I do know is that there is a relationship of some sort between Grey and that spinster authoress, Natalya Beauvisage. Philadelphia is her home; she lives with her parents. As long as Grey remains interested in her, he will postpone his return to England, and you and I will be forced to live in fear."

"What in God's name can we do about it?"

"David, darling, are you witless?" She gave him a charming smile. "You will court Miss Beauvisage yourself and woo her away from Grey. I, meanwhile, will convince him that I have sold most of the Hartford jewels. We'll hide them somewhere until he's gone. You know Grey. Once he realizes that his little flirtation with that insipid bluestocking is doomed, he'll grow bored with his situation here and return home to obtain the divorce he yearns for."

"What makes you believe that this woman would throw Grey over for *me*?" David queried, thoroughly dazed by her speech.

"Because, my dearest, you will make her see that Grey is a rake who will break her heart," Francesca replied patiently. "You will treat her tenderly, attentively, appealing to her vanity. You know his style with women; it's hardly romantic. Once she realizes what she's been missing, she'll forget all about him."

He shook his head. "This has the ring of utter insanity to me. What if Grey appears when I am with her? Dear Christ, I'd die a hideous death!"

"Come over here," Francesca commanded. When he obeyed, she took him in her arms and stroked his graying hair. "Now then, darling, can you not see the sport in this plan? Have you not spent your entire life resenting Grey and longing for revenge? I am offering you one more opportunity to have it. You mustn't be afraid. I'll see to it that Grey is otherwise occupied when you are with Miss Beauvisage. You know that you can depend on me. Haven't I seen to everything since the day we met?"

"Yes," he acknowledged in a muffled voice.

"Once Grey has gone home to get his divorce, we will be truly free. You haven't forgotten our dream? Don't you want to marry me any longer?"

"Oh, my darling," David said passionately, "you know that I do!"

Slipping one sleeve down, Francesca bared her breast. "Then you haven't any choice, have you? Say yes, my angel, and you may have all of me, for the rest of your life."

"Yes," he breathed.

"I'm not certain I heard you, darling."

"Yes! Yes, I'll do it!"

"That's better." She offered him her taut, rouged nipple, and he took it into his mouth, sucking eagerly. Francesca dropped her head back and allowed herself a secret smile. "Much better. . . ."

"Talya?" Kristin poked her head into her mother's dressing room. Clad in a blue-and-white-striped round gown, a short blue spencer, and a chip-straw bonnet with striped ribbons, she looked fresh and lovely. "There you are!"

"I was just looking for a bonnet of Maman's to wear today. I am riding into Philadelphia, and don't want anything too large for fear it might come loose in the wind." Wearing only a chemisette and petticoat, Natalya turned from the shelves lined with Caro's stylish hats and held up a small pale gray bonnet lined with rose sarsenet. "This is perfect! I had hoped she didn't take it with her."

"It feels odd not to have them here, doesn't it?" Kristin said wistfully. "Hollis has asked me to visit Bartram's Botanical Gardens with him. He's bringing a basket lunch for us to share on the banks of the Schuylkill. Do you think Maman would approve?"

"Why would she not?" Natalya exclaimed, delighted. "Krissie, I can't tell you how pleased I am that you are keeping company with Hollis Gladstone. I like him very much."

Blushing uncertainly, Kristin replied, "I find that I like him myself, more and more. And, Talya, he likes *me*, not as an ornament, but as a person! He seems to understand me, and I can speak frankly to him, which is very gratifying."

"Then you've recovered from your infatuation with Grey St. James?"

"That horrid, rude man? I've forgotten him completely!"

Rather taken aback, yet relieved, Natalya kissed her sister and wished her a happy outing. Alone again in the familiar dressing room, she looked around and thought of her mother. Only one day had passed since Alec and Caro had left for Connecticut, but it seemed much longer. Natalya's eyes misted as she remembered her mother's parting words, spoken as she leaned from the carriage window and reached out to caress her elder daughter's cheek. "I know that you will be changed when we return, and I am glad for it. If you listen to your heart, darling Talya, and remain true to yourself, the future will unfold as it is meant to."

A noise from the hallway broke into Natalya's reverie and she returned to her bedchamber to see the hall door opening.

"There you are, Charlotte!" she exclaimed, smiling as her maid entered the room. "I thought perhaps you'd gotten lost."

"Aye, I nearly did, it's been so long since you've had need of me," the girl replied sulkily, nearly tripping over the edge of the rug as she approached her mistress. In her arms she carried a lovely riding gown of rose linsey-woolsey finished up the front with dove-gray braiding. "I don't mind telling you that I've never been treated this way before. In his lordship's house, I was respected and valued. Everyone knew that I was one of Mrs. Thistle's best maids." Carlotte fairly scowled as she repeated, "Everyone knew! There are rules in England, you know, but I can see that you don't hold with such over here. You'd look after yourself if it weren't so bloody difficult to fasten the backs of your gowns, and once I even peeked in from the corridor and saw your sister attending you! How d'you think that made me feel?"

Natalya tried to look sympathetic. "Charlotte, I must be honest with you." She held up her arms as the maid slipped the habit over her head. "We do things differently here. I've never really had a maid of my own, although I could have, because I find it simpler to look after myself. It has nothing to do with my regard for you or your abilities, Charlotte, so you mustn't take offense. . . ."

Natalya paused as a thought struck her. There was a hierarchy among the servants even at Belle Maison, and she had unwittingly made it difficult for Charlotte to assume her rightful position as ladies' maid by not keeping her occupied with tasks to perform. "I am sorry if I've been thoughtless . . . but I'm not certain I want to change," she said. "There will always be duties for you here, but I doubt that I would ever want to have you dancing attendance upon me."

"I see." Charlotte pressed her lips together and fussed with her mobcap. "You've made yourself quite plain, mistress. Perhaps I should seek employment elsewhere."

Natalya turned back from the mirror in surprise. "If you feel that strongly about it, perhaps you should, for your own happiness must come first. I do want you to know, however, that I shall always be grateful for the care you gave me when

I fell ill during our voyage to America. And if you do decide to leave, I shall miss you, Charlotte.''

"I appreciate that, mistress, but you don't *need* me any longer." Looking downcast, the girl walked slowly toward the door. "I believe I'll go into the city today if there is nothing more you require of me."

"That sounds like a splendid idea, for it is a beautiful day! Do avail yourself of my carriage. I am planning to ride myself."

"That's kind of you, mistress, and I'm grateful."

Charlotte Timkins closed the door and stood in the corridor for a long moment. Hesitantly she reached into the deep pocket of her apron and drew out a folded piece of parchment covered with writing in a swirled hand. ''At least there's someone who needs me,'' she muttered despondently, then set off to prepare for her excursion to Philadelphia.

Grey St. James was sitting at his desk in the sun-drenched study when Jasper Speed appeared in the doorway. The man-servant noted that his master's dark head was bent over the piece of paper on which he was writing, so he cleared his throat discreetly and waited.

As Grey dripped hot wax onto the folded note and sealed it with his ring, he said quietly, ''Yes, Speed?''

"I believe that you may have a visitor, sir. She is stabling her horse at the moment, and—''

"Is it my wife?" His eyes like sharpened steel, Grey rose to his feet in one fluid movement and strode to the garden doors before Speed could reply. There he beheld Natalya walking from the stable. It was as if the golden sunlight shone only upon her, and she was radiant.

Speed knew that his master had seen her, for the taut lines of his face softened, his gaze warmed, and a smile played over his mouth. In that moment Speed knew the truth. "I take it, sir, that this visit is not altogether unwelcome?"

"Hmm? Oh, quite right, Speed," he said, glancing back distractedly. "Not unwelcome in the least."

When Natalya reached the edge of the garden, Grey went

out to greet her. "To what do I owe this honor?" he asked, with just a touch of irony.

"I shan't be coy," she replied gaily. "I came to see you because I missed you. You've missed me as well, haven't you? It's all right, you can admit it; it's written all over your face."

An unfamiliar sensation of joy swelled within him as he clasped her fingers in his strong, brown hands. "You're very brash today, minx."

"Yes, I am, and I'm enjoying it immensely! Will you give me luncheon? I find that I have the most prodigious appetite of late."

Grey gazed down into her thick-lashed eyes, twin jewels of sparkling turquoise, and surrendered to her magic. "Come inside, Miss Beauvisage, and we shall see if we can discover a way to appease your hunger."

She loved the fond, mocking tone of his voice, loved the feel of her hand tucked in the crook of his masculine arm, loved the way his eyes crinkled slightly in the sunlight as they turned back toward the house. No detail escaped the embrace of Natalya's love. When they stepped into Grey's study and she spied Jasper, the light of her smile took him in, too.

"How good it is to see you again, Speed! It's quite apparent that you are well. Laviolet's cooking must agree with you."

Flushing, Speed glanced down at his expanding waistline, then chuckled. "Indeed, you are correct, Miss Beauvisage. Soon I shall be forced to have my clothes let out." He took a breath and added, "I hope you will not think me presumptuous for saying so, but you are looking extremely beautiful, and it is a great pleasure to have you visit us."

"Miss Beauvisage is an ardent admirer of presumptuousness, my dear Speed. It is second only to her love of audacity and high drama, so you can never put a foot wrong by behaving presumptuously toward her," Grey said, devils dancing in his eyes.

"Pay no attention to him," Natalya declared as she cuffed Grey's arm. "He is very bad, is he not? You, on the other hand, are terribly kind—and an estimable gentleman in all aspects. Grey is fortunate to count you as a member of his household.''

Speed's face was as red as his hair and he was quite speechless as he watched his master glower at his guest. Clearly their relationship had progressed far beyond that which he would have believed possible of so detached and dispassionate a man; for even as he arched a black brow at her, it was obvious that they were engaged in a sort of love play.

"If you have no further need of me, sir . . ." Speed mumbled, backing toward the door.

Dragging his eyes from Natalya's, Grey said, "Wait. I have an errand for you." He crossed to the desk and picked up the letter he had been writing. "Take this to my lady Altburne immediately and tell her that I require a response. Do not leave without her written reply. Understood?''

"Yes, sir.'' Speed had gone pale now, for he realized that his master had taken Natalya into his confidence. Shocked beyond words, he exited with the letter in his grasp.

"What a sweet man,'' Natalya said, untying the ribbons of her bonnet and lifting it from her honey-hued curls.

"Speed has become something of a friend as well as a manservant,'' Grey acknowledged. "I'm quite fond of him. Did you know that he lost his wife not long ago? He's the son of my former manservant, who took another position while I was in France. Speed was a farmer until his wife died in childbirth, followed by the baby boy. He needed a change, and I suspect that he viewed me as a worthy distraction.''

"Poor man!'' Natalya said sadly.

"I'm sure he wouldn't want your sympathy, minx. He's happy now, I think, and lives in the present rather than the past.'' His face darkened as he added, "Which is what I intend to do myself just as soon as this matter with Francesca is resolved.''

"Will you tell me what has happened? What did you write to her?''

"Bloody *nothing* has happened,'' Grey replied in a hard voice. "She hasn't responded to my first letter, so I wrote today to inform her that I will visit tomorrow at five o'clock and expect to find her at home.''

"Well, that's good news," Natalya rejoined cheerfully. "You're free today and doubtless yearning for something to take your mind off your troubles." She touched a finger to her breast. "I am at your service, sir!"

"Are you indeed?" There was an undercurrent of amusement in his tone, but the expression in his silvery eyes was far more complex. Slowly he lifted Natalya's hand and kissed the palm with lips that burned her tender flesh. "Let us visit Laviolet in the kitchen and see what she has to feed you."

"Are you not hungry also?"

Still holding her hand, he led her across the hall, murmuring, "Rather; but I doubt that food can satisfy me this afternoon. . . ."

Chapter Twenty-seven

May 17, 1814

SITTING ON A STOOL NEXT TO GREY IN THE SUN-washed kitchen, Natalya felt richly content. The long bleached table, accented by a glazed jug of blue French irises, was covered with dishes of food. There was a bowl of sliced bananas, melon, strawberries, and oranges all mixed together, a freshly baked loaf of spiced honey bread, a cold salad of shrimp, scallops, peas, and red peppers tossed with a creamy dill dressing, sweet potato pudding, an okra soup that Laviolet had just finished, wild blackberry pie, and a bottle of dry Vouvray wine.

Laviolet stood across the table preparing a leg of lamb for supper, smiling to herself as she pretended not to watch Grey and Natalya. They were eating and chatting amiably together, their hands brushing occasionally. It might be whispered about the house that Laviolet's employer was a libertine, but those days were clearly over. Grey St. James was in love; as besotted as the girl, if that was possible!

"I couldn't eat another bite," Natalya announced at last, glancing down rather sheepishly at her half-full plate. "I think I may have overestimated my capacity, but who could blame me? Everything looked so tempting and tasted sublime. Laviolet, you must not repeat this, but I am beginning to suspect that you are an even better cook than our own Hyla DuBois."

"When we are happy, all food tastes good," Laviolet replied, with quiet pleasure.

Grey, who had been eating bread and soup, glanced up and smiled at her. "We don't want to distract you from that leg of lamb by wandering into a philosophical discussion, so I suppose we'd best be on our way. Miss Beauvisage, would you care to take some exercise to aid your digestion?"

She saw the mischief in his eyes as he stood and offered her his hand. "That would be lovely, Mr. St. James. Thank you again for luncheon, Laviolet."

As they strolled down the wide corridor toward the stair hall, Natalya whispered, "We dare not venture outdoors, Grey. It wouldn't do at all for Francesca to see us together. What manner of exercise did you have in mind?"

"I thought a brisk stroll up the stairs would do nicely," he replied conspiratorially, and placed his hand at the small of her back to guide her.

Her heart began to pound with anticipation, for she yearned shamelessly for his touch and the sensation of his body against her own. It was bliss to share Grey's company, to talk and laugh with him and feel the bond between them strengthening, but there was more to love, and she desperately needed to feel that completion.

Grey made no pretense of his intentions. He led her directly into his bedchamber and closed the door. During his adult years he had known many and varied forms of lust, but he had never felt like this before. His physical need had never been so intense, and yet it was much more than that. When he turned to Natalya and she came into his arms, a sweet, cleansing heat passed forcefully between their bodies.

Natalya pressed her face against his shirt and held fast to his shoulders for fear her knees would give way. When his lips brushed her hair, and she turned her face up to him, Grey lifted her for a long kiss that went straight to her heart, branding it with fire.

Somehow they found their way to the bed. Smiling into each other's eyes, they shed their clothing. Natalya fumbled with the intricate folds of his snowy cravat, then Grey deftly unfastened her riding gown. Standing before him in her chemisette, she felt like a bride.

"You are utterly perfect," he said in a husky voice, touching his thumb to the rosy nipple that swelled against the thin muslin of her bodice. "Utterly perfect for me."

Natalya realized that she believed him. No longer did she fear that she was not young enough, that her mouth or breasts were too full, or her eyes the wrong color. Grey loved her just as she was; in fact, he *preferred* her this way. He'd hinted many times that she was precisely his idea of womanly beauty, but Natalya had never dared believe it until now. Newly confident, she slid the chemisette from her body and stood naked and proud before him.

Arousal, raw and deeply primitive, surged through Grey at the sight of her. Pulling off the rest of his clothes, he reached for her, and the contact of their warm, bare bodies was pleasure beyond description. His sun-bronzed hands wandered down the graceful line of her back, over her full hips and the curves of her buttocks. Natalya felt her breasts swelling against the crisp black hair covering his hard chest. When he pressed her hips to his, she found that she thrilled to the sensation of his fully erect manhood, hot and insistent against her belly. They began to kiss hungrily, and it came to Natalya that an innocence born of the tenderest emotions infused each caress of their mouths and hands.

As he lifted her onto the bed, it seemed to Grey that he was making love to a woman for the first time. What had changed? He knew only that he had never dreamed of feeling thus; his heart had opened and he was beginning to understand all that he had missed by keeping it locked so securely all these years. . . .

"Darling Natalya," he said gravely, staring into her luminous eyes, "I love you."

Garbed in an exquisite gown of pale green India muslin with a long pearl necklace encircling her neck, Francesca entered her downstairs parlor with an air of grandeur. She wore her auburn curls in a Grecian knot offset by two emerald-studded combs that had been favorites of the deceased Countess of Hartford.

"My dear Miss Timkins," she exclaimed warmly, walking

toward the Sheraton sofa with her hands outstretched. "I cannot tell you how delighted I am that you could visit me today."

Red-faced and nervous, Charlotte stood up and bobbed a curtsy. "Pleased to be here, your ladyship." She hardly knew how to react to so effusive and familiar a greeting from the woman who had briefly presided over Hartford House. Although Charlotte had been in awe of Francesca then, as far as she knew the viscountess had never noticed her existence.

"Do sit down, my dear. I'll ring for tea. My cook makes the most delicious little cakes, and I'll wager you're famished after the long ride from that . . . farm in the hinterlands." Her lips pursed in obvious distaste.

When a serving girl had brought tea and tiny frosted cakes, Francesca waited until she and Charlotte were alone again before confiding, "These American servants are quite hopeless! I cannot tell you, my dear Charlotte, how elated I was to discover that *you* of all people were in Philadelphia."

Charlotte wondered how her ladyship had learned this, but she was far too shy to ask. In fact, Francesca had sent one of her own lackeys out to Belle Maison the previous day, ostensibly to apply for a position there. He'd happily discovered that the Beauvisages had left for Connecticut and lingered to casually quiz the servants. When at last he returned to Pine Street with the information that Natalya's ladies' maid was a Miss Charlotte Timkins who had come with her from England, Francesca was intrigued. The name sounded vaguely familiar, but for what reason? It was David who remembered that the girl had been employed at Hartford House like her mother before her.

"She's a bumbling child, very eager to please," he'd told Francesca. "She spilled tea on me once and burst into tears, begging me not to tell my father."

Now that she saw Charlotte, Francesca remembered her. Out of regard for Mrs. Timkins, Mrs. Thistle had been training the woman's daughter for the world upstairs beyond the kitchen. Sometimes she had been allowed to watch Francesca's own ladies' maid perform her elaborate duties.

"You must tell me how you came to America," Francesca

continued blithely, pretending not to notice that Charlotte's hand was shaking violently as she attempted to sip her tea.

"Well, my lady, I actually came with his lordship. That is— your husband! I mean, if he is still your husband. I wouldn't know about such things, it's not my place. At any rate, he was bringing Miss Beauvisage home, and I came along as her ladies' maid." Overcome by curiosity, she asked, "Does his lordship know that *you* are here as well?"

"Oh, yes, of course! You see, that was part of his plan all along. Perhaps you are not aware of it, my dear Charlotte, but Lord Altburne is a very evil man. That was why I was forced to run away when I had the opportunity. But through devious means he has discovered my whereabouts. His lordship means to harm me . . . and I have reason to suspect that your new mistress is in league with him."

Charlotte gasped and nearly dropped her cup and saucer. "Oh, my lady, that is terrible! But I hardly think that my mistress is capable of evil—"

"Dear sweet innocent Charlotte!" Sighing, Francesca shook her head sadly. "How trusting you are. You have been very sheltered and know nothing of people of this sort, who are masters at hiding their true natures. Have another cake."

Her eyes like saucers, Charlotte accepted the proffered cake and popped it in her mouth, chewing furiously. "My lady, is it not possible that you could be mistaken?"

"I fear not, my dear," Francesca replied regretfully. "You see, I have evidence."

"Oh!" The girl's brow wrinkled as she tried to accept what she had been told. "It seems . . . impossible, but—"

"Surely you do not accuse me of lying?"

"Oh, no, my lady!"

Francesca sat down beside Charlotte, patting her plump hand. "I understand that this has been a terrible shock for you, my dear girl. Tell me, have you been very happy in the employ of Miss Beauvisage?"

"Now that you mention it—no, my lady, I haven't. She's nothing like a proper English lady. In fact, she would rather do for herself than call on me."

"But, don't you see, that's because she doesn't want you to
see what she's really doing."

"It is?" Charlotte squeaked. "I never thought of that. Do
you know, my lady, I've been feeling more and more unhappy,
deprived of the duties I was raised to perform. More than
anything, I must be *needed*."

"Well, my dear girl," Francesca replied, slipping a kind
arm around the maid's shoulders, "I understand exactly how
you feel. But, now you must cheer up, because *I* need you,
and we have important work to do!"

Leaning back against pillows plump with goose down, Natalya sipped from a goblet of wine and breathed deeply of the
fragrant breeze that wafted in from the garden. "I would say
that I am happy," she murmured, gazing into Grey's eyes,
"but that seems a very small word for such an overwhelming
feeling."

He wrapped his hand around her slim fingers and lifted them
to his mouth. "I never would have believed that I could vol-
untarily engage in such a conversation with a woman," he
said, with a self-deprecating smile. "I never believed that this
could really happen in life. I thought true love was for fools."

"And now?" she prodded, joyously anticipating the answer.

Grey gave her a dazzlingly white grin. "I know that I was
the fool. The love I feel for you is, quite possibly, the first
honest and valuable emotion of my life. It is as if I've been
walking under a dark cloud of cynicism for so long that I
assumed it was hovering over everyone." Impatient with the
gap between their bodies, he drew her against him, kissing her
brow and her soft, unruly curls. "When I met you, I was
skeptical of your enthusiasm for life. I resisted the desires of
my heart, even though I could not bear to part from you. I
used to think that love was a game that I had to win, but now
I have discovered freedom in surrendering—" Grey's eyes
stung and his voice caught for an instant. "The cloud has
disappeared, and there is only golden light, all around."

Tears clung like stars to Natalya's lashes as she set aside her
wine and straddled Grey's thighs, perfectly at ease in her na-

kedness. "I do not regret the years I wasted doubting love,"
she declared, "because I think God was keeping me safe for
you. In the past, I believed that I could never give any man
power over me. I treasured my independence. And yet, with
you, I felt differently almost from the beginning. When you
took charge of me, I *liked* it, even though I could not admit it
in my mind. I was so confused! All I knew was that I felt
secure when you were near, and more keenly alive than I had
ever imagined possible. It was quite alarming." She ran her
fingers through the soft mat of hair on his brown chest. "Oh,
Grey, do you not think that we were meant to be mates?"

Although no promise of marriage had passed his lips, Natalya trusted him, and that was a gift he did not take lightly.
"Yes, minx, I believe that is what God intends for us."

Smiling, she caressed his tousled, silver-freckled hair and
the lean line of his jaw. "I can feel the light all around us, too.
We're going to have a wonderful life together, and I shan't take
one moment of it for granted. Where shall we live?"

In the magical world they had created in this testered bed,
the reality of Grey's marriage to Francesca seemed a barrier
that could be easily pushed aside. He gave himself permission
to dream. "You'd love Briar Hill, the country estate that will
one day be mine. It's in Hampshire, one of the most idyllic
regions of England. But . . ." His face darkened and he glanced
toward the window. "I'm not at all certain that I want any part
of the life that's been created for me back home. Even that
word—*home*—seems hollow compared to the warm, loving example of family and home I've witnessed at Belle Maison."

"Won't you tell me more about your family?" Natalya asked
gently. "I do need to understand." Returning to a less distracting place beside him, she nestled in the circle of his embrace,
her breasts warm against the tapering line of Grey's chest.

He sighed harshly. "It's all so different from what you're
used to. Growing up, I learned about duty. As a nobleman
from birth, and the heir to an earldom, I was groomed to
believe that I was better than other people. England's upper
class is fraught with beliefs that have little to do with humanity." He reached for his wine and took a long drink before

continuing, "My life was very cold and regimented, especially after my mother died, though I don't remember her as being a particularly warm person. How could she be, married to my father?"

"What is he like?"

"Extremely remote, although I must own that I have begun to find him rather amusing of late. Perhaps it's because it no longer matters to me that he scarcely remembers I'm alive, let alone cares." His tone was distant. "However, when one is a little boy and craving a word of kindness or encouragement from one's father, it's hardly amusing to hear, 'Fine, fine, yes, quite, and do visit me again if you happen to be passing by,' spoken without so much as a backward glance."

Natalya's heart ached with Grey's pain. Kissing his shoulder, she exclaimed, "What a horrid man!"

"Not precisely. He simply doesn't know any other way to behave." Grey shrugged. "And once I realized that he could not give me what I needed, that I could never measure up to his standards no matter what I did, I taught myself not to care. I threw myself into the heartless but amusing pastimes of a titled rake: gambling, wenching, drinking, sporting, and other activities in that line. Then I went to fight Boney, and you know the rest."

"But have you no other family besides your father?"

"My mother died giving birth to my sister, and my brother, David, was lost in the battle of Salamanca two years ago. I have other more distant relations, but none I particularly admire."

"How very disheartening. Were you close to your brother?" Natalya sensed that these questions were painful for him, but she also knew that it was important for him to share with her the details of his past so that they could go forward.

"No. David and I were not close. As the elder son and heir, I received what little attention my father had to give, and David quite justly resented that. Also, to be honest, he could not equal me in other areas. He was not as tall or strong as I, nor did he excel in the meaningless but fashionable pursuits I described earlier. He lacked the streak of reckless daring I possessed, which is a quality that is highly valued in London society.'' Grey paused, and a shadow momentarily crossed his face. ''Sometimes I think that he wanted to die in battle. What did he have to return to? Knowing what I do now, I would try to change things between us, but we cannot go back, can we?''

''And what of the life *you* returned to?''

He shook his head. ''Everything had changed, just as you warned me it might. There was one good friend left to me, but nothing else was the same. Also, discovering that Francesca had made off with Mother's jewels didn't improve my spirits.'' Shivering slightly in the breeze, he turned on his side and pressed the length of his strong body against Natalya's welcoming softness. ''This is a devil of a conversation for us to be having. Let me close by saying that whatever regrets I had about my return to London were dispelled after I arrived here. When I met your family and entered their home, I realized that nothing had been real before. My past had been a maze of smoke and mirrors.'' He kissed her deeply, his passion mounting. ''*This*, my darling, is life as it is meant to be.''

During the hours when the sun mellowed before accepting the twilight, Natalya lay safe in Grey's arms, napping peacefully. He awoke first, almost surprised to find that she was not a dream—and even more surprised to realize that he had no regrets about all that had transpired between them. She fit against him as naturally as their thoughts and conversation flowed together. Natalya was right: God had created her as his mate.

''I feel *wonderful*,'' she said suddenly.

Grey saw that she was looking at him with alert turquoise eyes, a smile playing over her mouth. When she began to stretch, still in the circle of his arms, he bent to trail kisses from the hollow of her belly to the pink crests of each beautiful breast. ''I could make love to you forever and still crave more,'' he said huskily, his fingers straying lower to caress her intimately.

Later, Natalya bounded out of bed and ran to the garden windows. ''Oh, Grey, look what a beautiful evening it's going to be! Let's go outside for a walk. I've been wanting to give you a proper tour of Society Hill, and I have so much energy!''

"But—"

"Have no fear, my love, I shall not be recognized." Her face shone with an impudent smile. "I'll disguise myself. No one will know me. I'll borrow clothes from—Fedbusk!"

Grey fell back on the pillows, laughing. "*Fedbusk!* You're outrageous!"

"Perhaps, but you must admit it is an inspired notion."

Half an hour later they were standing in the stair hall. Grey was drawing on his gloves, and Fedbusk himself was glowering at Natalya, apparently unamused by her comical appearance. Since they were nearly the same height, she fit easily into one of Fedbusk's butler costumes. The length of the black coat and breeches was nearly perfect, but Natalya had tied one of Grey's black cravats around the waistband of the breeches, which ballooned around her thighs. Grey had helped her tie the white stock, which looked charming against her delicate, sun-tinted face. She wore her own white stockings, handkerchiefs stuffed into Fedbusk's buckled shoes, and a wide-brimmed black hat in the Quaker style that covered her hair and the upper part of her face.

" 'Tis bad enough that *I'm* forced to wear those clothes, but when you give them to a woman, I cannot approve," Fedbusk grumbled. "And, I'd like to know, sir, why it is that I am locked in this bleedin' house when *she's* allowed to parade around town with you in *my* clothes!"

Grey calmly raised his eyebrows. "Hold your temper, old fellow. Miss Beauvisage is wearing these clothes because they render her unrecognizable. Perhaps if you were to don *her* garments, I could permit you to roam at liberty."

"Have you taken leave of your senses . . . sir?" Fedbusk spluttered.

"A jest, old chap," Grey reassured him, biting back a smile. "Try to be patient for one more day. After I recover the jewels from Lady Altburne tomorrow night, it won't matter if she knows that you're in Philadelphia. Until then I'd rather not take unnecessary risks. I simply don't trust the woman, and the less she knows, the better I'll feel."

"It's a mighty queer arrangement, if you ask me," declared the grizzled seaman.

"I believe you've previously registered that same opinion," Grey observed dryly.

Speed came out of the kitchen then, hurrying down the hall with a piece of spiced honey bread in one hand and a folded note in the other. "There you are, sir. I've been waiting to give this to you." He turned over the paper to his employer, then glanced at Natalya, widened his eyes, and grinned. "I say! You're quite a sight, Miss Beauvisage. May I remark that you look much more attractive in those clothes than Fedbusk?"

"You're too kind, Mr. Speed," she replied, smiling at him under her lashes and sketching a curtsy.

"Humdudgeon," Fedbusk grunted.

Grey, having read the note, folded it and handed it back to Speed. "Excellent. Our appointment is fixed for tomorrow at five o'clock."

"Lady Altburne conveyed the reply to me personally, sir, and said to tell you that she is looking forward to your visit with great pleasure."

"I don't doubt it one bit," Natalya said, frowning under the wide brim of her Quaker hat.

Fedbusk threw open the door. "Are you two going or not?"

"Don't be jealous, minx," Grey whispered as they stepped outside. "It doesn't suit you."

"Oh, I'm not jealous. I trust you implicitly. I just don't trust *her*."

Then Francesca was forgotten. Strolling down Spruce Street next to Grey, she felt positively frolicsome. Passing carriages held occupants who had fawned over Natalya and her book at the Hampshires' party and now only glanced quizzically at the odd little black-clad Quaker man with the spring in his step.

"Isn't this fun!" she exclaimed to Grey. "I only wish I could hold your arm. I want to touch you all the time."

He gave her an affectionate smile and caught himself before he reached out to caress her cheek. Walking down the wide, straight street lined with horse chestnut, lime, and maple trees, Natalya pointed out residences of friends and famous Americans. Society Hill, with its beautiful mansions and quaint row houses, had been the home at various times of Benjamin Franklin, George Washington, Alexander Hamilton, and such illustrious Philadelphia family names as Willing, Powel, Chew, Bingham, Biddle, and Penn.

"You know," Natalya explained, "Society Hill didn't get its name because it's a wealthy neighborhood. It comes from the Free Society of Traders, which was granted a charter by William Penn around 1680 and set up a warehouse and office near the waterfront." She continued to instruct him as they walked along the river, peeked at the *Wild Rover*, then started west on Pine Street.

Noting a street sign, Grey remarked, "This is the street where Francesca lives. Perhaps we ought to walk in a different direction."

They had just turned north on Third Street when a plain hired carriage passed by. Natalya noticed the occupant, who was craning his neck to stare at them. "Grey, do you know a thin man with gray hair and gold spectacles?"

"I don't believe so. Why do you ask?"

"Well, the man in that carriage going down Pine Street was staring at us as if he'd seen a ghost. Assuming that I am unrecognizable, I would deduce that he was looking at you."

Grey shrugged, remembering the description Stringfellow had given of Francesca's gentleman friend. There was no point in worrying Natalya, so he merely said, "Perhaps I reminded him of someone else."

They were approaching a huge mansion set back from the street behind a high fence. "This is the Washington Benevolent Society now, I'm told, but when I left for France William Bingham still lived there. He's moved to France now himself; apparently he's never fully recovered from the death of his wife, Anne. The Mansion House was the centerpiece of President Washington's Republican Court when Philadelphia was America's capital, and Anne Bingham was an elegant and lovely hostess. Don't you find it rather sad that everything could change so quickly? Twenty years ago all of American society vied for invitations to the Binghams' lavish parties, and Anne and William had power, beauty, wealth, and influence. Now . . . it's all over, and they are both gone." Natalya paused, gazing pensively at the Mansion House. "Of course, Meagan Hampshire knew them rather well and says that Anne's beauty was superficial. Perhaps that was their undoing."

"Unfortunately I am all too familiar with people of that sort," Grey said. "They rarely come to happy ends." He pointed up the street, glad of a distraction. "Isn't that your grandmother's house?"

"Yes. Might we visit her for a few minutes? I've been thinking of Grandmama a great deal these past two days, and there is something I need to say to her."

They strolled up the neat brick footpath to the home of Antonia Beauvisage, and Grey stood back as Natalya knocked. This time Mrs. Reeves answered the door. The pink-cheeked cook was nearly as old as her mistress and provided Antonia with welcome companionship. "Ah, Miss Natalya!" she exclaimed, as if the young woman's appearance were perfectly commonplace. "It's lovely to see you, and you, too, Mr. St. James. Mrs. Beauvisage is in the library."

Antonia, having overheard, met them in the hallway. She was looking especially pretty in an old-fashioned gown of azure blue silk trimmed with Alençon lace. Her expression, however, was apprehensive as she regarded her granddaughter through her tiny spectacles. After greetings were exchanged, she said in hushed tones, "I would invite you inside, but Mr. Saunders is here. We have been enjoying a lively game of backgammon. I must tell you frankly, my dear, that I was rather disappointed in your behavior when we encountered you at the garden party. I will not bring you into the same room with Barton if you are going to stare at him as if—"

"Grandmama, please don't go on," Natalya said, looking distraught. "That's why I've come . . . to speak to you about Mr. Saunders, and then, I hope, to speak to him."

"Perhaps I should join Mr. Saunders and allow you both some privacy," Grey interjected. He went into the library and took Antonia's chair at the game table.

"This won't take long, Grandmama, and I can say it standing right here. It was horrid of me to behave as I did when you introduced me to Mr. Saunders. I may have *said* nothing uncivil, but I am perfectly aware that my feelings were written on my face.''

"Barton is a very kind and sensitive man, Talya. He has been so good to me—'' Antonia's voice caught as tears pricked her eyes. ''I understand that you were accustomed to thinking of me only with your grandfather, and, of course, so was I. When he died, there was a tremendous void in my life. God was generous enough to bring Barton, a man whom I could never compare to my grand Jean-Philippe. I have a great deal of love in my heart, nurtured during more than sixty years of marriage, and it makes me happy to have someone to care for again. It's true that I have a large and loving family, but all of you have lives of your own. . . .''

Natalya put her arms around her grandmother. ''I understand! Oh, Grandmama, I beg your pardon for my selfishness, and I want you to know that I have only good wishes for you and Mr. Saunders. You see, I have finally opened my own heart to love, and I understand many things now that confused me before.''

''Is it Mr. St. James?'' Antonia smiled in delight, her green eyes sparkling. ''Aha! I sensed as much the moment I first saw the two of you together. Now then, Talya, what on earth possessed you to put on that ridiculous costume? The hat, in particular, is singularly unflattering.''

Laughing, Natalya kept an arm around her grandmother's waist and steered her toward the library. ''I fear that you are correct as usual, Grandmama. Why don't we join the gentlemen so that we can all become better acquainted?''

''Nothing could please me more, my darling girl.''

Chapter Twenty-eight

May 17–18, 1814

FRANCESCA SAT AT HER DRESSING TABLE, THE BOX containing the Hartford jewels open before her. She touched each priceless piece, gazing into the glittering depths of the gems and holding them against her cheek. Beautifully crafted gold, flawlessly cut diamonds, sapphires, emeralds, rubies, amethysts, warm and luminous pearls; all were here, and they belonged to her. It was more difficult for Francesca to part with these treasures than any human being. Promising that they would soon be back safely in her care, she reluctantly closed the box, locked it, and returned the key to its hiding place.

Francesca had mixed emotions about giving the jewels to David, even for a day. She had made the suggestion so that he would feel more secure and believe that they truly were operating as partners in this scheme. In fact, David could scarcely have been more in the dark, and Francesca intended that he stay there. Her real reason for sending him to Belle Maison had more to do with keeping him well out of the way during her meeting with Grey than with any notion that David's "wooing" might induce Natalya Beauvisage to forget his quite unforgettable brother. Of course, Francesca's schemes invariably were multilayered, and this was no exception. Grudgingly realistic, she had to consider the possibility that her own plan for tomorrow evening's assignation with Grey might go awry, in which case she would be glad that the jewels were hidden outside of this house.

"Ah, there you are, my love," David said as he entered Francesca's bedchamber. Coming up behind her, he bent to press a kiss to the nape of her neck. "If possible, you are even more stunning than when last we met. That shade of green is infinitely becoming, and those ropes of pearls are perfect accessories," David declared, adding with a chuckle, "even if I did give them to you myself."

Smelling liquor on his breath, Francesca forced a smile. "It's lovely to see you, too, dear." She gestured toward the carved box. "I've prepared the jewels for you to keep in your rooms. Since Grey has no idea that you are alive, let alone in Philadelphia, that should be the safest place."

David St. James wore a preoccupied expression as he sat on the edge of the curtained bed and pushed his spectacles up on his nose. "I've seen my brother."

"You've—*what*?" Francesca's heart began to race and her face went pale. "What the devil do you mean? You haven't spoken to him? You couldn't be *that* stupid!"

He blinked, momentarily taken aback by her venomous tone. "I say, darling, sheathe your claws. Have you forgotten that you *love* me?"

"Don't play with me, David," she ground out between perfect white teeth. "I'm much better at it than you, and I'll always win in the end."

"See here, there's no cause for threats. I've done nothing wrong." David leaned back instinctively, alarmed by the light in her eyes. "I saw Grey from my carriage, on my way here. He was walking north on Third Street in the company of a very odd-looking little man."

"What sort of odd-looking little man?" she demanded impatiently.

"How should I know? A Quaker, I suppose, or whatever they call 'em." He got up to pour himself a brandy. "Queer little fellow wearing oversize clothes and a big black hat. Walked and laughed like a girl. Can't imagine why Grey would be in the company of such a bizarre—"

"It was that insufferable spinster!" cried Francesca.

"Eh?" He turned from the cellaret, looking thoroughly perplexed. "You didn't tell me the wench goes in for men's clothing. Deuce take it, what's happened to Grey's taste in females? And I hope you don't actually still expect me to pretend to romance someone wearing breeches and a Quaker hat, because I really must protest—"

"Oh, David, do be quiet!" She had begun to pace, making a conscious effort to calm herself. David might be obtuse, but even so it wouldn't do to mishandle him. "I don't know for certain that it was Natalya Beauvisage, I'm just guessing. Perhaps she was in disguise to protect herself from my eyes. Grey is just devious enough to think of such a thing, and if he did, it means that matters have gone farther than I feared. You really mustn't lose any more time, David. You'll have to visit Miss Beauvisage tomorrow."

"What? Do you intend that I simply turn up on her doorstep, introduce myself, and demand that she fall in love with me?"

She stopped beside him and slipped her arms around him, kissing an especially sensitive spot below his left ear. "Darling, I cannot get Grey out of our lives without your help. Do, please, try to cooperate. . . ."

"All right. Of course." As always, David felt himself melting as she carefully applied her lips and fingers.

"Now, do you really think that I would send you off without a plan? I have enlisted the help of Miss Beauvisage's maid, Charlotte Timkins, who will take your message to Belle Maison and vouch for your character, good looks, pleasing personality, and all the rest. She'll say that she knew of you in England."

"And what reason shall I give for this visit?" David managed to inquire as Francesca drew off his coat and began to untie his cravat.

"I think that a daringly romantic approach would be most effective." She opened his shirt, loosed her breasts, and rubbed against him, the long pearl necklaces pressed between their bodies. In a husky voice she continued, "Charm her first with your manners and breeding. Take wine to her and see that she drinks it. Then, when she is lulled into pleasant complacency, you will become more ardent—eloquently passionate, expressing your admiration for her ridiculous book and declaring that you fell deeply in love with her as you read it.''

He was guiding her toward the bed, fumbling with the fastenings at the back of her gown. ''You're brilliant, as always, my goddess, but what if my declaration of love does not draw the desired response from Miss Beauvisage?''

''Then, you will become a bit more *forceful*,'' Francesca replied, first kissing and then biting his mouth. ''We cannot spare the time for a drawn-out seduction. You must compromise that creature immediately, and Charlotte will appear to witness the event. Loyal, of course, to her true master, she will go to Grey and report Miss Beauvisage's indiscretion.''

David could scarcely think as Francesca pulled at his trousers with one hand and found his aching manhood with the other. ''I don't mean to be difficult, but it occurs to me that there's a devilish lot that could go wrong. What if Charlotte recognizes me and sounds an alarm? Or what if—''

''Don't be a bore, darling.'' She removed her hand from his crotch and rose up on an elbow to stare down at him, her green eyes slanting upward at the corners. ''That silly maid hasn't seen you for years, and you've changed far too much. Besides, she thinks you're dead, too. And furthermore, she is loyal to me. She thinks Grey and that wench are quite beastly, she's happy to be needed again, and happier still to be well paid for her efforts. Just take the jewels to your rooms, hide them, and appear at Belle Maison tomorrow at five o'clock. Do as I tell you and leave the thinking to me. Everything will be just fine!''

David gazed at her breasts, which were mere inches from his face, dragged her hand back to his groin, and nodded. ''I am your humble servant, madame. In any event, what've I to lose? My life, perhaps, but I'm not altogether certain it's of much value.'' Pulling her into his arms, he muttered, ''*Seize* the moment, hmm?''

''An excellent philosophy,'' Francesca agreed, trying not

to smile as her husband's brother kissed her ravenously. With any luck, this would be the last time she'd have to endure his ardent pawing. . . .

The forenoon was too sumptuous to resist, Natalya decided as she closed the cottage door and looked around the garden. The tulips and daffodils were fading, but pink and white peonies were opening to take their place. Delicate lilies of the valley clustered in shady spots, and there were borders of forget-me-nots, tufted pansies, primroses, and blue phlox in full, glorious bloom.

Breathing in the perfumed air, Natalya told herself that she could not be expected to write on a day like this. Everything seemed changed now that she was able to let her love for Grey sing over her nerves, her heart, her mind, knowing that he felt the same. It was as if there were an invisible link binding their souls even when they were apart. Never had she known such joy; it filled her and made her want to laugh aloud. Now, more than anything, she longed to call for her horse and ride into Philadelphia, but Grey had insisted that she remain here until his meeting with Francesca was over. Once he had recovered the jewels and settled the issue of ending their marriage, he had told Natalya, they could be together openly.

She dropped onto a carved stone bench under the plum tree, smoothed her white muslin skirts, and turned her face up to the sun. It was possible, she had discovered, to amuse herself endlessly by recalling each moment she and Grey had spent together since their meeting in France. It made her smile now to think of them struggling in the alcove at Château du Soleil while Grey pressed a dirk between her breasts. How he had excited her, despite her rage, even then!

Last night had been sublime. Their time with her grandmother and Barton Saunders was merry, since all four were under the spell of romance. Grandmama had served a warm loaf of Russian rye bread, made from her own mother's recipe, with sliced ham, white cheese, and rosy ripe peaches. Learning that Antonia had left Russia in her youth, Grey quizzed her about her homeland, charming her thoroughly.

It was dark when Natalya and Grey rose to bid Antonia and Barton good night. When she discovered that they had walked to her house, Antonia insisted that they borrow her landau so that Grey could escort her granddaughter back to Belle Maison quickly and conveniently.

Under the light of a full moon, they drove slowly through Society Hill, turning onto Chestnut Street so that Natalya could point out the State House, where the Continental Congress had adopted the Declaration of Independence. Crossing Sixth Street, they next beheld the Congress Hall and Philadelphia's first truly impressive theater. The high Palladian window in the center of the Chestnut Street Theatre was ablaze with the light from chandeliers as people entered for that evening's performance of a light opera called *The Sailor's Return*. A boy with an oyster barrow lingered under the corner gaslight, and nearby stood a frail-looking girl selling violets. The richly garbed playgoers ignored her, but Grey bade their driver stop. He jumped down to the flagged pavement and paid a grand sum for two nosegays.

"Go home to bed, little one," he commanded, bestowing a flashing smile upon the urchin, "and tomorrow use this money to buy good food, a hot bath, and a proper gown."

"Aye, sir, I will," she mumbled, dumbfounded.

Back in the landau, he handed the violets to Natalya. "One bunch is for you, love, and the other is for your charming sister. Tell her I am sorry for the way I behaved at the garden party, and that I shall personally beg her pardon when next we meet."

Natalya's heart ached with love as she pressed the tiny, fragrant flowers to her nose and stole a glance at his moon-silvered profile. Distraction soon appeared, however, in the form of the Pump House, a luminous white building with a round tower in the middle. It was located in High Street's huge Centre Square, which had been fenced in and meticulously landscaped, with the added attraction of a fountain by William Rush.

"So that is your famous Waterworks!" Grey exclaimed. "An amazing achievement."

"It is, isn't it," she agreed. "The water flows through a conduit from the Schuylkill, then a steam engine pumps it to huge tanks in the upper story here. From this Pump House, the water travels through wooden pipes to homes and hydrants all across Philadelphia."

"All of Europe would be agog," he remarked.

Sitting now on the garden bench, her eyes closed against the sunlight, Natalya smiled as she relived the moment. She loved Grey's keen intelligence and curiosity. He no longer pretended to be cynical or bored but seemed rather to attack life with humor and a singular flair that she found intensely appealing. She drew in her breath at the memory of their parting the night before. When the landau pulled up in front of Belle Maison, Grey had pressed her onto the narrow, velvet-upholstered seat and pretended to ravish her. His starlit face had been cheerfully wicked as he loomed above her, white teeth agleam, then swooped down to demand kisses that took her breath away. Their joyous love seemed a tangible thing, alive between them in the cool night air. When at last he let her up and escorted her from the carriage to the front door, he'd held her gently, almost reverently, caressing her back as they'd exchanged bittersweet kisses of parting.

"Be patient," he had whispered, "until tomorrow night. I will come to you then, after the other business is finished." Pressing his lips to the delicate pulse point at the base of her neck, he'd murmured, "I love you, Natalya . . . with all my heart."

The sun was warm on her muslin bodice, and Natalya felt her nipples tighten in response to the memory of his touch. Tonight seemed impossibly distant. How could she wait so many hours?

"Mistress Natalya?" Charlotte's voice seemed to come from far away. "Are you sleeping?"

Opening her eyes with an effort, Natalya smiled dreamily. "Perhaps a little. What is it, Charlotte?"

"I have a letter for you, from a lovely English gentleman I met at a bookshop yesterday," she recited woodenly, her cheeks crimson. "He had your book, mistress, and asked the shopkeeper how he might meet you. It was bold of me, I know, but I went up to him and said that I was in your employ, and we chatted for a bit. Such a nice man, very elegant and cultured, and quite taken with you after reading *My Lady's Heart.* I discovered that he was an old friend of the earl's second son, David. I couldn't recommend him more highly, mistress! He said that he might send you a letter, and begged me deliver it. It's just arrived.'' Relieved to come to the end of her speech, Charlotte held out the letter.

Natalya shaded her eyes against the sunlight and looked curiously at her maid. ''Are you quite well, Charlotte? You seem to be rather . . . nervous.''

''Nervous?'' Her face felt as if it were on fire. ''I—I think I may be catching a chill, actually.'' Pressing the letter into Natalya's hands, she added, ''I'd better go inside and put on a shawl.''

She watched the girl dash clumsily through the maze of garden paths, then shook her head and broke the seal on the letter. It read:

My dear Miss Beauvisage,

   Pray excuse my audacity; I am aware that you are quite above my touch, but I cannot resist daring to hope that you may receive me. I am an ardent admirer of your writing gifts, as well as a visitor in your fair city, and it would be the crowning moment of my sojourn in America if I could return to England having spent a few minutes in your esteemed presence.

   I shall be near your home this afternoon and will call at approximately four o'clock. Might I hope for a cup of tea and your inscription in my copy of *My Lady's Heart?* Begging your indulgence, I remain,

   Your humble admirer,
   David Standish

It seemed very odd to Natalya. How could this Mr. Standish make such a fuss over someone he had never met? Was this what celebrity meant? She might suspect him of some sort of romantic delusions, but he sounded respectful—and Charlotte's recommendation could not have been more glowing.

What swayed her in the end was the realization that Mr. Standish's visit would help to fill the hours until she could be with Grey. She was also intrigued by Charlotte's reference to the man's friendship with David St. James. Perhaps he could tell her more about Grey's family.

Hyla had gone with Natalya's parents to Connecticut, but the elderly cook's best kitchen maid, Lydia, had remained behind, and she fixed a lovely afternoon meal for the two sisters to share on a little table in the garden. Natalya was bursting to tell Kristin about Grey, but she wanted to wait until the problem of Francesca was behind them. She had even put the other nosegay of violets in water, planning to deliver them when she broke the news to Krissie in the morning.

"The most mysterious thing has happened!" the younger girl exclaimed as she produced an envelope to show her sister. Kristin's name was written on the outside in a flowery scrawl. "Someone has sent me two tickets for tonight's performance of *The Sailor's Return*. This is not Hollis's writing, so I suspect that they are a gift from his aunt, with whom we are dining tomorrow evening. I know you must feel that I am never at home anymore, and I feel terribly rude leaving you each night while Maman and Papa are away, but I hope you will understand. . . ."

"Oh, Krissie," Natalya assured her, "I couldn't be more pleased for you—and Hollis. As it happens, my own life has been rather eventful of late, so I haven't been languishing here in your absence. And nothing could make me happier than knowing that your courtship with Hollis is progressing so well."

"I'll own that I am quite surprised myself, but I feel a sort of warm contentment when we are together. It's nothing like I imagined I would feel. . . ." Kristin smiled shyly and took a sip of lemonade. "I expected to be swept off my feet by someone dashing and handsome, yet this seems more *real* somehow. It's very sweet; a quiet sort of romance, with an understanding between us that deepens each day." After a brief pause, she glanced down at her plate and added, "I must confess, too, that I feel attracted to him now in a way I never would have believed possible. When he touches me and we kiss, it's simply wonderful!"

Natalya beamed. "I don't mean to speak too soon, Krissie, but I believe that Hollis Gladstone is the perfect man for you."

"I think you may be right, Talya. Now, you must tell me what has been happening to you!"

"I—am not free to speak, yet, but tomorrow I should be able to tell you. . . ."

"It's Grey St. James, isn't it?" Kristin crowed. The sight of Natalya's answering blush made her laugh. "You needn't respond; I can see it in your face. How thrilling! But of course, I knew all along how you felt about him."

"How can you say that?" her sister cried in outrage. "You were chasing after him yourself, mooning over him!"

"Oh, I was just having a bit of fun. I was only a child then."

"Krissie, the Hampshires' garden party was only three days ago!" Natalya exclaimed.

Rising gracefully from the table, Kristin replied, with infinite wisdom, "Perhaps, but that is the way of life. Three days ago I was a girl, and now I am transformed."

Natalya would have laughed if she hadn't seen the truth in her sister's words. She herself felt as if she had lived years in the past few days. "Yes, what you say may very well be true. And now, off with you, puss! I'm sure you have a thousand things to do to prepare for your evening at the theater. I, on the other hand, have nothing more to anticipate than a visit from a man who is an admirer of my books. He wrote to me and begged for an audience." She made an uncertain little moue.

"But, is that wise?" Kristin asked, with an air of mature concern. "What if this man is a toad? Papa is gone, and Pierre with him—and the other servants are just boys."

"Charlotte met this fellow in a bookshop and knew of him in England. She insists that he's perfectly respectable; in fact, she could not praise him highly enough. All I have to do is give him tea and write my name in his copy of *My Lady's*

Heart, then send him on his way." Seeing that her sister still looked uncertain, Natalya added, "If it will make you feel better, you can meet him yourself before you go out."

Natalya had hoped that Charlotte might be prevailed upon to serve tea during David Standish's visit, then pop in and out while he was there to lend an air of propriety to the interview. However, when she made this suggestion to Charlotte, the girl began to stutter.

"Oh—well—mistress, I don't think so . . . that is, I'm not certain—I mean, I'm not feeling well!" She had just finished fastening the back of Natalya's demure white gown with heather ribbons and was reaching for the white lawn tucker that would conceal her bosom. "I've—I've a fierce pain in my belly."

"Oh, my!" Natalya said, looking over her shoulder at Charlotte with a mixture of concern and bewilderment. The girl had always been a bundle of nerves, but today her behavior was exceptionally hectic. "Why aren't you in bed, Charlotte? If you are ill—"

"It's just gotten worse, mistress, during these past minutes."

In truth, Charlotte reflected nervously, she had been given specific instructions by Lady Francesca to stay well out of the way during Mr. Standish's visit to Belle Maison, and she was glad to obey. She had hated to lie to her mistress about everything, especially when she spoke so kindly and was so concerned. But her ladyship had told her it was necessary . . . and her ladyship had paid her a great deal of money and even promised to take her on later as foremost ladies' maid—and it seemed impossible that her ladyship would lie. . . .

"If you don't mind, then, mistress," Charlotte murmured, "I do believe I'll go and have a little lie-down." Averting her eyes guiltily, she sidled toward the door.

"Charlotte?"

"Yes'm?"

Natalya smiled and said gently, "I do hope you feel better."

Her face flamed. "Oh, I shall. 'Twas doubtless something I ate."

"If you do recover before long . . . perhaps you might look in on Mr. Standish and me. I'm certain that he is a fine gentleman, but my sister will be out, and I do feel a bit uneasy about being alone with him."

Charlotte nodded, bolted from Natalya's bedchamber, and fairly tumbled down the back stairway to the main floor. As she crossed through the dining room, she heard a knock at the front door and glimpsed, through the window, a carriage in the drive. Kristin Beauvisage, dressed to go out, hurried down the center staircase to open the door, so Charlotte slipped out into the garden. She wanted nothing more than to reach her sunny little room in the servants' quarters behind the kitchen, but a lackey whom she recognized from Lady Francesca's house was coming toward her from the drive.

"Charlotte Timkins?" he inquired in a low voice, glancing around furtively. When she nodded, he produced an envelope from his waistcoat pocket. "Ye're to read this without delay."

He seemed to disappear into thin air, and Charlotte felt her heart begin to pound as she stared at the envelope. Clutching it, she ran all the way to her room, nearly tripping en route over a grapevine, which would have sent her facefirst into a cluster of rose bushes. At last, seated safely on her neat, narrow bed, she opened the envelope and saw more money inside. Next to it was a note penned in a familiar, swirling hand:

My dear Charlotte,

I have one other *tiny* favor to ask of you, so that we may be certain nothing can go amiss. After Miss Beauvisage's visitor arrives, do please wait in the back of the house in case you hear any commotion, or hear her cry out. Mr. Standish has come to compromise her, thereby ending the adulterous affair between her and my husband. A messy business, I realize, but the only solution where right may prevail in the end. When you see that this has been accomplished, you must go to Lord Altburne, remind him that you are ultimately loyal to him, and tell him what you have seen.

Also, dear Charlotte, if you imagine that you recognize Mr. Standish, say nothing. You must *trust* me.

There was no signature, but none was needed. Charlotte's head throbbed and she burst into tears.

Smiling politely, Kristin ushered Natalya's caller into the center stair hall. She had sent a young housemaid to fetch her sister and was now uncertain how to proceed.

"I understand that you are English, Mr. Standish?"

"That is correct." David squinted slightly, having taken off his spectacles so that he might affect a quizzing-glass instead. His high, starched collarpoints grazed his chin, and he wore a cravat tied with extreme intricacy. Producing his quizzing-glass with a flourish, he peered through it at Kristin, who was clad in a lovely evening dress consisting of a British net frock over a blue satin slip. It was cut low around her breasts, and she drew her shawl closer to her body in response to his appreciative gaze.

"I am a great admirer of your sister's writing talents," David went on, drawing out *My Lady's Heart* from under his coat. "She has a singular gift, but clearly God has blessed *you* with extraordinary beauty!"

Kristin took a step backward. Her carriage was waiting and she was already late, but she deplored the idea of leaving Natalya alone with this person. She was about to tell him that her sister was too ill to see him when Natalya herself appeared on the staircase.

"Mr. Standish?" she inquired, descending quickly with a smile of greeting. "I am Natalya Beauvisage. It's a pleasure to meet you."

"Ah!" David exclaimed as he took her hand at the foot of the stairs. "I see that I have been hasty in my judgment. God has blessed you not only with artistic talent, but also with beauty as breathtaking as your sister's!"

Rodney had left the carriage and appeared now at the door. "Are you ready to depart, miss?"

Kristin glanced despairingly toward Natalya. "I could change my plans. . . ."

"Nonsense," she pronounced. "Mr. Standish and I are just

going to have a cup of tea and then I'll write for the rest of the evening. I'll see you when you return later.''

Kristin bade them a reluctant good-bye and preceded Rodney to the carriage, barely noticing as he helped her in. As they started off down the sweeping drive, she sat back and tried to dismiss the unsettling feeling in her stomach. Perhaps she had only imagined that David Standish seemed to smell of evil.

Chapter Twenty-nine

May 18, 1814

"NOW THEN, MR. STANDISH, MAY I OFFER YOU A cup of tea?" Natalya inquired as she led him into the north parlor. Perching on the edge of the Chippendale settee, she gestured toward a nearby wing chair, hoping that her visitor would take the hint. Instead he sat beside her and lifted his quizzing-glass.

"No need to bother the servants, Miss Beauvisage. I'd be happier with a bit of brandy, and don't mind pouring it myself. Why don't I get you a sherry?" Without waiting for her assent, he went to the cellaret and availed himself of its contents, returning moments later with two generously filled glasses. "Ah, this looks delicious after that tedious ride from Philadelphia. To your health, my dear!"

Natalya eyed the goblet of sherry dubiously, but she wanted to get through this as amicably as possible. She touched the rim of her glass to his, took a sip, and then ventured, "I understand that you knew the Earl of Hartford's son in England."

David nearly choked. "Who told you that?"

"My maid, Charlotte, whom you met in the bookshop yesterday. When she gave me your note, she recommended you highly, and said she knew of you when she was employed by the earl."

"Oh!" Silently damning Francesca for not informing him of her detailed scheming, he managed to regain his composure. "Yes, I am acquainted with the family. David St. James was an excellent fellow."

"I know his brother, Grey," she confided. "What a tragedy David's death must have been."

"Alas, how true!" Shaking his head, David drank liberally from his glass. "He was far the more worthy of the two sons, if I may say so. Don't suppose that Grey wasted a moment grieving for him."

"Oh, no, I think you're wrong. I believe that he was more affected by the loss than even he knows, and he has told me that he would change his relationship with his brother if he could go back."

Her visitor looked pained for an instant, then squinted at her through his quizzing-glass. "Indeed? It doesn't signify in the least now, though, does it? And I didn't come out here to discuss a lot of English nobles. I came to acquaint myself with *you*, dear lady. Has anyone told you how beautiful you are? One imagines that a female author will be plain and all too maidenly, but you're nothing like that. . . ."

When Mr. Standish moved to narrow the space between them, Natalya felt a sudden wave of panic. All her instincts told her that her admirerer was about to become inappropriately ardent. She began to pray that Charlotte would recover from her indigestion and burst clumsily into the room to rescue her.

When Francesca heard Grey's step on the stairs, she stood behind her bedchamber door and waited for him to knock.

"Francesca," he called in demanding tones. "Why the devil has your butler sent me up here? Come downstairs and we'll conduct this interview in your parlor."

"Grey, dear, just join me inside for a moment, then we can go downstairs," she replied. "I have the jewels here, and would rather not show them to the servants."

He stood for a moment, considering, then sighed and opened the door. Striding into the spacious room, he looked around for Francesca. "Fiend seize it—"

Quickly and quietly she closed the door, locked it, and slid the key underneath it to the hallway. Grey whirled around in time to see her straightening. Clad only in her Chinese silk wrapper, her hair flowing loose over her shoulders, she met his flinty stare with fiery emerald eyes. "Darling," she murmured, with a secret smile, "you're late."

"What the devil are you up to this time?"

"I think it's time that you and I forget what has happened these past two years. Let us return to the way it was between us." Her voice and expression were seductively feline. "I know you haven't forgotten. How could you?"

Grey was standing conveniently near the bed, taut and handsome in a dark blue coat, white cravat, snug buckskin breeches, and riding boots. Her eyes devoured him as she walked to the side of the bed.

"You must be mad," Grey muttered impatiently. "Just give me the jewels, Francesca."

She stared at his hand, which was gripping the bedpost in anger. A scar stood out across it, white in contrast to his bronzed skin. She sensed the tight rein Grey held on his dangerous temper, and this excited her beyond measure. Shrugging, she let the wrapper fall to the floor in a liquid, silken pool, then lay back naked across the bed like a work of art. "Remember, Grey?" she taunted hoarsely, stretching her arms over her head, conscious of the way her breasts stood up and her belly flattened. "Take me again. No one could ever love me as you did. I'll do anything you want, anything. . . ."

As Francesca opened her thighs and lifted her hips toward him, Grey knew a nearly overpowering urge to wrap his hands around her neck and tighten his grip until she could no longer breathe, move, smile, whisper, or plot evil against another human being.

"Have you taken leave of your senses?" he demanded, a muscle moving in his jaw.

"Why, of course not, darling," Francesca purred, caressing herself. "As you can plainly see, and are intimately aware, I am quite myself . . . perfect in every way."

He reached down, scooped up the silk wrapper, and threw it over her. "Get the hell up and give me my mother's jewels, damn you! I wouldn't touch you if you were the last woman on earth, so spare yourself the effort.''

Her eyes hardened as she rose slowly to a sitting position. "It's that insipid little spinster, isn't it? Has she deluded you into thinking that you can be faithful to one woman?" Harsh laughter broke from her, filling the bedchamber like poison. "Believe me, darling, it's not in your nature. She'll never be able to satisfy you the way I can, and you're a fool to give up the chance to take me back. Can't you see, we're perfectly suited. We're alike, you and I—hard-hearted and in love only with pleasure. Oh, you may think you've changed, but I know better. Men like you *never* change! It's in your blood, my wild devil, and a conventional marriage to a maiden with a lot of romantic notions would bore you to tears and eventually drive you mad. I'm the only woman, the only woman—''

Grey gripped her arm with such force that she gasped in pain. "That's quite enough. *You're* the one who's mad, and I thank God that I've found my way into a better world.'' His voice lowered to a menacing tone. "Give over the jewels, madame.''

Francesca began to laugh again, this time maniacally, straining upward so that their faces were inches apart. "What if I said that you would have to earn them first?''

"Nothing on this earth could induce me to touch you in the manner you suggest," Grey replied, with deadly calm.

"Well, nothing on this earth could induce me to part with my jewels," she spat. "Did you really imagine that I would be so foolish as to keep them in this house? If so, my dear husband, you woefully underestimate me!''

A vein pulsed in his forehead as he released her and turned to look around the bedchamber. Raking a hand through his hair, he realized that it would be pointless to search for the jewels. She was right: they would certainly not be anywhere he would think to look. And his disgust with Francesca was so overpowering that he couldn't bear to spend another minute here. Without a backward glance, he strode to the door, turned the knob, and found it locked.

"Oh, dear," she cooed from the bed, "I've locked it and lost the key."

Realizing that he would surely murder her if he remained there to argue, Grey stepped back, pretended the paneled door was Francesca, and brought his booted foot against it with deadly force. It splintered, the lock broke, and he took his leave.

When she heard the front door slam, Francesca flew off the bed in a rage, grabbed an exquisite Sevres vase that David had given her for her birthday, and threw it against the wall. As it smashed into a million pieces, she uttered a long, primitive scream.

Why? Why was it that she, who had never been denied anything in her life, was now frustrated at every turn? It was maddening!

Calming herself took an act of will, but at last Francesca was able to consider her situation dispassionately. She sat at her dressing table and stared at herself in the mirror, pondering what was to be done about Grey . . . and her own future.

Soon the answer came to her, and she smiled at her own brilliance. If she could not regain her place as Grey's wife, she would see him dead. Then she could marry David, and they would return to England together. *David* would be heir to the earldom, Grey would be out of the way, and before long that nasty old earl would die and all the Hartford estates and holdings would belong to her.

Of course, it would mean killing that silly authoress, too, but that didn't bother her in the least. David was already with her. Francesca would join them, wait for Grey to walk into her trap, and all her problems would be solved by day's end.

Throwing on her wrapper, she went into the hallway to call for her carriage, then ran back to her dressing room and selected a gown of bloodred velvet. Perfect, thought Francesca, feeling utterly and deliciously mad; the evening promised to be thrilling beyond belief. Slipping her feet into white kid slippers and rushing toward the door, she gave one fleeting thought to Grey, who might just be persuaded to beg her pardon before he died.

As he walked from Francesca's house to his own on Spruce Street, Grey couldn't wipe the memory of her eyes from his mind. When he had married her in London, she had been provocative and even wicked at times, but something had happened to her since then. Was it possible that she actually *had* tripped over the brink into true madness? And, if so, what did that mean to him? Of course, he could more easily obtain a divorce, which required an act of Parliament, but did his involvement end there? He saw her again, naked, laughing crazily, taunting him, and realized that Francesca was fully capable of attempting to harm him or someone else. Was there some way of returning her to her father in England, of having her confined?

Deep in thought, Grey scarcely noticed the carriage in front of his house. Fedbusk met him at the door, clearly disgruntled.

"Your supper's ready, sir."

"Good. I'm ravenous," Grey replied, and started past him toward his study, where he usually took his meals when alone.

"I tried to tell 'em that you wouldn't have time," Fedbusk grumbled, following him, "but they said they'd wait anyway."

"What are you prattling about?" Preoccupied and hungry, Grey had no patience for Fedbusk's cryptic mutterings.

"Them, sir," he said, pointing toward the parlor. "Somebody Gladstone and a girl."

Suddenly feeling as if he were suffocating in the warm May evening, Grey stripped off his coat and strode into the parlor to discover the identities of his uninvited guests. Whoever they were, he fully intended to send them away. The stocky, sandy-haired man who stood when he entered the room looked vaguely familiar, but then Grey's eyes fell on Kristin Beauvisage and he bit back the curt greeting.

"Ah, Miss Beauvisage, how nice of you to drop by." Forcing a smile, he crossed the parlor and was introduced to Hollis. "On any other evening, I would consider it an honor to sit down and visit with you both, but I'm afraid you've come at rather an awkward time. I do hope you won't think me unforgivably rude if I—''

"Mr. St. James," Kristin broke in, "are you on your way to Belle Maison?"

"Eventually. I have some matters to attend to first."

"I know this will sound preposterous, and perhaps Hollis is right when he says that I am being overanxious, but there is a man visiting my sister, and—''

Grey's jaw hardened and his eyes grew steely. "What man?"

"He's English; an admirer of Natalya's book, he says. I'm sure he's perfectly harmless, but I just had an odd feeling about him, and I felt that I couldn't enjoy the theater tonight unless I made you aware—''

"What does he look like?" Grey interrupted.

"He was rather slight, and older. He has thinning gray hair . . .''

"Spectacles?"

"No, a quizzing-glass, but now that you mention it, I wouldn't be surprised if he normally does wear them, because he was squinting.''

Grey smiled. "As you say, there's probably nothing to worry about, but if it will make you feel better, I'll ride out now and make certain this fellow isn't attempting to compromise your sister's virtue.''

"He hardly seems capable of that''—Kristin laughed as they walked toward the door—"but I appreciate your understanding. I do hope you don't think I'm terribly silly for bothering you.''

"Nothing could be farther from the truth!" Still wearing his most charming smile, Grey led them to the front door and bade them good night.

When Fedbusk trundled back into the stair hall to remind his master that supper would soon be inedible, he stopped short at the sight of Grey's stormy expression. "You look like the devil himself, sir, and I doubt that a cold supper will do much to cheer you up.''

"Get me my coat!" Grey shouted. "And be quick about it!''

* * *

Overcome by an attack of conscience and curiosity, Charlotte Timkins crept into the house through the servants' entrance and stood in the darkened hallway, listening.

For the past hour she had lain on her bed, thinking alternately about Lady Francesca and Natalya Beauvisage. Money, titles, and promises were all well and good, but there was something about her ladyship that didn't set right. And Miss Beauvisage, for all her independent ways, was kind and genuine. Charlotte felt truly guilty when she remembered her mistress's face, concerned and sympathetic, after she had lied about being ill.

Now, in the back of the house, she wondered what she should do. If she disobeyed her ladyship's instructions, she would surely be punished somehow. The truth about her spying and the money she'd taken would come out, and then Miss Beauvisage wouldn't want her, either. And yet how could she betray someone who was so honest and good? It was a terrible dilemma.

Muted voices drifted to her from the north parlor. Charlotte tiptoed toward the stair hall, somehow managing not to trip or break anything on her way.

"Mr. Standish, I really must ask you to leave now," Natalya was saying, a note of alarm in her voice. "I must insist. Do not touch me again, sir!"

"You're old enough to know about the pleasures of the flesh," a man's voice replied loudly. "And I can teach you things you never dreamed of, my beauty."

"Loose me or I shall scream!"

He laughed. "But there's no one to hear, is there? The servants are all eating supper, and your parents are away."

"How do you know about my parents?" Natalya's voice rose with real panic. "Who are you? What do you want with me?"

Charlotte froze, beads of perspiration breaking out on her forehead as she waited in vain for the man's response. There were sounds of a struggle, followed by a thump, as if bodies had toppled onto the floor. Her heart pounding in her ears, she

peered into the shadowy room and saw a man in a frockcoat
and brown pantaloons lying on top of her mistress on the beautiful English rug in front of the settee. His hand covered her
mouth, but Charlotte could hear Natalya's muffled cries mingled with the man's muttered replies.

Tears of sympathy for her poor mistress pricked her eyes.
Without thinking, she picked up a brass candlestick from the
nearby Pembroke table, crept soundlessly toward the figures
struggling on the carpet, and struck the man on the back of
the head. He fell forward without a sound, and Natalya pushed
him away, weeping.

Charlotte was staring, her eyes like saucers, at the evil visitor who lay prostrate before her. "A ghost! God save us all,
it's a ghost!"

As she shrank back against the settee, Natalya managed to
whisper, "What? Who is he? Tell me, Charlotte!"

"Mistress, it's the Earl of Hartford's second son, David St.
James!"

"But, it can't be! He's been dead for two years!"

He had begun to stir, and Charlotte jumped backward in
terror. "He's a ghost, that's what!"

A voice spoke from the stair hall, high-pitched with wicked
amusement. "Hardly, you silly twit."

Natalya whirled around to behold Francesca St. James
standing in the arched doorway. Clad in a gown of bloodred
velvet with a black mantelet, her auburn tresses flowing around
her shoulders in wild disarray, she was pointing a pistol at
them. Somehow Natalya marshaled the wits and strength to
stand and meet her venomous gaze. "Madame, I must ask you
to put away that weapon and leave my house."

Francesca threw back her head and laughed as if her rival
had made a huge jest. "My dear Miss Bluestocking, has no
one taught you that the person holding the weapon issues the
orders? I must ask you and your loyal servant to stand against
this wall." When the women did not immediately obey, her
face twisted with fury. *Do as I say—now!*"

Putting an arm around the trembling Charlotte, Natalya
obeyed. Her gown was torn at the shoulder, the lawn tucker

crumpled and forgotten under the settee, and her hair was tumbling down in loose curls, but she lifted her head proudly and returned Francesca's stare.

"I say," David groaned, sitting up and rubbing the back of his head. "I've a cursed big lump coming on."

"Stop blubbering, you bloody fool. Get up and help me," Francesca snapped. When David had struggled to his feet and crossed to her side, weaving slightly, she said, "My reticule is inside the front door. There's a knife in it. Cut strips from the draperies so that we can bind their hands and feet."

"What do you mean to do?" David inquired.

"I just told you!" she spat.

"But, why? You aren't going to harm them, surely?"

"Of course, you idiot! I've seen your insufferable brother, and it's plain that the only solution is to do away with him, which means doing away with his lover as well. I've no doubt that he has kept her informed of my existence in Philadelphia and the bad blood between us, so—"

"You want to *kill* Grey?" he repeated blankly.

"Don't look so shocked! If you had the wits God gave a *stoat*, you would see that it is the only solution. You needn't pretend you haven't hated him all your life, and now we shall both be rid of him. The title will be yours, darling, we shall be married, and we can return to England. I'll say I discovered you wandering about in France suffering from memory loss. Isn't it *perfect*?"

David felt numb as he stared into her burning eyes. "Well, yes, I suppose so."

"You were the man she ran away with," Natalya whispered incredulously. "You faked your death in battle and stole your own brother's wife!"

"Do not speak again or I shall shoot you immediately," Francesca said in tones of ice.

Having retrieved the evil-looking knife from Francesca's reticule, David set about slicing strips from the silk draperies. The light was fading quickly and Francesca urged him on, then handed him the pistol as she bound Natalya's and Charlotte's wrists.

"Now what do you intend to do?" David asked, watching her in confusion. "You don't mean just to shoot them in cold blood, do you?"

"Imbecile!" She threw him an irritated glance over one shoulder, then gagged Natalya and Charlotte with strips of silk. "We shall wait for Grey. I know my beloved husband, and I feel certain that he'll come rushing out here tonight to cleanse himself of the memory of our earlier encounter. My effect on him was undeniable. He was clearly aroused, but seems to have temporarily developed a conscience. No doubt he'll believe that a visit with his little spinster will absolve him of all his wicked thoughts." Francesca pushed Charlotte down to the floor and began to tie her ankles together. "We'll wait for him to walk into our trap, tie him up as well, and then let him watch his lover die first. . . ."

David was listening in horrified fascination when Francesca's head snapped up. "What's wrong?" he asked.

"Listen!" she hissed, scrambling to her feet, the knife clutched in one hand.

Natalya's heart gave a painful wrench as she recognized the sound of hoofbeats on the drive. Please God, she prayed, don't let it be Grey. Don't let it end for us this way! Francesca had forgotten to bind her ankles, and she wondered if there was anything she could do. The silk that bound her wrists had been made into draperies by Caro at least twenty years ago, and she had threatened to replace them because of age even before Natalya went to France. Now, as she tugged and pulled her wrists apart, Natalya felt the fabric begin to tear.

A sharp knock sounded at the front door, followed by Grey's achingly beloved voice. "Natalya? . . . Is anyone at home?"

Smiling, Francesca whispered to David, then slipped into the stair hall and stood behind the door, just as she had earlier in her own bedchamber. Grey knocked again, then tried the door, opened it, and stepped into yet another trap.

Instantly Francesca was behind him, the blade of her knife pressed between his shoulder blades. "Lift your hands up for me, darling, unless you want your lover to die," she purred.

All the muscles in his lean body tightened, but Grey remained silent and did as she bade him. The point of the knife cut into his coat, nudging him forward into the dimly lit north parlor. ''Damn you, Francesca,'' he breathed when he glimpsed Natalya, gagged and bound beside Charlotte on the floor.

Then David St. James stepped out of the shadow, shaking visibly as he pointed the pistol at his brother.

Lifting his eyebrows, Grey remarked with pointed irony. ''Ah, there you are, David. Not dead at all, I perceive, but come to rescue me. How can I convey my gratitude?''

''Hold that pistol steady, you dolt,'' Francesca commanded her lover, who had begun to sweat profusely under Grey's cool gaze. ''Pull back the hammer and shoot Miss Beauvisage instantly if she makes a suspicious move.'' Still gripping the knife, she reached for the remaining strips of silk and prepared to tie her husband's wrists behind his back.

Natalya fought an urge to weep in the face of Grey's bravado and the fate that loomed before them both. Then she heard it: a tiny, familiar click in the paneled wall. Grey winked at her as relief flooded her body.

In the next instant, a panel in the wall sprang open and Fedbusk and Speed burst into the parlor, brandishing pistols. Their color was high, and they wore reckless grins.

''Don't none of you move!'' Fedbusk commanded, his feet spread as if he were back on the *Rover*'s quarterdeck. ''Now then, wench,'' he drawled, staring at Francesca, ''I never did like you, and I've always wished I could say so to your face! Now that I have, take that knife from 'is lordship's back and toss it across the floor toward us.''

''Go to the devil,'' she snarled, then turned her eyes up on the quaking David. ''Shoot Grey! Shoot him now! Don't let him win again!''

David's finger hooked around the trigger as he sobbed, ''I cannot. He is my brother!'' When he drew it back, the pistol exploded, and Francesca stared down in stunned disbelief as a crimson stain blossomed and blended with the bloodred violet of her bodice.

Horrified, Natalya watched as Grey's wife tumbled to the

floor at her feet and lay motionless. Fedbusk and Speed ran
up behind David and were divesting him of his weapon just as
Natalya ripped free of the rotting silk that bound her wrists
and scrambled to her feet. She could hear Charlotte making
incoherent whimpering sounds behind her gag, and she helped
the young maid up, trying to move her away from the dead
woman.

David St. James was sobbing, clinging to his brother. "Hold
on, old man," Grey said in a voice rough with tenderness. "I
must see to the ladies."

Sagging limply against Natalya, Charlotte glimpsed a movement over her mistress's shoulder. It was Francesca. Smeared
with blood, she was reaching up, wild-eyed, clambering to her
knees, the knife in one hand, her other fingers transformed
into scarlet-streaked claws that grasped Natalya's white muslin
skirts, pulling with inhuman strength.

Caught off-balance, Natalya staggered backward. Grey
dashed toward her from across the parlor, but the blade was
already slashing into Natalya's gown. Charlotte, her wrists still
bound, threw herself past her mistress and drove Francesca
back.

Emitting one last striek, Francesca toppled onto her own
knife and died at last.

Chapter Thirty

 May 26, 1814

GREY SAT ON THE EDGE OF ALEXANDRE BEAUVISage's massive cherry desk, gazing out the windows of his office at the shipyards below. Both men had removed their coats and were indulging in glasses of Madeira. Spread across the desk were plans for other ships.

"When this war is ended," Alec was saying, "and I believe that will be soon, I can stop outfitting my vessels as warships and turn to more exciting designs. I think we're about to enter a new age, when ships can be built to be faster and more efficient than ever. Have you seen the French luggers that have been trading in our waters recently? This newest design"—he pointed toward the central drawing—"is based on them."

"Your work is fascinating," Grey said. He stared intently at the plans, then looked up to find that Beauvisage was watching him. "No doubt your son will join you in business when the war is over."

"I rather doubt it." Alec smiled and gave a Gallic shrug. "Étienne seems to take after his maternal grandfather. Farming is his passion, and he and his wife, Marianne, have purchased land adjoining her family's farm in northern New York State."

"Are you disappointed, sir?"

"Not at all." Lighting a cheroot, he wandered to the window and gazed down at the men toiling over the wooden skeletons of ships while the Delaware River glittered in the distance. "Étienne must do exactly as *he* pleases. It is his life, not mine, certainly, and my only wish is that he seek happiness and fulfillment." Alec glanced back at the Englishman with a wry smile. "Of course, it would add to *my* happiness and fulfillment if I could find a young man who honestly loves this work and would enjoy learning from me, sharing with me, and eventually carrying on in my place." He paused, then arched a white brow meaningfully. "I don't suppose, my good friend, that you have entertained any thoughts of remaining in Philadelphia?"

Grey felt a rush of emotion that had been unknown to him a season ago. When discussing their love, Natalya spoke of the grace of God, explaining that grace meant "unmerited favor." He found himself thinking of that phrase almost hourly now that the cloud surrounding Francesca's death had lifted and he and Natalya were planning their life together in earnest. He had no idea why God had blessed him with Natalya. The added gift of her openhearted family filled him with wonder.

"Yes, sir, I would like to remain in Philadelphia," he answered the older man. "In fact, that is the reason I came to see you today. When you and Mrs. Beauvisage returned from Connecticut yesterday, there was so much to tell you—so much had transpired in your absence. Yet it didn't seem right to discuss Natalya . . . our own romance, in the same conversation with Francesca's plots."

"And now?" Alec prodded gently.

"I have the honor of asking for your daughter's hand in marriage, sir. She has taught me all that I know about love," Grey said, a smile playing over his mouth, "and I shall do everything in my power to see that nothing dampens her natural joy in living. I have made one devil of a mistake already, and hope I can claim to be insightful enough to have learned from it."

"A worthy speech," Beauvisage said approvingly, his turquoise eyes warm with pleasure and affection. Closing the space between them, he placed an arm about Grey's shoulders. "I will dare to speak for Caro and tender our approval for this marriage on one condition . . ."

"Yes, sir?"

"That you'll stop calling me sir immediately!" He gave a shout of laughter. "You must call us Alec and Caro or, better still, Papa and Maman, but no more of this sir and Mrs. Beauvisage nonsense! Agreed?"

Grey was shocked to feel tears sting his eyes. "I—I am quite undone . . . Alec. In all honesty, I must tell you that my own father, my own family, is totally unlike this one. Formality is a very old habit, one I may not be able to break immediately."

"I know," Alec replied, with grim understanding. "Do not forget that I am acquainted with your father. In his defense, I should say that he doubtless could not give his children what he did not have to give. That formality you speak of was instilled in him from birth . . . but underneath it all, I believe Lord Hartford does have a heart. He saved my life, you know."

"Odd, isn't it—that thirty-year link between our two families?"

Beauvisage nodded, then turned to his desk and began rolling up the sheaf of papers. "You said that Lady Altburne was buried in St. Peter's churchyard?"

"Yes. Natalya felt that she must have been mad, and therefore not responsible for the harm she tried to inflict. I tended to agree—that Francesca was mad, at any rate. It seemed the right thing to do, giving her a decent burial. . . ." Grey's eyes darkened. "I just wanted the matter resolved so that we could begin to move onward, away from the horrific memories."

"And your brother?" Alec asked softly. "What's to become of him?"

"Actually we've made a peace of sorts. I rather felt that Francesca had put a sort of spell on him that was broken when she ordered him to murder me. He's had a difficult life, and I had a great many regrets when I thought he was dead. Natalya has helped me to see his behavior in a more positive light. It will take time, but I hope that eventually we can be brothers more truly than we were before the war." Grey reached for his Madeira, took a drink, then turned the glass absently in his hands. "At any rate, I'm sending him home to England. The *Wild Rover* sails tomorrow, and David will have the unpleasant but unavoidable task of informing Francesca's family of her death. I don't know how he'll explain his own role in it, or his whereabouts these past two years to our father.'' One corner of his mouth quirked ironically. ''Our father is difficult to shock, and believe me, I've tried. David may well get no more from him than: 'So, you're alive, after all. Good of you to inform me, and do let me know if you die again.' ''

Alec chuckled and led the way toward the door. ''I promised Caro that I'd come home early today. It seems that Kristin has someone she wants us to formally meet. I hope you'll join us for supper as well. You must go through it all again, I fear— begging both of us for Natalya's hand in marriage as if you and I never discussed it. Caro would have our heads if she thought we *men* had been conducting a secret conference!''

In the corridor, Grey shrugged into his coat, laughing as he tried to imagine Caroline in a fit of temper. Then he glanced back at the paneled door that bore Alec's engraved nameplate. Above it was the bare strip left when Jean-Philippe Beauvisage's plate had been removed after his death.

''I would be proud to see your name there one day, Grey,'' Alec said simply, watching him. ''Consider carefully, though, without regard for my feelings. You must join me only if that is your true heart's desire.''

''Just exactly *what* are you two females plotting now?'' Grey thundered in tones of mock outrage.

Natalya and Charlotte, who had spread swatches of fabric across his bed and were conferring intently, looked up in surprise at the sound of his voice. Charlotte literally jumped at the sight of Grey's powerful body filling the doorway, his raven hair wind-ruffled and his eyes stormy as he glared at them. ''My lord!'' she squeaked.

Natalya's lips curved in a winsome smile. ''Charlotte dear, you mustn't call him that. You know that he is pretending to be a commoner.''

''I would venture to guess,'' he accused, refusing to take her bait, ''that the moment I was out the door this morning you two scurried up here and began scheming ways to change *my* bedchamber, my private domain, my bastion of—"

"You're quite right, my love," Natalya broke in, hurrying over to hug him. With her honey-hued curls and pale yellow gown, she resembled a sunbeam. "I thought we might do *our* bedchamber over in shades of Wedgwood blue and lemon. Come and look at the fabrics we have to choose from." Pulling his hand, she drew him to the bed. "Charlotte is helping me tremendously. I intend that she shall never again have reason to doubt how much we need and appreciate her."

Charlotte, seeing the mischievous light in Grey's eyes, realized that he had been teasing all the time. It had been another of their love games, as Jasper Speed called the little dramas Grey and Natalya seemed to find so amusing.

"I suppose that means that I shall be denied the pleasure of dressing and *undressing* my wife?" Grey inquired, arching a brow at Charlotte.

The girl's plump cheeks went crimson, but she summoned the pluck to retort, "You're having me on, sir, and I know it! Do you mean for me to answer back in kind?"

"Bravo," Natalya cried, clapping her hands merrily. "The victorious Miss Timkins!"

"I believe I'll take myself off and see if Mrs. Pritchard needs help in the kitchen." Charlotte backed toward the door, nearly lost her footing where the rug ended, and laughed. "Not that I'm any handier in the kitchen than I am anywhere else! I just hope that I can manage, after the two of you marry and I have to live here, to keep from falling headfirst down that treacherous staircase!"

When they were alone, Grey closed the door and returned to Natalya's side. In the next instant she was lying across the bed, pinned beneath his hard, lithe body. "I have missed you," he murmured suggestively.

"Surely, sir, you do not mean to ravish me in broad daylight," Natalya exclaimed, beaming as his lips grazed her throat. "How dare you take such liberties! This is—oh!—shocking behavior!"

"And you love it. . . ." Grey's breath was warm and arousing against her ear.

Her giggles were muffled by his demanding kiss, and her arms twined about his broad shoulders as passion flared and swept between their bodies like a brushfire. Grey always seemed to know exactly what she needed most at any given moment; now his fingers tugged at Natalya's shallow bodice to free her aching breasts. His mouth and hands were tantalizingly gentle, then a little rough, then tender again, until Natalya was writhing beneath him, her gown drawn up around her thighs, her hips arching against the telltale stiffness concealed within his snug trousers. Her cheeks were pink, her full lips moist, her response unabashedly ardent.

When at last his hand slipped down to stroke her swollen womanhood, she gazed into his silvery eyes and began to unfasten his trousers. He seemed to be bigger each time they made love, and Natalya thrilled to feel him, hot and hard, in her tiny hands.

"Good God, what a woman you are," Grey whispered hoarsely.

"All you'll ever need, my love," was her audacious reply.

"Conceited, too"—he chuckled—"but quite correct." He thrust into her then, filling her until she gave a little cry.

Natalya matched his rhythm with a feverish intensity, as if the bond between them strengthened each time their bodies fused. Physical ecstasy came easily with Grey, sometimes just from a single kiss or caress, and now she felt the storm in her loins crest and break in a shower of pure bliss. Panting, her hands in his hair, she pressed hot kisses to his face and shoulders, until he paused only briefly, then drove suddenly into her to the hilt, and made the deep groaning sound she loved best.

Not long after that, Grey swung his legs over the side of the bed, strode to the mirror, and began to rearrange his clothes. "I nearly forgot the time," he remarked.

Her curls in disarray and her gown crumpled, Natalya sat up and exclaimed, "Well, I feel rather ill used!"

"Do you?"

"No." A dimple winked beside her mouth.

"Vixen." As he retied his cravat, Grey commented, "As you know, the *Wild Rover* sails at dawn, and Fedbusk is going on board shortly. I must bid him farewell, and then I have a dinner engagement."

"What! With whom?" she challenged.

"Your family."

"Papa invited you? How lovely. I assume he agreed to our marriage?" Natalya rose and stood beside him, brushing out her hair.

"Yes, but he said that I must ask him and your mother together." Glancing down, Grey smiled at her delicate, lively countenance and caressed the soft curve of her cheek. "As you predicted, my keen-witted minx, your father asked if I would care to join him in business. I feel as if I am standing under a shower of blessings."

Natalya paused in the act of pinning up her hair. "That's what you truly want, then? You wouldn't prefer to return to England?"

"No." He slipped into his coat. "I cannot predict how I will feel after my father dies, but that may be twenty years from now. He's as healthy as a horse. What about you? Do you object to staying in Philadelphia?"

"Heavens, no! As I've told you before, I love being home again. It was the best thing for me, going away for so many years, because it made me see Philadelphia and my own family with fresh eyes. I shall adore living here in this house I love, married to *you*, and raising our children with their relatives so close by. I've already decided on the bedchamber that I shall transform into my study. It has the loveliest view of the garden. I cannot write without a view, you know!"

As they descended the elliptical staircase, Grey said, "Your father suggested that we wait to be married until the fall. Rumor has it that the British fleet will be attacking along the coastline this summer, and Philadelphia may be a target. It is Alec's wish that we wait until the danger is past, so that as much of your family as possible can attend, including your brother and his wife and baby." He gave her a sidelong grin. "I suspect that your papa has deduced that we have no intention of languishing in a state of chastity until our wedding night."

"He knows we are far too hot-blooded for such nonsense," Natalya agreed. "And I would rather wait until autumn. I actually feel as if we are already married, certainly in a spiritual sense, and the wedding will be an occasion to celebrate our love. I *do* want Étienne and his family to be with us, as well as my darling aunt Natalya, Papa's sister, who lives in Charleston, and all the other family members I haven't seen for so long." On the bottom step, she waited for Grey to turn back and hold her in his arms. "I think that the added weeks of preparation will be good for us. I can divide my time between Belle Maison and here, preparing for our marriage more gradually, and you will have some time alone to adjust to your new life in America. That's important."

Although he yearned for her when they were apart, Grey knew she was right. "You're very wise."

"I may have lingered overlong on the vine, but I'll be a better wife than some silly chit of eighteen," Natalya declared, kissing him.

He smiled into her soft aqua eyes. "Believe me, love, if you had been plucked any earlier, you wouldn't have been ripe. You're delicious and fascinating now, and will only improve with each passing year. . . ."

"*Ahem!*" Fedbusk stood impatiently at the edge of the stair hall, dressed in his favorite loose white breeches, striped jersey, blue coat with brass buttons, and a flat-brimmed hat of black canvas waterproofed with tar. "I been waitin' to say good-bye."

"Fedbusk, how grand you look!" Natalya cried, running to his side. "I know that you must be longing to be back on board the *Rover*, but I hope you will remember that we shall miss you, and that you have been a tremendous help to us here."

He nodded, blinking as if something had gotten into his eyes. "Aye, miss. It's good of you to say so."

"You haven't forgotten my letter? You'll deliver it personally?"

"I promise."

"What letter?" Grey interjected, standing behind his be-trothed.

"Must you know everything?" She glanced up at him, then gave Fedbusk a conspiratorial wink. "I'm sending a letter to London with dear Fedbusk, that's all. Where are the jewels?"

"David's taking them on board. I had to trust him, but I've instructed Fedbusk to follow through and make certain they are returned safely to my father."

"Well, I'd best be off," Fedbusk said gruffly. "Never had any use for good-byes. Tell Speed I've gone, but I'll be back."

"You will?" Natalya could not contain her delight.

" 'Course I will. The master needs me." He looked up at Grey with piercing eyes. "Always has."

"Exactly so," Grey confirmed, reaching out to shake his friend's weathered hand. "Have a safe voyage, old fellow, and return when you feel the urge."

"When the time's right," Fedbusk agreed, the corners of his eyes crinkling slightly as he gave Natalya a last look. Then he opened the door and marched out into the sunlit afternoon.

Natalya and Grey stood together in the stair hall. "I'll miss him," Grey said after a moment.

"The house won't be quite the same without him," she agreed, sighing. "Where is Speed?"

"I left him with David. My brother still seems dazed by all that's happened, and I thought he could use a bit of assistance with his packing. Speed will return after he's seen David on board the *Rover*."

They wandered down the hallway, stopping in the kitchen to let Laviolet know that she could go home since Grey would be dining at Belle Maison. Natalya told Charlotte that they would be leaving soon and advised her to gather their fabric samples and the notes they had made.

Grey then took Natalya's hand and led her into the garden. "We have a few minutes, and there is something I'd like to say to you before we join your family."

They sat down on a bench bordered by oxeye daisies, and Grey stretched out his lean, muscular legs. Natalya enjoyed the sweetness of the silence between them as they watched mother birds gather food for their babies. Grey stroked her slim fingers, touching each one as if it were precious to him. "We haven't spoken very much about . . . that night," he said. "I know that we'd both prefer to put that horror behind us, but I also know that you must think about it."

Natalya hesitated, vulnerable in her desire to find the right words. "I do, yes, but somehow *she* does not seem connected to *us*. She was part of another life for you, and that night is rather like a nightmare that lingers long after one wakes." She leaned against his shoulder. "It needn't haunt us, though, Grey. What we have is made of love and light, and it was as if she came from a different world. . . ."

"Hell, I believe it's called," Grey remarked, with a trace of irony, then squeezed her hand reassuringly. "I suppose you're right. That entire episode does seem like a nightmare, and although I cannot help feeling somewhat responsible—"

"Oh, no, you must not," Natalya declared emphatically. "Francesca's madness was her own; you had no part in it. All you did was marry her in haste, which was foolish, but nothing more than that."

He shook his head. "When I remember what she did to you, how frightened your eyes were, and how close she came to harming you . . ." A shadow of pain darkened his eyes.

"Perhaps that ought to be the lesson in that night," Natalya mused. "If remembering it helps us to remain grateful for each other and our love, there may be some value in it after all."

Reaching into the pocket of his waistcoat, Grey said, "I asked David to leave me one piece of the Hartford jewels." He drew out a ring consisting of a simple, perfect, pear-shaped diamond set on a narrow band of gold. "David assured me that she never touched it because she considered it too plain, but I have always loved this ring. Will you wear it to mark our betrothal?"

Natalya stared at the exquisite heirloom Grey held between his thumb and forefinger. "Oh . . . It's beautiful!" Her eyes brimmed with tears that spilled onto her pink-stained cheeks. "I love it, Grey, and I would be so proud to wear it!"

Smiling, he slipped it onto her slender finger, then gathered her onto his lap and held her fast. Natalya wept against his white shirt, hiccupping, then began to giggle softly.

"My own adorable minx," Grey murmured, framing her face between his bronzed hands and kissing her eyes, the tip of her nose, and finally her salty lips. "I may not be fit to be your husband, but I cannot contemplate a future without you. You are part of me. If I begin to behave like a brute—"

"I shall box your ears," Natalya promised. "Never fear, however. We shall have such fun that you will soon forget how to be a scoundrel."

Grey knew that this was an outrageous declaration, but he believed her.

EPILOGUE

These two
Imparadised in one another's arms,
The happier Eden, shall enjoy their fill
Of bliss on bliss.

JOHN MILTON
(1608–1674)

Belle Maison
September 25, 1814

THE BEAUVISAGE HOME WAS A HIVE OF CELEBRA-tion and reunion on the day of Grey and Natalya's wedding. Servants, including Pierre and Hyla, the Stringfellows, and Laviolet Pritchard, labored in the sun-washed garden arranging flowers, decorations, and white-draped buffet tables laden with champagne and food. Male voices could be heard inside the back cottage, where Grey and the other men had been banished. Female laughter floated out to the garden through the upstairs windows. The entire upper floor of Belle Maison had been taken over by women.

Natalya stood in the center of her bedchamber wearing a ruffled chemise cut very low in front and a creamy satin petticoat encrusted with lustrous pearls and fiery diamonds. Her burnished gold curls were piled loosely atop her head, a cluster of long ringlets falling over one shoulder. Charlotte was pinning lilies of the valley, which had been forced in the hothouse for this occasion, here and there amid the curls, while Caro adjusted the petticoat and stood back to have a look.

"Your great-grandmère must be beaming with pleasure as she watches over us," she whispered. "How proud she would be!"

"As soon as I knew we would be married here, I began thinking about this gown," Natalya replied. "I knew that Great-Grandmère had given it to you to wear on your wedding

371

day, Maman, but I scarcely dared hope that it would be so perfectly preserved after nearly ninety years. . . ."

"This is so romantic!" exclaimed Marianne Beauvisage.

Étienne's wife was sitting on the high field bed, petite and lovely in a chemise gown of white muslin with a violet spencer that set off her glossy black hair. On her lap she held little Faith, who was sitting up rather unsteadily and clapping. With her baby in tow, Marianne had traveled down from New York for the wedding, praying that her husband might somehow find a way to join them for his sister's wedding. One of the most exciting moments thus far had been his appearance on the doorstep of Belle Maison. Tanned and handsome in his uniform, he'd explained that General Strickler had given him leave to come north from Baltimore because of his heroic conduct during the attack on Fort McHenry.

After the nation's capital had been savaged by the British in August, every city on the eastern seaboard had spent the next few weeks fearing that it would be next. Rising to the occasion, Philadelphia had begun to dig entrenchments, enlist recruits, and sew uniforms. To everyone's relief, however, the British had passed over them, striking instead at Baltimore. The Beauvisages had guessed that Étienne's regiment might be there, and though they'd learned that the British ships had been turned back, they'd been unsure of Étienne's fate until last night, when he'd materialized at Belle Maison.

Marianne had the dreamy look of a new bride herself, and it was difficult for her to be away from her husband even for this hour. When a knock sounded from behind the secret panel in the bedchamber wall, Caro said, "I'll wager that's my son, sneaking over here from Grandmère's cottage."

Marianne, who knew nothing of Belle Maison's hidden passageways, laughed in disbelief. "How could Étienne be in the wall?"

"Cover yourselves," her husband called, "because I'm coming in!"

Étienne, who was just three years Natalya's senior, often remarked that he had lived the first eighteen years of his life "with Talya in my pocket." She had forced him to play with her, he had alternated between resentment and protectiveness, they had shared dreams and fights and high-spirited pranks, and there had always been a special bond between them. Now, as he stepped into her bedchamber, Étienne smiled at Marianne but went first to his sister.

"How beautiful you are, Talya," he declared, holding her hands and smiling into her eyes.

"I'm only half dressed!" She laughed. "But, after all the names you called me when we were children, I must say that it's satisfying to extract a compliment from you."

"I don't think potato face fits you anymore," Étienne admitted, joining in her laughter.

She looked up at her brother, who was tall and dark like their father, and touched his cheek. "I missed so much these past six years. It makes me indescribably happy that this wedding has brought together so many people I love. I wish that Uncle Nicky and Aunt Lisette and James and Adrienne could be here, but they've written us a splendid letter, promising to visit in the spring. How fortunate we are to have such a wonderful family, with new members added like branches on a tree. I have a new sister, and a beautiful *niece*—"

"And I am about to gain a brother," Étienne agreed, with a grin. Taking Faith from her mother, he kissed her plump cheek and added, "Grey even *looks* like my brother!"

Just then Kristin came in from her room across the hall. As her sister's bridesmaid, she had chosen a gown of pale pink satin designed in a more current fashion, but embroidered with pearls and bits of crystal in patterns similar to those on her great-grandmère's wedding gown. In her black curls she wore a garland of pink rosebuds and lilies of the valley.

"How do I look?" she asked, doing a little pirouette inside the doorway. As she spun around, she glimpsed her brother and gave a cry of outrage. "Étienne! What are you doing here? Don't you know that no men are allowed upstairs before the wedding?"

"I couldn't resist exploring the secret passageways again, and before I knew it, here I was," he replied, with a disarming grin.

"That's no excuse." She turned to Caro. "Maman, you must make him go. He's probably spying and will tell all the men what we're wearing!"

"You sound just as you did when you were five years old," Étienne observed dryly. When Faith made a cooing sound, he patted her bottom and added, "Even my daughter agrees, don't you, sweetheart?"

Caro motioned to Kristin to join them and smiled radiantly at her three children. "Now, I won't have you quarreling. This is a mother's dream, having the three of you together again on such a joyous occasion."

"I was only teasing, Krissie," her brother said, leaning down to kiss her cheek. "Actually, although I was missing my wife and daughter, I also came to tell you all that guests are beginning to arrive. Believe it or not, André and Devon Raveneau are here from Connecticut—"

"What?" Caro exclaimed. "They've come back from England, then? How exciting! I wrote to invite them to the wedding, but I never dreamed they would be able to come."

Étienne nodded. "Apparently they'd just returned home when your letter arrived and they decided to travel down on a whim. Lindsay is with them, too, but she's now Mrs. Coleraine, arm in arm with her new husband. Nathan remained in London, but Mouette and her children sailed back to America with the others. Seems she was recently widowed. . . ."

"Goodness," Caro murmured. "I'll have to go down soon and greet them. Such a lot of news in their family!"

"Papa's with them, hearing about their adventures in Britain," Étienne assured her, "and the Hampshires have just arrived, so Lion and André and Papa are having quite a reunion."

"Is Aunt Natalya coming with Grandmama?" Kristin inquired. "She was supposed to arrive in Philadelphia last night."

"Well, we'll soon see," Caro said.

Natalya, her face shining with pleasure, declared, "This is the most splendid day of my life! Étienne, you must go now so that I can finish dressing. It seems an eternity since I've seen Grey, and I am prodigiously anxious to become his wife."

Handing his daughter back to Marianne, Étienne remarked, "Allow me to assure you, beautiful sister, that your future husband shares your impatience." He stepped into the opening in the wall and called, "Farewell, ladies!"

The wedding guests were all assembled in the garden, which was still bright with the colors of dahlias, asters, phlox, butterfly bushes, chrysanthemums, and autumn crocuses. It was a glorious afternoon, cool and sunny, and the guests were in a festive mood. Caro was chatting animatedly with her sister-in-law, Natalya Beauvisage Andrews, and the Raveneaus and newly married Coleraines, when Alec drew out his watch and pointed. Bishop William White emerged from the cottage, followed by Grey and Jasper Speed. The three men stood at the end of the garden's main brick footpath, and Grey surveyed the crowd.

Many of the guests from the Hampshires' party were here, including Charles Willson Peale, his sons, and a group of Natalya's childhood friends. Susan Hampshire was chatting gayly with a redheaded Irishman named Patrick O'Hara, who had crossed the Atlantic with the Raveneau family. Minutes after meeting, Susie and Patrick appeared to be in a world of their own, while the Hampshires looked on in consternation. Antonia Beauvisage, Barton Saunders, and Hollis Gladstone stood in the front row behind a cluster of rosebushes, where they were joined by Étienne, Marianne, and little Faith Beauvisage. Also present were two of Alec's sisters, Danielle and Katya, and their families. His third sister, Natalya, was with Caro.

Grey felt completely relaxed under the scrutiny of the assembled guests although he wondered how long it would take for him to sort them all out. His impeccably tailored suit was black, his shirt and cravat white as snow against his bronzed face, and his waistcoat was threaded with silver like his hair, which gleamed in the sunlight. Jasper Speed stood proudly beside his master, one hand against the pocket that held the golden band Grey would place on the finger of his bride.

"It's rather a shame," he whispered to Grey, "that there's no one here from home . . . you know, from your side."

"I hope we're all on the same side now," he replied, flashing a grin. "And, you are here, my friend."

Caro had slipped into the house with her sister-in-law, who had been her own first friend at Belle Maison thirty years ago. "Here comes your namesake," she whispered to Natalya Andrews, and they looked up to behold her daughters sailing down the stairs with Charlotte Timkins fussing in their wake.

Natalya looked spectacular in her great-grandmother's wedding gown, a Watteau-style *robe à la françois* of rich creamy satin that perfectly complemented her warm complexion and honey-hued curls. The loose overdress, edged with pearls and diamonds, was open to reveal a matching petticoat, and the plunging neckline culminated in a dazzling profusion of jewels. She carried a bouquet of lilies of the valley, pink rosebuds, and lilies, and her face glowed with joy and anticipation.

"Good lord, Caro, she looks exactly like you!" the older Natalya gasped. "And, in Grandmère's gown . . . it's almost eerie!"

"She has Beauvisage eyes," Caro replied softly, even as her own vision misted.

Alec had entered through the garden doors and came up behind his wife, slipping his arms around her waist. "My sister is right," he whispered, staring at Natalya and remembering his own wedding.

Natalya met her parents and aunt at the foot of the stairs, embracing each of them in turn. "Aunt Natalya, I am so glad you could come. How I have missed you!"

"It's a happy day . . . and you are marrying a devastatingly attractive man!"

"I know." She nodded, smiling shyly. "I can scarcely wait."

"Well, he is waiting, so we'd best get on with it," Alec said. "Caro, you and Natalya had better join the others in front."

The two ladies exited, and Kristin was just preparing to step out into the sunlit garden, when a carriage came clattering up the drive. Almost immediately, the front door flew open and Fedbusk burst into the house, sunburned and grimy.

"God's eyes," he cried. "I was afraid we were too late!"

"Fedbusk!" Natalya exclaimed, tears springing to her eyes. "You came back for our wedding! Grey will be overjoyed to see you."

" 'Tis not only me, miss." Stepping to one side, he bowed his head as a tall, austere-looking man with white hair entered the house and walked through the stair hall toward Natalya and her father.

"I cannot believe my eyes," Alec said softly. "It's Lord Hartford." He hurried forward to greet Grey's father and bring him back to Natalya's side.

"This must be the bride," his lordship said, with a thin smile. "You ought to know, my dear, that it was your letter that persuaded me to go to all this trouble. I was quite . . . moved, one might say, by what you wrote. Decided that my son deserved congratulations for making such an exceptionally fine choice."

Fedbusk looked on in horror as Natalya Beauvisage hugged the Earl of Hartford, a man whom no one ever touched. Her eyes were brimming with tears as she drew back to say, "I hope to be a true daughter to you, my lord. I love Grey with all my heart, so you and I already have that in common."

Although he smiled only slightly, Hartford's ice-blue eyes seemed to thaw as he regarded her. "Don't press me too hard my dear. I'm not one for emotion—but I do like *you*."

"They're waiting for us," Alec said gently. "I'll take Lord Hartford and . . ."

"Fedbusk, Papa," Natalya supplied, beaming.

"And Fedbusk out to join your mother and the rest of the family, then I'll return for you, my darling."

Grey was beginning to feel restless and warm in the sunshine when he saw Alec Beauvisage appear again in the garden. His heart seemed to stop as he stared, first at a travel-stained Fedbusk, and then at someone who looked incredibly like his own father. Where had Fedbusk come from, and who was that man?

"Blister me, sir, it's his lordship!" Speed whispered at Grey's shoulder.

"That is impossible."

Taken aback by his master's decisive response, Speed fell silent. The old man paused at the front of the crowd, then walked up to them.

"I can hardly blame you for looking as if you'd seen a ghost," Hartford said to his son in tones of mild irony. "However, it is I. Father of the groom, I perceive, hmm?" He was about to return to the others, then turned back. "Grey, that bride of yours is an exquisite woman. I like her immensely."

Somehow Grey found his voice and replied, "I'm glad, Father. Thank you for coming."

With that, the earl went back to stand beside Caroline. A few moments later Kristin appeared, followed by Natalya on her father's arm. Grey couldn't believe his eyes; she looked like a vision from a childhood fairy tale, her lush beauty mingling with rich satin, pearls, flowers, and sparkling gems. As she reached his side and smiled at him through tears of joy, he sensed as well the spiritual embrace of her family, their friends, and, miraculously, his own father.

He took his bride's hands as the minister began to speak. My heart is full, he thought, gazing at her with pure love in his eyes. They had already come so far together, and they would spend the rest of their lives finishing the journey.